Wicked Epic Adventures

another WALLACE the BRAVE collection

Will Henry

Andrews McMeel
PUBLISHING®

to Willy B.

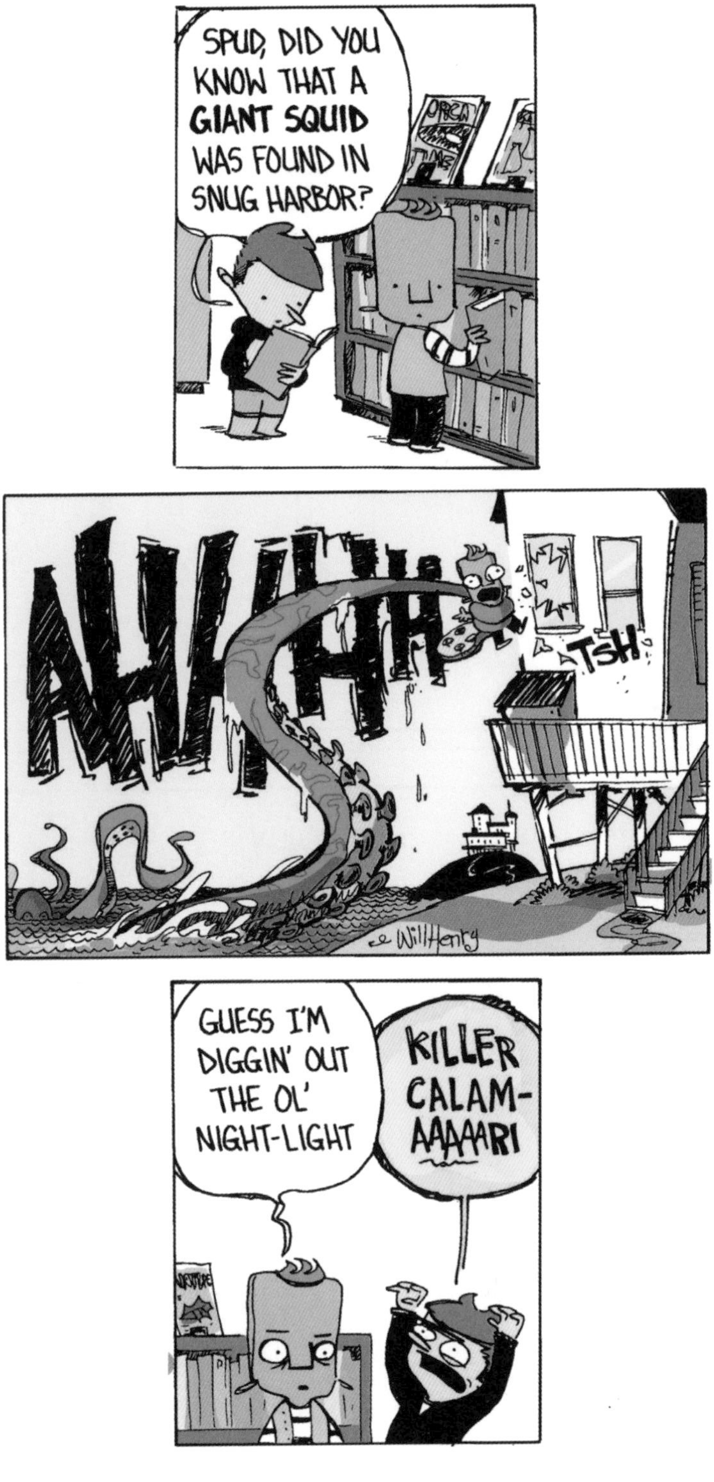
SPUD, DID YOU KNOW THAT A **GIANT SQUID** WAS FOUND IN SNUG HARBOR?
AHHHH
TSH
GUESS I'M DIGGIN' OUT THE OL' NIGHT-LIGHT
KILLER CALAM-AAAAARI

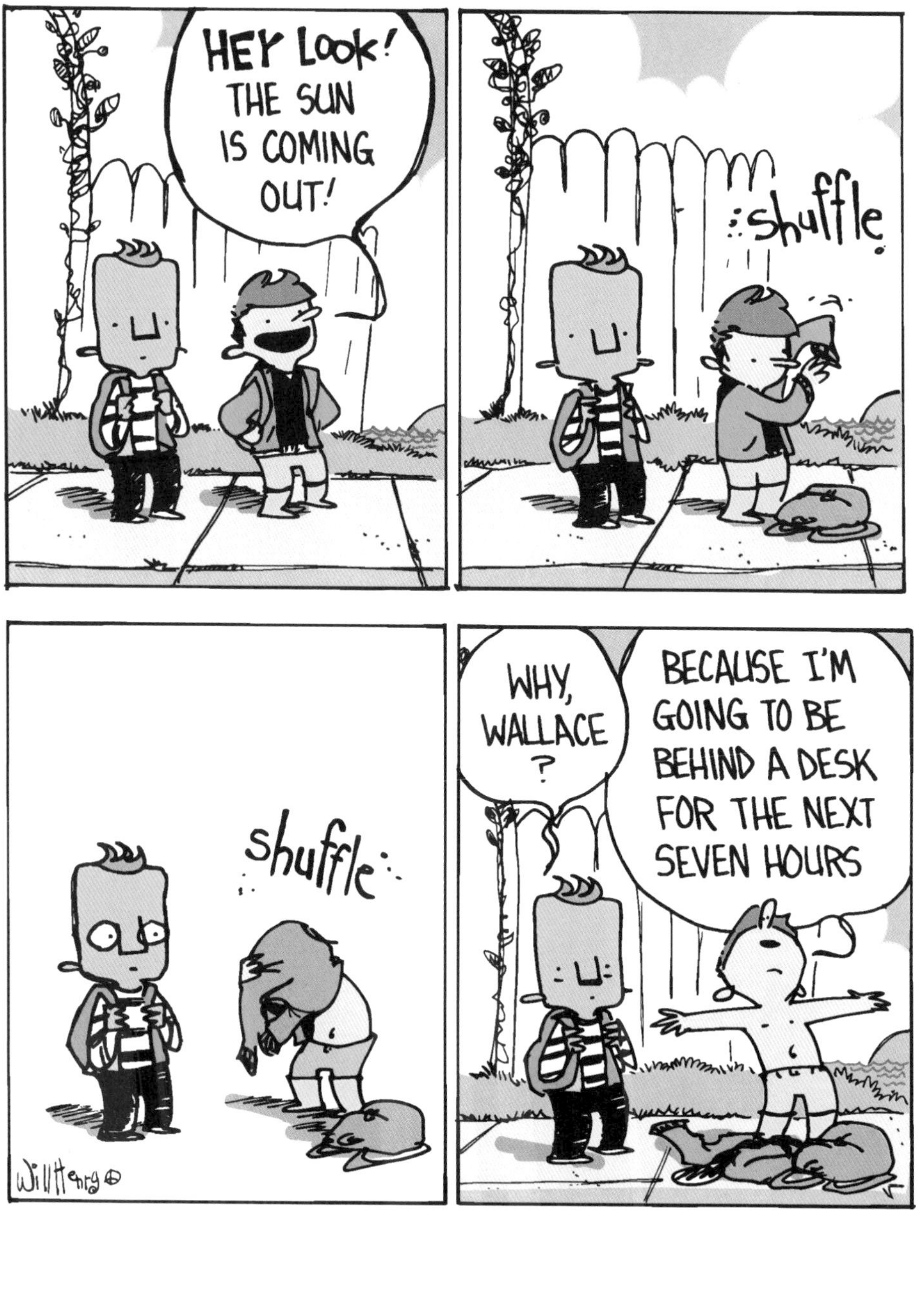
HEY LOOK! THE SUN IS COMING OUT!
shuffle
shuffle
WHY, WALLACE?
BECAUSE I'M GOING TO BE BEHIND A DESK FOR THE NEXT SEVEN HOURS
Will Henry

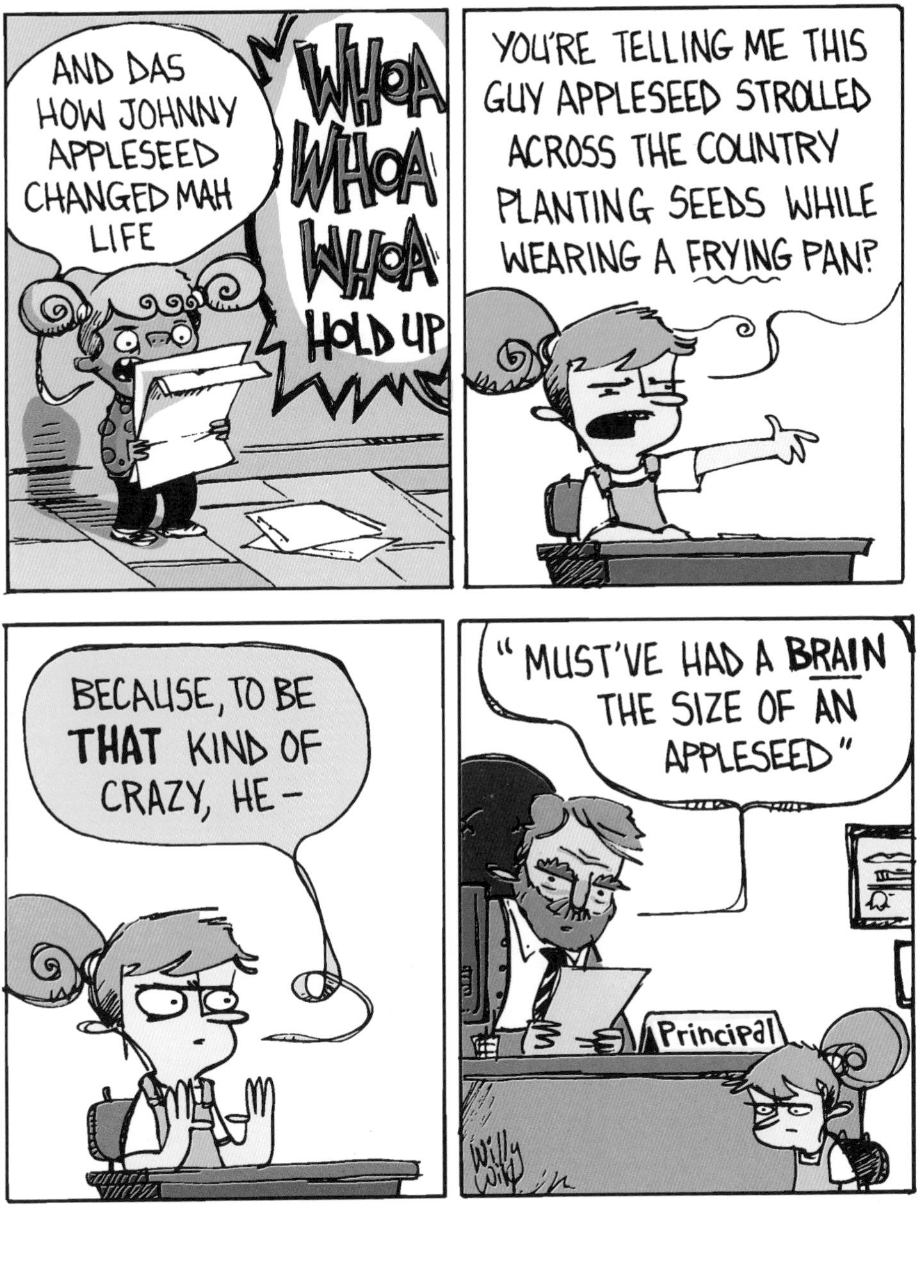
AND DAS HOW JOHNNY APPLESEED CHANGED MAH LIFE
WHOA WHOA WHOA HOLD UP
YOU'RE TELLING ME THIS GUY APPLESEED STROLLED ACROSS THE COUNTRY PLANTING SEEDS WHILE WEARING A FRYING PAN?
BECAUSE, TO BE THAT KIND OF CRAZY, HE-
"MUST'VE HAD A BRAIN THE SIZE OF AN APPLESEED"
Principal
Willy Wiki

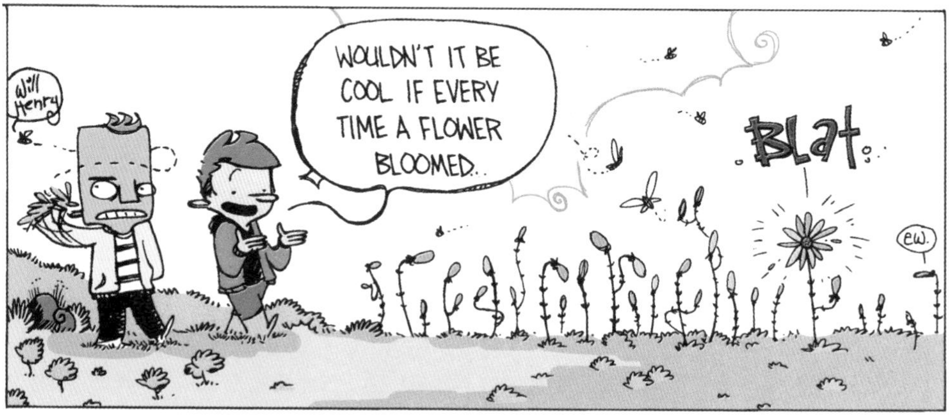
Will Henry
WOULDN'T IT BE COOL IF EVERY TIME A FLOWER BLOOMED...
BLAT
EW.

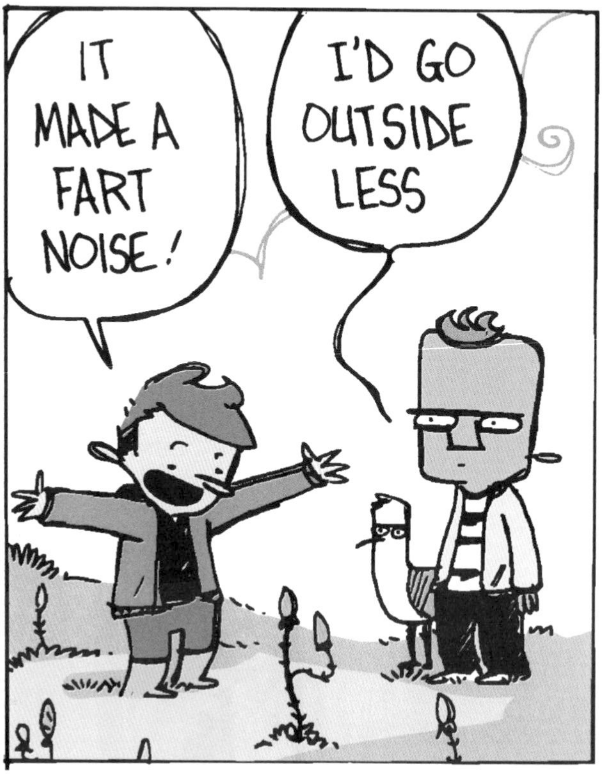
IT MADE A FART NOISE!
I'D GO OUTSIDE LESS

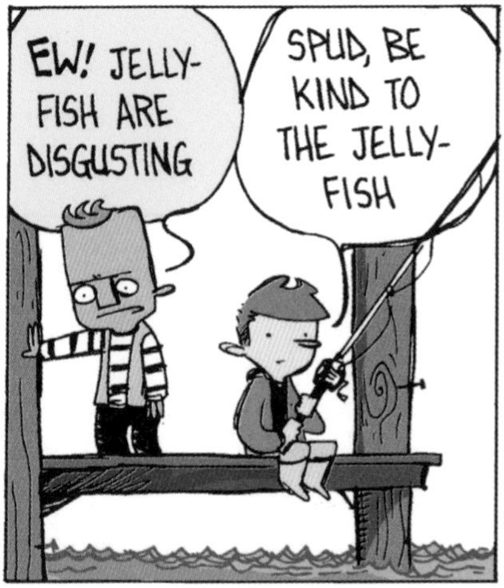
EW! JELLY-FISH ARE DISGUSTING
SPUD, BE KIND TO THE JELLY-FISH

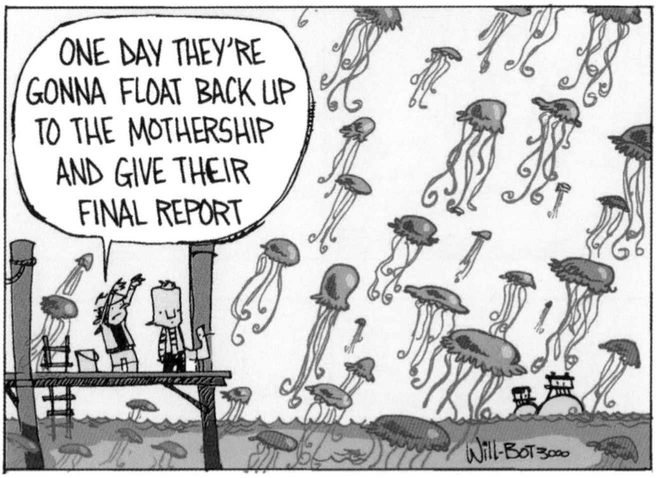
ONE DAY THEY'RE GONNA FLOAT BACK UP TO THE MOTHERSHIP AND GIVE THEIR FINAL REPORT
WILL-BOT3000

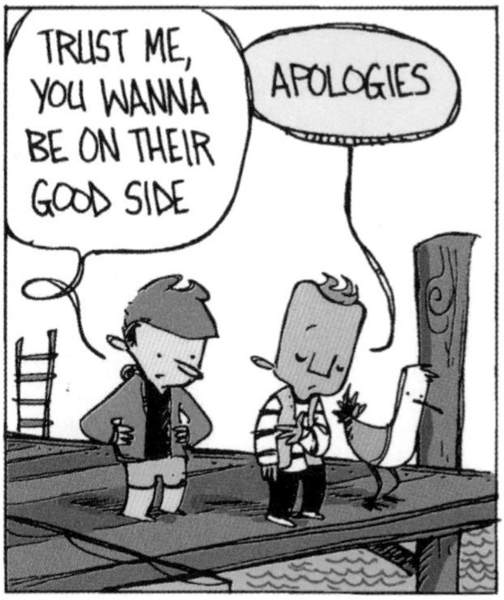
TRUST ME, YOU WANNA BE ON THEIR GOOD SIDE
APOLOGIES

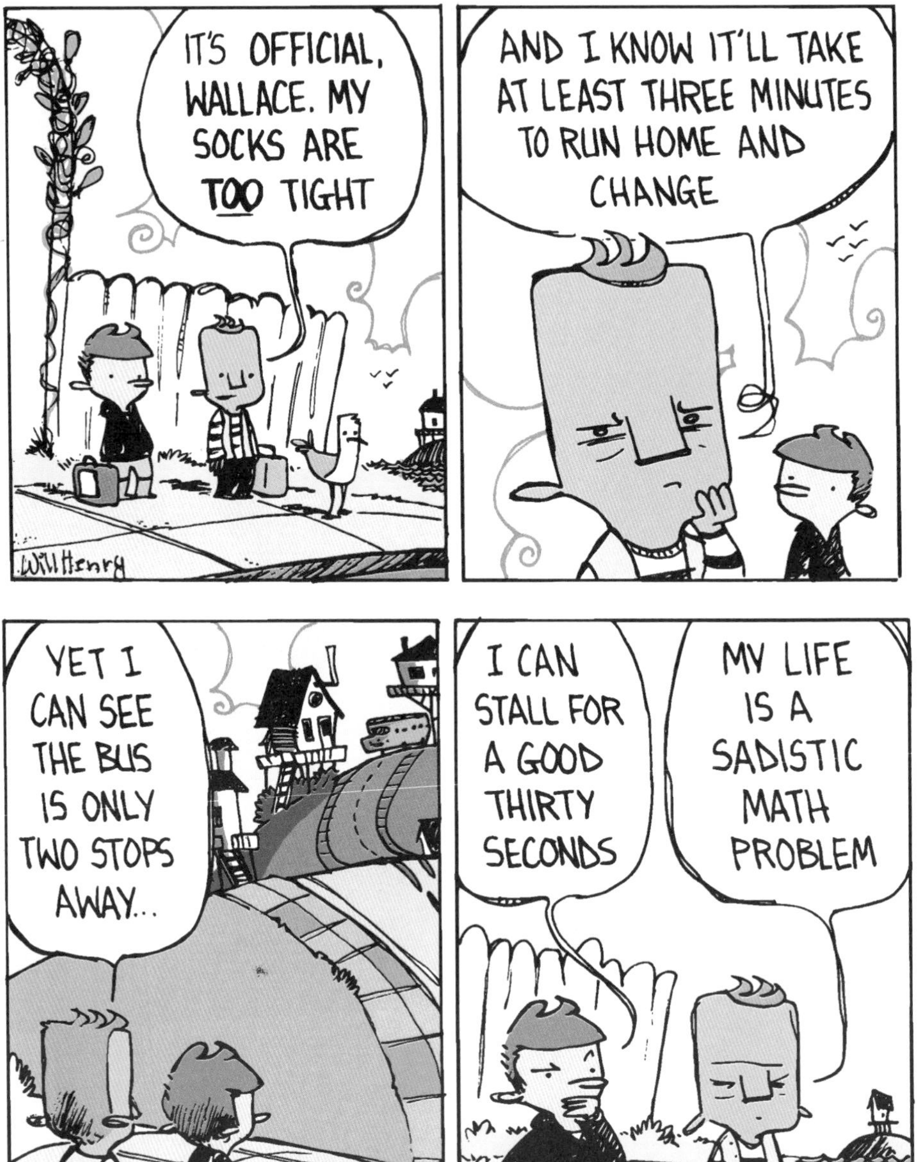
IT'S OFFICIAL, WALLACE. MY SOCKS ARE TOO TIGHT
WillHenry
AND I KNOW IT'LL TAKE AT LEAST THREE MINUTES TO RUN HOME AND CHANGE
YET I CAN SEE THE BUS IS ONLY TWO STOPS AWAY...
I CAN STALL FOR A GOOD THIRTY SECONDS
MY LIFE IS A SADISTIC MATH PROBLEM

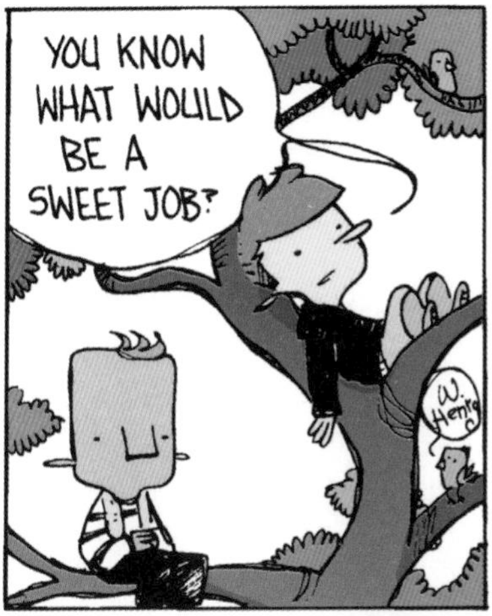
YOU KNOW WHAT WOULD BE A SWEET JOB?

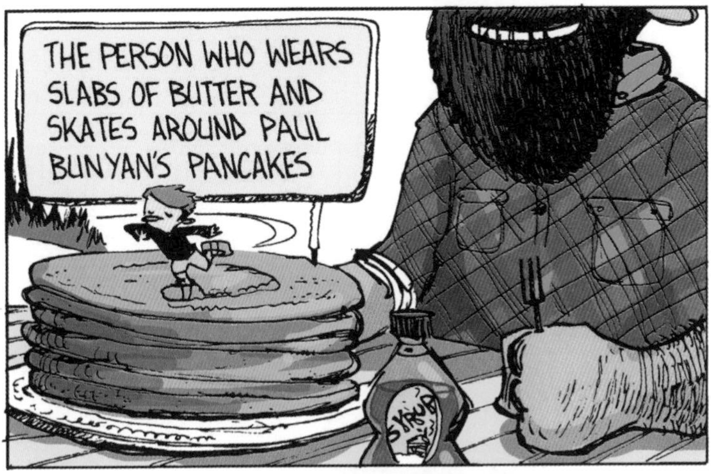
THE PERSON WHO WEARS SLABS OF BUTTER AND SKATES AROUND PAUL BUNYAN'S PANCAKES
SYRUP

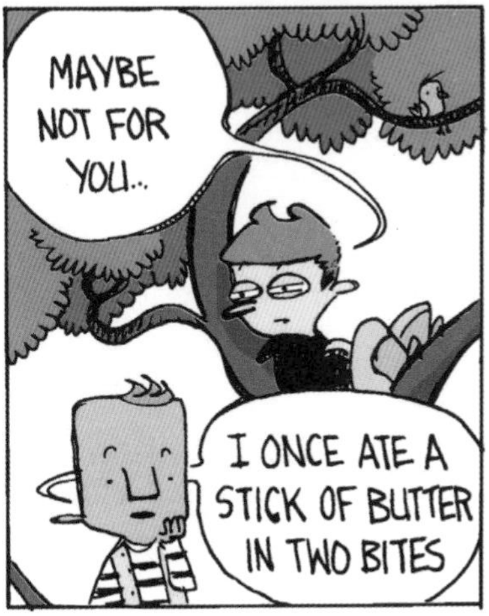
MAYBE NOT FOR YOU...
I ONCE ATE A STICK OF BUTTER IN TWO BITES

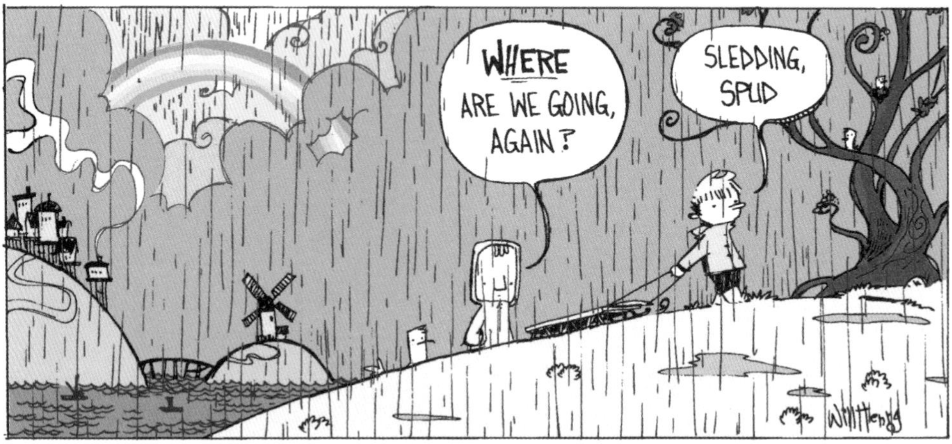
WHERE ARE WE GOING, AGAIN?
SLEDDING, SPUD

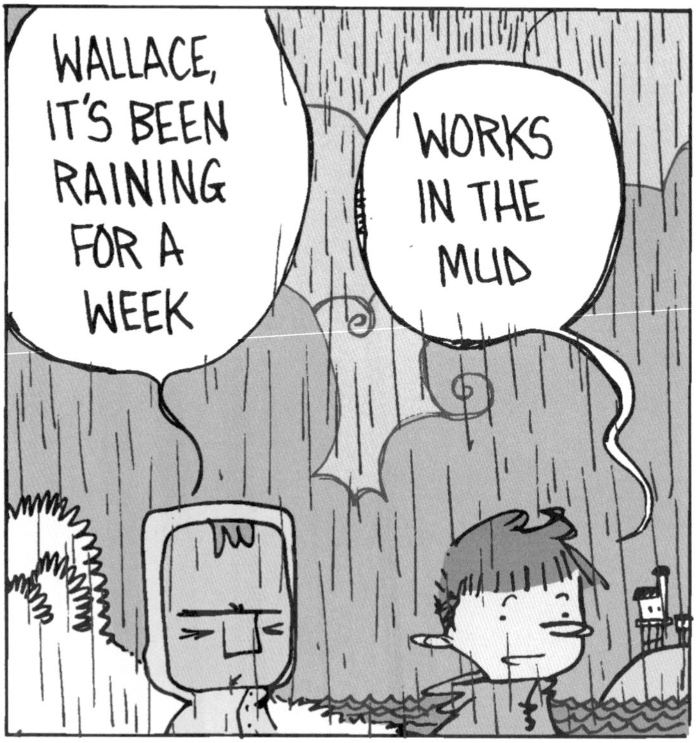
WALLACE, IT'S BEEN RAINING FOR A WEEK
WORKS IN THE MUD

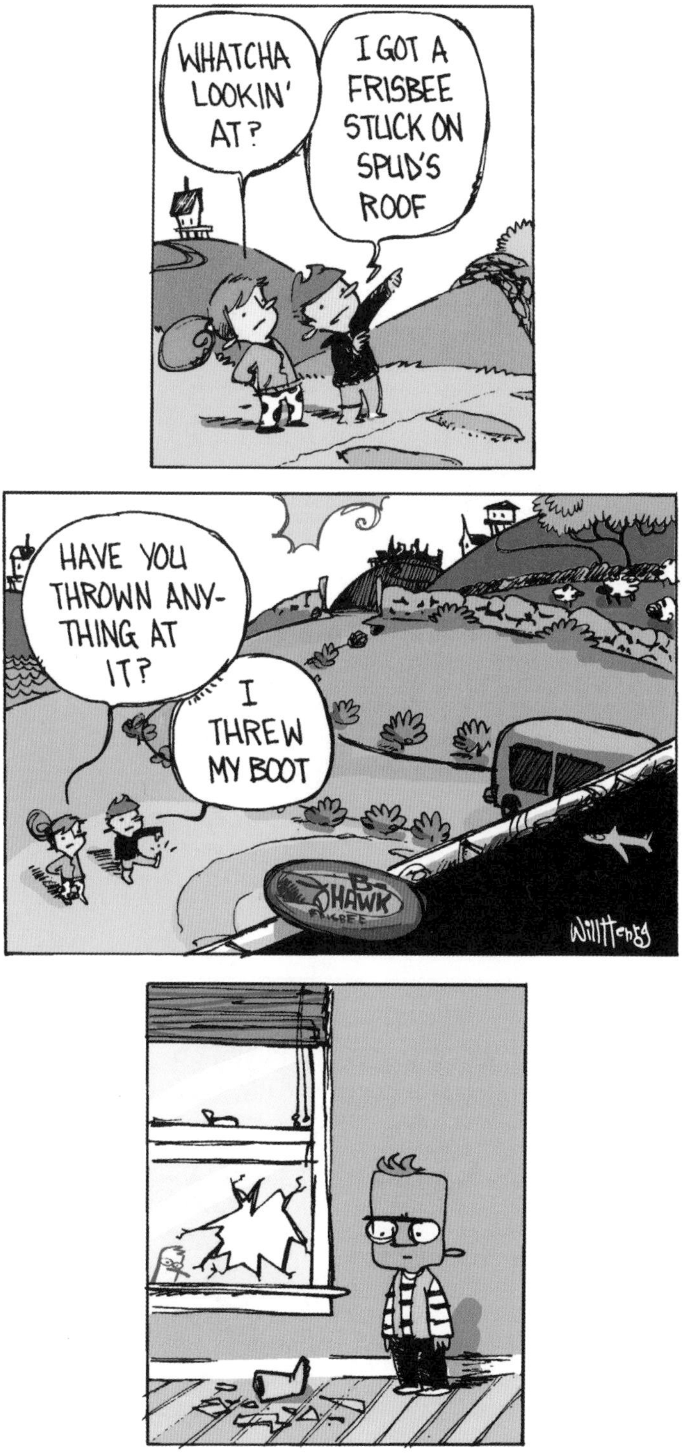
WHATCHA LOOKIN' AT?
I GOT A FRISBEE STUCK ON SPUD'S ROOF
HAVE YOU THROWN ANY-THING AT IT?
I THREW MY BOOT
B-HAWK

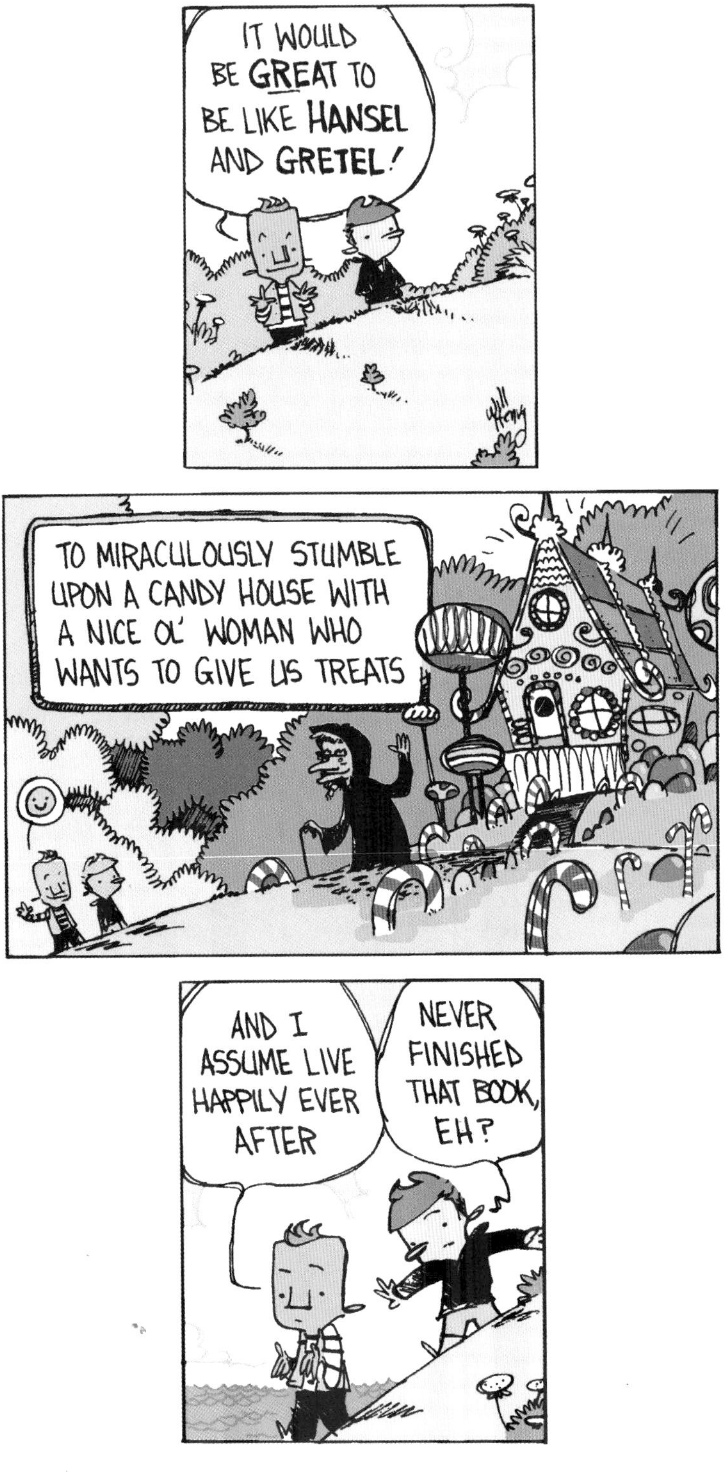
IT WOULD BE GREAT TO BE LIKE HANSEL AND GRETEL!
TO MIRACULOUSLY STUMBLE UPON A CANDY HOUSE WITH A NICE OL' WOMAN WHO WANTS TO GIVE US TREATS
AND I ASSUME LIVE HAPPILY EVER AFTER
NEVER FINISHED THAT BOOK, EH?

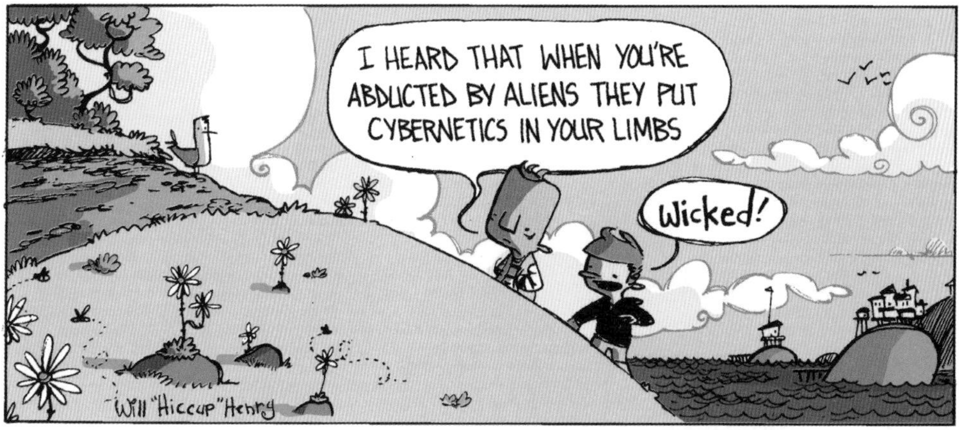
I HEARD THAT WHEN YOU'RE ABDUCTED BY ALIENS THEY PUT CYBERNETICS IN YOUR LIMBS
Wicked!
Will "Hiccup" Henry

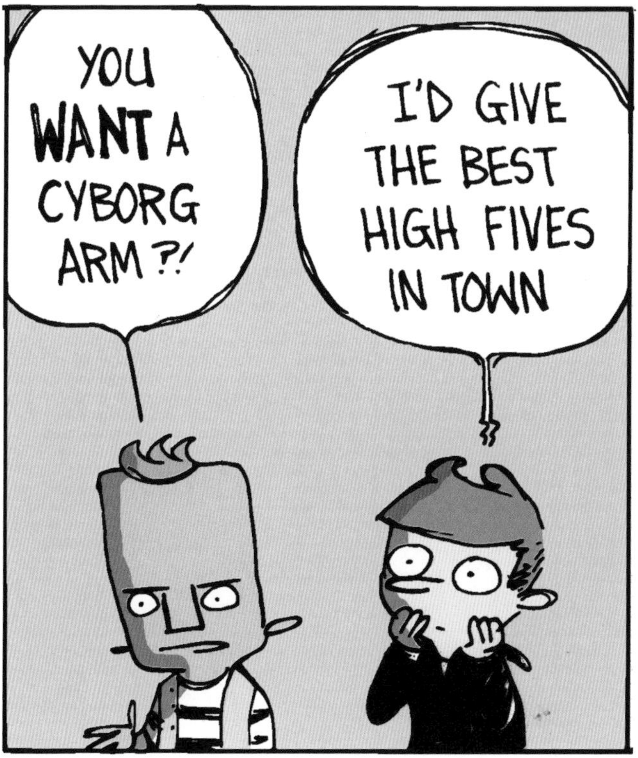
YOU **WANT** A CYBORG ARM ?!
I'D GIVE THE BEST HIGH FIVES IN TOWN

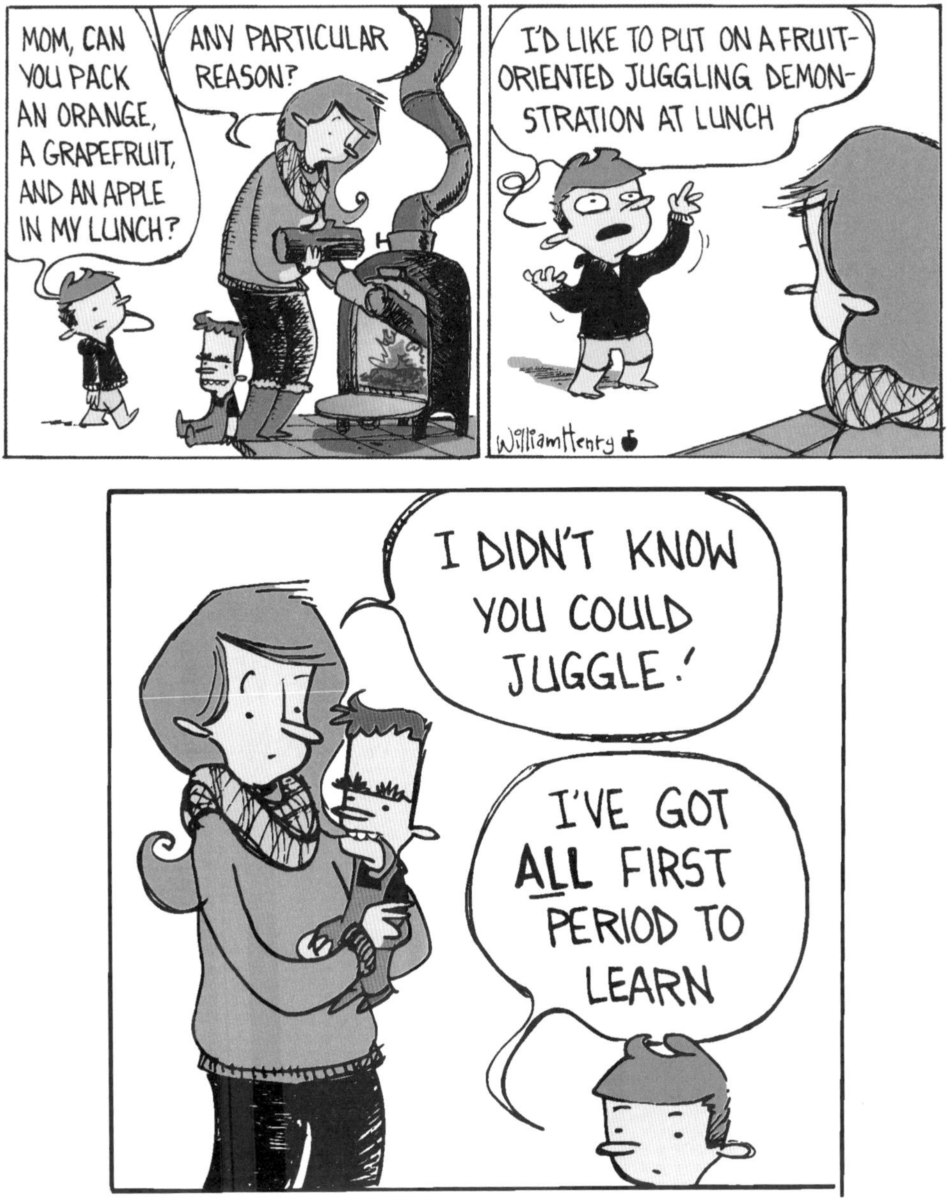
MOM, CAN YOU PACK AN ORANGE, A GRAPEFRUIT, AND AN APPLE IN MY LUNCH?
ANY PARTICULAR REASON?
I'D LIKE TO PUT ON A FRUIT-ORIENTED JUGGLING DEMON-STRATION AT LUNCH
WilliamHenry
I DIDN'T KNOW YOU COULD JUGGLE!
I'VE GOT **ALL** FIRST PERIOD TO LEARN

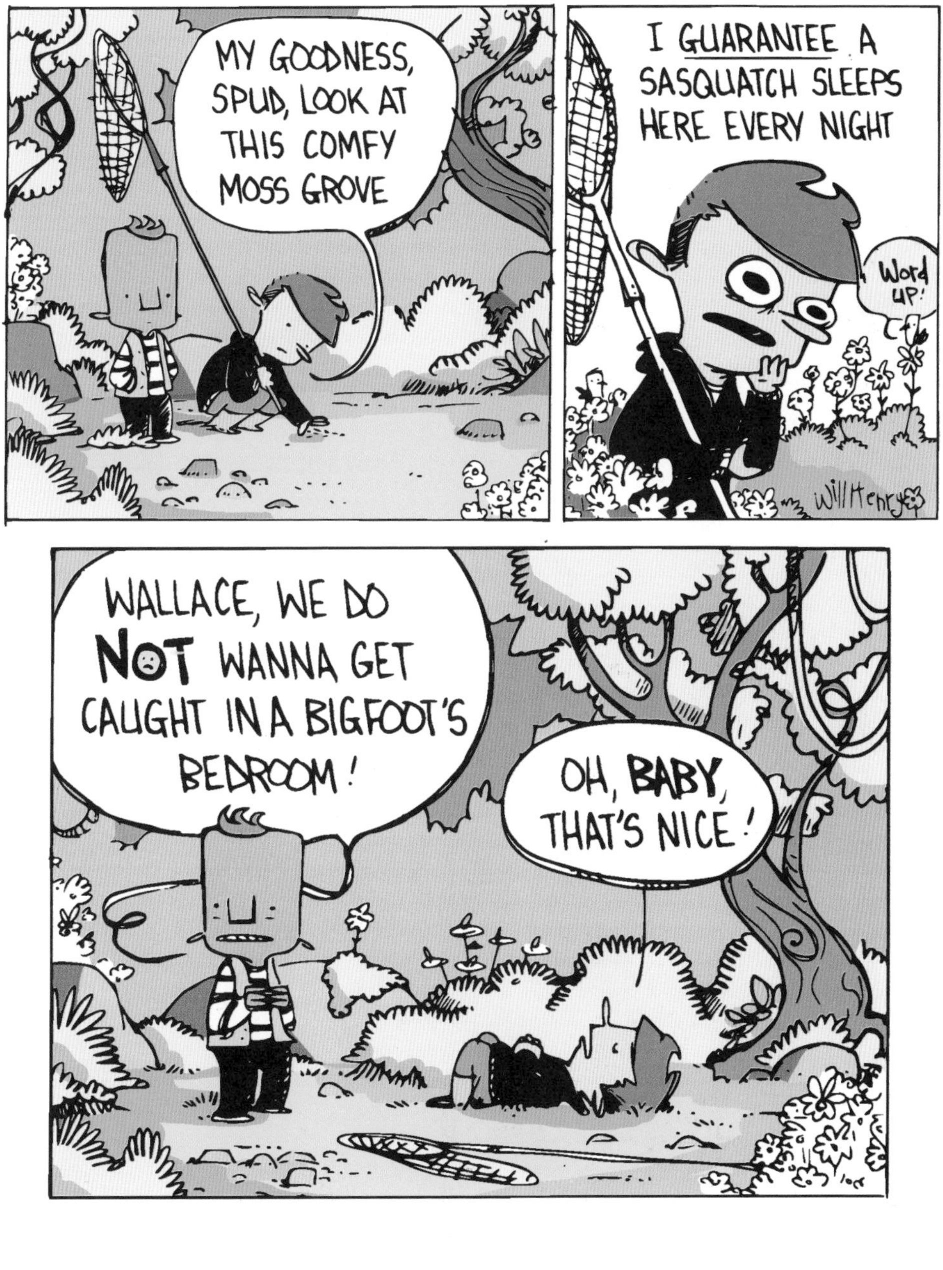
MY GOODNESS, SPUD, LOOK AT THIS COMFY MOSS GROVE
I GUARANTEE A SASQUATCH SLEEPS HERE EVERY NIGHT
Word up!
Will Henry
WALLACE, WE DO NOT WANNA GET CAUGHT IN A BIGFOOT'S BEDROOM!
OH, BABY, THAT'S NICE!

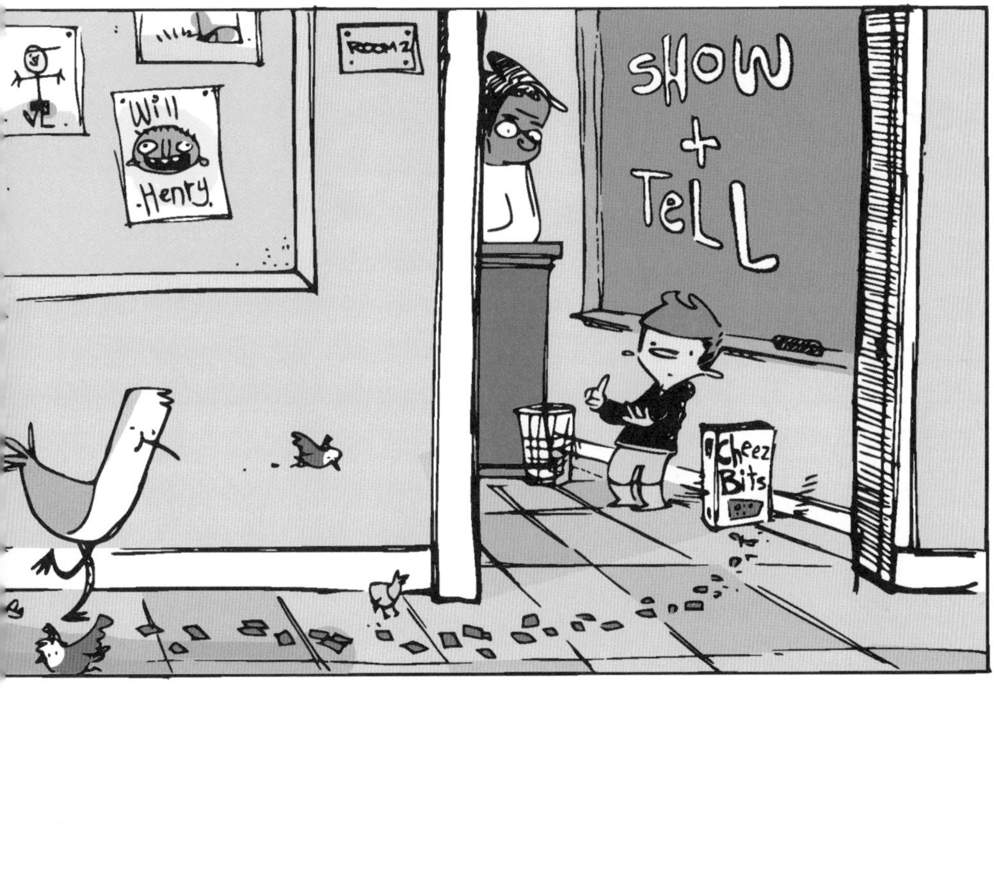
ROOM 2
Will
Henry
SHOW
+
TeLL
Cheez
Bits

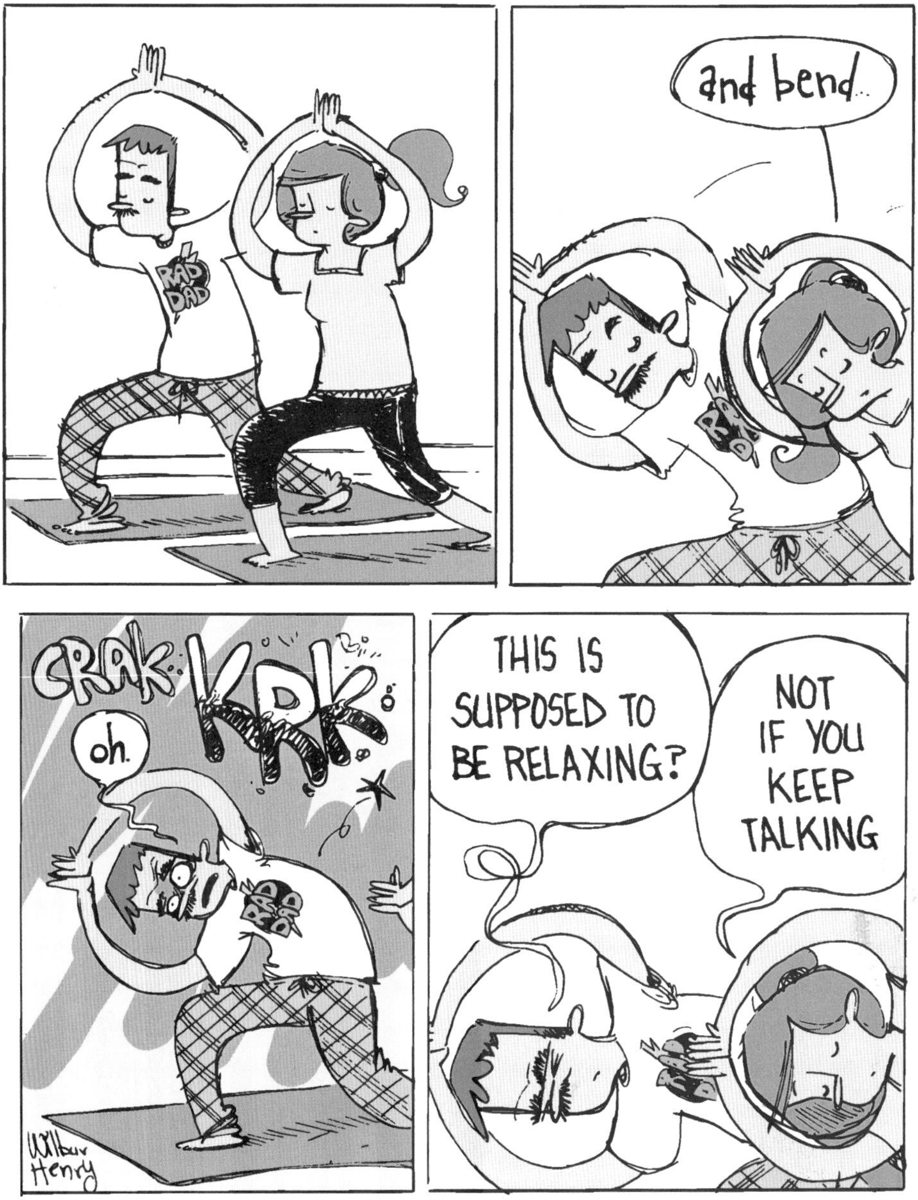
RAD DAD
and bend...
CRAK KRK
oh.
THIS IS SUPPOSED TO BE RELAXING?
NOT IF YOU KEEP TALKING
Wilbur Henry

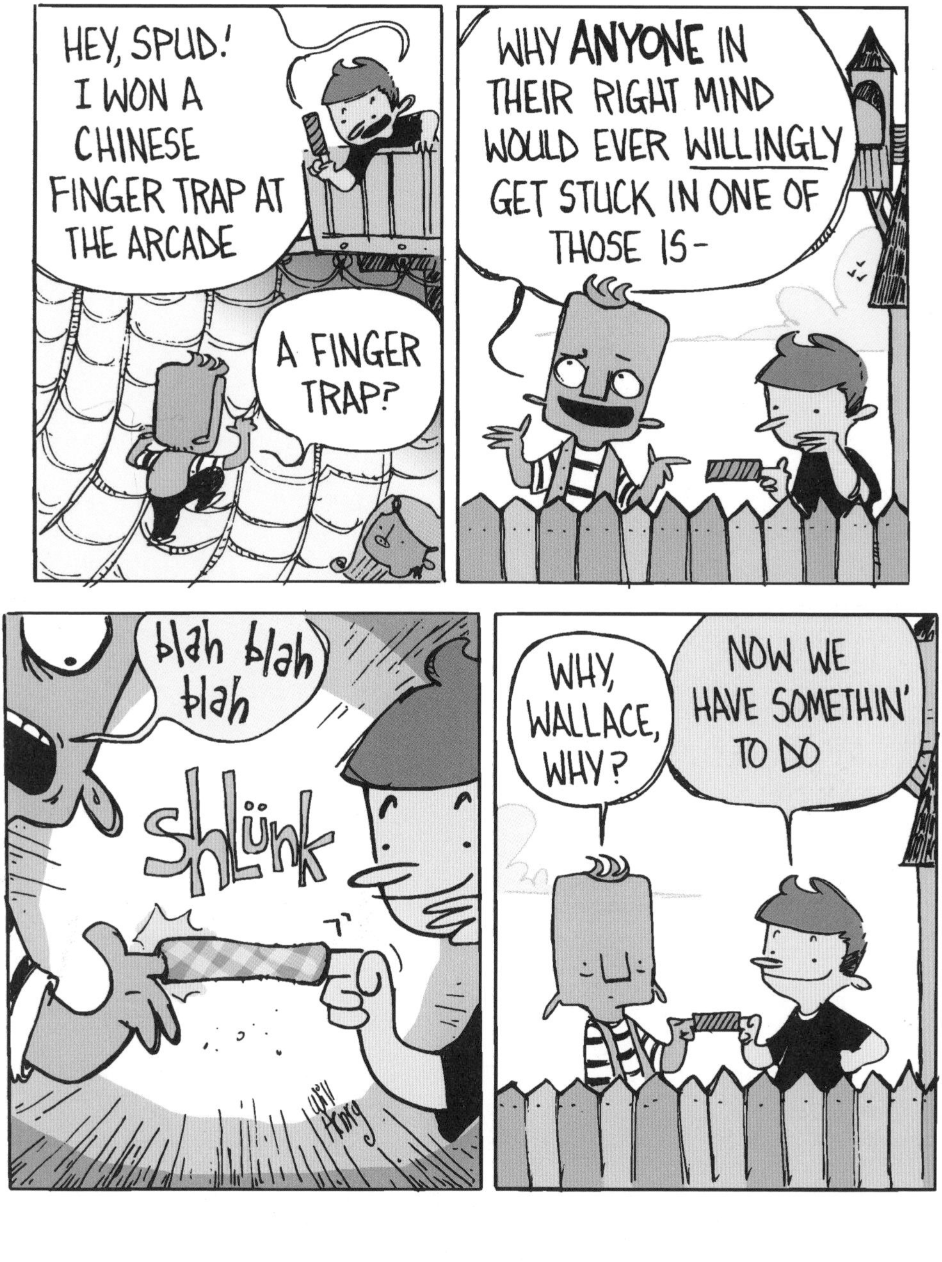
HEY, SPUD! I WON A CHINESE FINGER TRAP AT THE ARCADE
A FINGER TRAP?
WHY ANYONE IN THEIR RIGHT MIND WOULD EVER WILLINGLY GET STUCK IN ONE OF THOSE IS-
blah blah blah
shlünk
WHY, WALLACE, WHY?
NOW WE HAVE SOMETHIN' TO DO

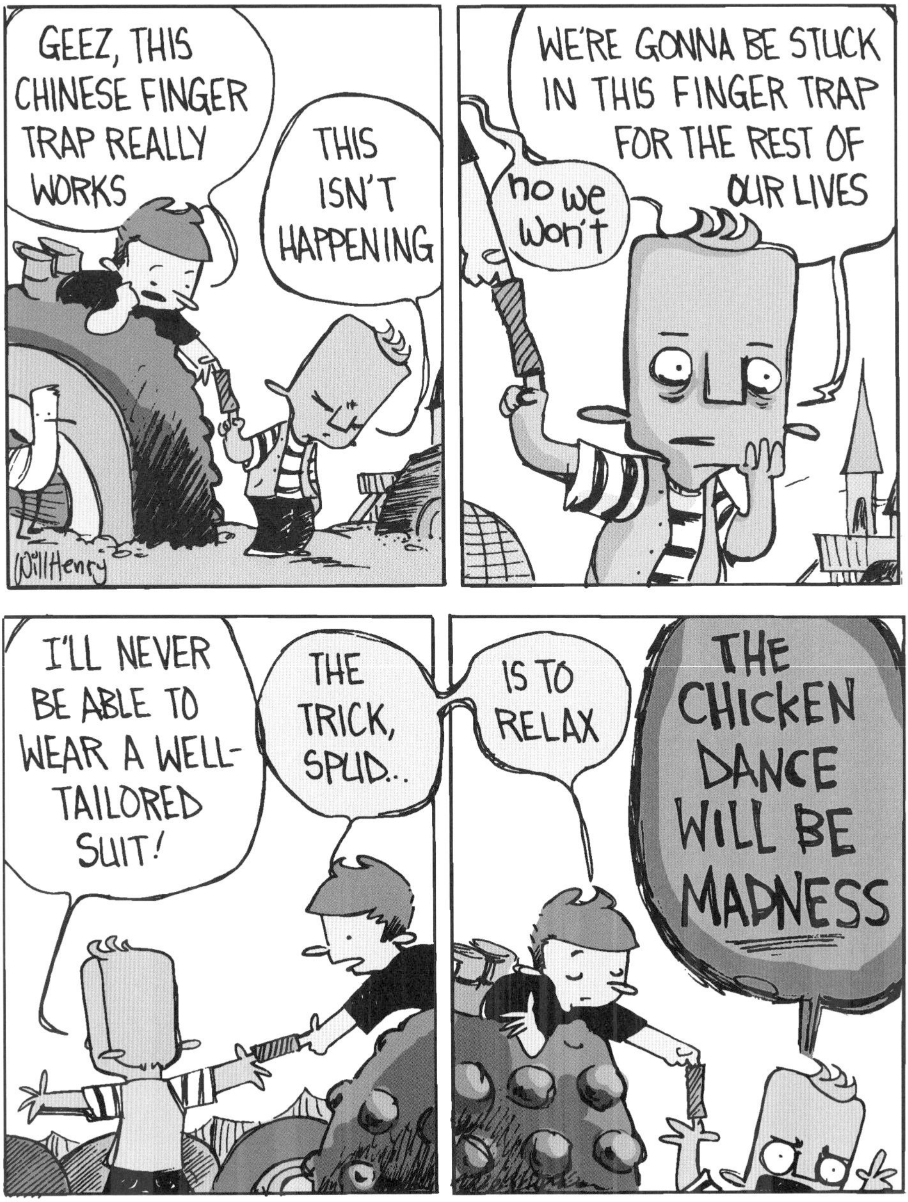
GEEZ, THIS CHINESE FINGER TRAP REALLY WORKS
THIS ISN'T HAPPENING
WillHenry
WE'RE GONNA BE STUCK IN THIS FINGER TRAP FOR THE REST OF OUR LIVES
no we won't
I'LL NEVER BE ABLE TO WEAR A WELL-TAILORED SUIT!
THE TRICK, SPUD...
IS TO RELAX
THE CHICKEN DANCE WILL BE MADNESS

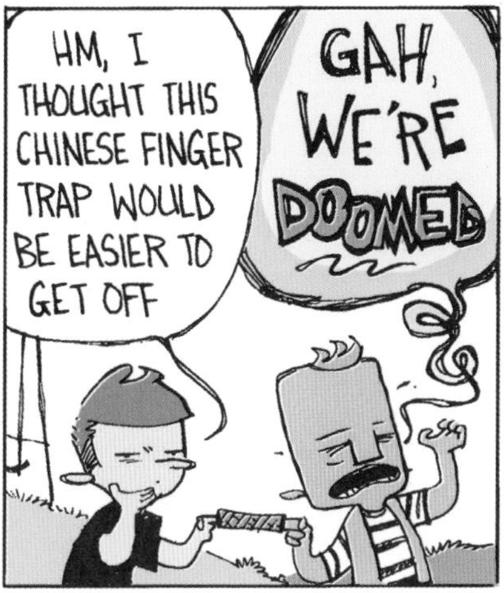
HM, I THOUGHT THIS CHINESE FINGER TRAP WOULD BE EASIER TO GET OFF
GAH, WE'RE DOOMED

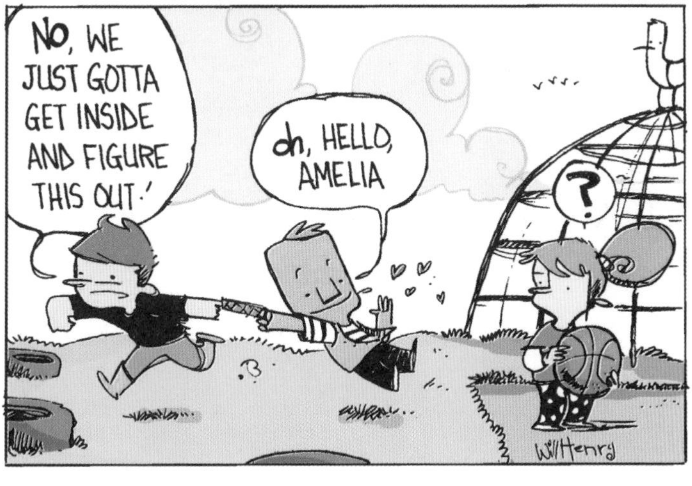
NO, WE JUST GOTTA GET INSIDE AND FIGURE THIS OUT!
oh, HELLO, AMELIA
?
WillHenry

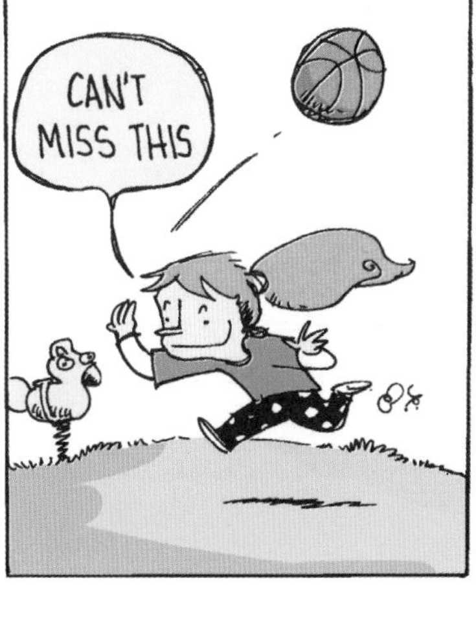
CAN'T MISS THIS

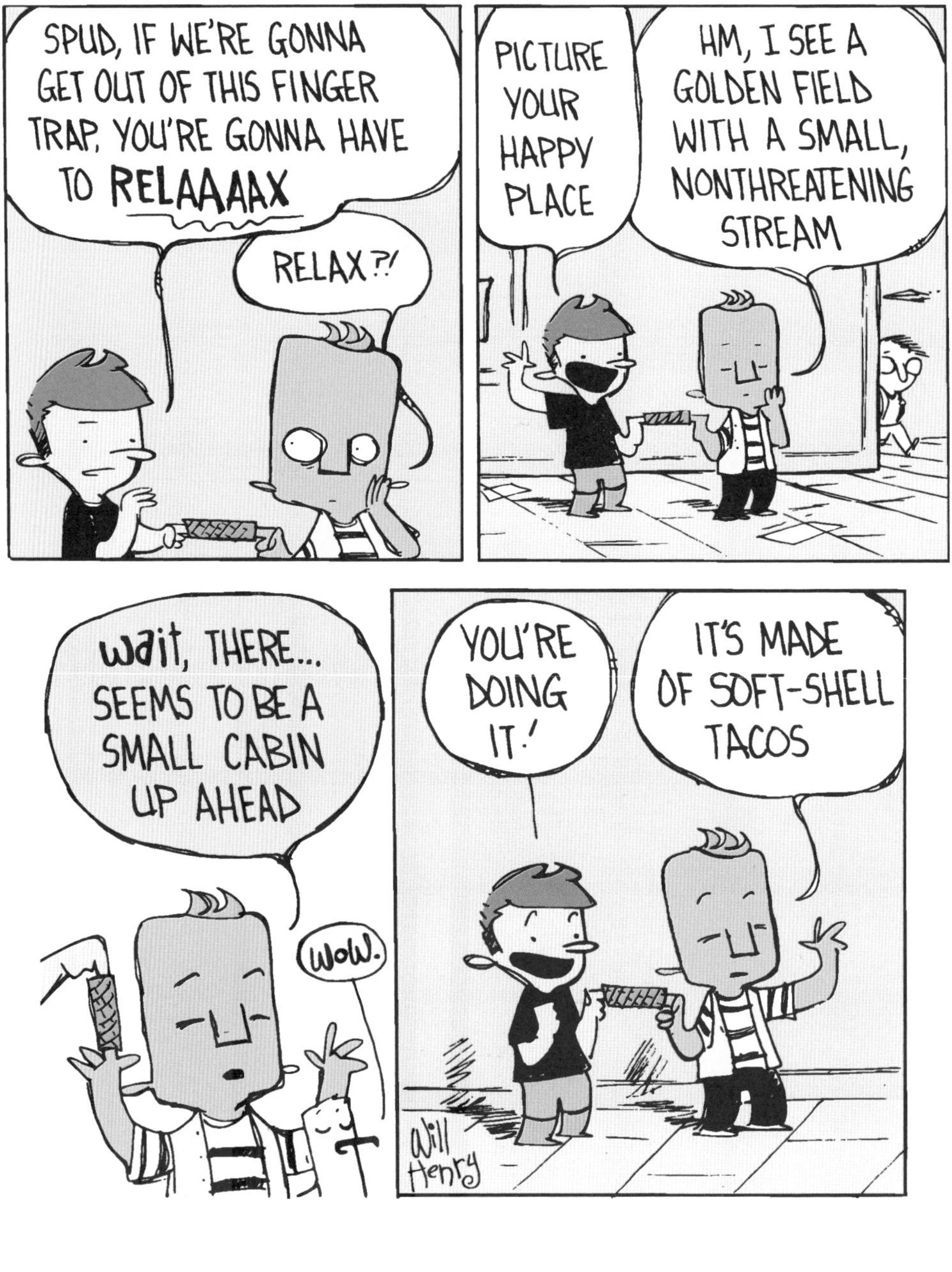
SPUD, IF WE'RE GONNA GET OUT OF THIS FINGER TRAP, YOU'RE GONNA HAVE TO RELAAAAX
RELAX?!
PICTURE YOUR HAPPY PLACE
HM, I SEE A GOLDEN FIELD WITH A SMALL, NONTHREATENING STREAM
wait, THERE... SEEMS TO BE A SMALL CABIN UP AHEAD
WOW.
YOU'RE DOING IT!
IT'S MADE OF SOFT-SHELL TACOS
Will Henry

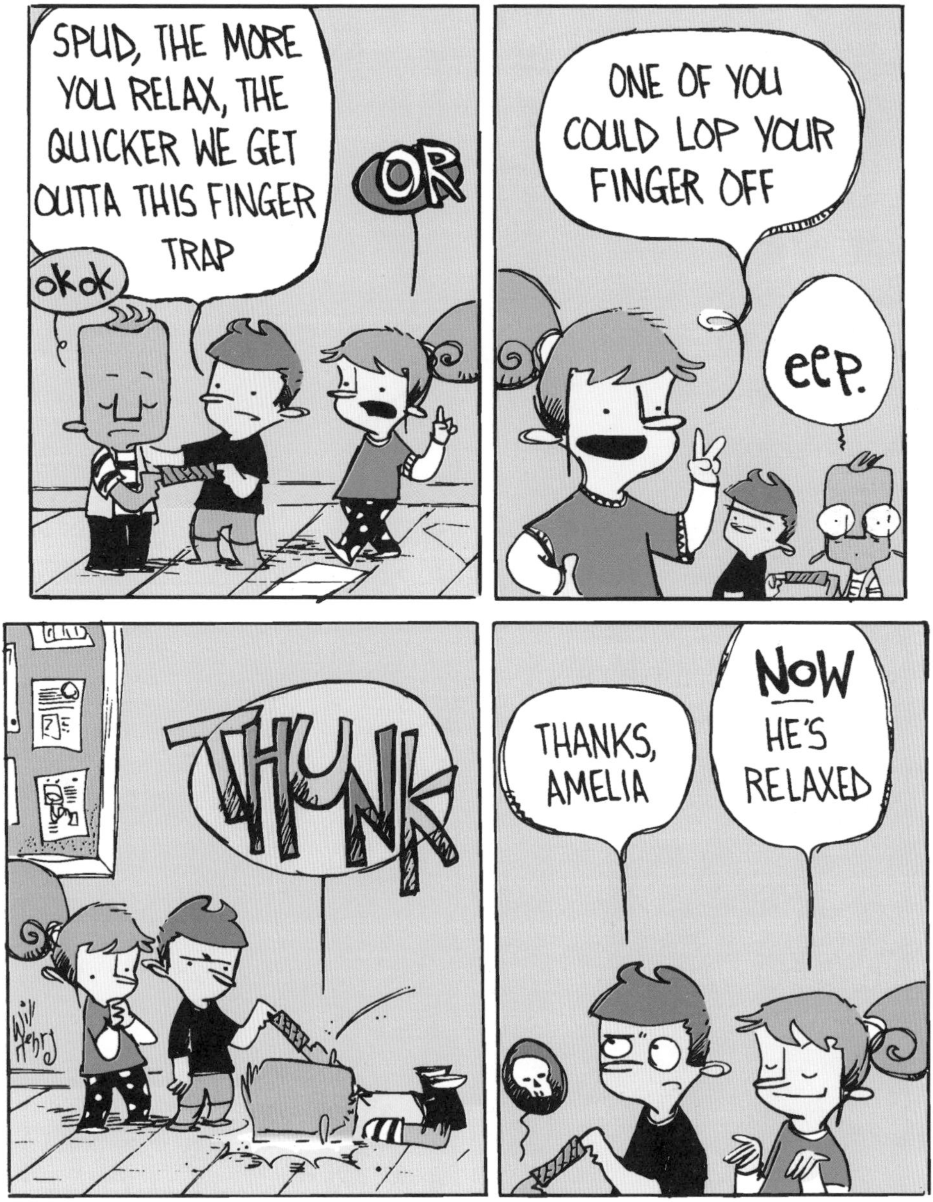
SPUD, THE MORE YOU RELAX, THE QUICKER WE GET OUTTA THIS FINGER TRAP
okok
OR
ONE OF YOU COULD LOP YOUR FINGER OFF
eep.
THUNK
THANKS, AMELIA
NOW HE'S RELAXED

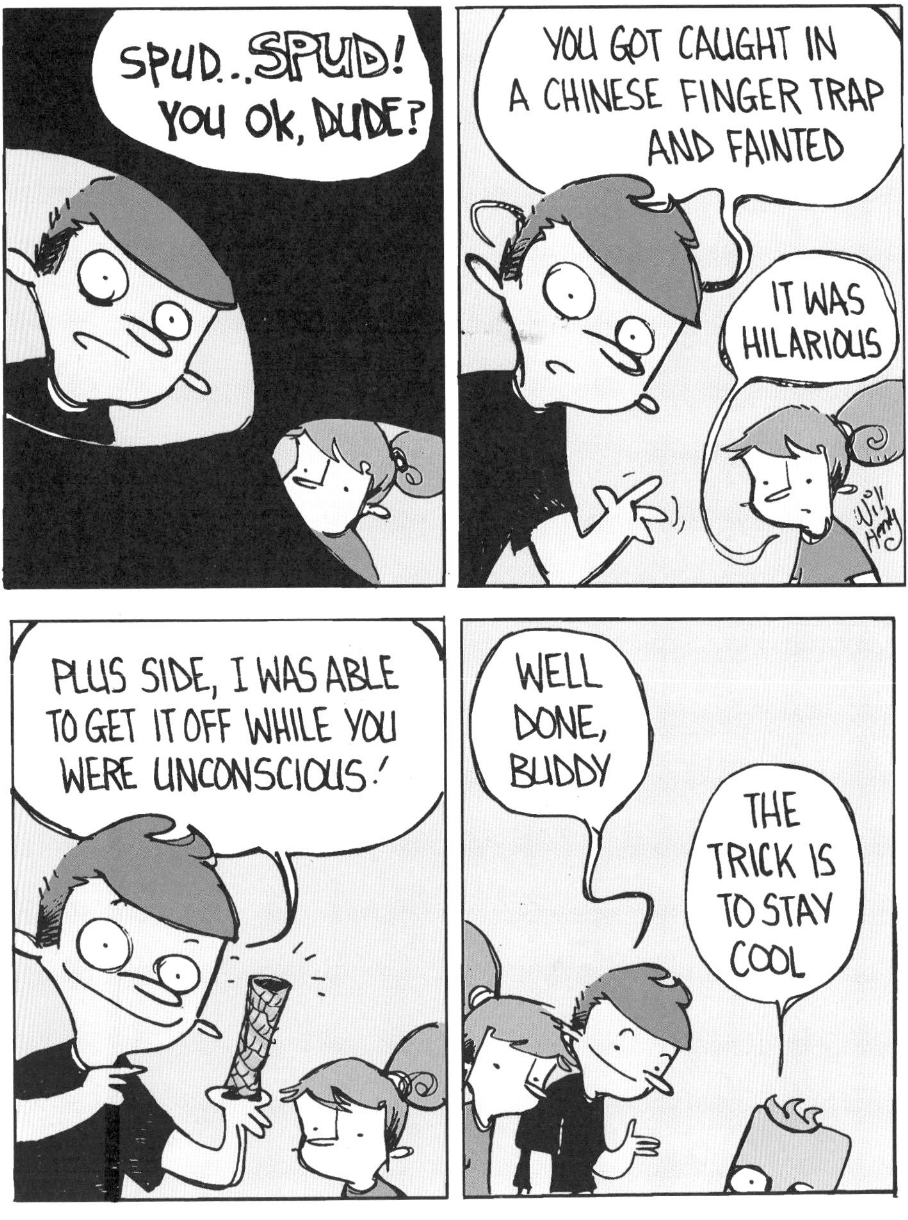
SPUD...SPUD!
YOU OK, DUDE?
YOU GOT CAUGHT IN A CHINESE FINGER TRAP AND FAINTED
IT WAS HILARIOUS
PLUS SIDE, I WAS ABLE TO GET IT OFF WHILE YOU WERE UNCONSCIOUS!
WELL DONE, BUDDY
THE TRICK IS TO STAY COOL

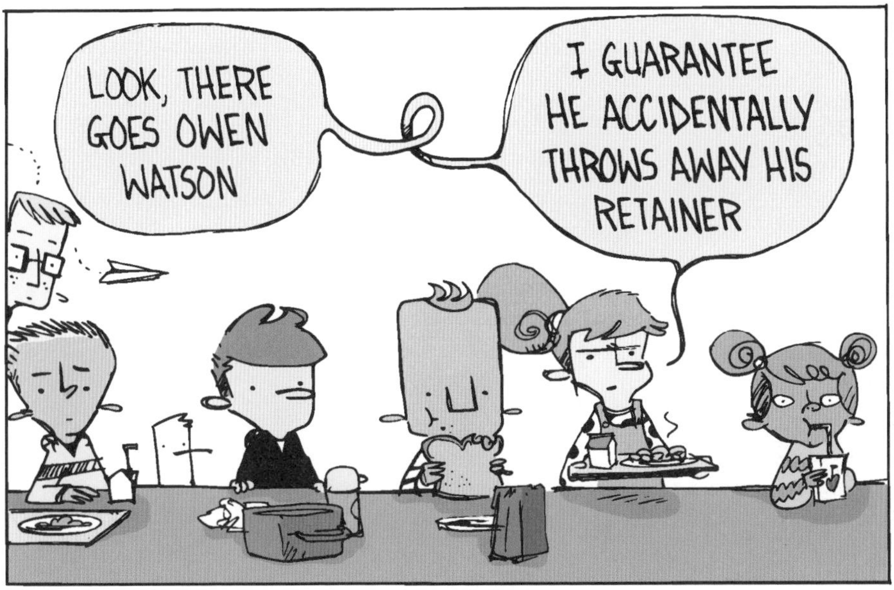
LOOK, THERE GOES OWEN WATSON
I GUARANTEE HE ACCIDENTALLY THROWS AWAY HIS RETAINER

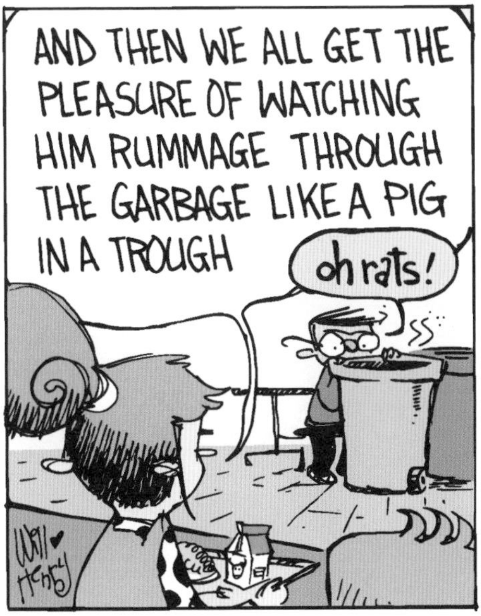
AND THEN WE ALL GET THE PLEASURE OF WATCHING HIM RUMMAGE THROUGH THE GARBAGE LIKE A PIG IN A TROUGH
oh rats!
Will Henry

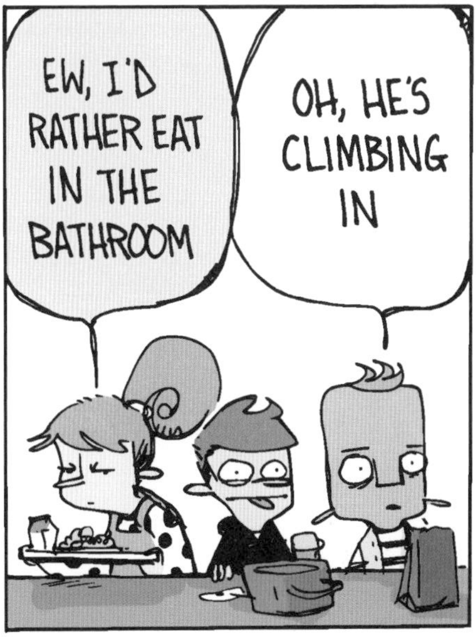
EW, I'D RATHER EAT IN THE BATHROOM
OH, HE'S CLIMBING IN

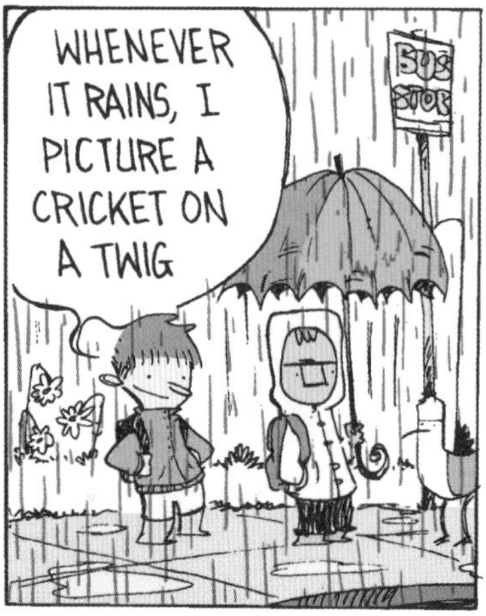
WHENEVER IT RAINS, I PICTURE A CRICKET ON A TWIG
BUS STOP

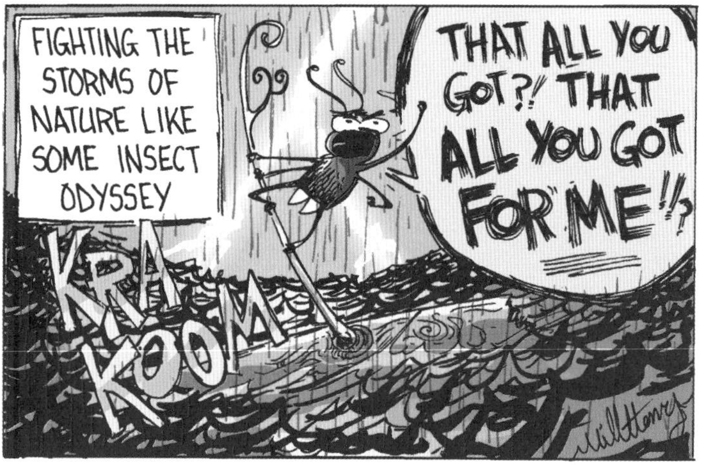
FIGHTING THE STORMS OF NATURE LIKE SOME INSECT ODYSSEY
THAT ALL YOU GOT?! THAT ALL YOU GOT FOR ME!?
KRA KOOM

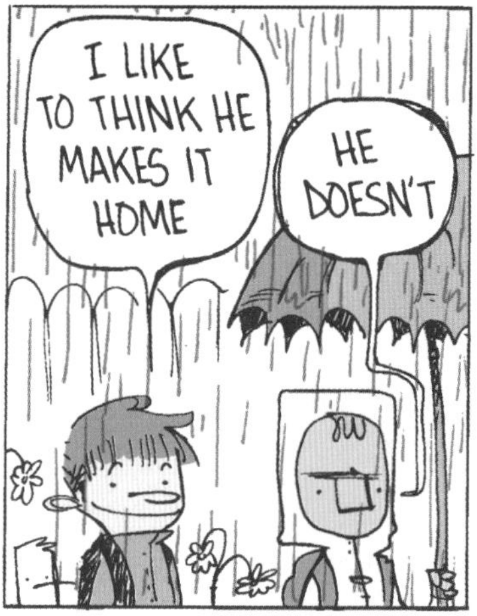
I LIKE TO THINK HE MAKES IT HOME
HE DOESN'T

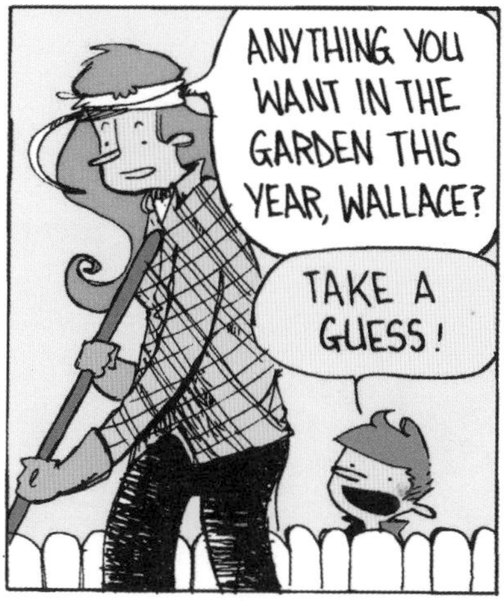
ANYTHING YOU WANT IN THE GARDEN THIS YEAR, WALLACE?
TAKE A GUESS!

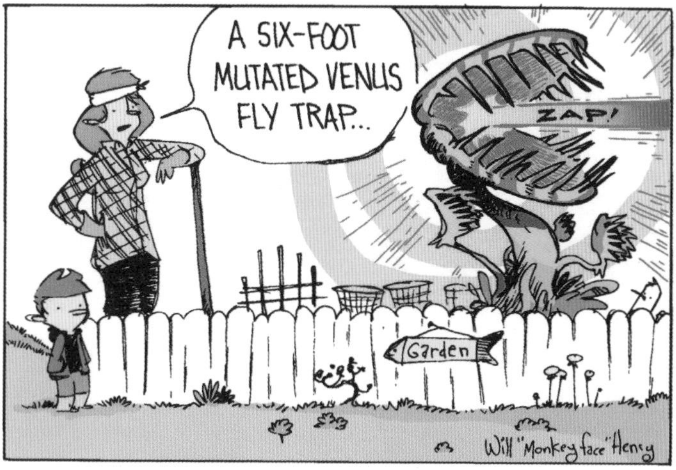
A SIX-FOOT MUTATED VENUS FLY TRAP...
ZAP!
Garden
Will "Monkeyface" Henry

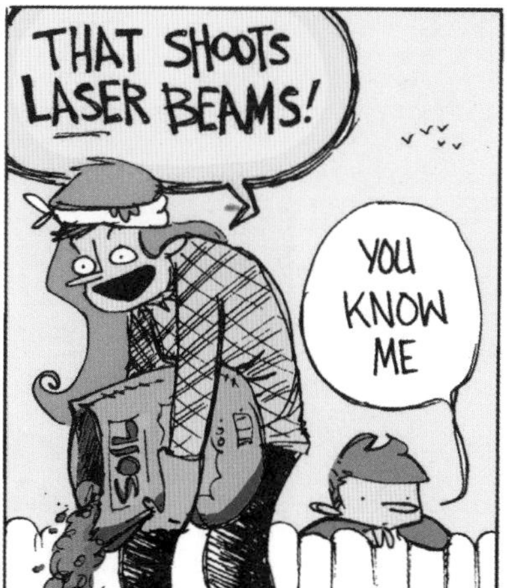
THAT SHOOTS LASER BEAMS!
YOU KNOW ME

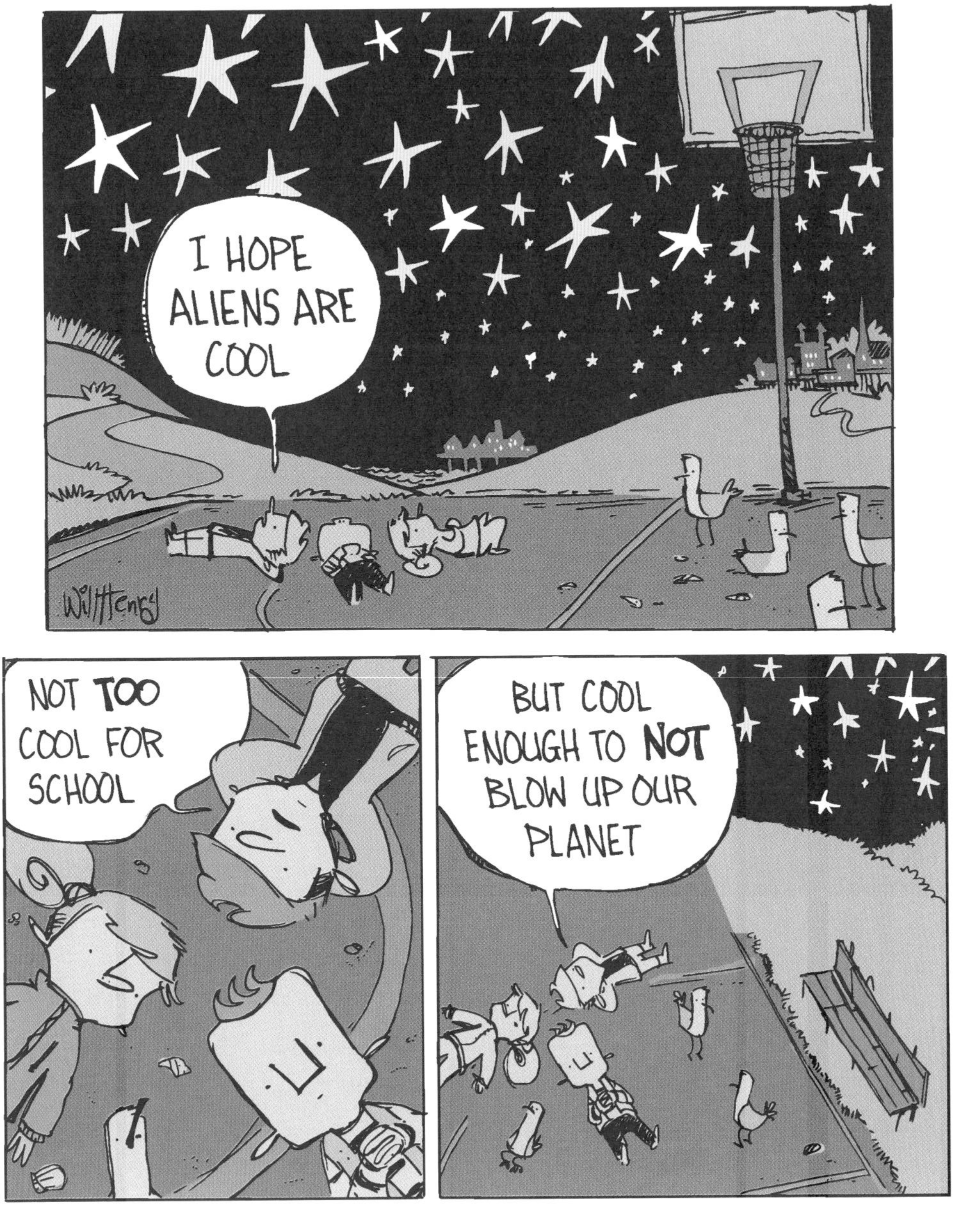
I HOPE ALIENS ARE COOL
WillHenry
NOT **TOO** COOL FOR SCHOOL
BUT COOL ENOUGH TO **NOT** BLOW UP OUR PLANET

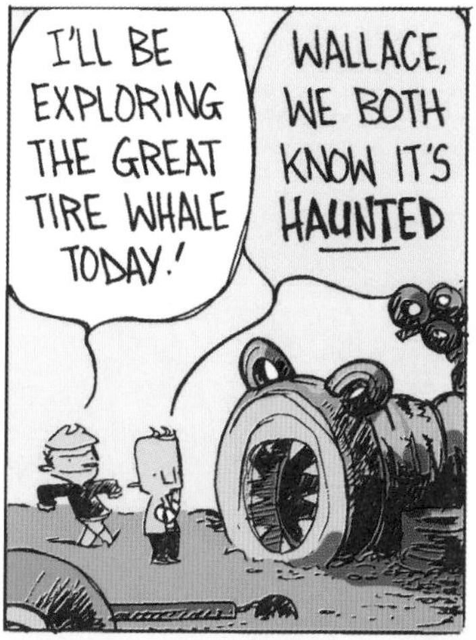
I'LL BE EXPLORING THE GREAT TIRE WHALE TODAY!
WALLACE, WE BOTH KNOW IT'S HAUNTED

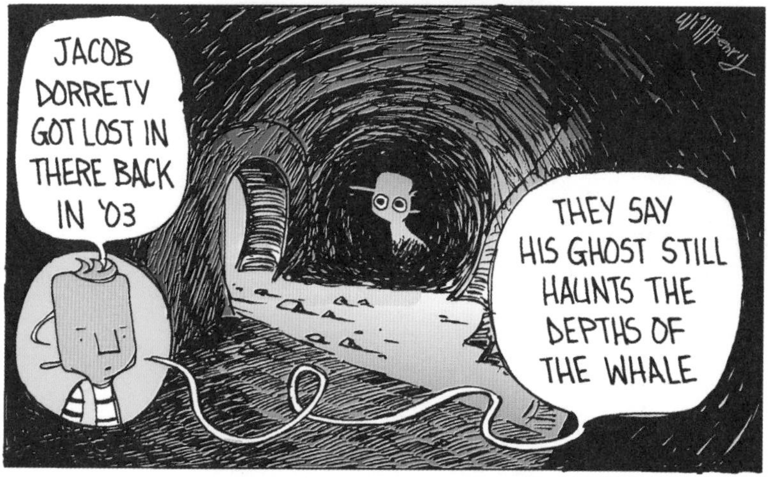
JACOB DORRETY GOT LOST IN THERE BACK IN '03
THEY SAY HIS GHOST STILL HAUNTS THE DEPTHS OF THE WHALE

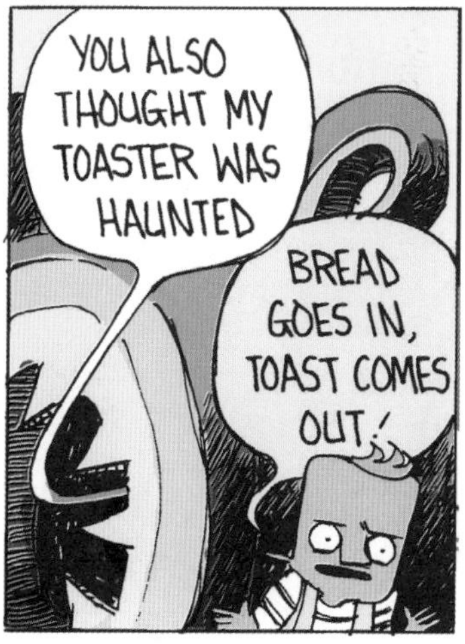
YOU ALSO THOUGHT MY TOASTER WAS HAUNTED
BREAD GOES IN, TOAST COMES OUT!

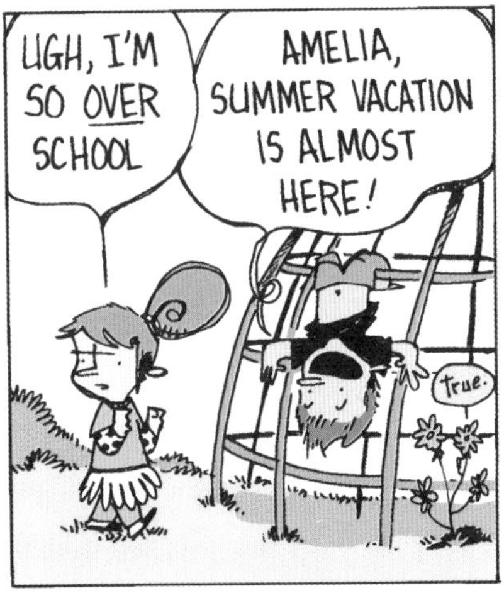
UGH, I'M SO OVER SCHOOL
AMELIA, SUMMER VACATION IS ALMOST HERE!
true.

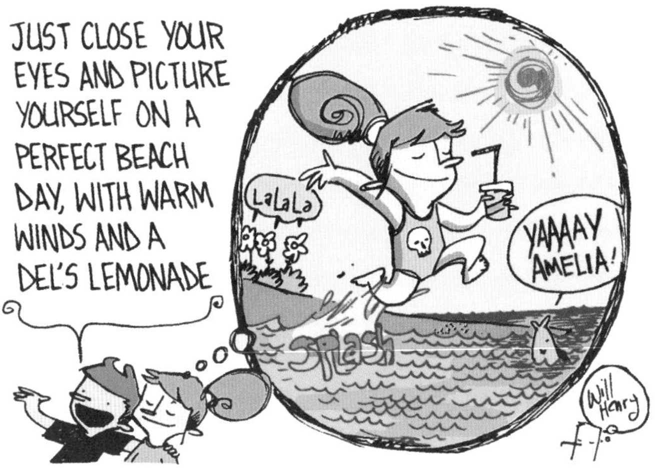
JUST CLOSE YOUR EYES AND PICTURE YOURSELF ON A PERFECT BEACH DAY, WITH WARM WINDS AND A DEL'S LEMONADE
LaLaLa
YAAAAY AMELIA!
SPLASH
Will Henry

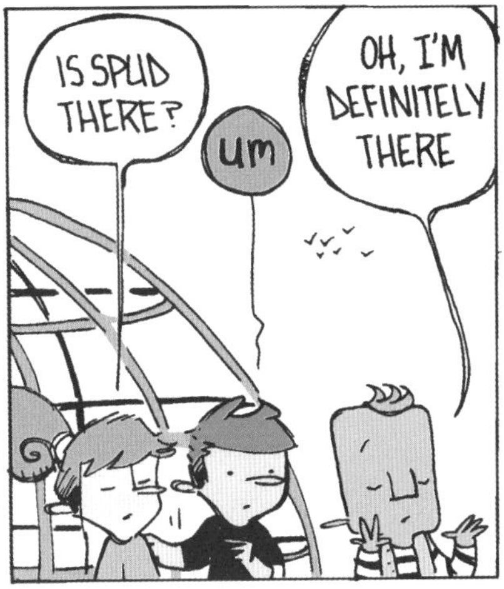
IS SPUD THERE?
UM
OH, I'M DEFINITELY THERE

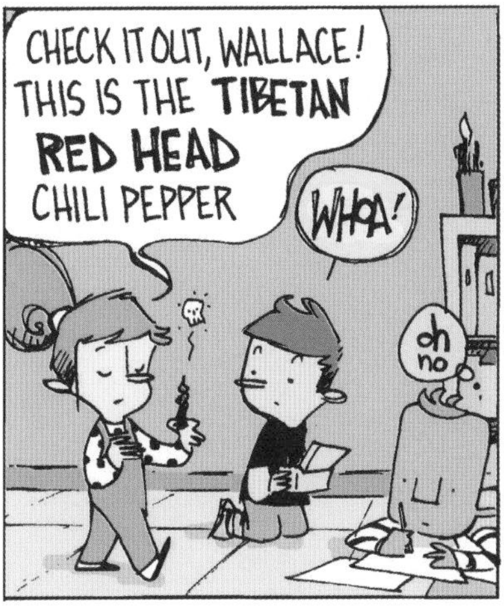
CHECK IT OUT, WALLACE! THIS IS THE TIBETAN RED HEAD CHILI PEPPER
WHOA!
oh no

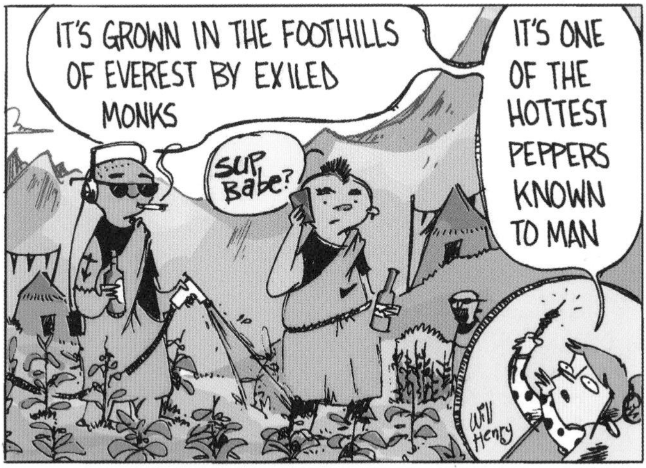
IT'S GROWN IN THE FOOTHILLS OF EVEREST BY EXILED MONKS
SUP Babe?
IT'S ONE OF THE HOTTEST PEPPERS KNOWN TO MAN
Will Henry

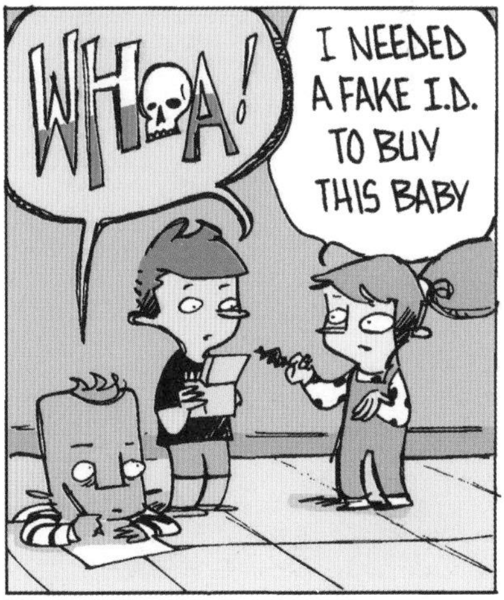
WHOA!
I NEEDED A FAKE I.D. TO BUY THIS BABY

SO, YOU'RE SAYING THIS CHILI PEPPER IS PRETTY HOT?
WALLACE, THAT IS A GROSS UNDER-STATEMENT

THEY SAY A SINGLE BITE OF THE TIBETAN RED HEAD WILL SEND YOU HURTLING NAKED THROUGH THE NINTH DIMENSION
wild
wild
wild
wild

AND I DARE YOU TO EAT IT
FINALLY SOMETHING TO DO TODAY
no.
willHenry

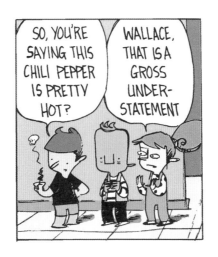

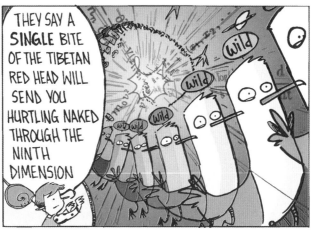

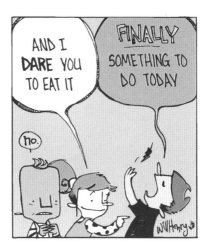

I DON'T KNOW WHAT THE FUSS IS ABOUT, THIS PEPPER IS BARELY-
WHAT HAVE I DONE?
THIS IS GONNA GET A BAZILLION VIEWS!

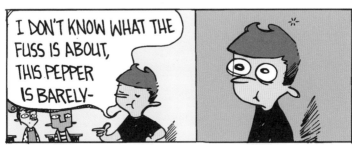

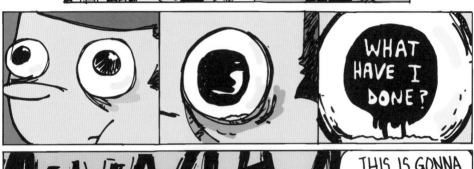

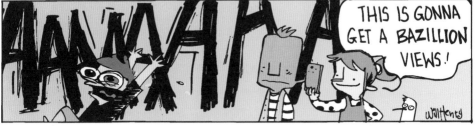

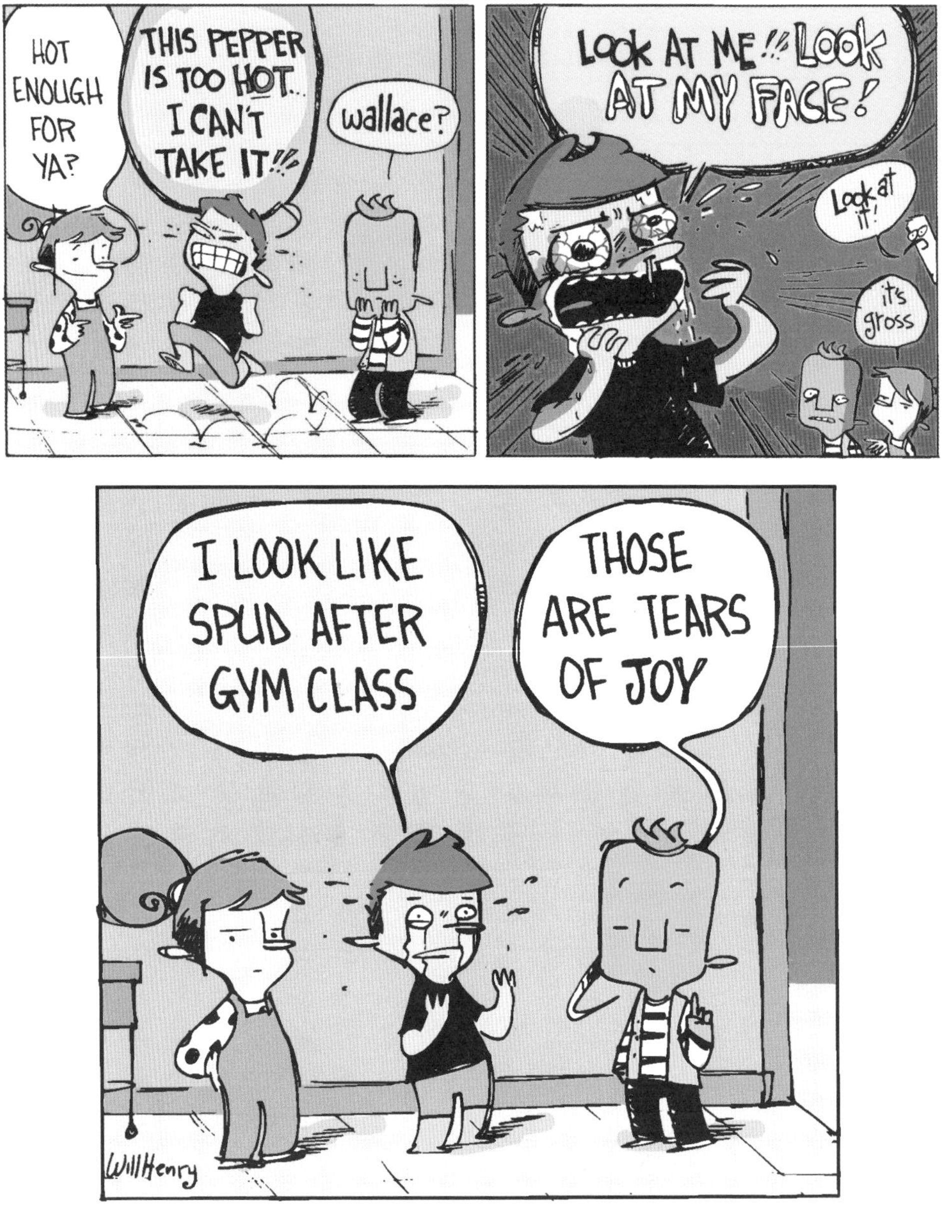
HOT ENOUGH FOR YA?
THIS PEPPER IS TOO HOT... I CAN'T TAKE IT!!
wallace?
LOOK AT ME!! LOOK AT MY FACE!
Look at it!
it's gross
I LOOK LIKE SPUD AFTER GYM CLASS
THOSE ARE TEARS OF JOY
WillHenry

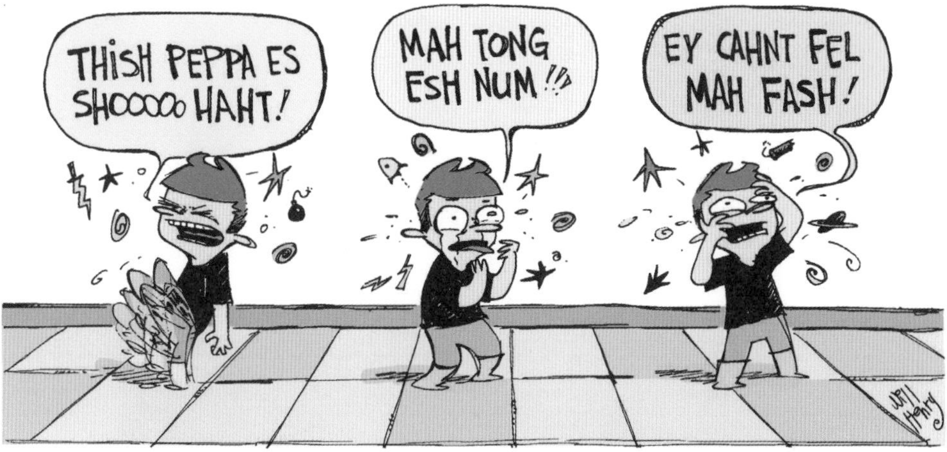
THISH PEPPA ES SHOOOOO HAHT!
MAH TONG ESH NUM!!!
EY CAHNT FEL MAH FASH!
WILL HENRY

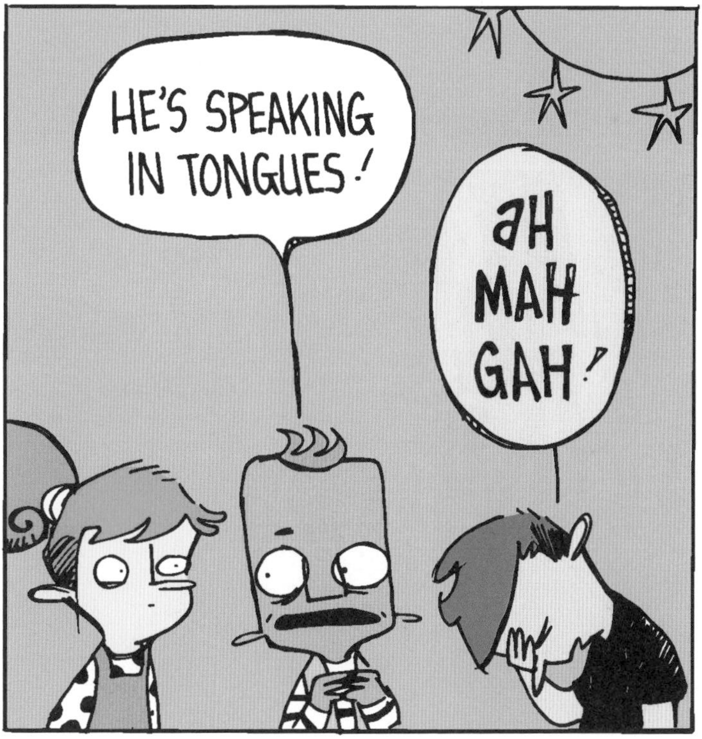
HE'S SPEAKING IN TONGUES!
AH MAH GAH!

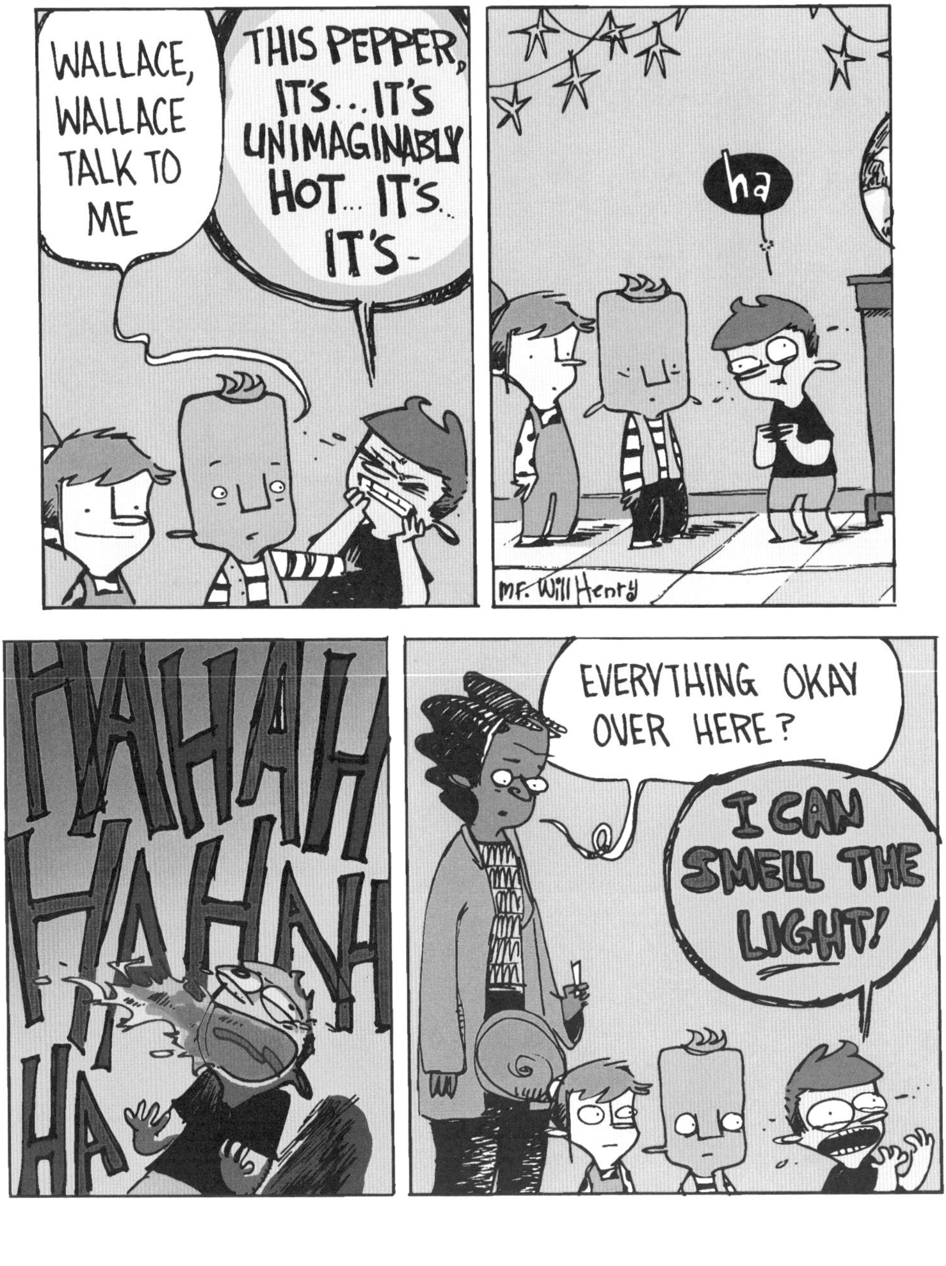
WALLACE, WALLACE TALK TO ME
THIS PEPPER, IT'S... IT'S UNIMAGINABLY HOT... IT'S... IT'S-
ha
MR. Will Henry
HAHAHAHAHAHAH HA HA
EVERYTHING OKAY OVER HERE?
I CAN SMELL THE LIGHT!

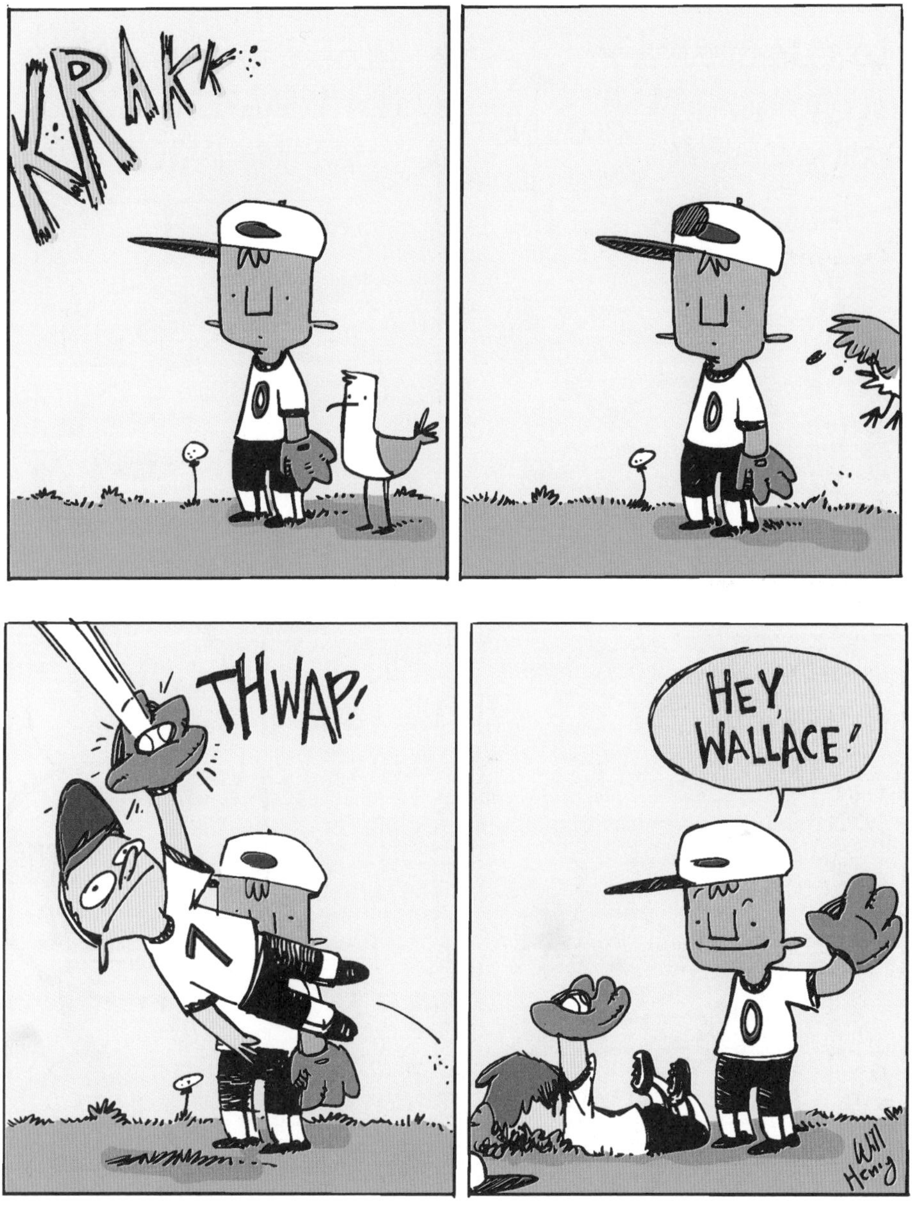
KRAKK
THWAP!
HEY, WALLACE!
Will Henry

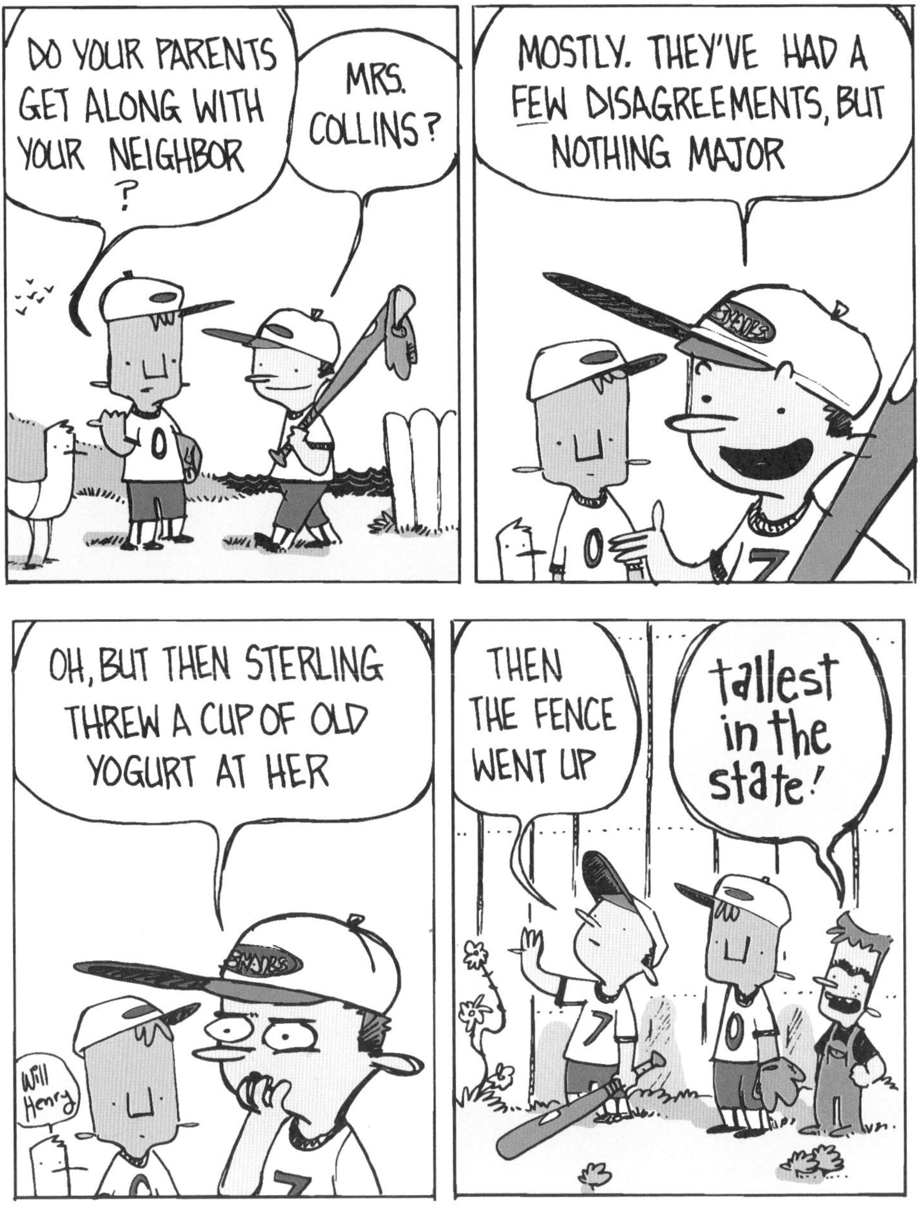
DO YOUR PARENTS GET ALONG WITH YOUR NEIGHBOR ?
MRS. COLLINS?
MOSTLY. THEY'VE HAD A FEW DISAGREEMENTS, BUT NOTHING MAJOR
OH, BUT THEN STERLING THREW A CUP OF OLD YOGURT AT HER
Will Henry
THEN THE FENCE WENT UP
tallest in the state!

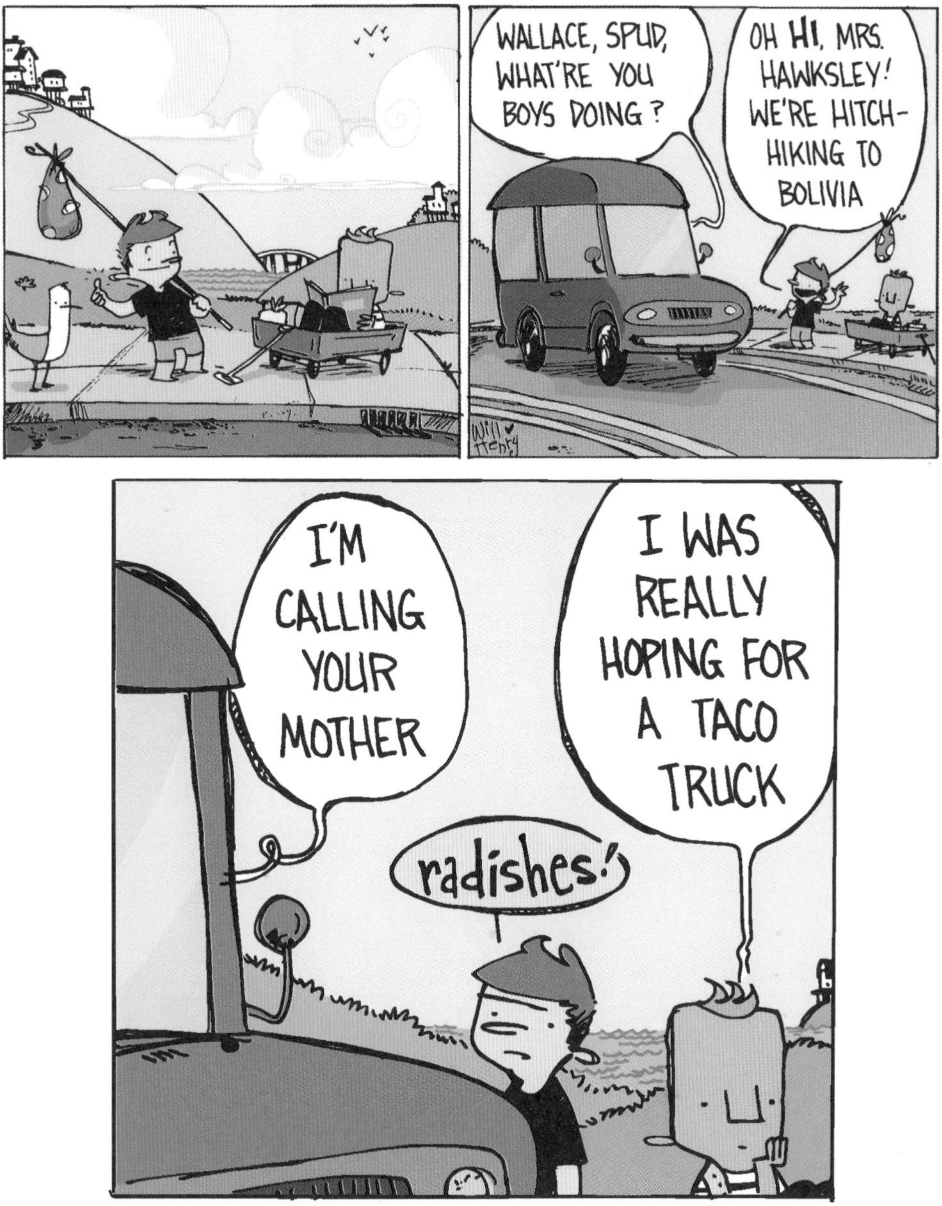
WALLACE, SPUD, WHAT'RE YOU BOYS DOING?
OH HI, MRS. HAWKSLEY! WE'RE HITCH-HIKING TO BOLIVIA
Will Henry
I'M CALLING YOUR MOTHER
radishes!
I WAS REALLY HOPING FOR A TACO TRUCK

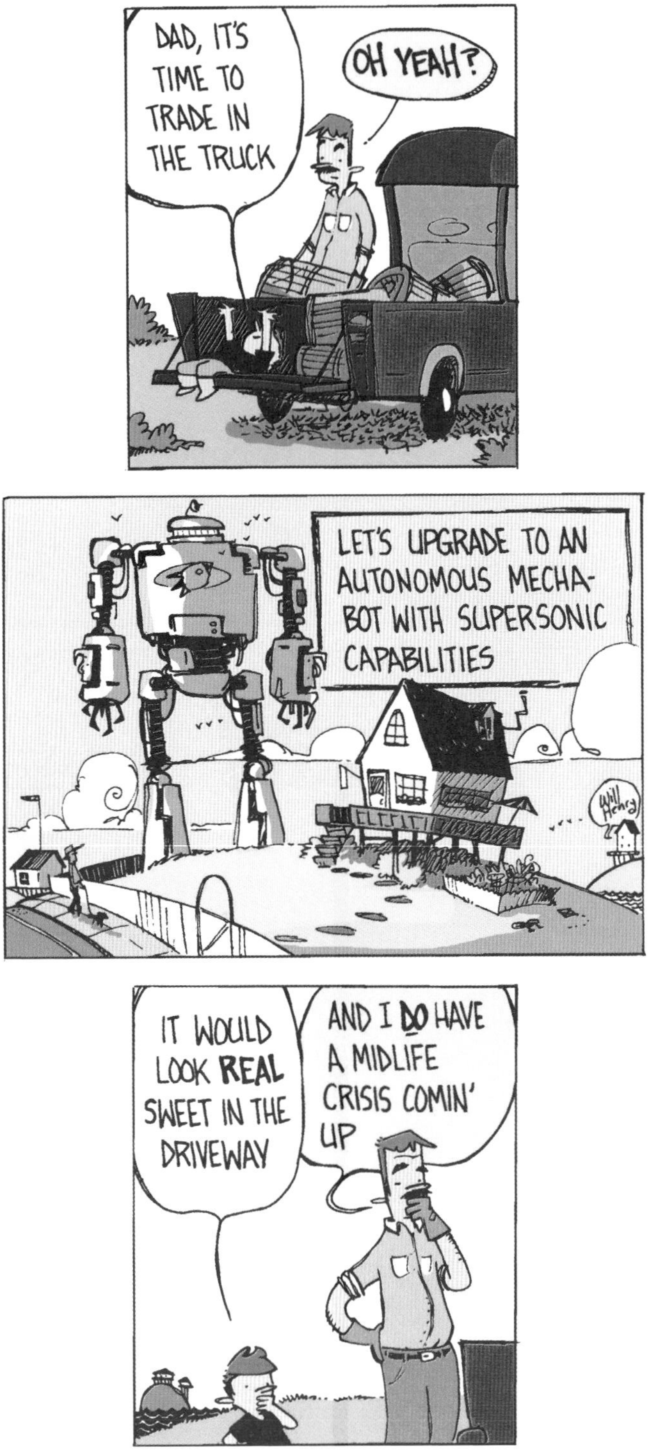
DAD, IT'S TIME TO TRADE IN THE TRUCK
OH YEAH?
LET'S UPGRADE TO AN AUTONOMOUS MECHA-BOT WITH SUPERSONIC CAPABILITIES
Will Henry
IT WOULD LOOK **REAL** SWEET IN THE DRIVEWAY
AND I **DO** HAVE A MIDLIFE CRISIS COMIN' UP

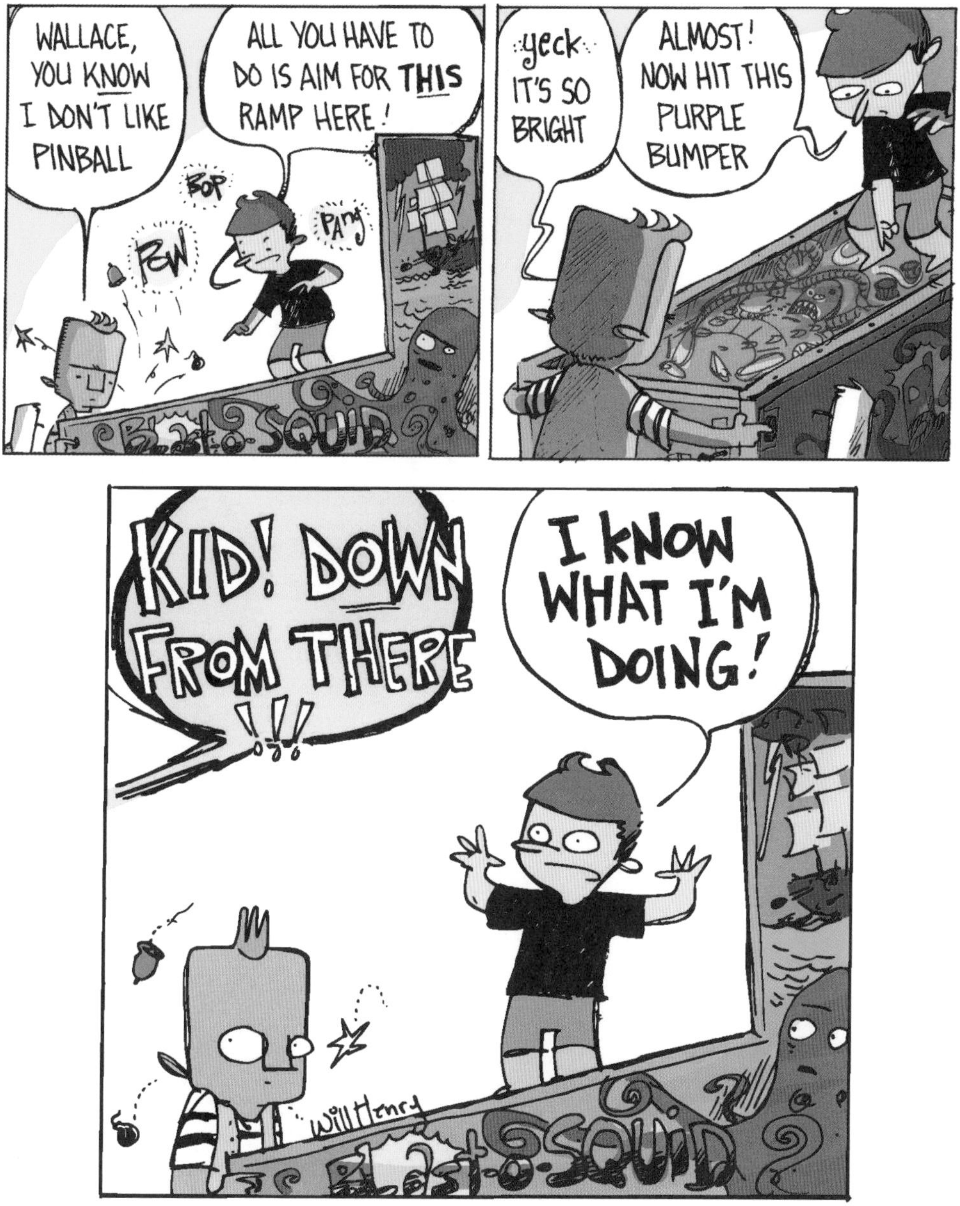
WALLACE, YOU KNOW I DON'T LIKE PINBALL
ALL YOU HAVE TO DO IS AIM FOR THIS RAMP HERE!
BOP
PANG
POW
BLAST-O-SQUID
yeck IT'S SO BRIGHT
ALMOST! NOW HIT THIS PURPLE BUMPER
KID! DOWN FROM THERE!!!
I KNOW WHAT I'M DOING!
Will Henry
BLAST-O-SQUID

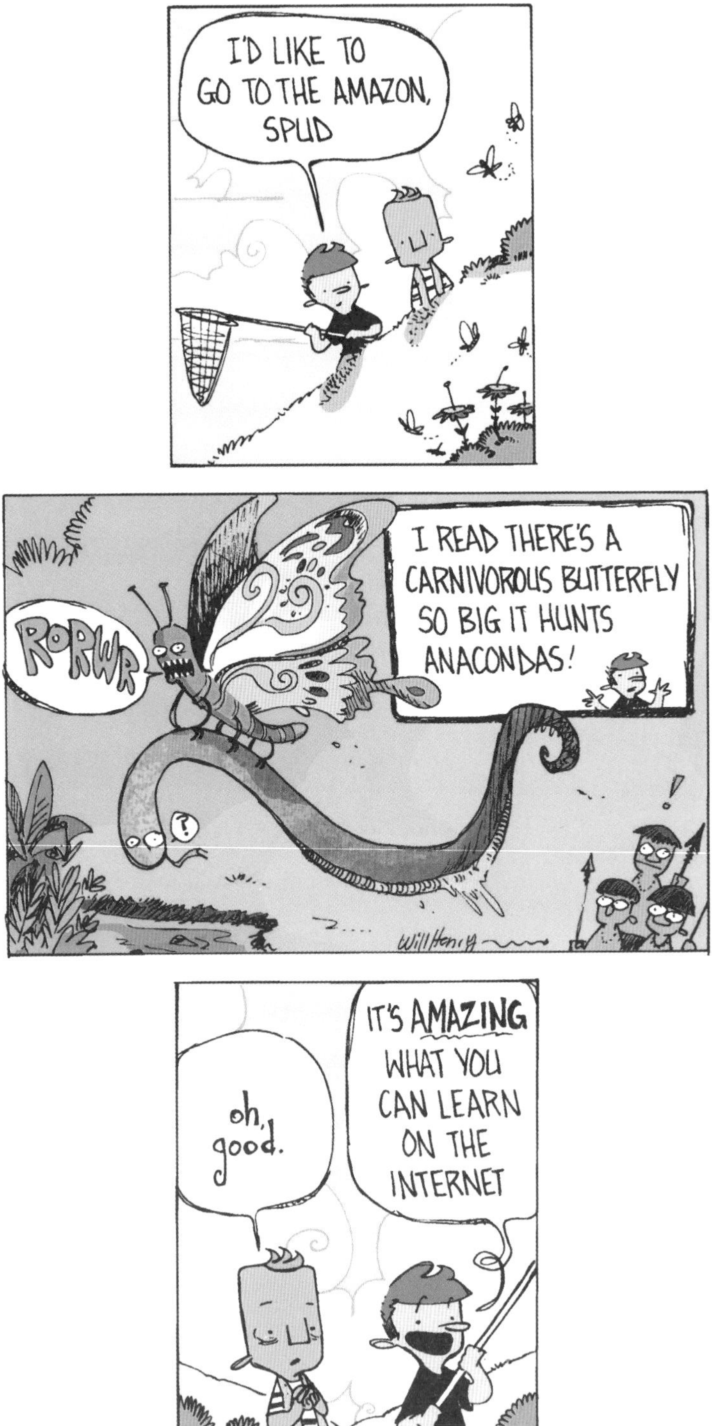
I'D LIKE TO GO TO THE AMAZON, SPUD
RORWR
I READ THERE'S A CARNIVOROUS BUTTERFLY SO BIG IT HUNTS ANACONDAS!
?
!
oh, good.
IT'S AMAZING WHAT YOU CAN LEARN ON THE INTERNET

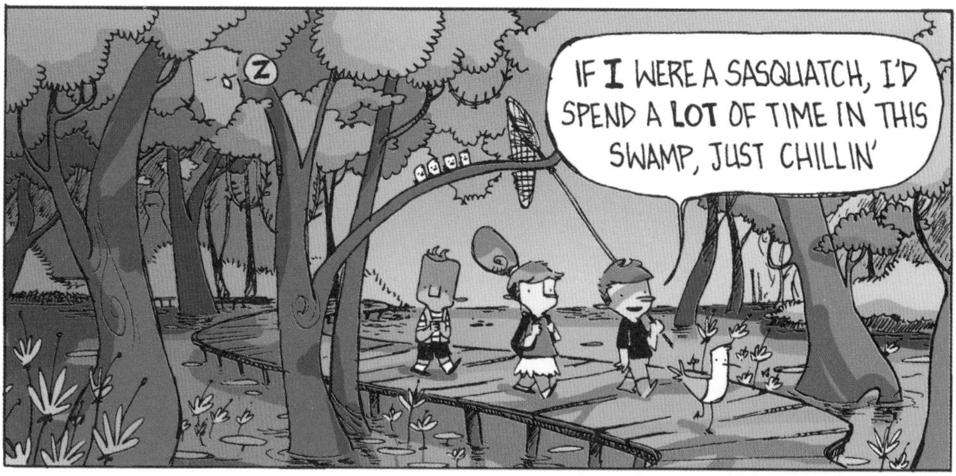
Z
IF I WERE A SASQUATCH, I'D SPEND A LOT OF TIME IN THIS SWAMP, JUST CHILLIN'

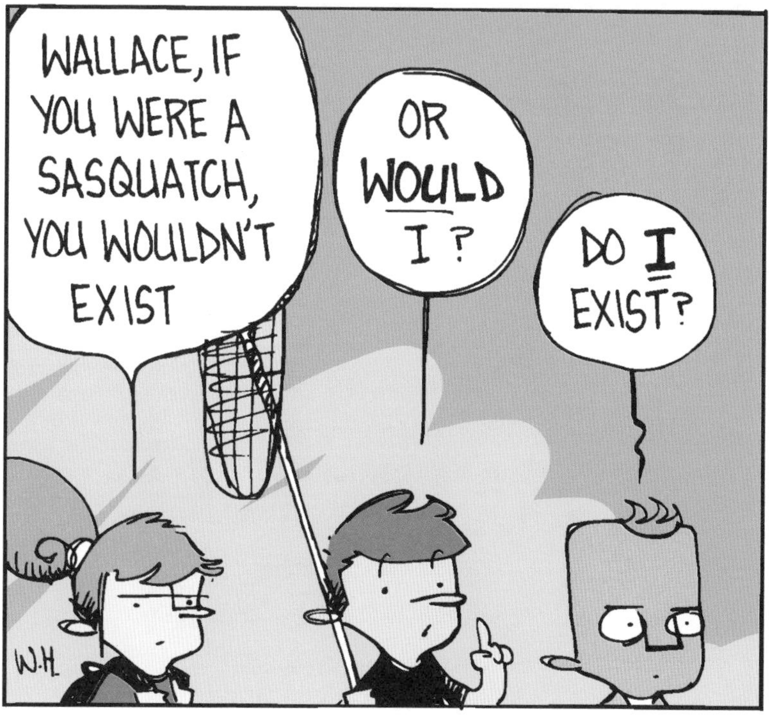
WALLACE, IF YOU WERE A SASQUATCH, YOU WOULDN'T EXIST
OR WOULD I?
DO I EXIST?
W.H.

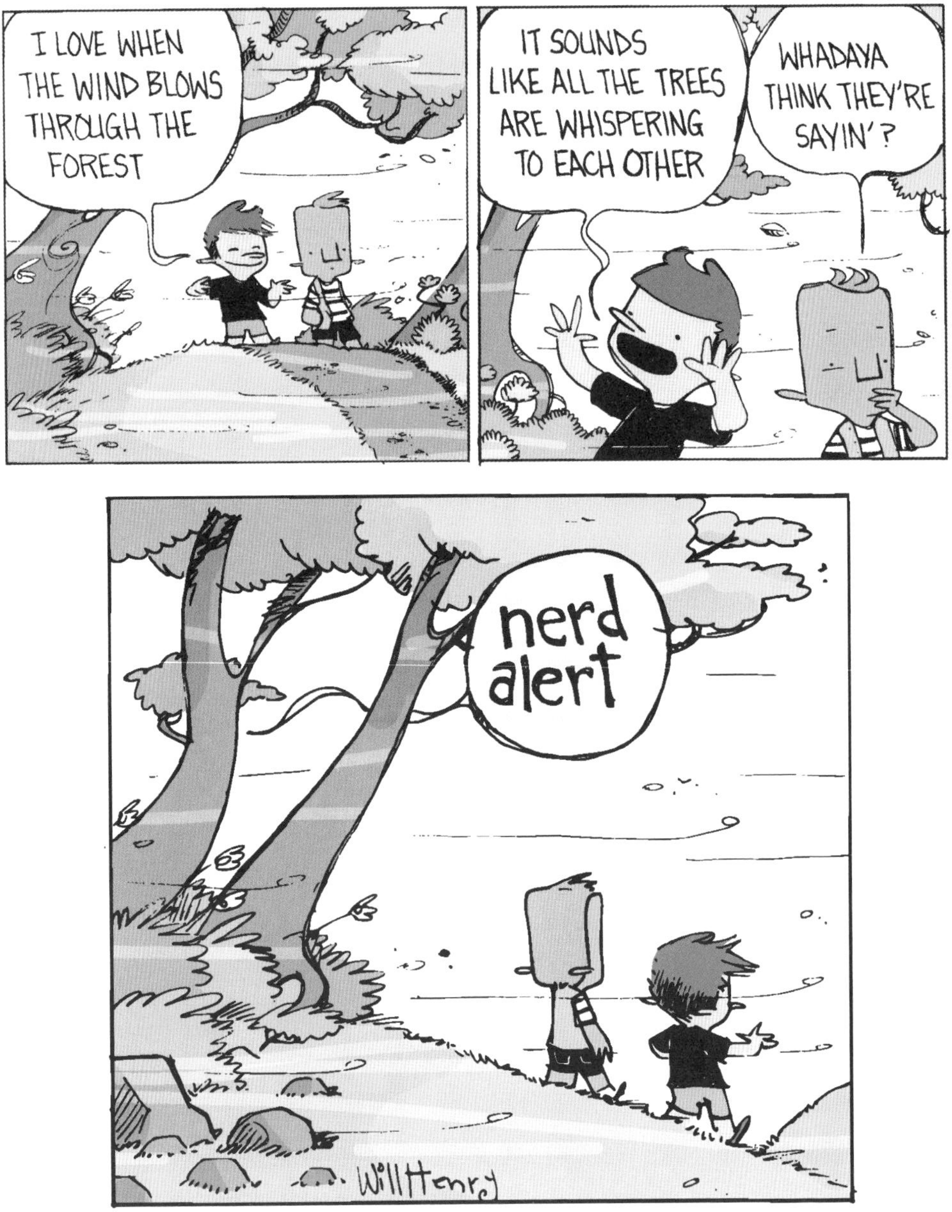
I LOVE WHEN THE WIND BLOWS THROUGH THE FOREST
IT SOUNDS LIKE ALL THE TREES ARE WHISPERING TO EACH OTHER
WHADAYA THINK THEY'RE SAYIN'?
nerd alert
WillHenry

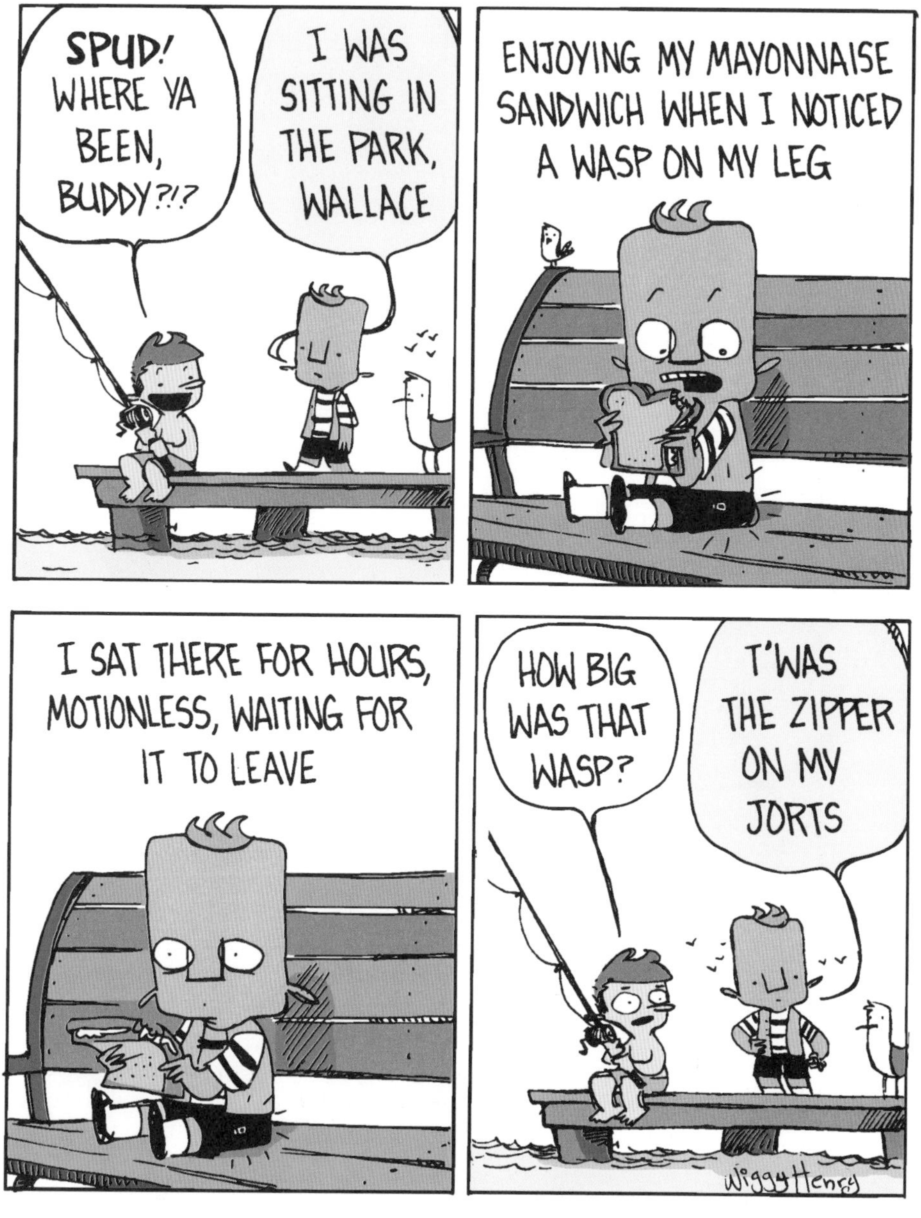

SPUD! WHERE YA BEEN, BUDDY?!?
I WAS SITTING IN THE PARK, WALLACE
ENJOYING MY MAYONNAISE SANDWICH WHEN I NOTICED A WASP ON MY LEG
I SAT THERE FOR HOURS, MOTIONLESS, WAITING FOR IT TO LEAVE
HOW BIG WAS THAT WASP?
T'WAS THE ZIPPER ON MY JORTS
Wiggy Henry

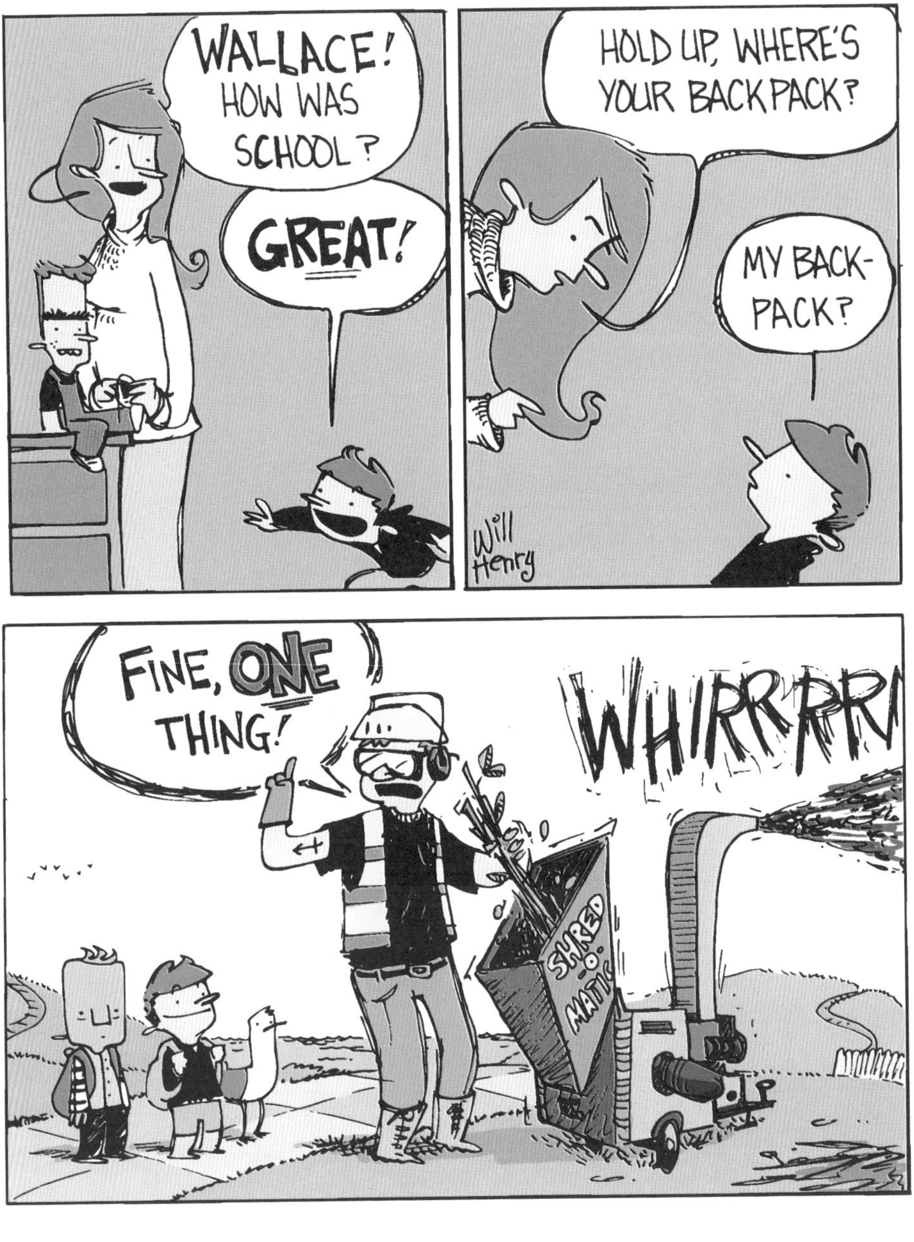

WALLACE! HOW WAS SCHOOL?
GREAT!
HOLD UP, WHERE'S YOUR BACKPACK?
MY BACK-PACK?
Will Henry
FINE, ONE THING!
WHIRRRRR
SHRED-O-MATIC

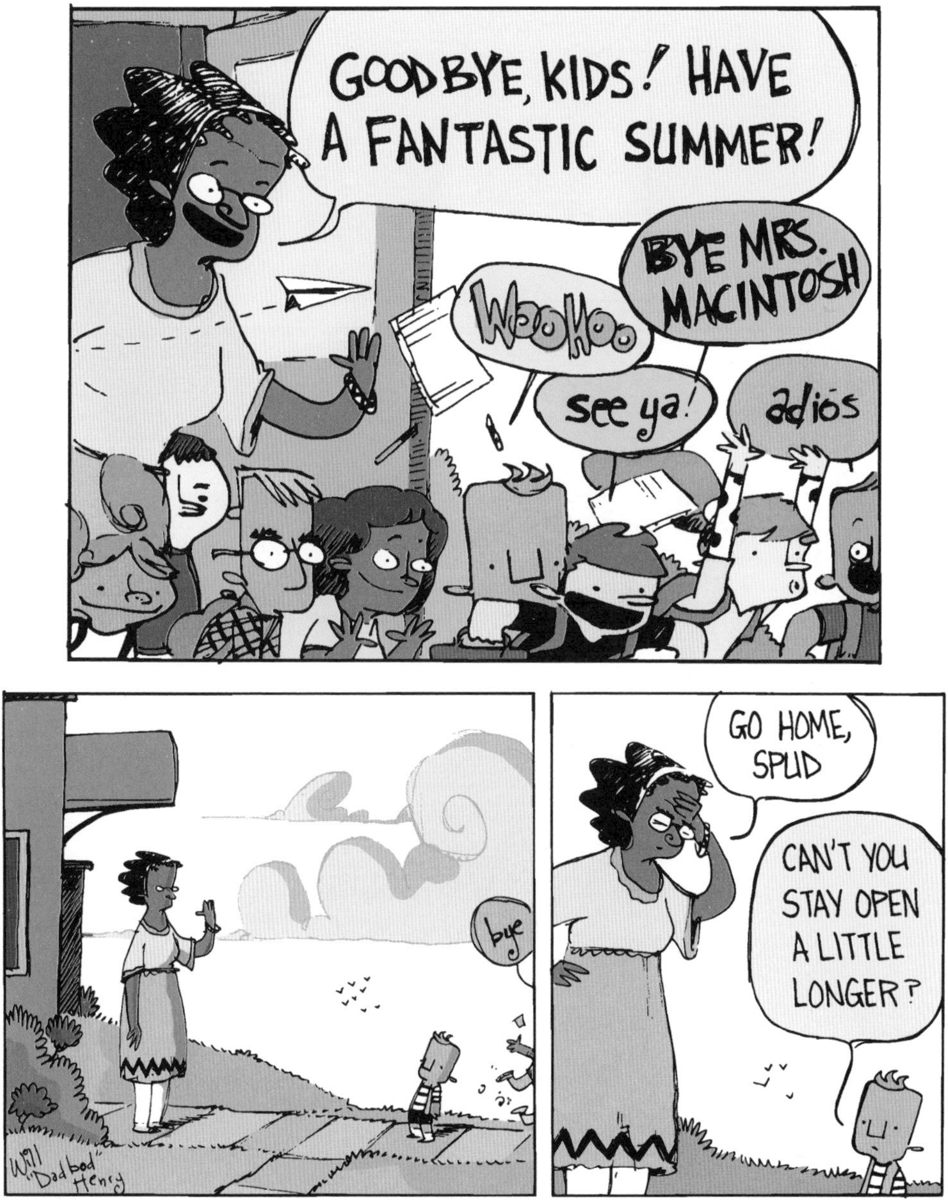
GOODBYE, KIDS! HAVE A FANTASTIC SUMMER!
WooHoo
BYE MRS. MACINTOSH
see ya!
adios
bye
Will "Dadbod" Henry
GO HOME, SPUD
CAN'T YOU STAY OPEN A LITTLE LONGER?

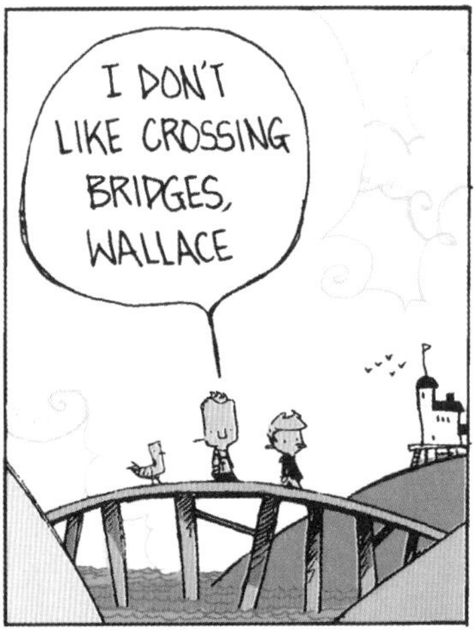
I DON'T LIKE CROSSING BRIDGES, WALLACE

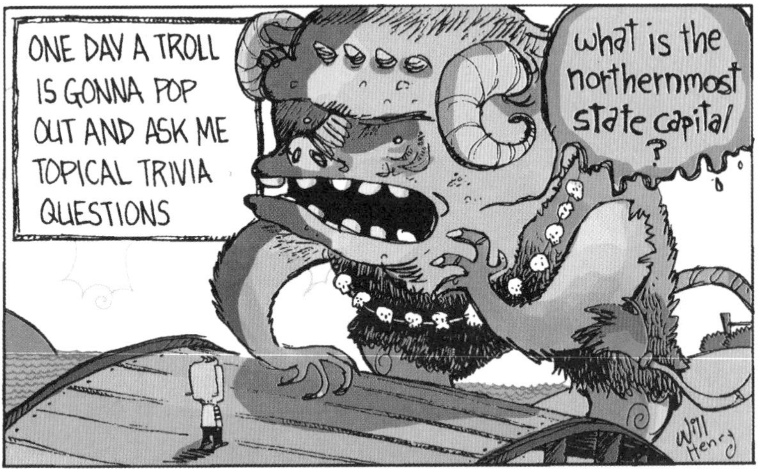
ONE DAY A TROLL IS GONNA POP OUT AND ASK ME TOPICAL TRIVIA QUESTIONS
what is the northernmost state capital?
Will Henry

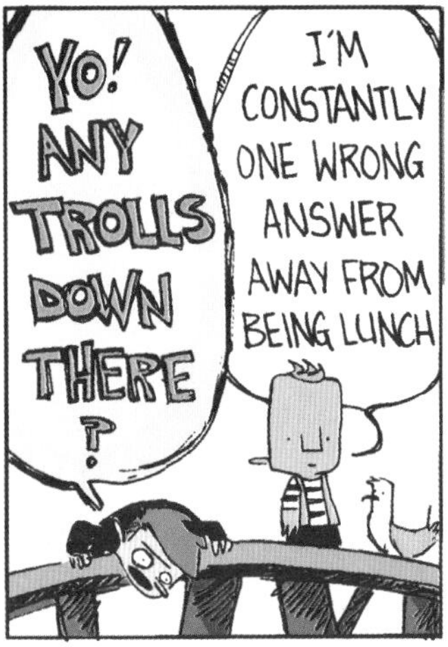
YO! ANY TROLLS DOWN THERE?
I'M CONSTANTLY ONE WRONG ANSWER AWAY FROM BEING LUNCH

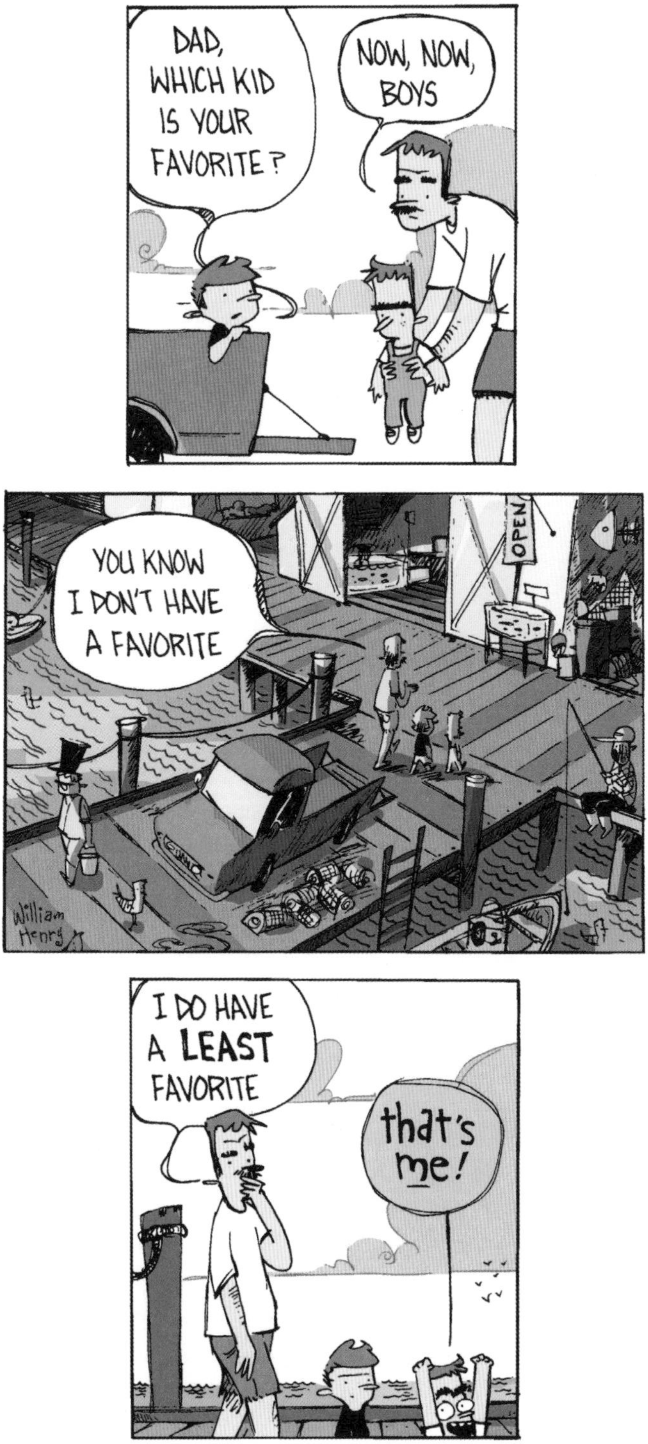
DAD, WHICH KID IS YOUR FAVORITE?
NOW, NOW, BOYS
YOU KNOW I DON'T HAVE A FAVORITE
OPEN
William Henry
I DO HAVE A **LEAST** FAVORITE
that's me!

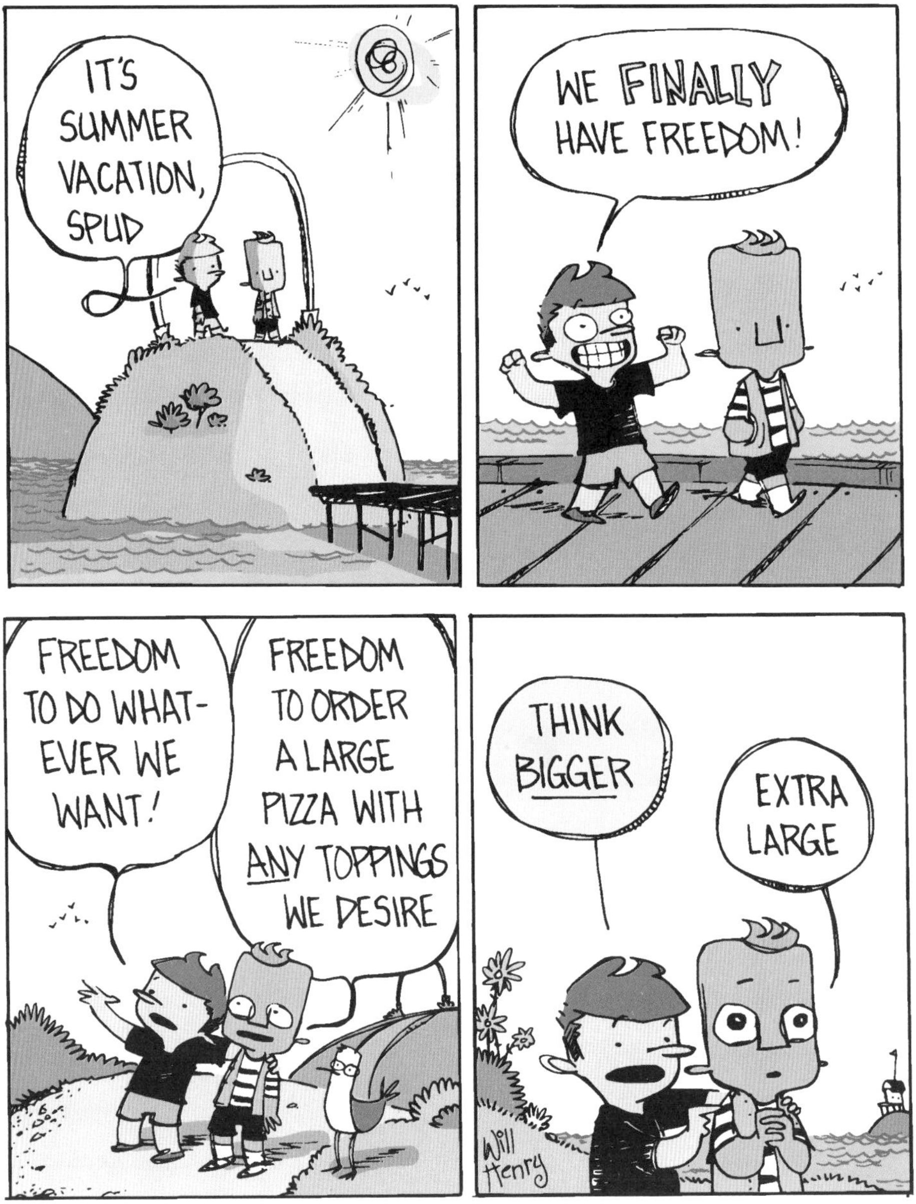
IT'S SUMMER VACATION, SPUD
WE FINALLY HAVE FREEDOM!
FREEDOM TO DO WHAT-EVER WE WANT!
FREEDOM TO ORDER A LARGE PIZZA WITH ANY TOPPINGS WE DESIRE
THINK BIGGER
EXTRA LARGE
Will Henry

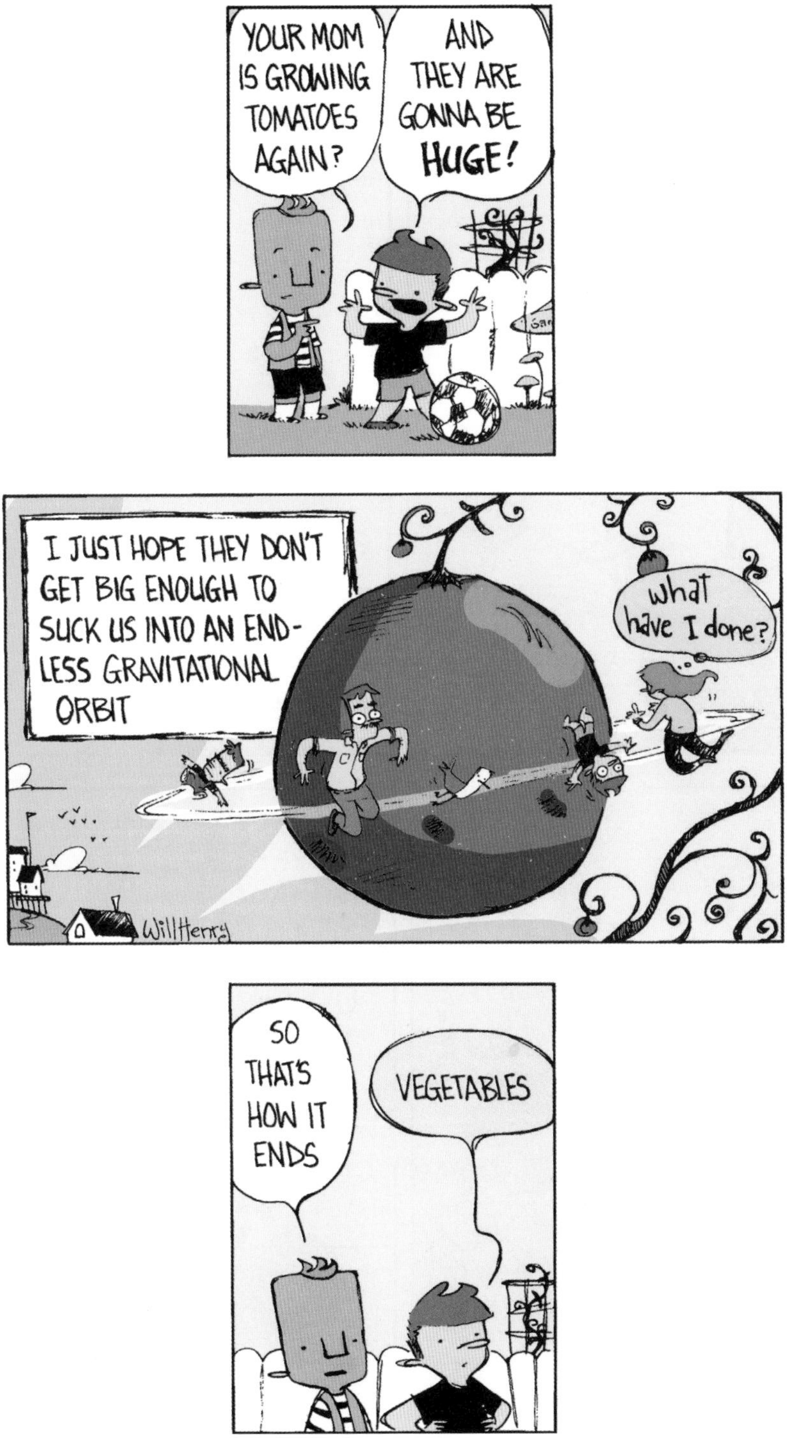
YOUR MOM IS GROWING TOMATOES AGAIN?
AND THEY ARE GONNA BE HUGE!
I JUST HOPE THEY DON'T GET BIG ENOUGH TO SUCK US INTO AN END-LESS GRAVITATIONAL ORBIT
what have I done?
WillHenry
SO THAT'S HOW IT ENDS
VEGETABLES

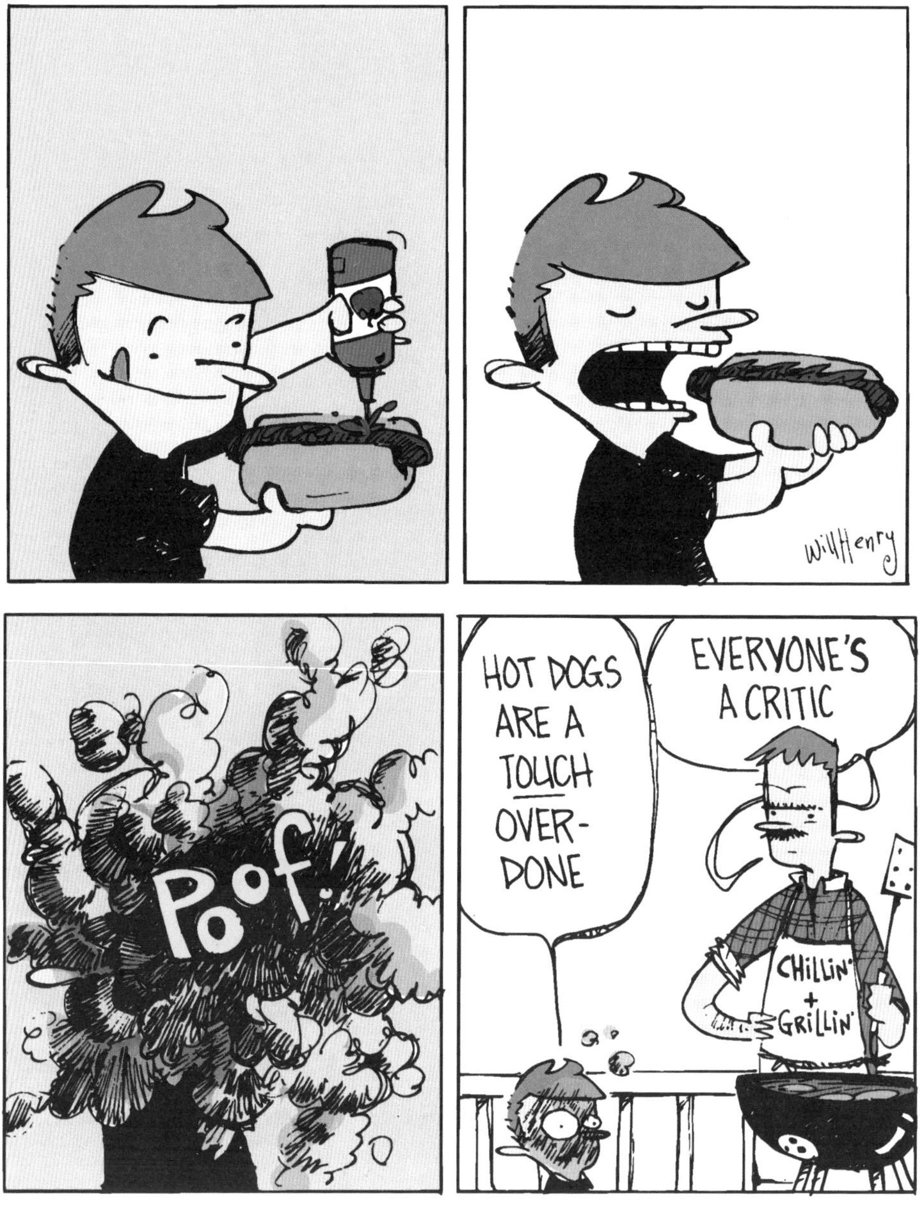
WillHenry
POOF!
HOT DOGS ARE A TOUCH OVER-DONE
EVERYONE'S A CRITIC
CHILLIN' + GRILLIN'

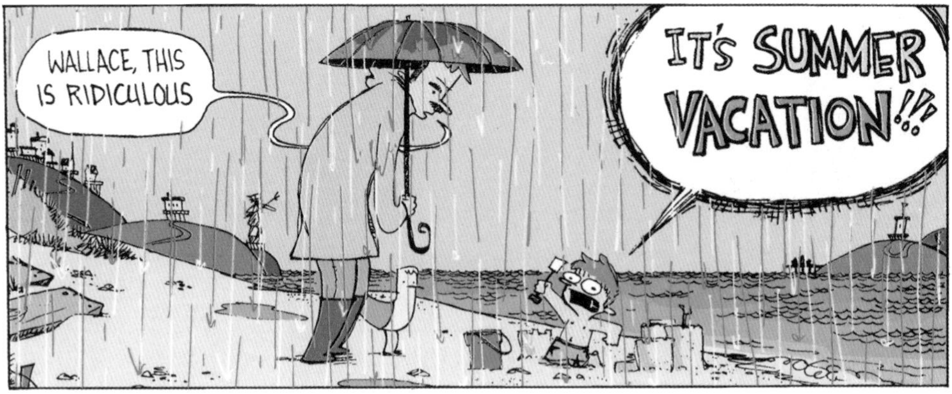
WALLACE, THIS IS RIDICULOUS
IT'S SUMMER VACATION!!!

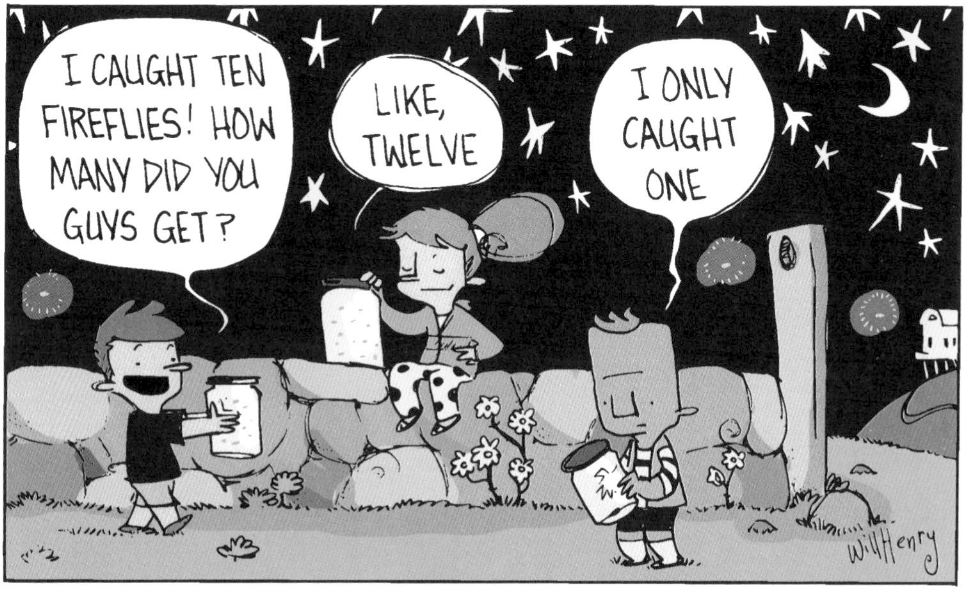
I CAUGHT TEN FIREFLIES! HOW MANY DID YOU GUYS GET?
LIKE, TWELVE
I ONLY CAUGHT ONE
WillHenry

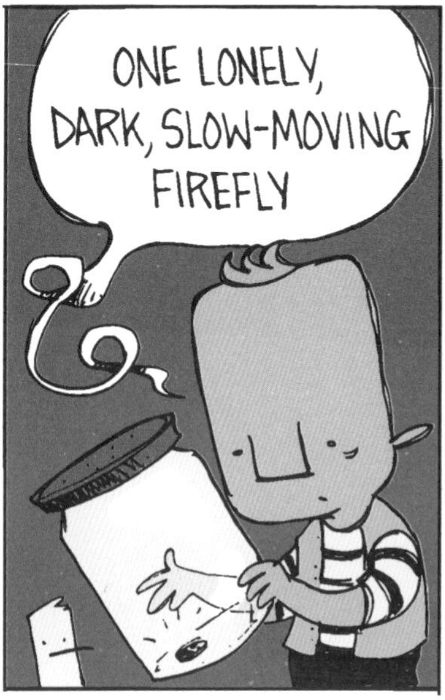
ONE LONELY, DARK, SLOW-MOVING FIREFLY

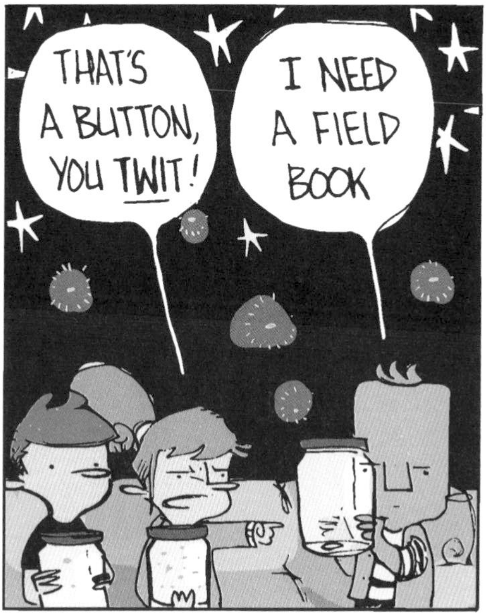
THAT'S A BUTTON, YOU TWIT!
I NEED A FIELD BOOK

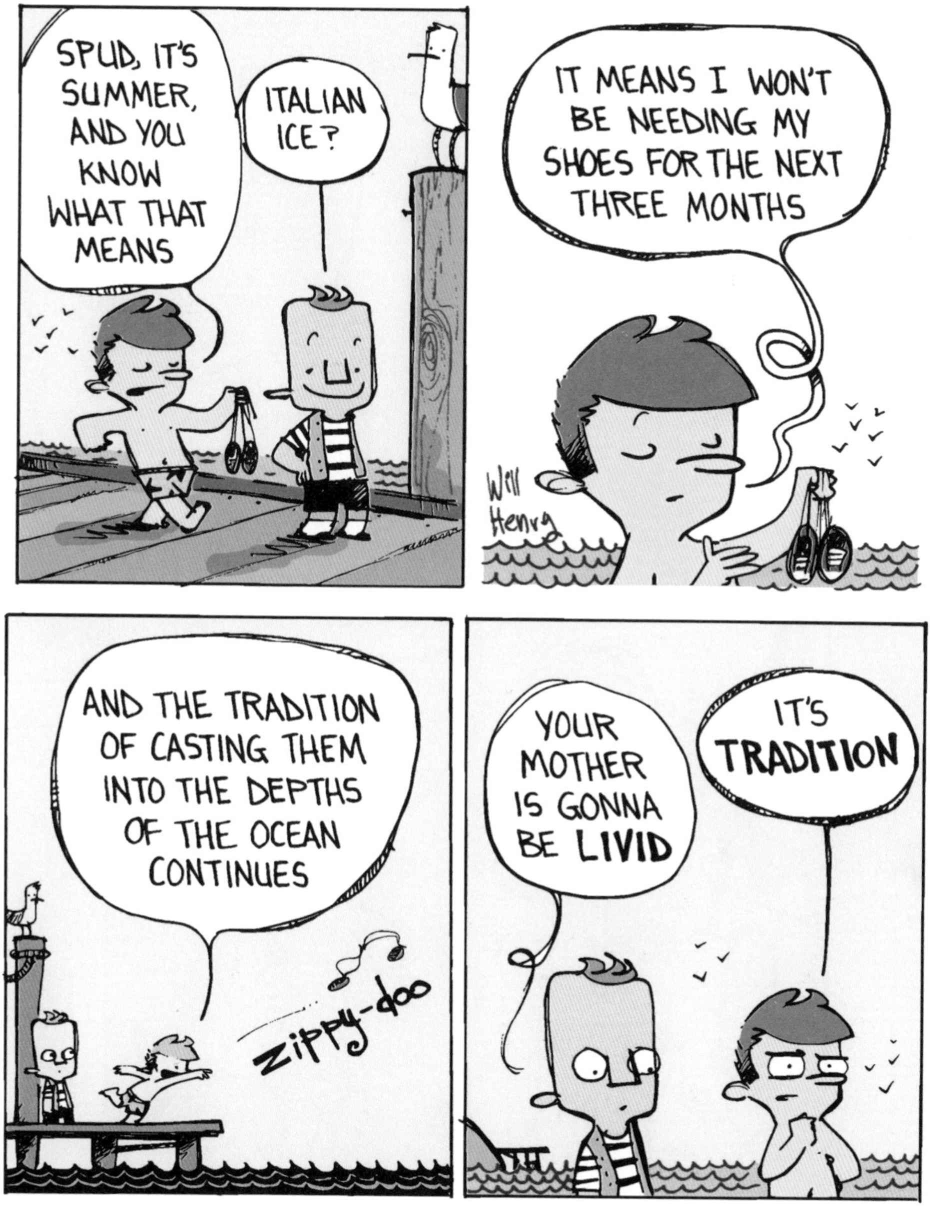
SPUD, IT'S SUMMER, AND YOU KNOW WHAT THAT MEANS
ITALIAN ICE?
IT MEANS I WON'T BE NEEDING MY SHOES FOR THE NEXT THREE MONTHS
Will Henry
AND THE TRADITION OF CASTING THEM INTO THE DEPTHS OF THE OCEAN CONTINUES
zippy-doo
YOUR MOTHER IS GONNA BE **LIVID**
IT'S **TRADITION**

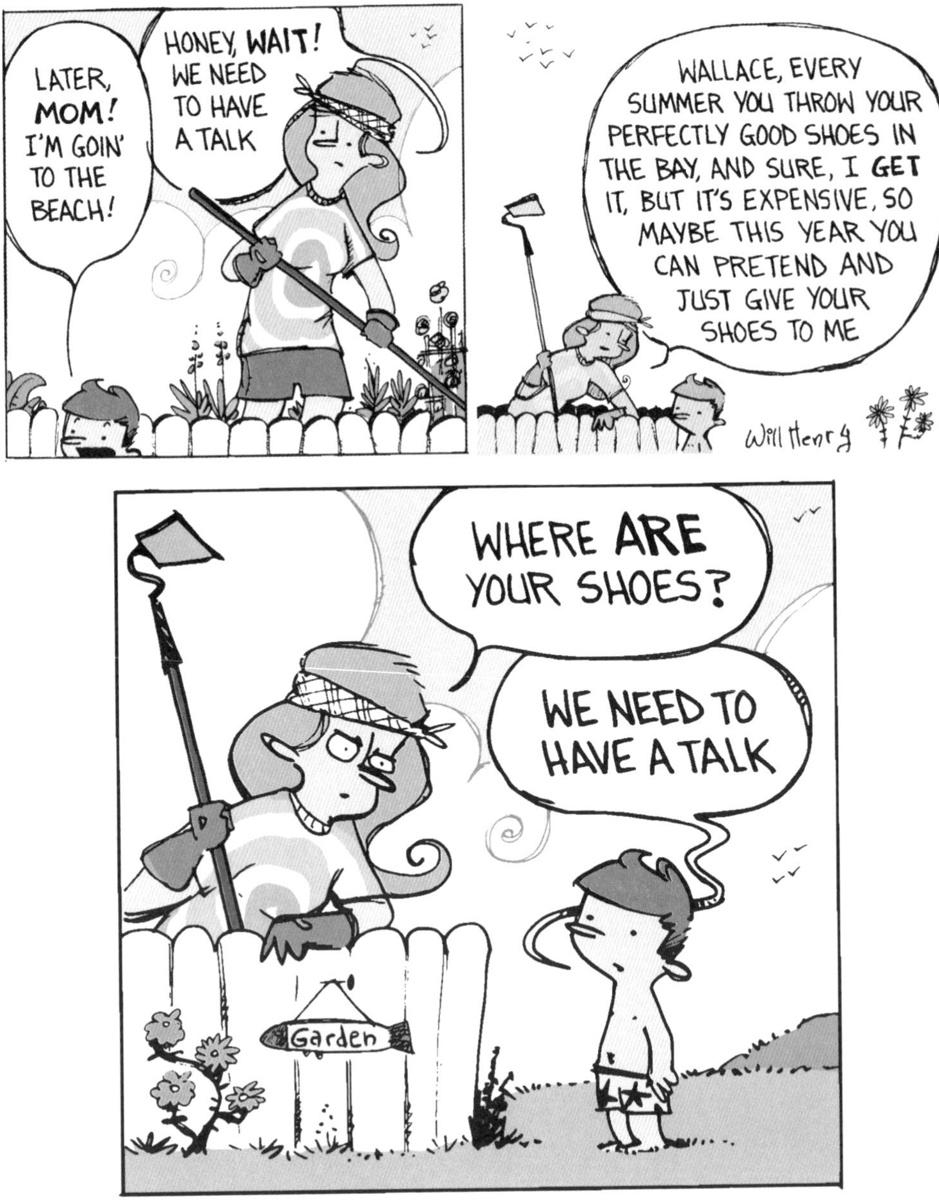
LATER, MOM! I'M GOIN' TO THE BEACH!
HONEY, WAIT! WE NEED TO HAVE A TALK
WALLACE, EVERY SUMMER YOU THROW YOUR PERFECTLY GOOD SHOES IN THE BAY, AND SURE, I GET IT, BUT IT'S EXPENSIVE, SO MAYBE THIS YEAR YOU CAN PRETEND AND JUST GIVE YOUR SHOES TO ME
Will Henry
WHERE ARE YOUR SHOES?
WE NEED TO HAVE A TALK
Garden

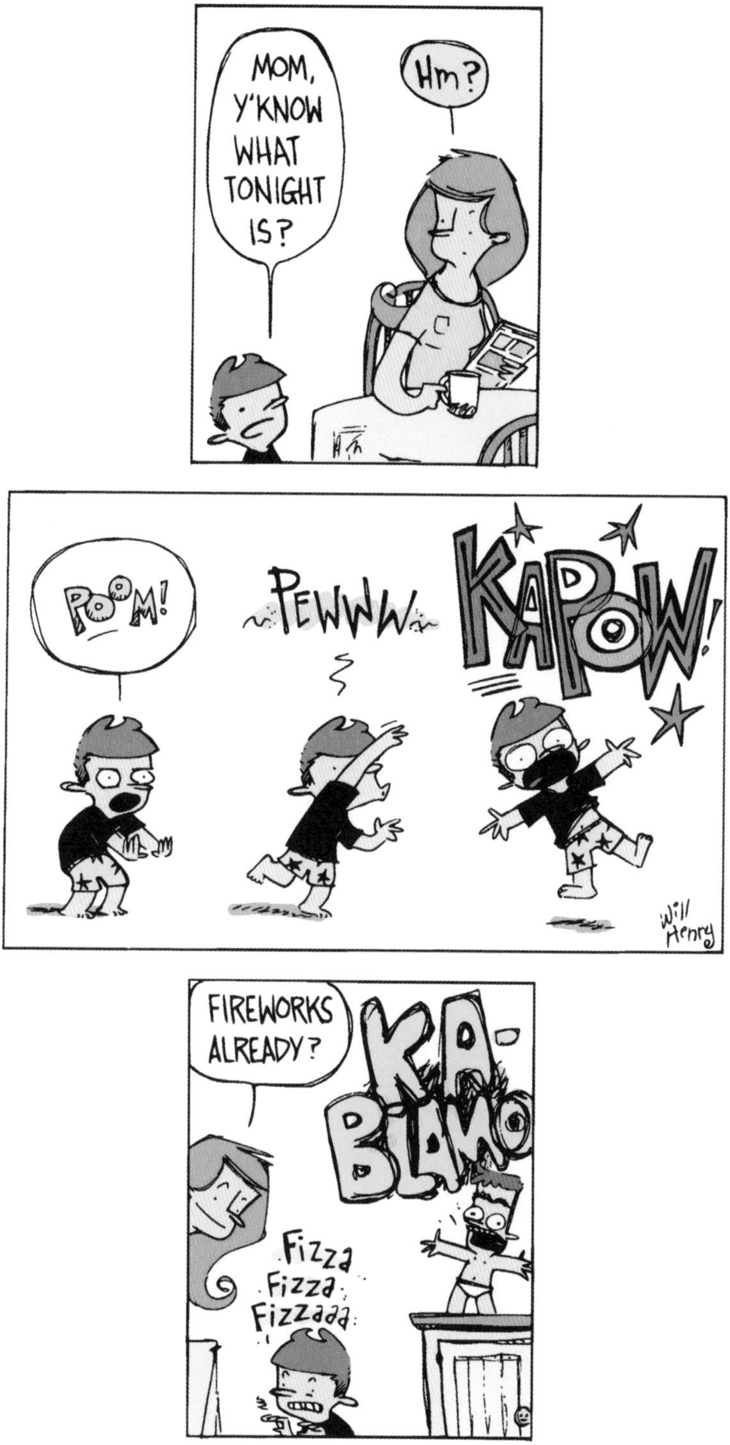
MOM, Y'KNOW WHAT TONIGHT IS?
Hm?
POOM!
PEWWW
KAPOW!
Will Henry
FIREWORKS ALREADY?
KA-BLAMO
Fizza Fizza Fizzaaa

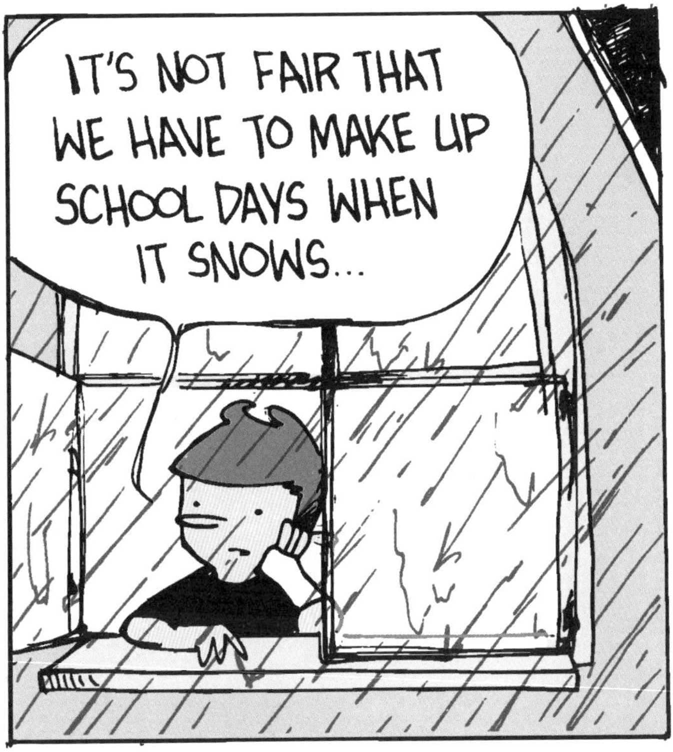
IT'S NOT FAIR THAT WE HAVE TO MAKE UP SCHOOL DAYS WHEN IT SNOWS...

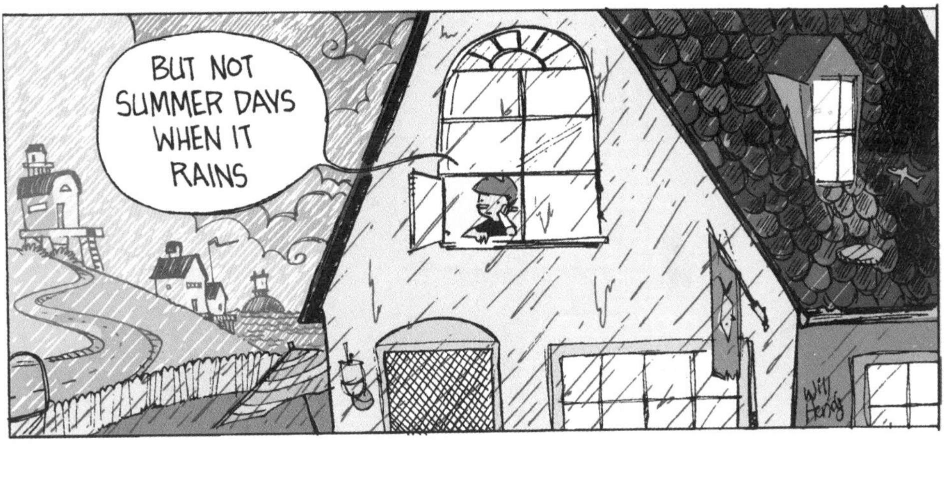
BUT NOT SUMMER DAYS WHEN IT RAINS
Will Henry

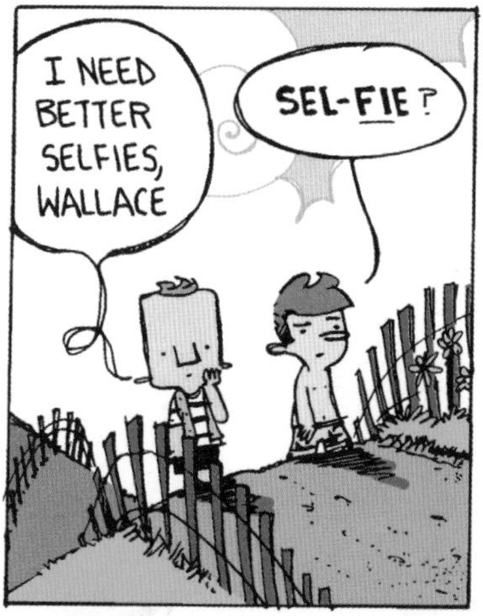
I NEED BETTER SELFIES, WALLACE
SEL-FIE?

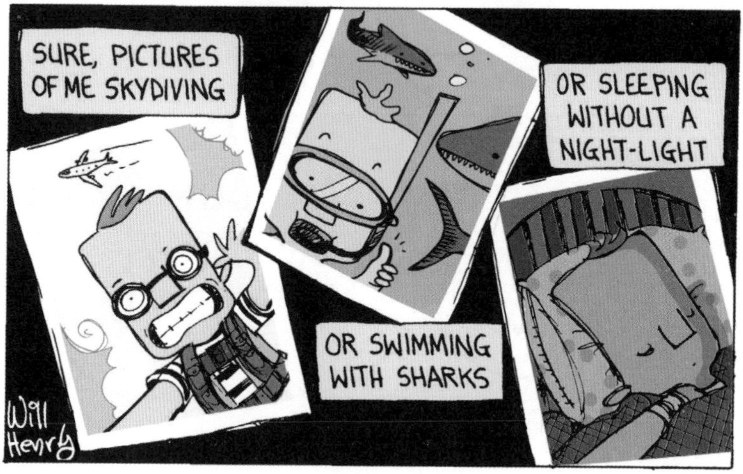
SURE, PICTURES OF ME SKYDIVING
OR SWIMMING WITH SHARKS
OR SLEEPING WITHOUT A NIGHT-LIGHT
Will Henry

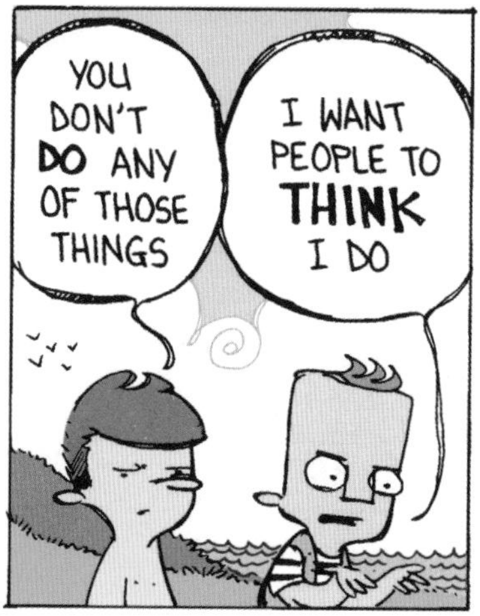
YOU DON'T DO ANY OF THOSE THINGS
I WANT PEOPLE TO THINK I DO

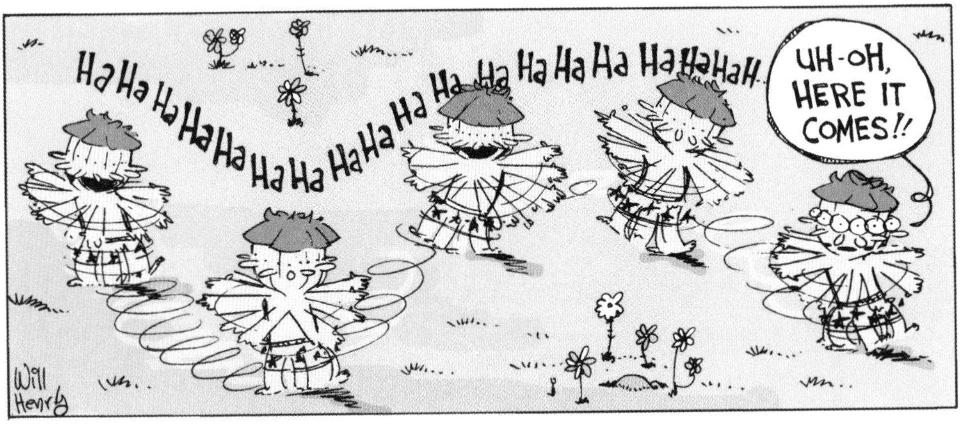
HaHaHaHaHaHaHaHaHaHaHaHaHa Ha Ha Ha Ha Ha HaHaHaH
UH-OH, HERE IT COMES!!
Will Henry

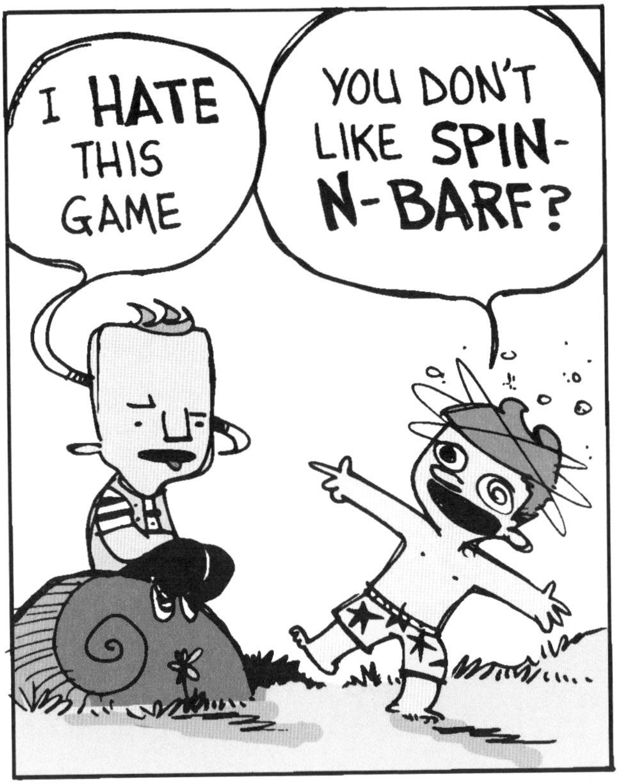
I HATE THIS GAME
YOU DON'T LIKE SPIN-N-BARF?

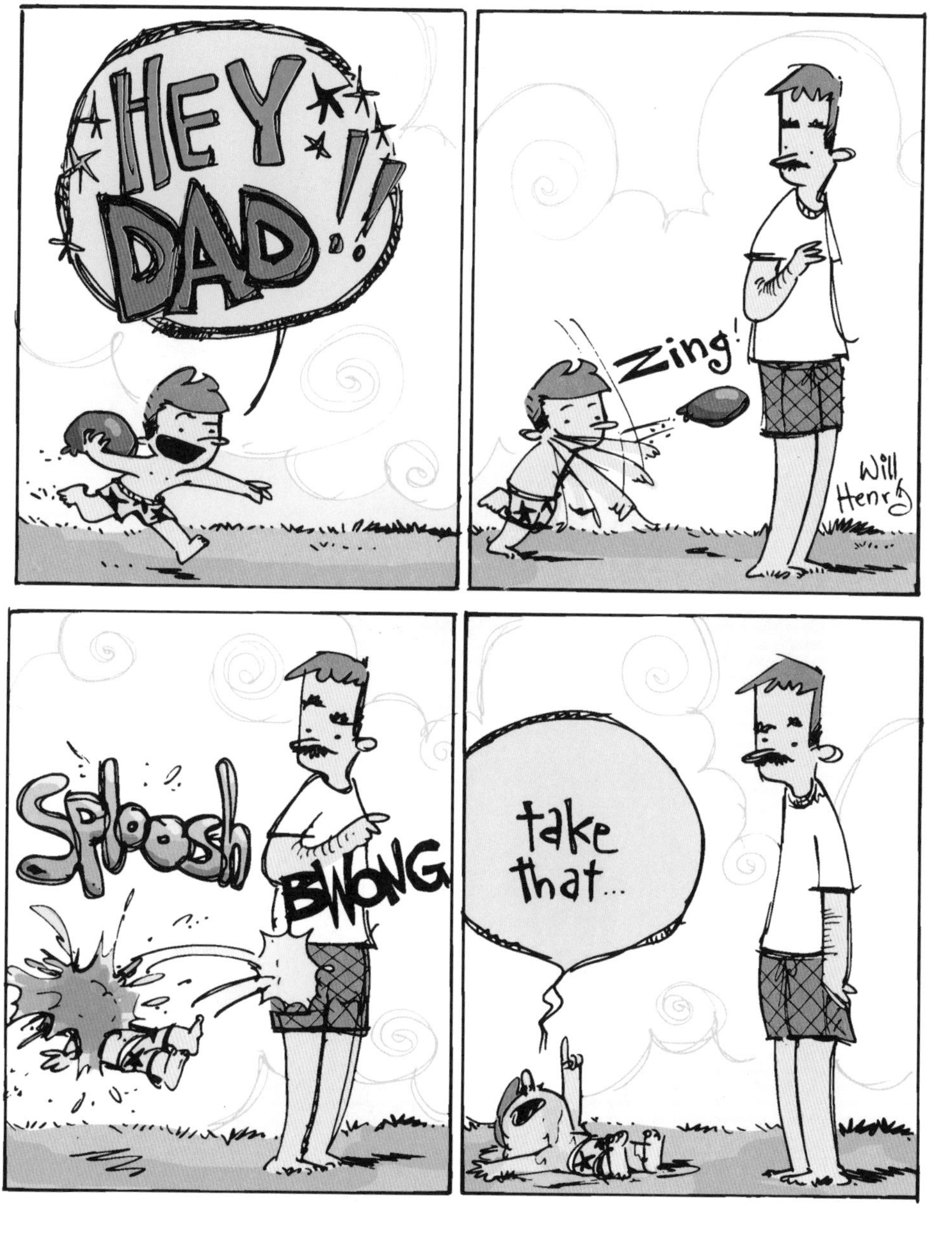
HEY DAD!!
Zing!
Will Henry
Sploosh
BWONG
take that...

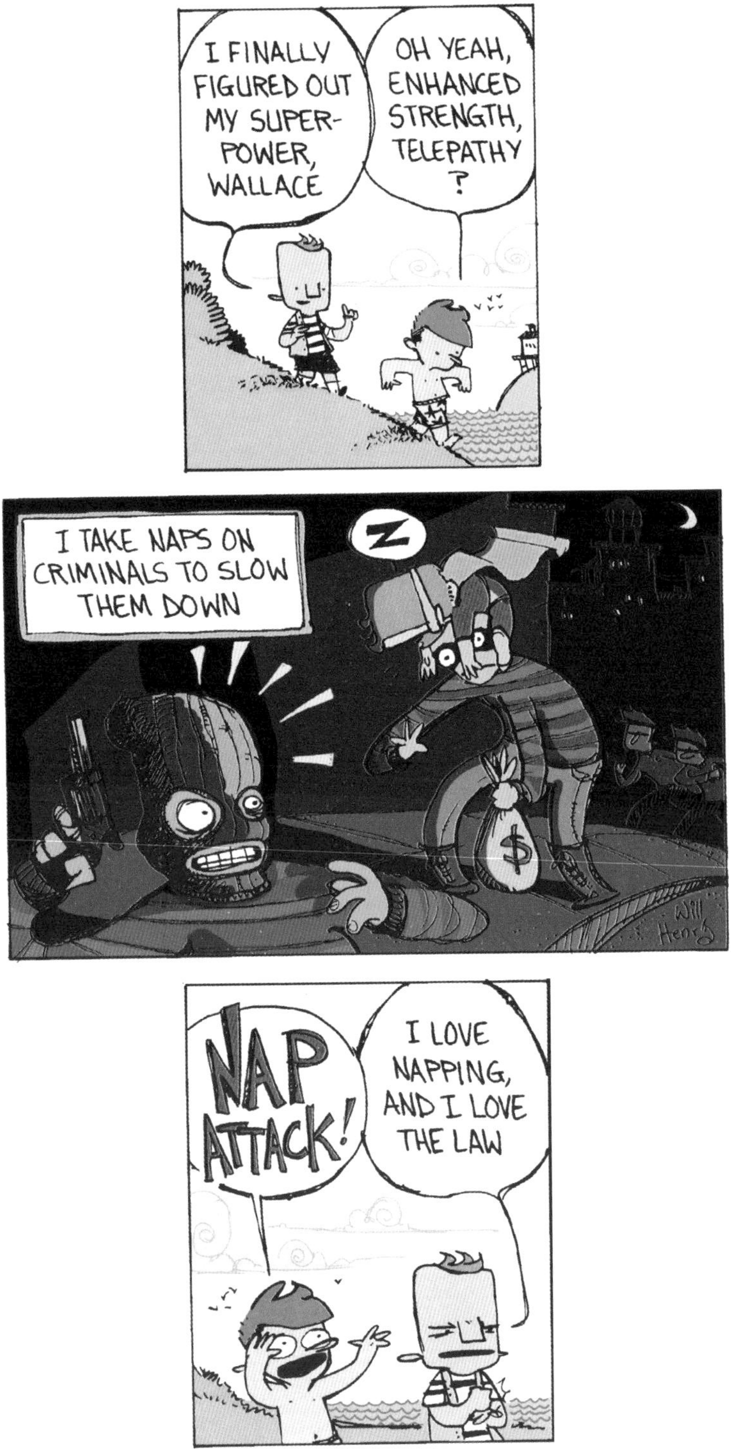
I FINALLY FIGURED OUT MY SUPER-POWER, WALLACE
OH YEAH, ENHANCED STRENGTH, TELEPATHY?
I TAKE NAPS ON CRIMINALS TO SLOW THEM DOWN
Z
NAP ATTACK!
I LOVE NAPPING, AND I LOVE THE LAW

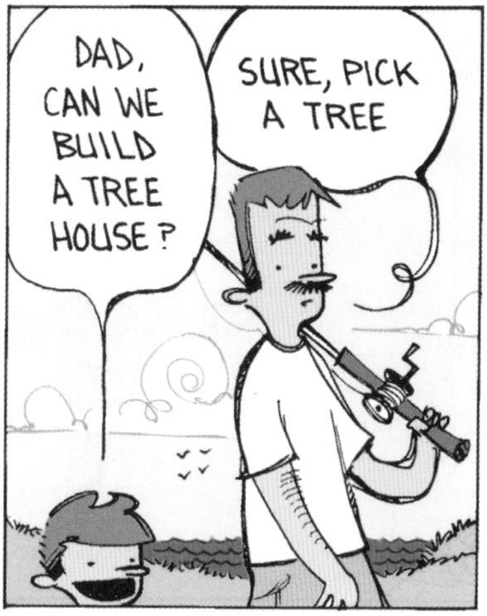
DAD, CAN WE BUILD A TREE HOUSE?
SURE, PICK A TREE

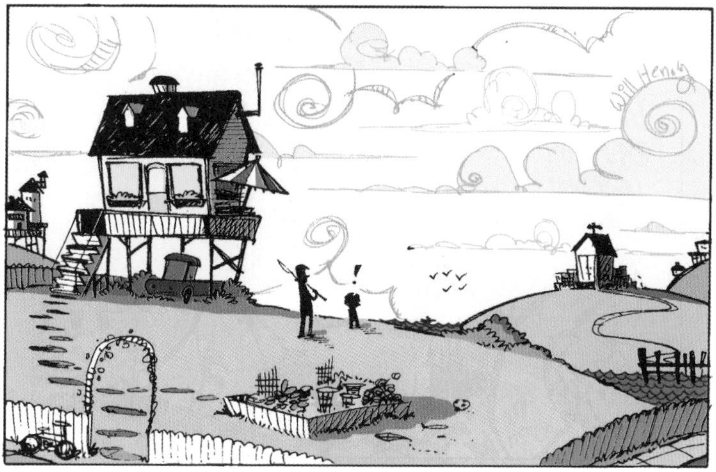

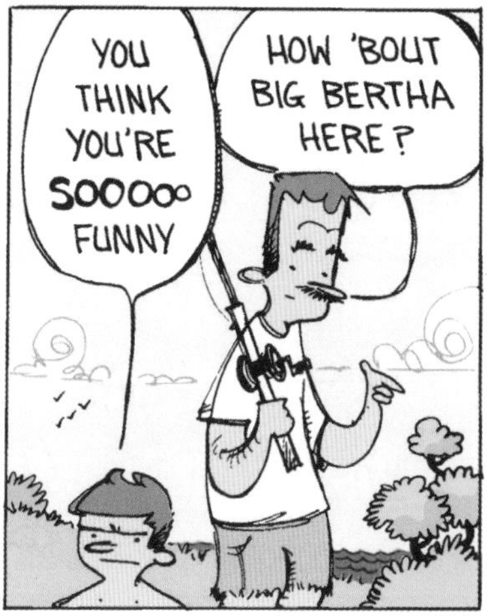
HOW 'BOUT BIG BERTHA HERE?
YOU THINK YOU'RE SOOOOO FUNNY

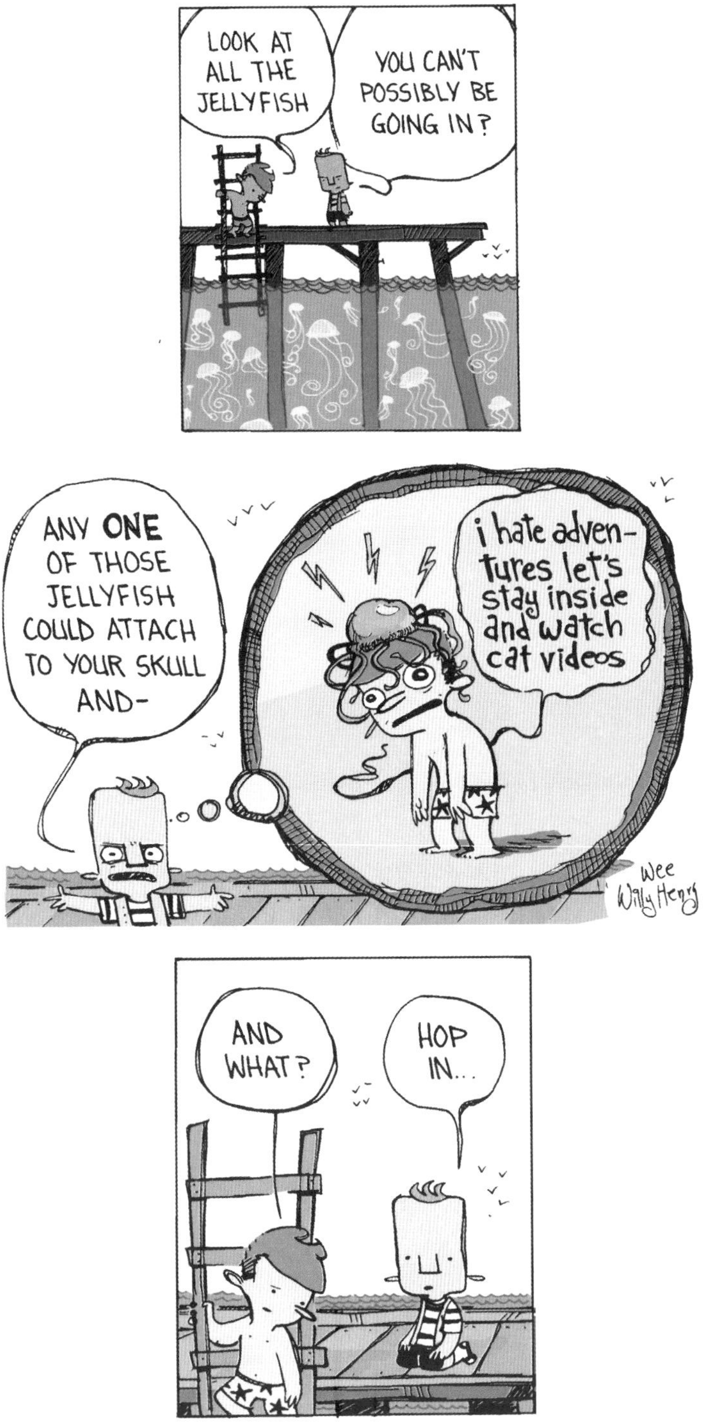
LOOK AT ALL THE JELLYFISH
YOU CAN'T POSSIBLY BE GOING IN?
ANY **ONE** OF THOSE JELLYFISH COULD ATTACH TO YOUR SKULL AND-
i hate adventures let's stay inside and watch cat videos
Wee Willy Henry
AND WHAT?
HOP IN...

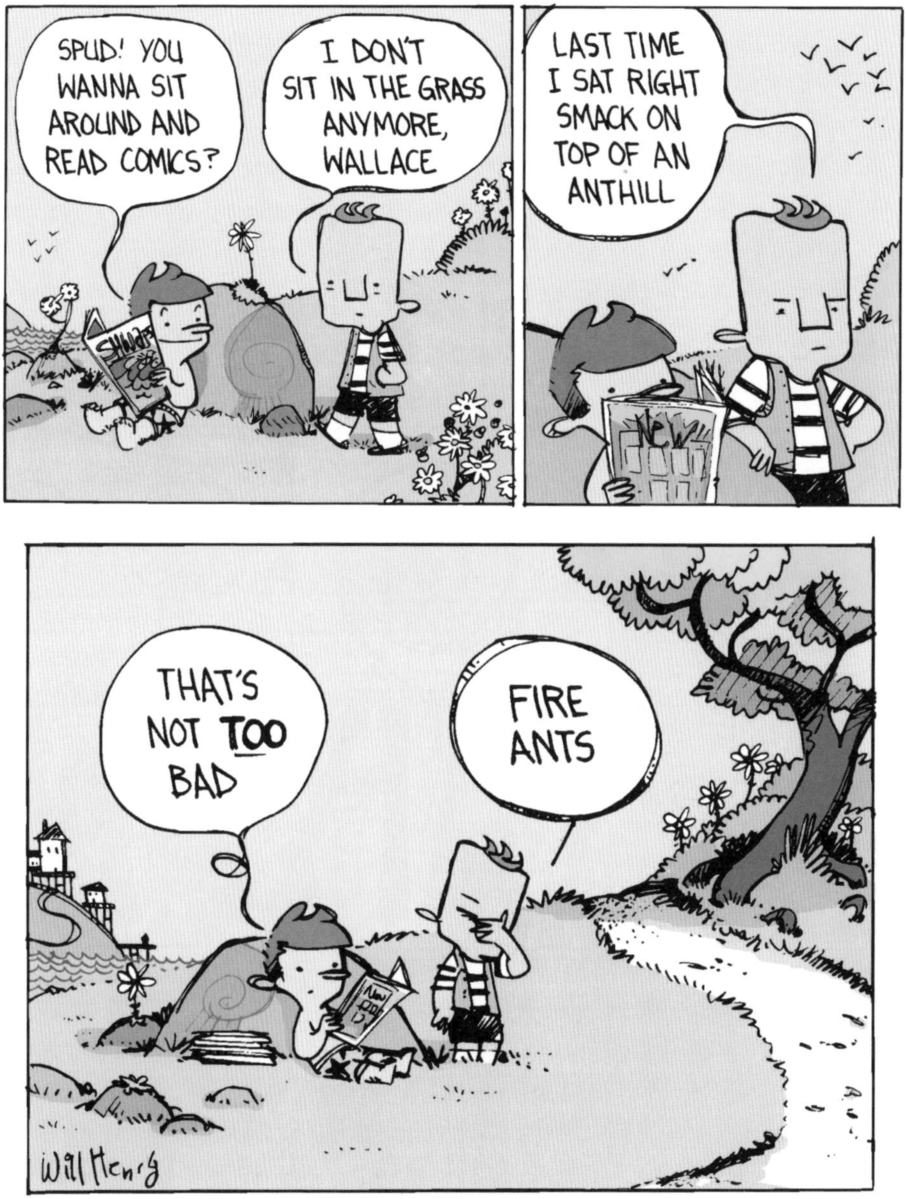
SPUD! YOU WANNA SIT AROUND AND READ COMICS?
I DON'T SIT IN THE GRASS ANYMORE, WALLACE
LAST TIME I SAT RIGHT SMACK ON TOP OF AN ANTHILL
THAT'S NOT TOO BAD
FIRE ANTS
Will Henry

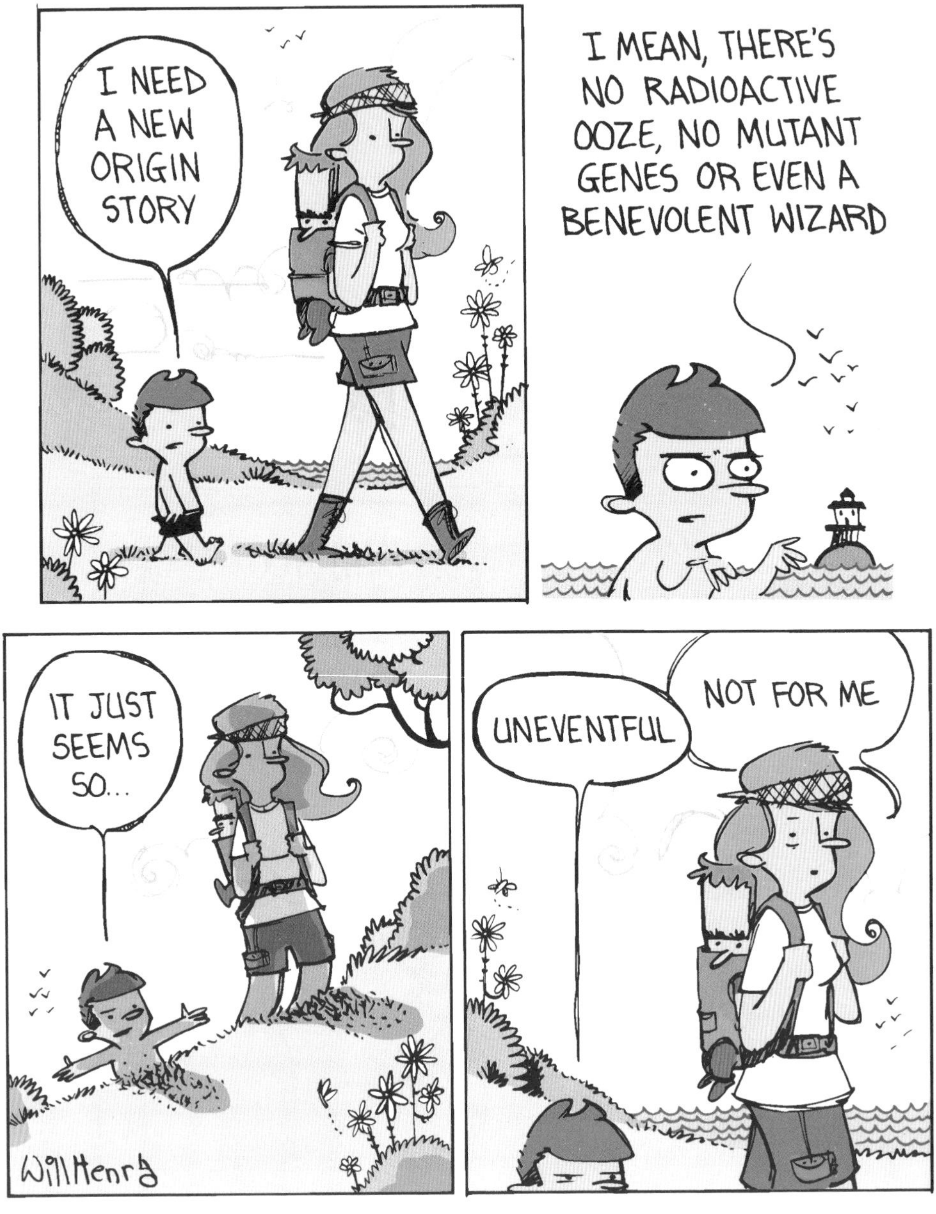
I NEED A NEW ORIGIN STORY
I MEAN, THERE'S NO RADIOACTIVE OOZE, NO MUTANT GENES OR EVEN A BENEVOLENT WIZARD
IT JUST SEEMS SO...
UNEVENTFUL
NOT FOR ME
Will Henry

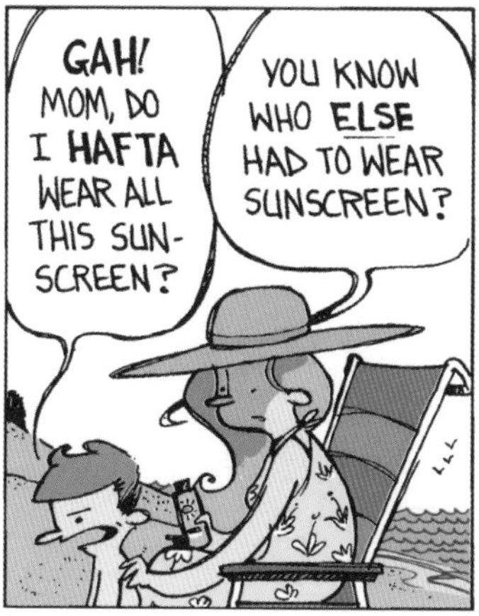
GAH! MOM, DO I HAFTA WEAR ALL THIS SUN-SCREEN?
YOU KNOW WHO ELSE HAD TO WEAR SUNSCREEN?

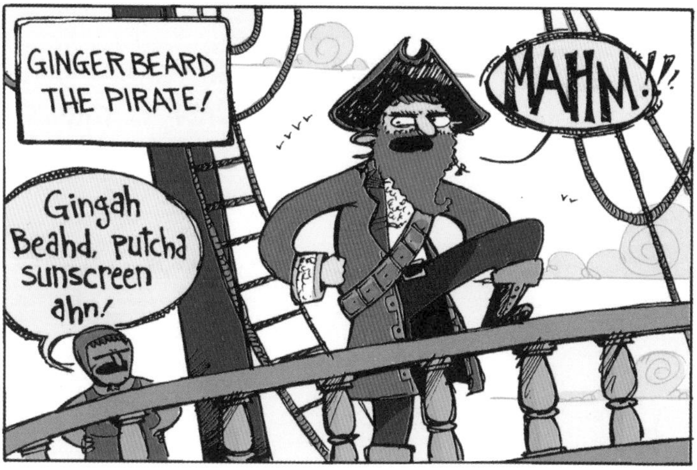
GINGER BEARD THE PIRATE!
Gingah Beahd, putcha sunscreen ahn!
MAHM!!?

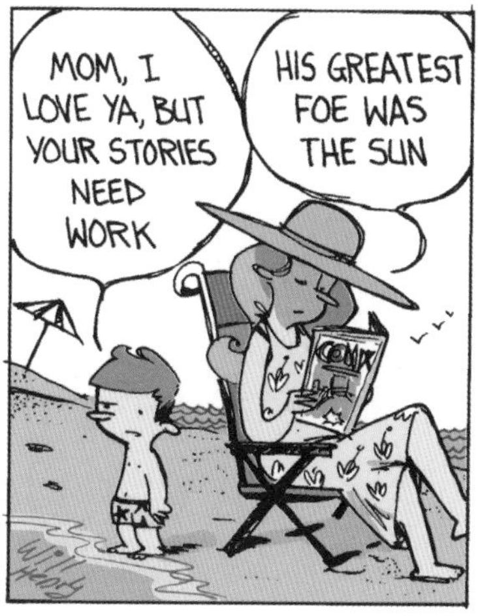
HIS GREATEST FOE WAS THE SUN
MOM, I LOVE YA, BUT YOUR STORIES NEED WORK

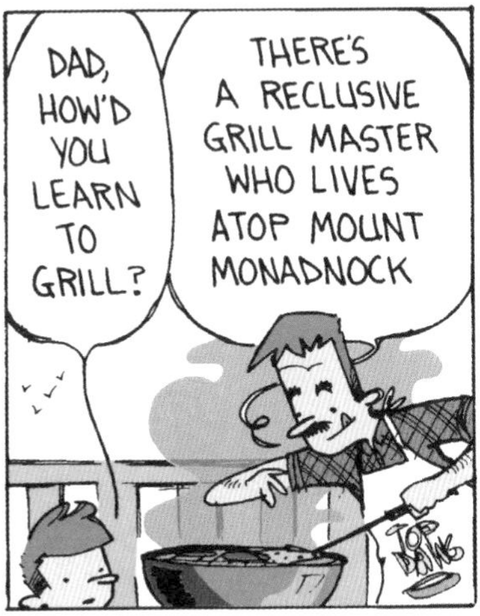
DAD, HOW'D YOU LEARN TO GRILL?
THERE'S A RECLUSIVE GRILL MASTER WHO LIVES ATOP MOUNT MONADNOCK
TOP DAWG

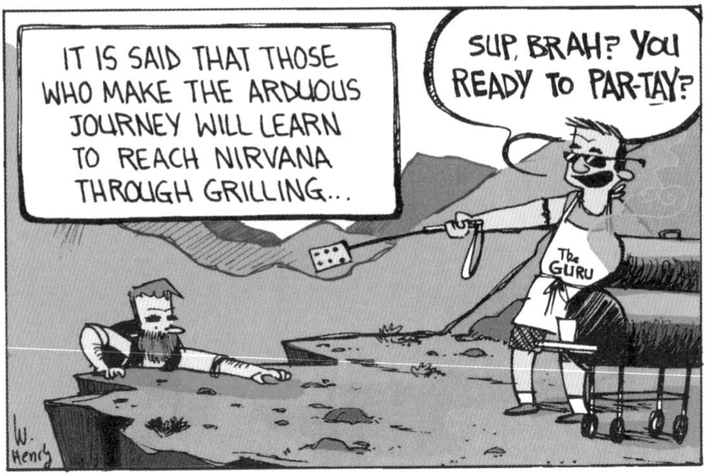
IT IS SAID THAT THOSE WHO MAKE THE ARDUOUS JOURNEY WILL LEARN TO REACH NIRVANA THROUGH GRILLING...
SUP, BRAH? YOU READY TO PAR-TAY?
The GURU
W. Henry

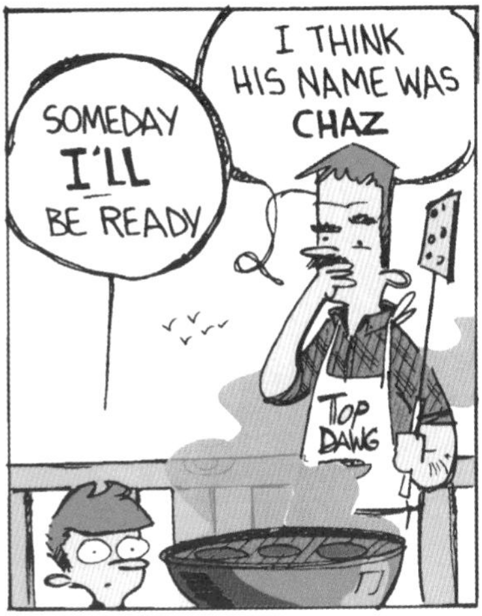
I THINK HIS NAME WAS CHAZ
SOMEDAY I'LL BE READY
TOP DAWG

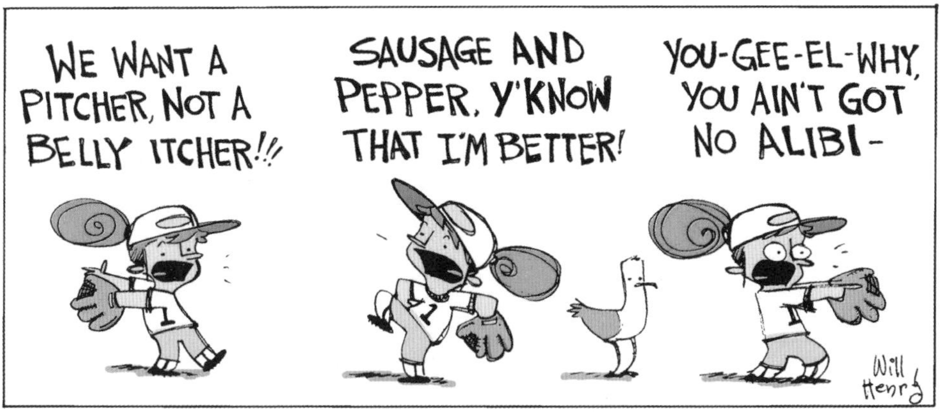
WE WANT A PITCHER, NOT A BELLY ITCHER!!!
SAUSAGE AND PEPPER, Y'KNOW THAT I'M BETTER!
YOU-GEE-EL-WHY, YOU AIN'T GOT NO ALIBI-
Will Henry

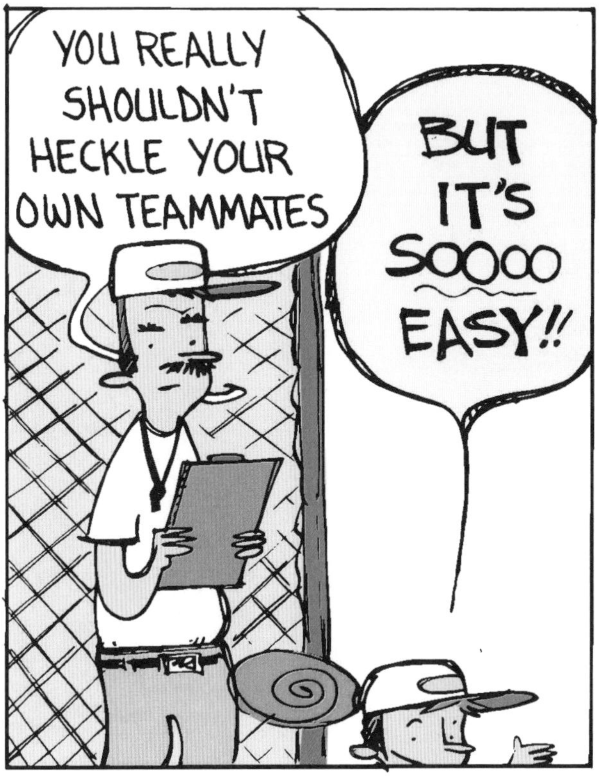
YOU REALLY SHOULDN'T HECKLE YOUR OWN TEAMMATES
BUT IT'S SOOOO EASY!!

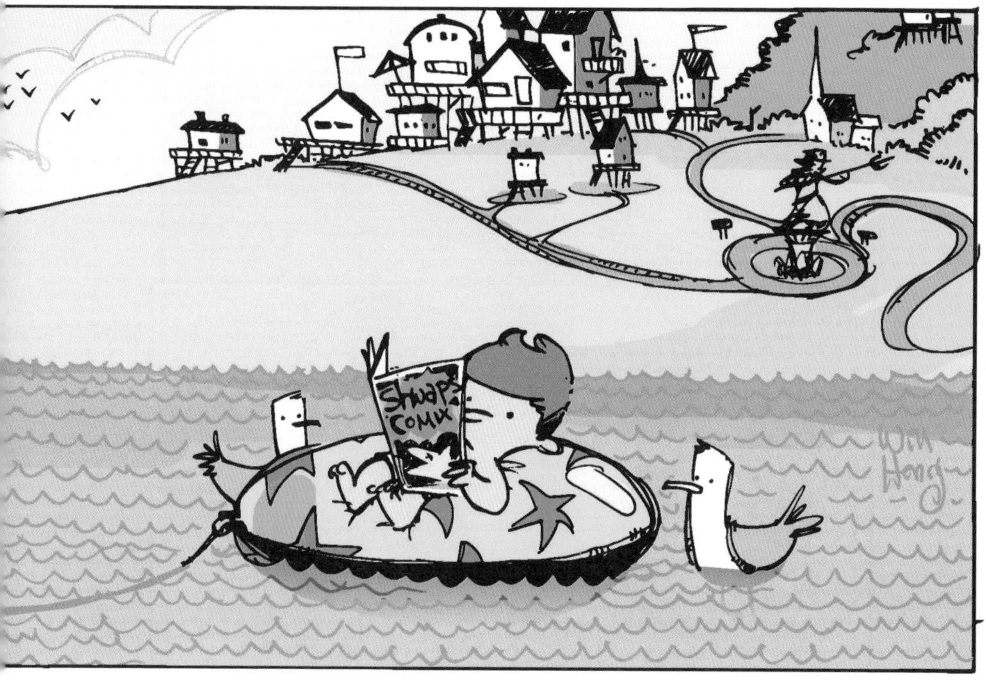
Shwap! COMIX
Will Hong

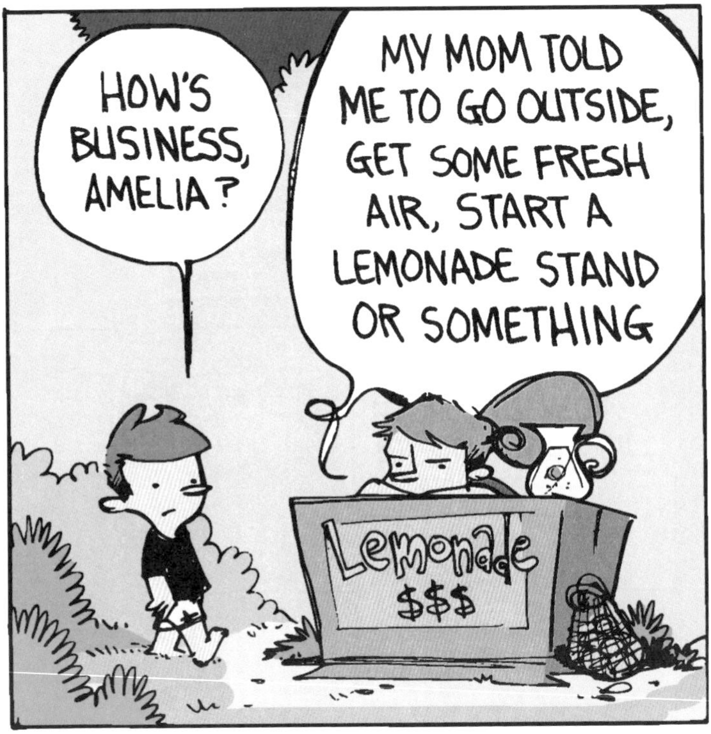
HOW'S BUSINESS, AMELIA?
MY MOM TOLD ME TO GO OUTSIDE, GET SOME FRESH AIR, START A LEMONADE STAND OR SOMETHING
Lemonade $$$

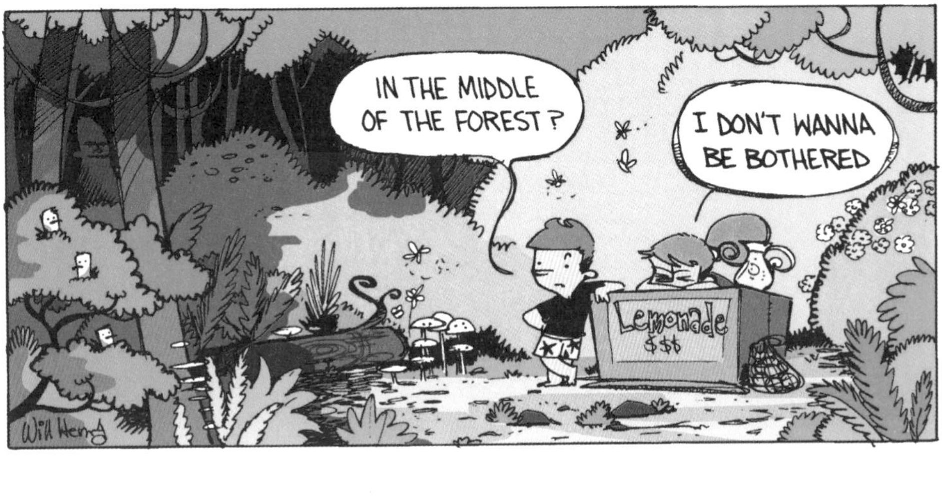
IN THE MIDDLE OF THE FOREST?
I DON'T WANNA BE BOTHERED
Lemonade $$$
Will Henry

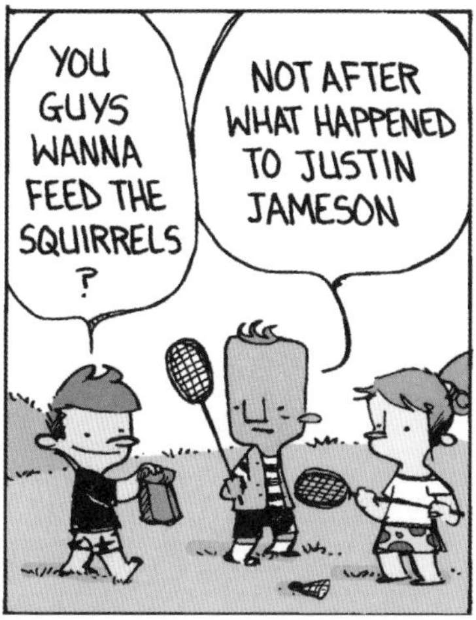
YOU GUYS WANNA FEED THE SQUIRRELS ?
NOT AFTER WHAT HAPPENED TO JUSTIN JAMESON

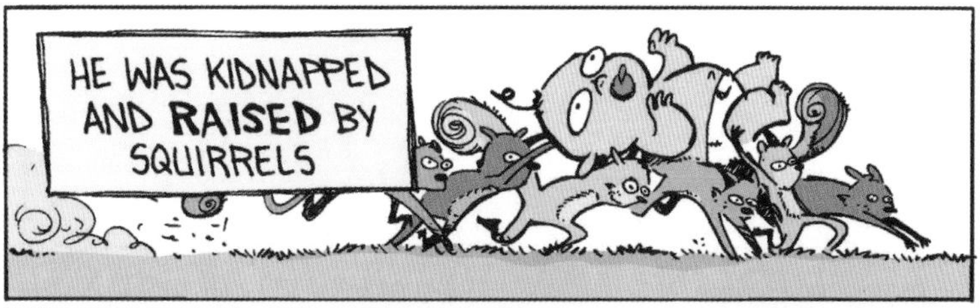
HE WAS KIDNAPPED AND **RAISED** BY SQUIRRELS

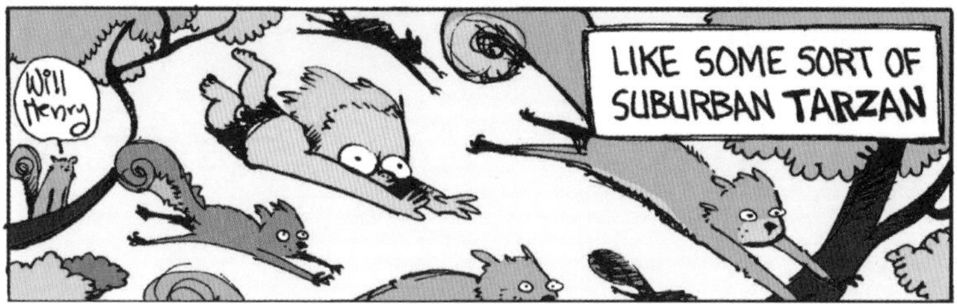
Will Henry
LIKE SOME SORT OF SUBURBAN **TARZAN**

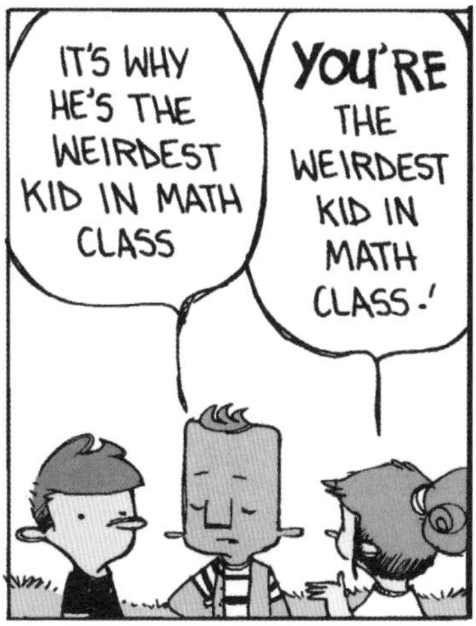
IT'S WHY HE'S THE WEIRDEST KID IN MATH CLASS
YOU'RE THE WEIRDEST KID IN MATH CLASS!

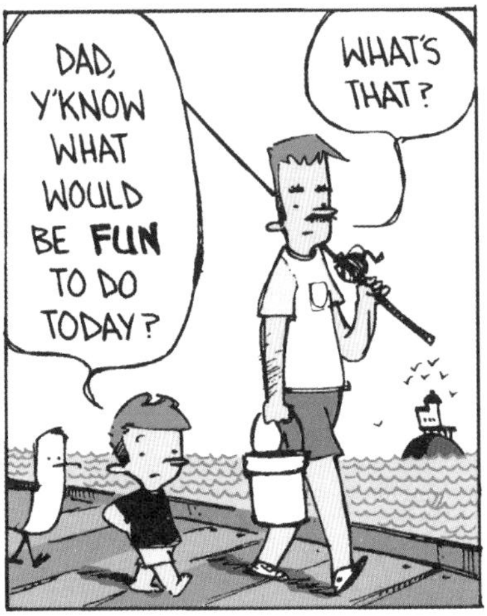
DAD, Y'KNOW WHAT WOULD BE **FUN** TO DO TODAY?
WHAT'S THAT?

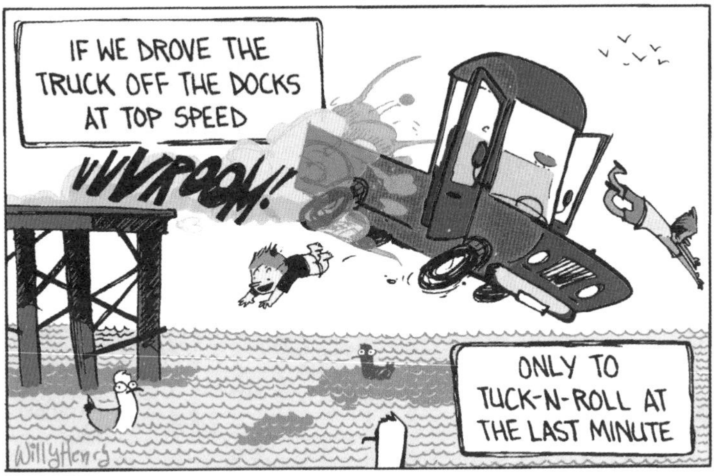
IF WE DROVE THE TRUCK OFF THE DOCKS AT TOP SPEED
VVVROOM!
ONLY TO TUCK-N-ROLL AT THE LAST MINUTE
WillyHenry

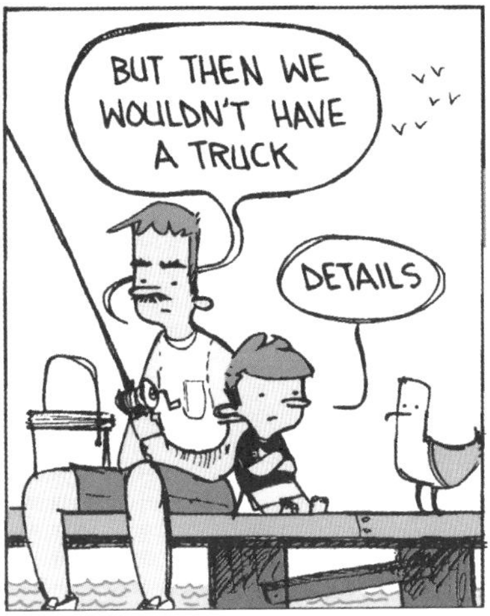
BUT THEN WE WOULDN'T HAVE A TRUCK
DETAILS

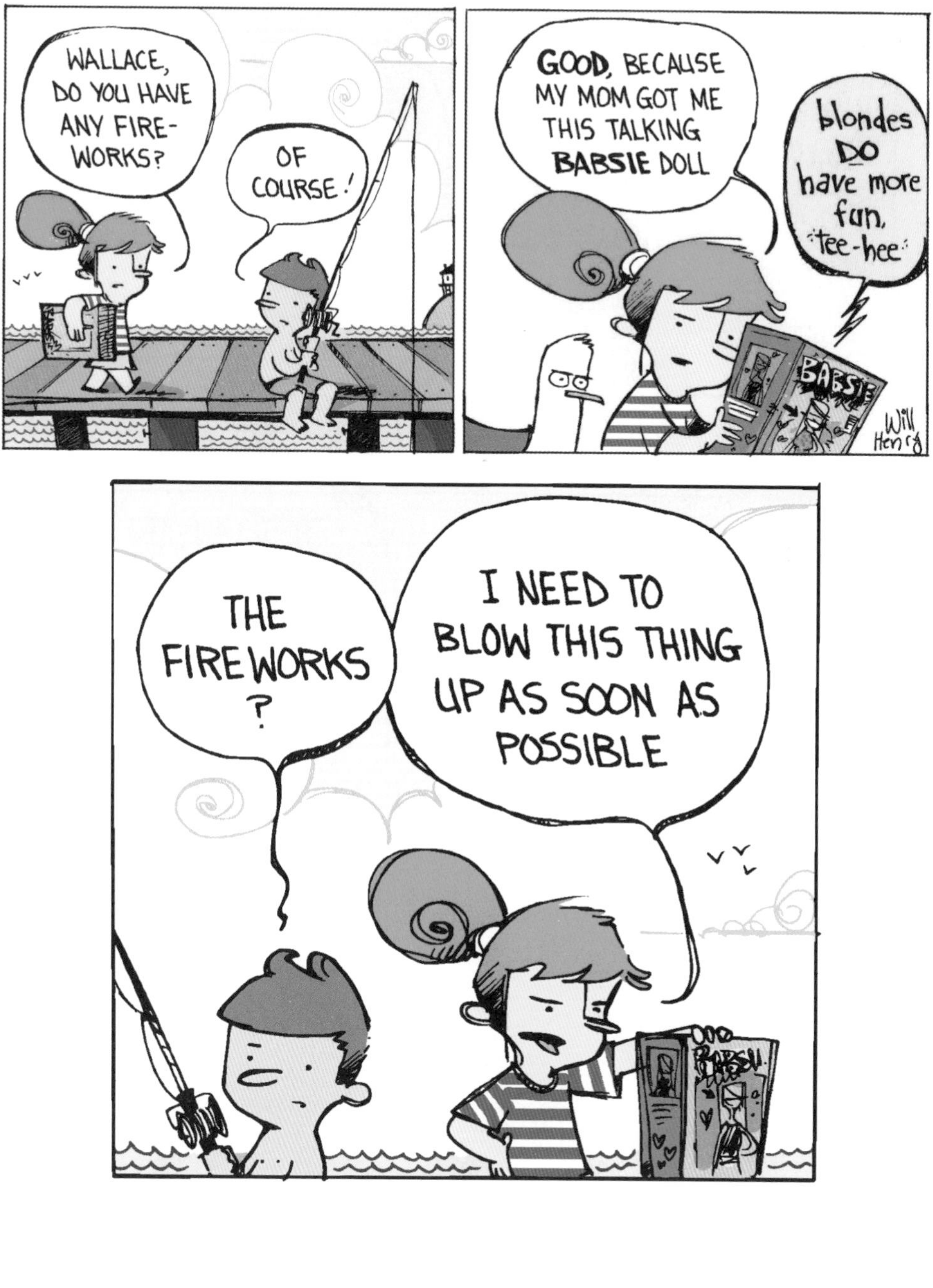
WALLACE, DO YOU HAVE ANY FIRE-WORKS?
OF COURSE!
GOOD, BECAUSE MY MOM GOT ME THIS TALKING BABSIE DOLL
blondes DO have more fun. tee-hee
BABSIE
Will Henry
THE FIREWORKS?
I NEED TO BLOW THIS THING UP AS SOON AS POSSIBLE

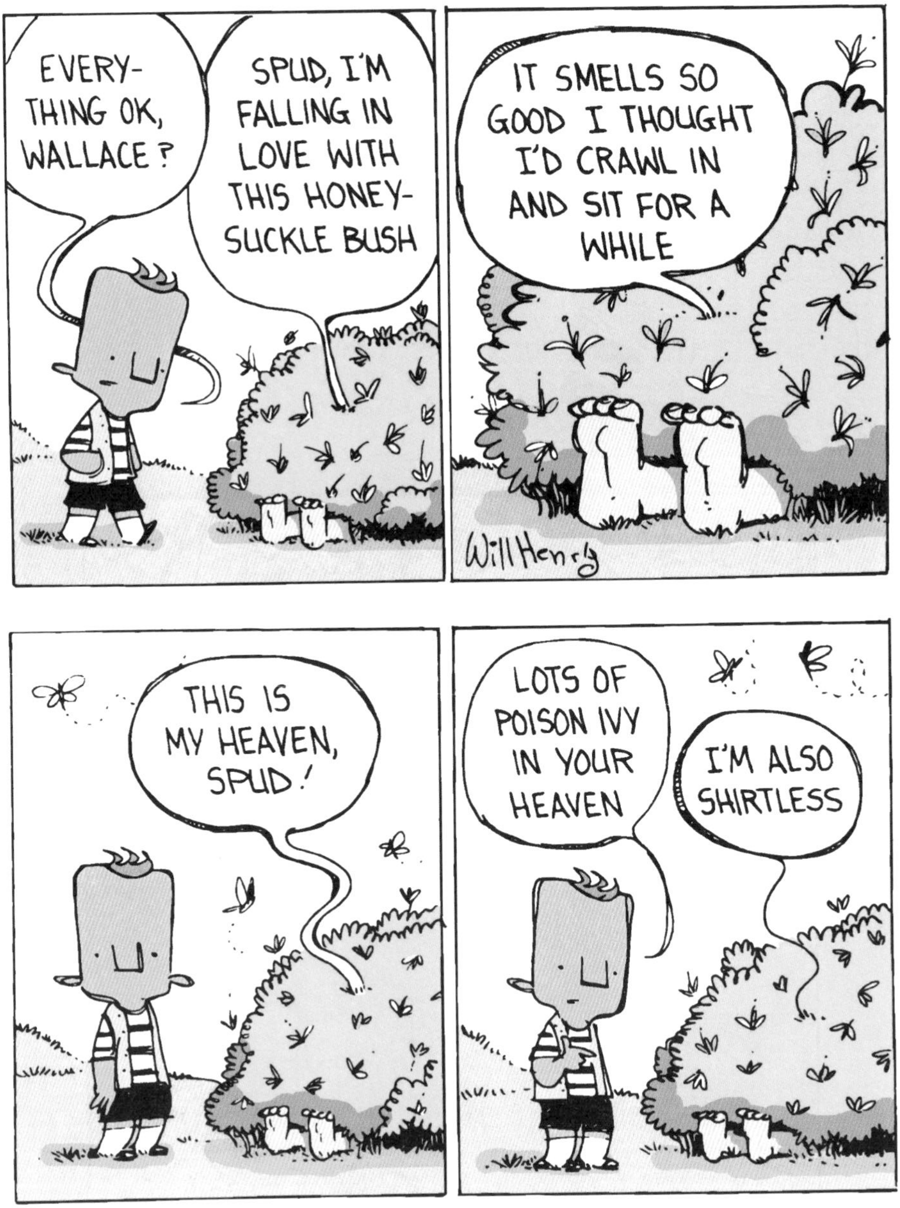
EVERY-THING OK, WALLACE?
SPUD, I'M FALLING IN LOVE WITH THIS HONEY-SUCKLE BUSH
IT SMELLS SO GOOD I THOUGHT I'D CRAWL IN AND SIT FOR A WHILE
Will Henry
THIS IS MY HEAVEN, SPUD!
LOTS OF POISON IVY IN YOUR HEAVEN
I'M ALSO SHIRTLESS

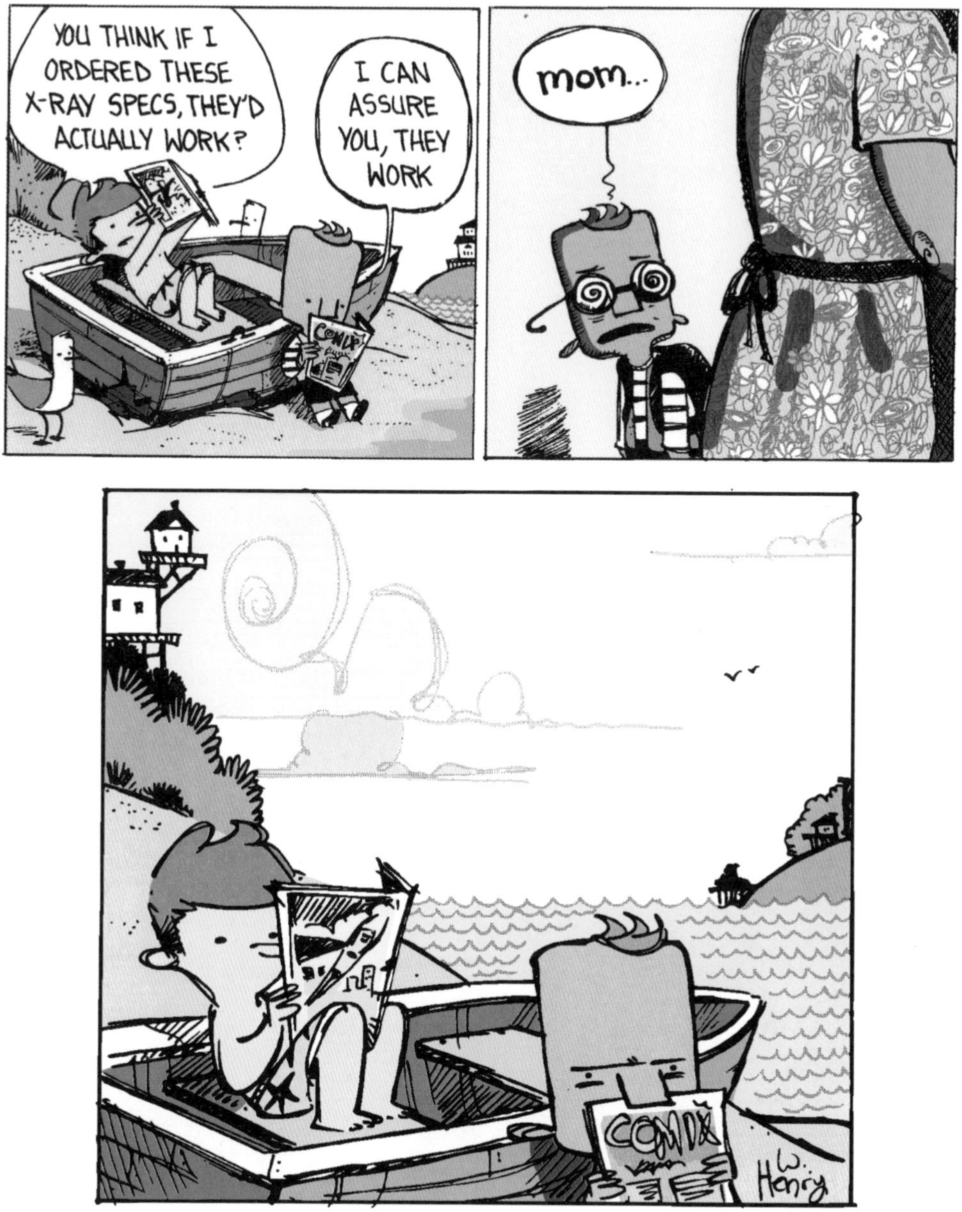
YOU THINK IF I ORDERED THESE X-RAY SPECS, THEY'D ACTUALLY WORK?
I CAN ASSURE YOU, THEY WORK
mom...
W. Henry

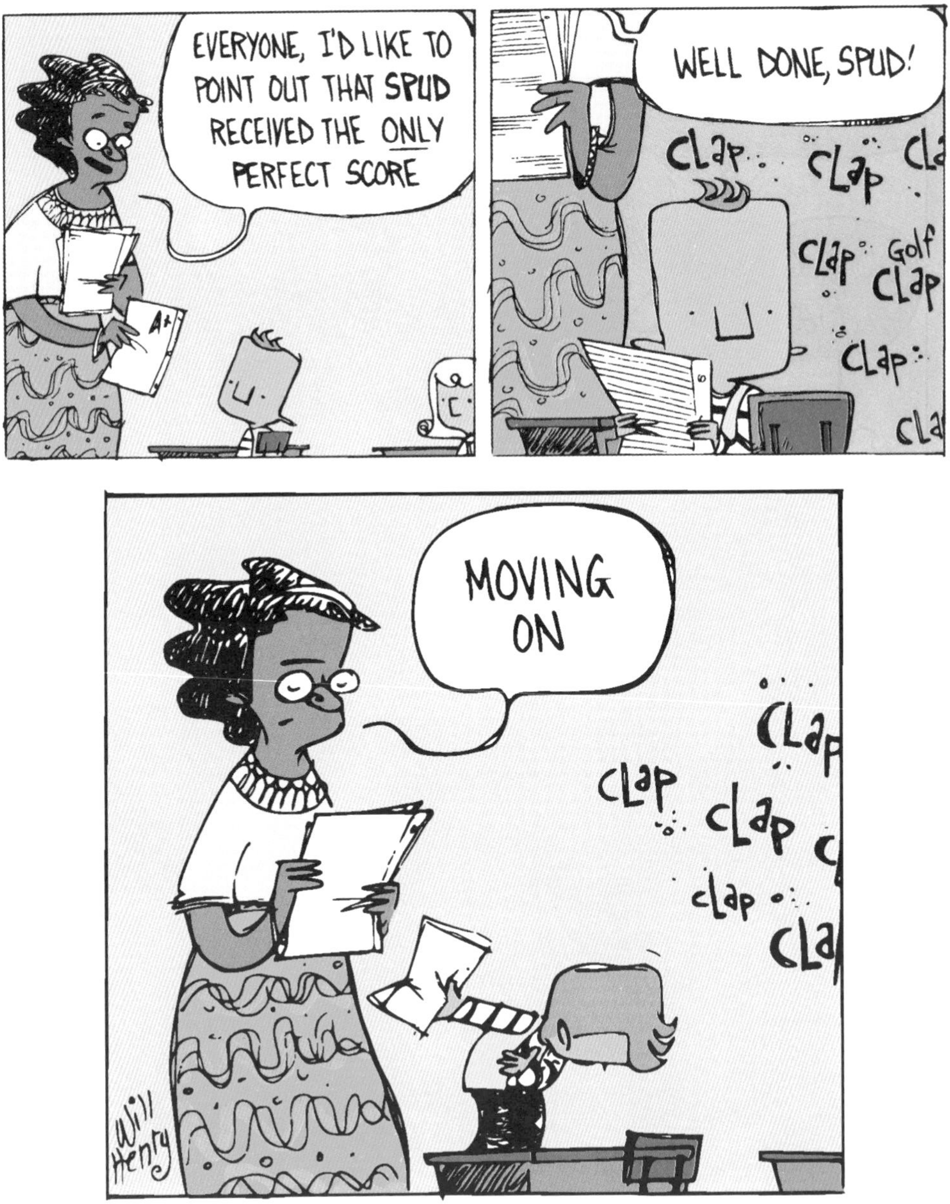
EVERYONE, I'D LIKE TO POINT OUT THAT SPUD RECEIVED THE ONLY PERFECT SCORE
WELL DONE, SPUD!
CLAP CLAP
CLAP Golf CLAP
CLAP
MOVING ON
CLAP
CLAP CLAP
CLAP
Will Henry

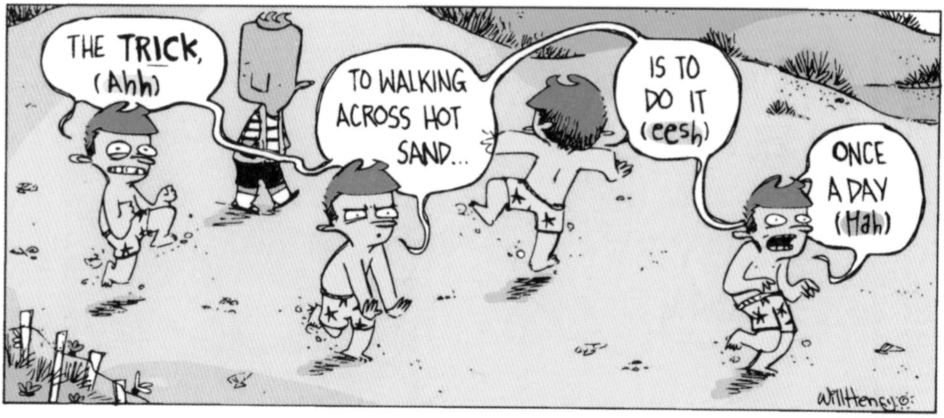
THE TRICK, (Ahh)
TO WALKING ACROSS HOT SAND...
IS TO DO IT (eesh)
ONCE A DAY (Hah)
WillHenry

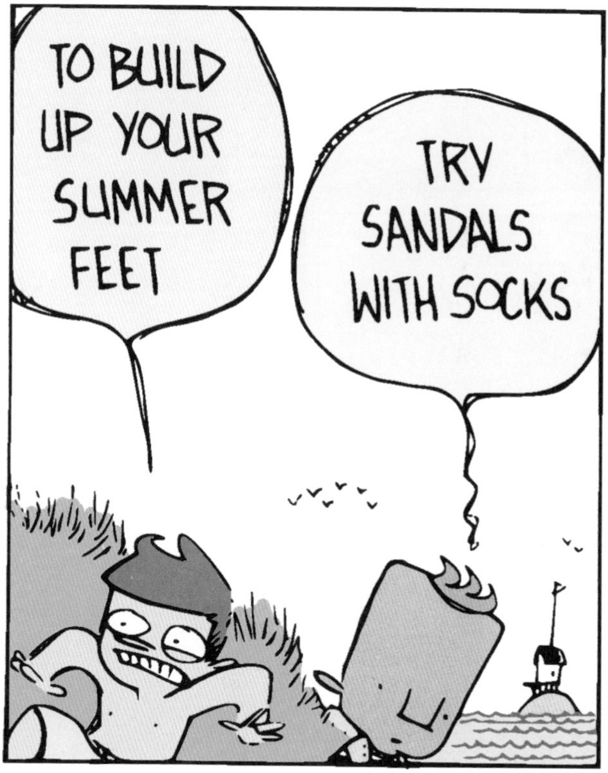
TO BUILD UP YOUR SUMMER FEET
TRY SANDALS WITH SOCKS

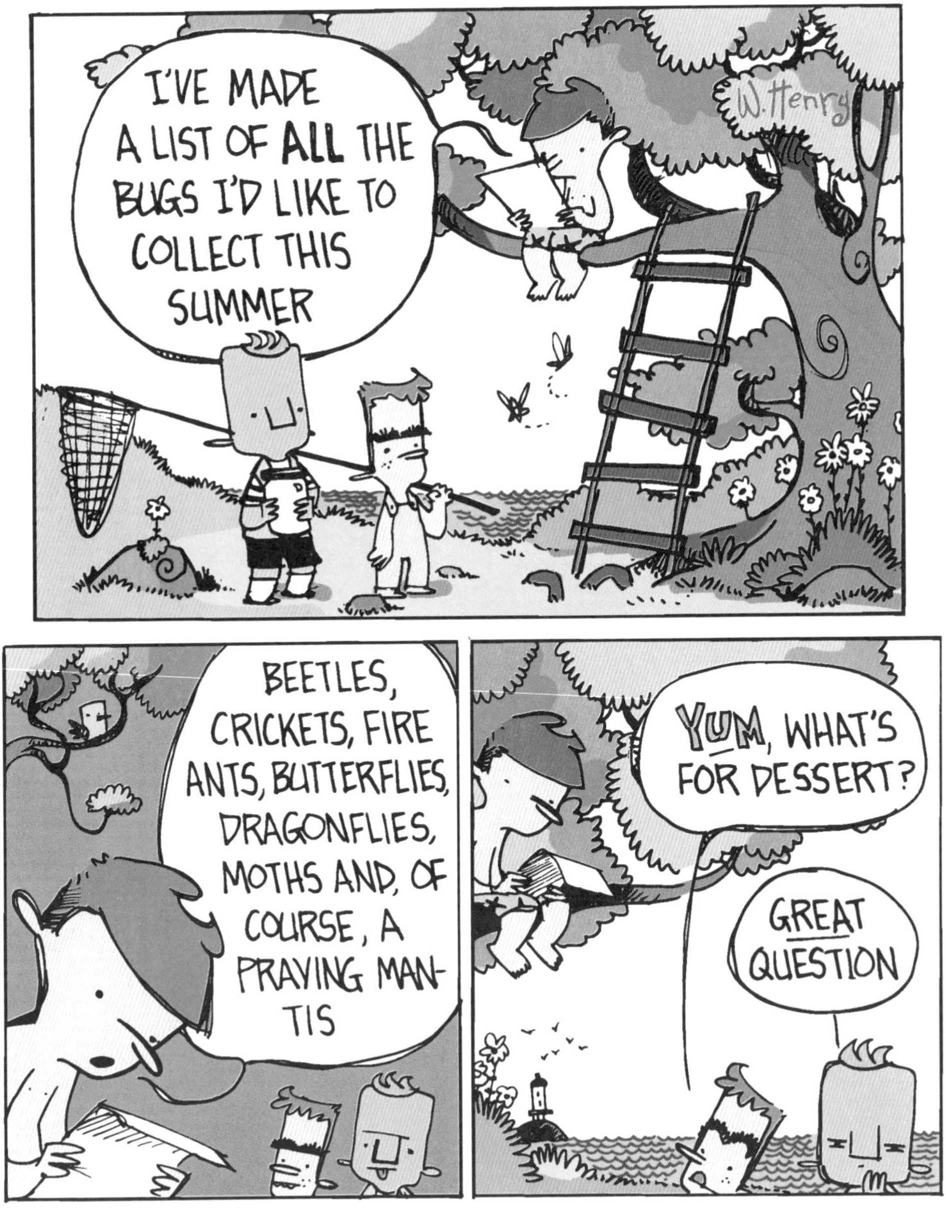
W. Henry
I'VE MADE A LIST OF **ALL** THE BUGS I'D LIKE TO COLLECT THIS SUMMER
BEETLES, CRICKETS, FIRE ANTS, BUTTERFLIES, DRAGONFLIES, MOTHS AND, OF COURSE, A PRAYING MAN-TIS
YUM, WHAT'S FOR DESSERT?
GREAT QUESTION

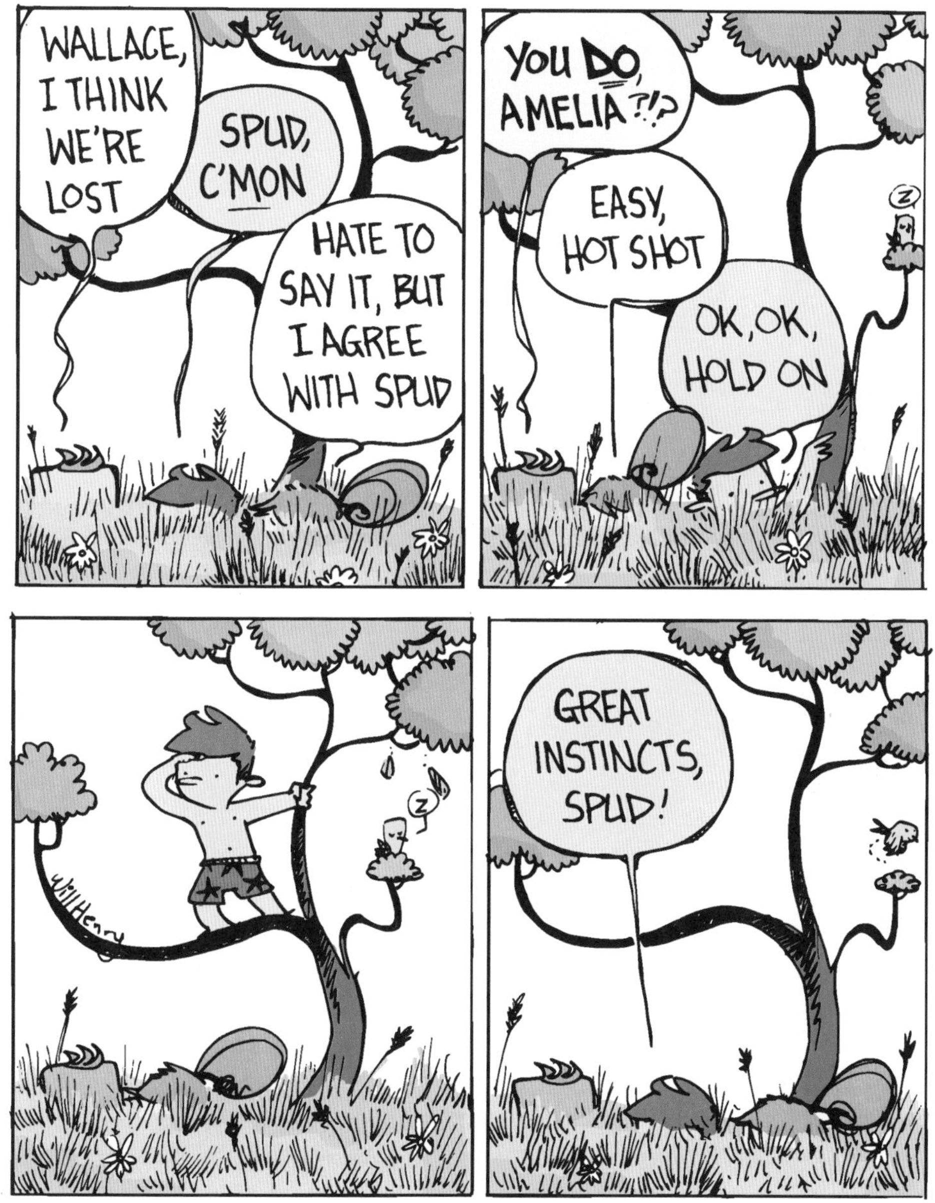
WALLACE, I THINK WE'RE LOST
SPUD, C'MON
HATE TO SAY IT, BUT I AGREE WITH SPUD
YOU DO, AMELIA ?!?
EASY, HOT SHOT
OK, OK, HOLD ON
Z
Z
WillHenry
GREAT INSTINCTS, SPUD!

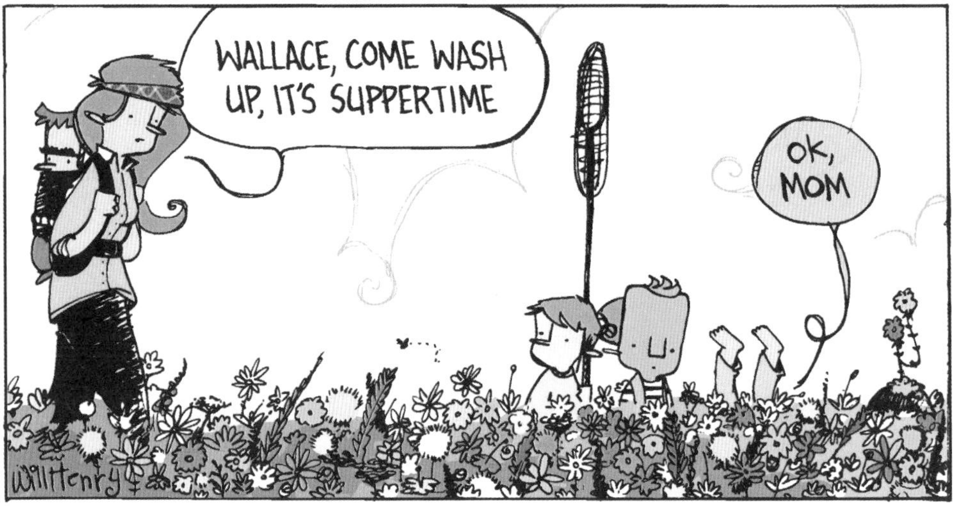
WALLACE, COME WASH UP, IT'S SUPPERTIME
OK, MOM
WillHenry

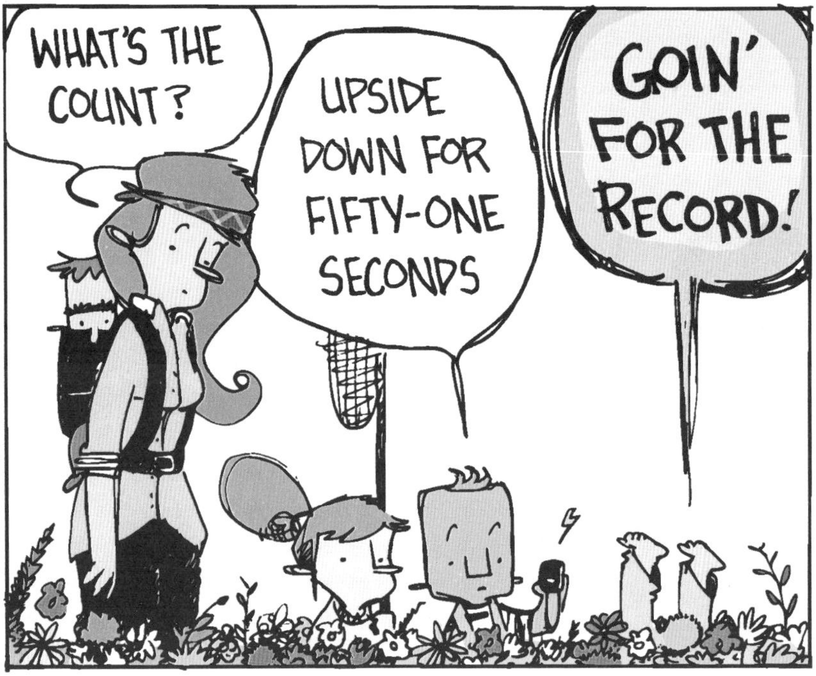
WHAT'S THE COUNT?
UPSIDE DOWN FOR FIFTY-ONE SECONDS
GOIN' FOR THE RECORD!

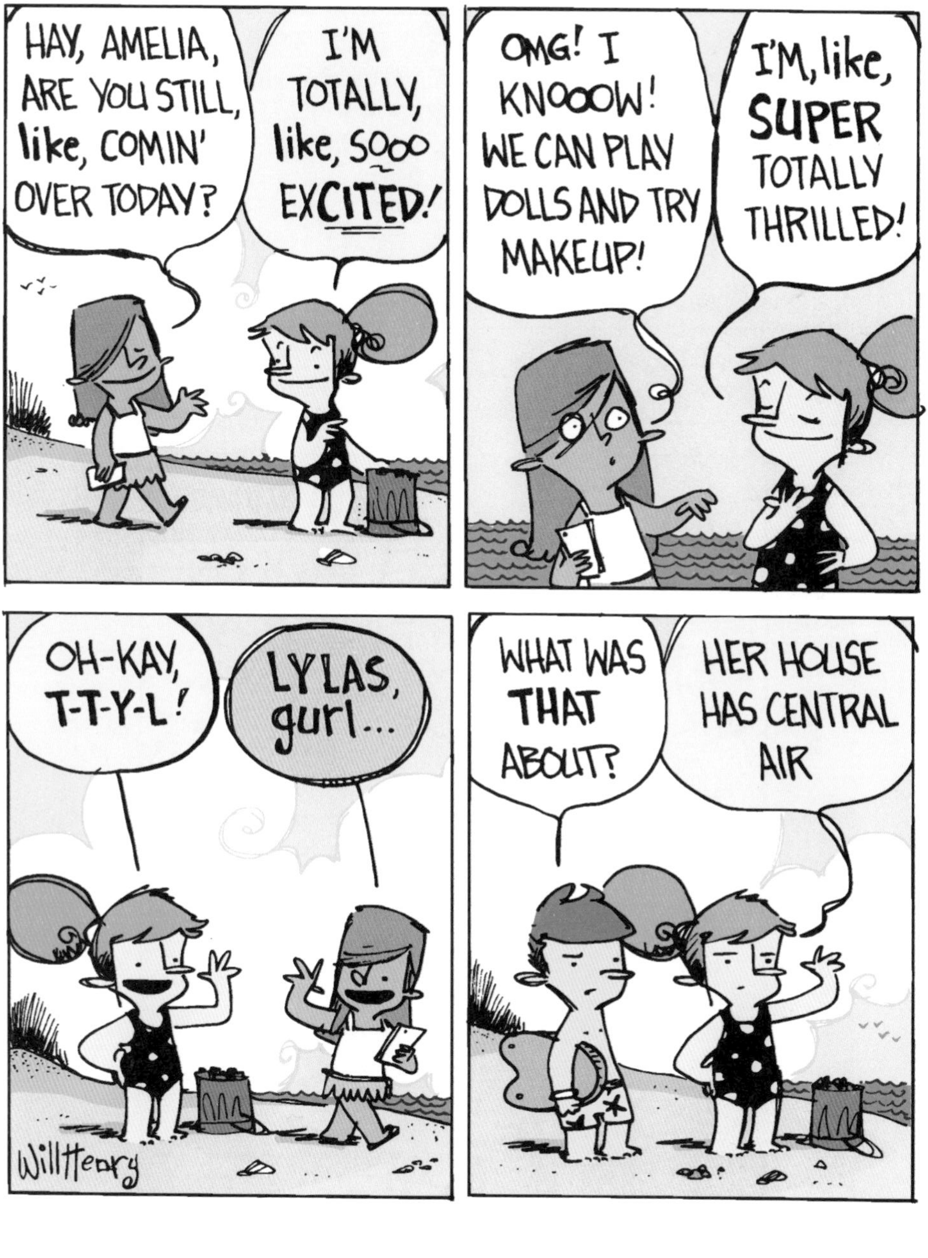
HAY, AMELIA, ARE YOU STILL, like, COMIN' OVER TODAY?
I'M TOTALLY, like, SOOO EXCITED!
OMG! I KNOOOW! WE CAN PLAY DOLLS AND TRY MAKEUP!
I'M, like, SUPER TOTALLY THRILLED!
OH-KAY, T-T-Y-L!
LYLAS, gurl...
WHAT WAS THAT ABOUT?
HER HOUSE HAS CENTRAL AIR
Will Henry

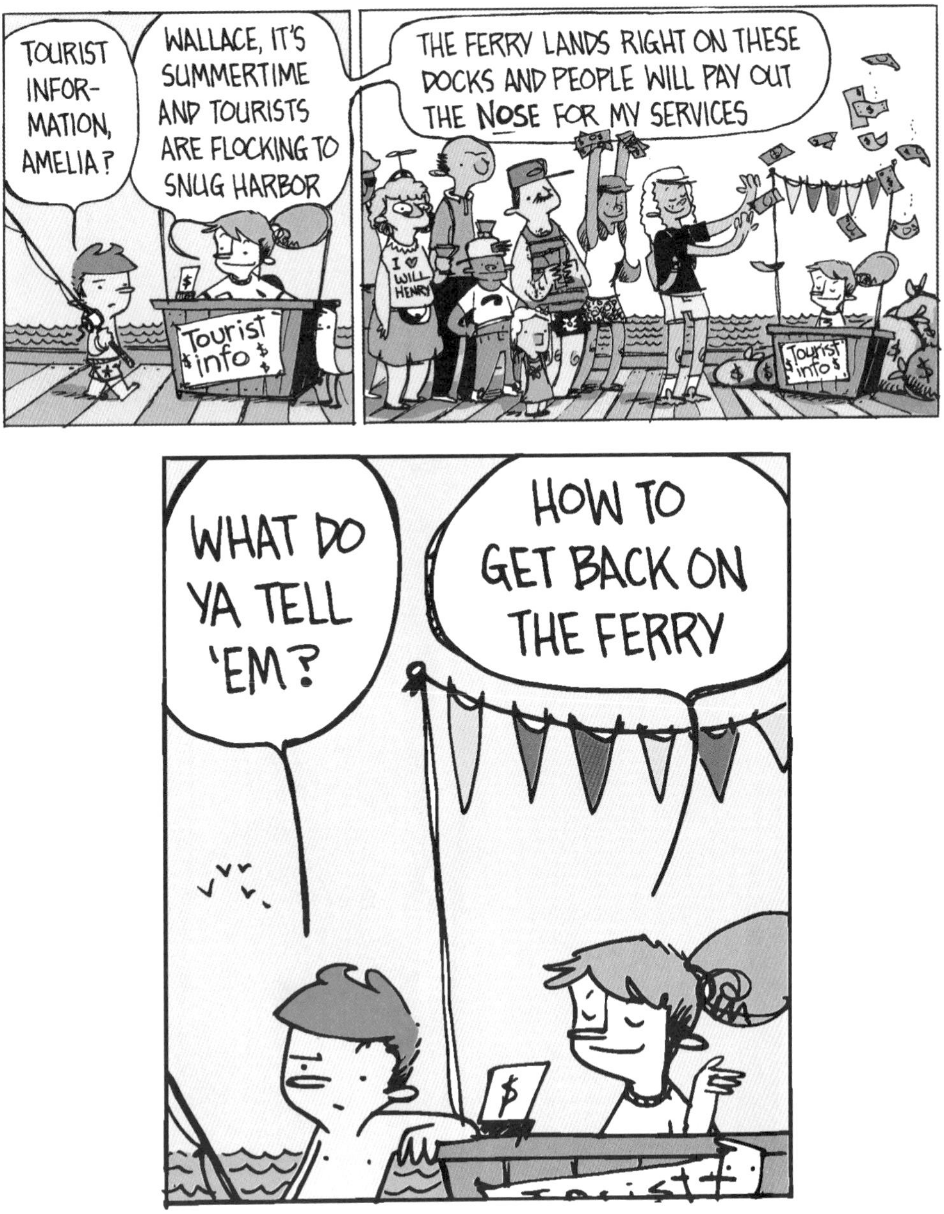
TOURIST INFORMATION, AMELIA?
WALLACE, IT'S SUMMERTIME AND TOURISTS ARE FLOCKING TO SNUG HARBOR
Tourist info $ $ $
THE FERRY LANDS RIGHT ON THESE DOCKS AND PEOPLE WILL PAY OUT THE NOSE FOR MY SERVICES
I ♥ WILL HENRY
Tourist info $ $
WHAT DO YA TELL 'EM?
HOW TO GET BACK ON THE FERRY
$

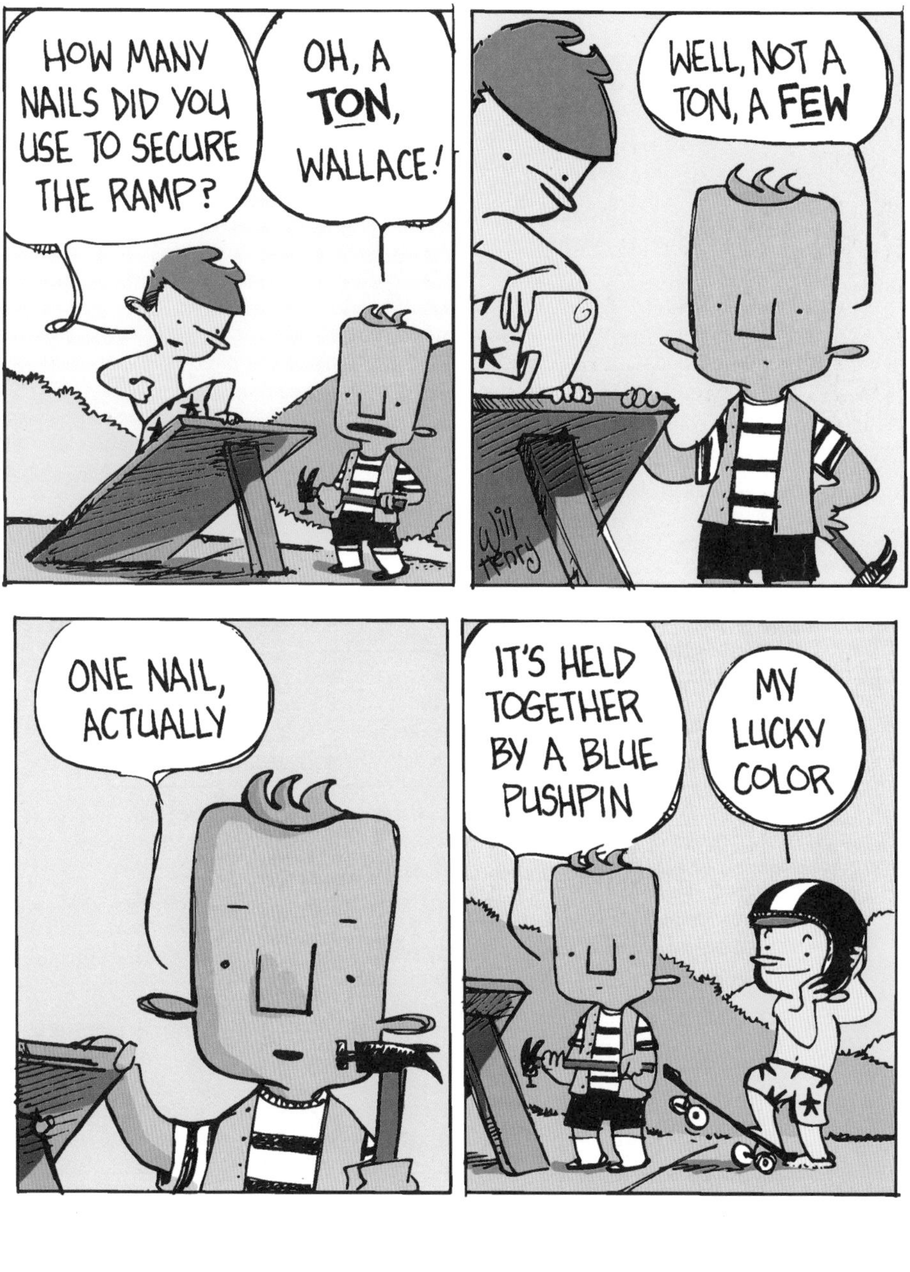
HOW MANY NAILS DID YOU USE TO SECURE THE RAMP?
OH, A TON, WALLACE!
WELL, NOT A TON, A FEW
Will Henry
ONE NAIL, ACTUALLY
IT'S HELD TOGETHER BY A BLUE PUSHPIN
MY LUCKY COLOR

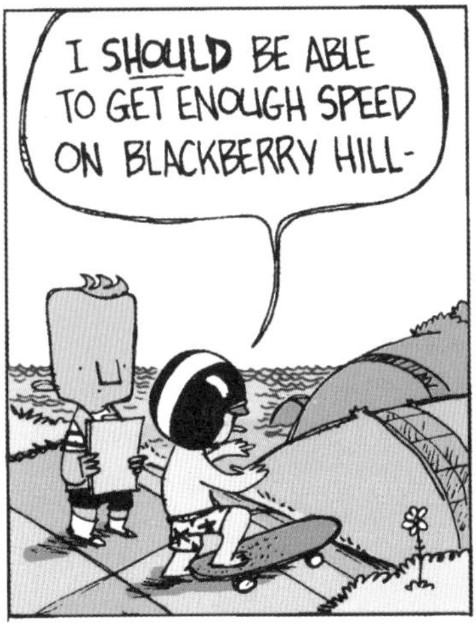
I SHOULD BE ABLE TO GET ENOUGH SPEED ON BLACKBERRY HILL-

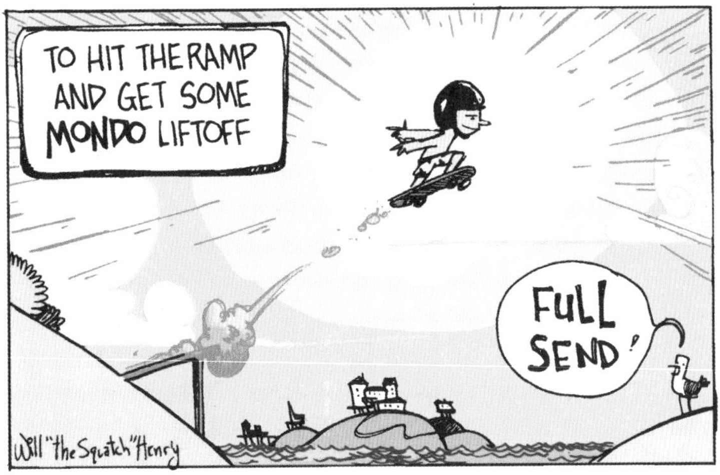
TO HIT THE RAMP AND GET SOME MONDO LIFTOFF
FULL SEND!
Will "the Squatch" Henry

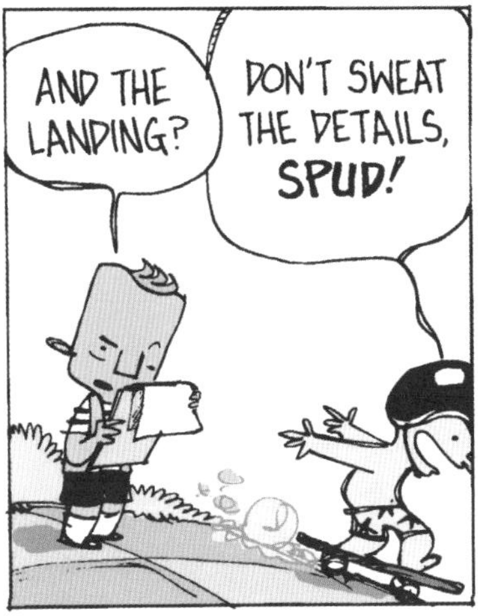
AND THE LANDING?
DON'T SWEAT THE DETAILS, SPUD!

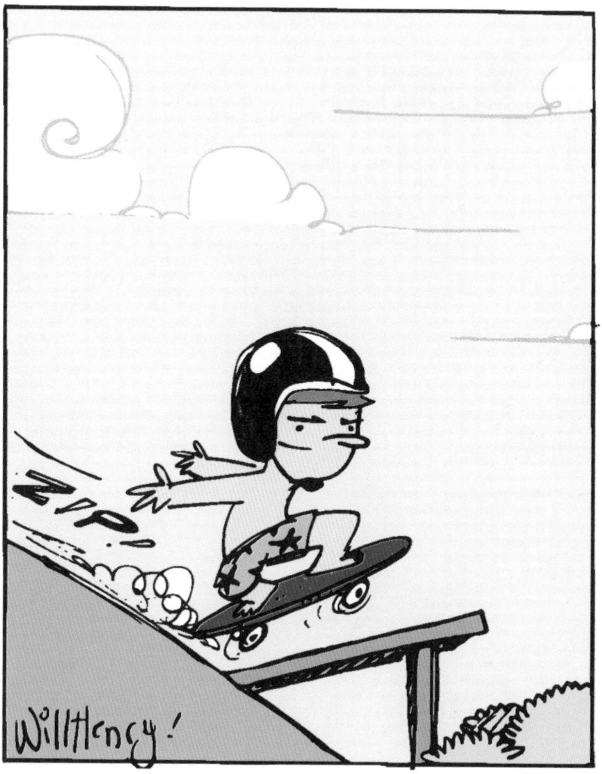
ZIP!
WillHenry!

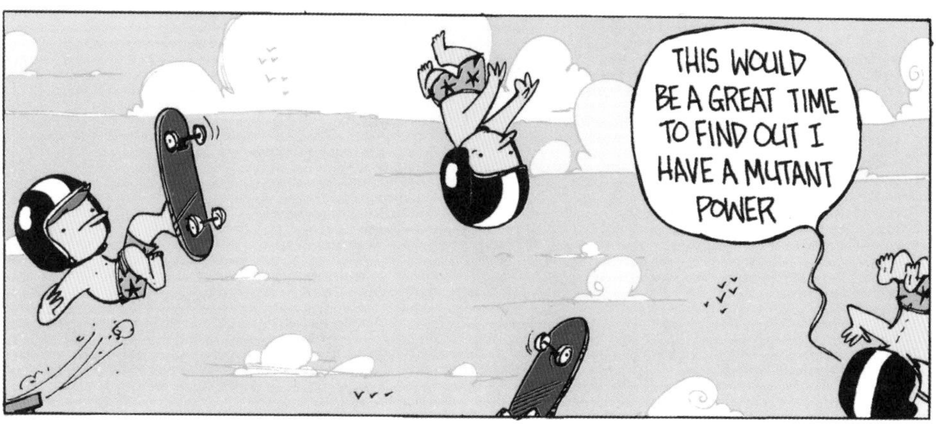
THIS WOULD BE A GREAT TIME TO FIND OUT I HAVE A MUTANT POWER

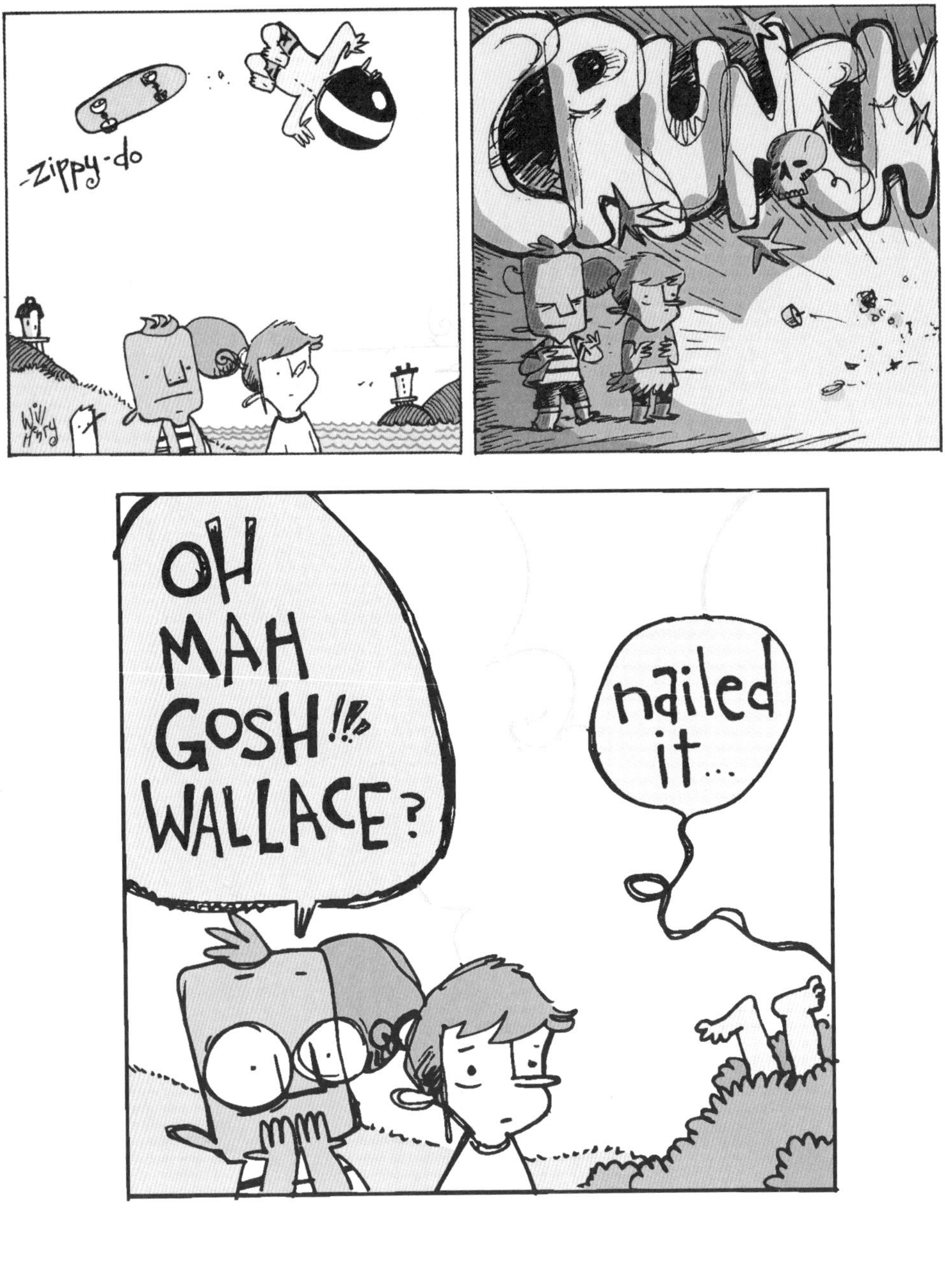
-zippy-do
Will Henry
CRUNCH
OH MAH GOSH!!! WALLACE?
nailed it...

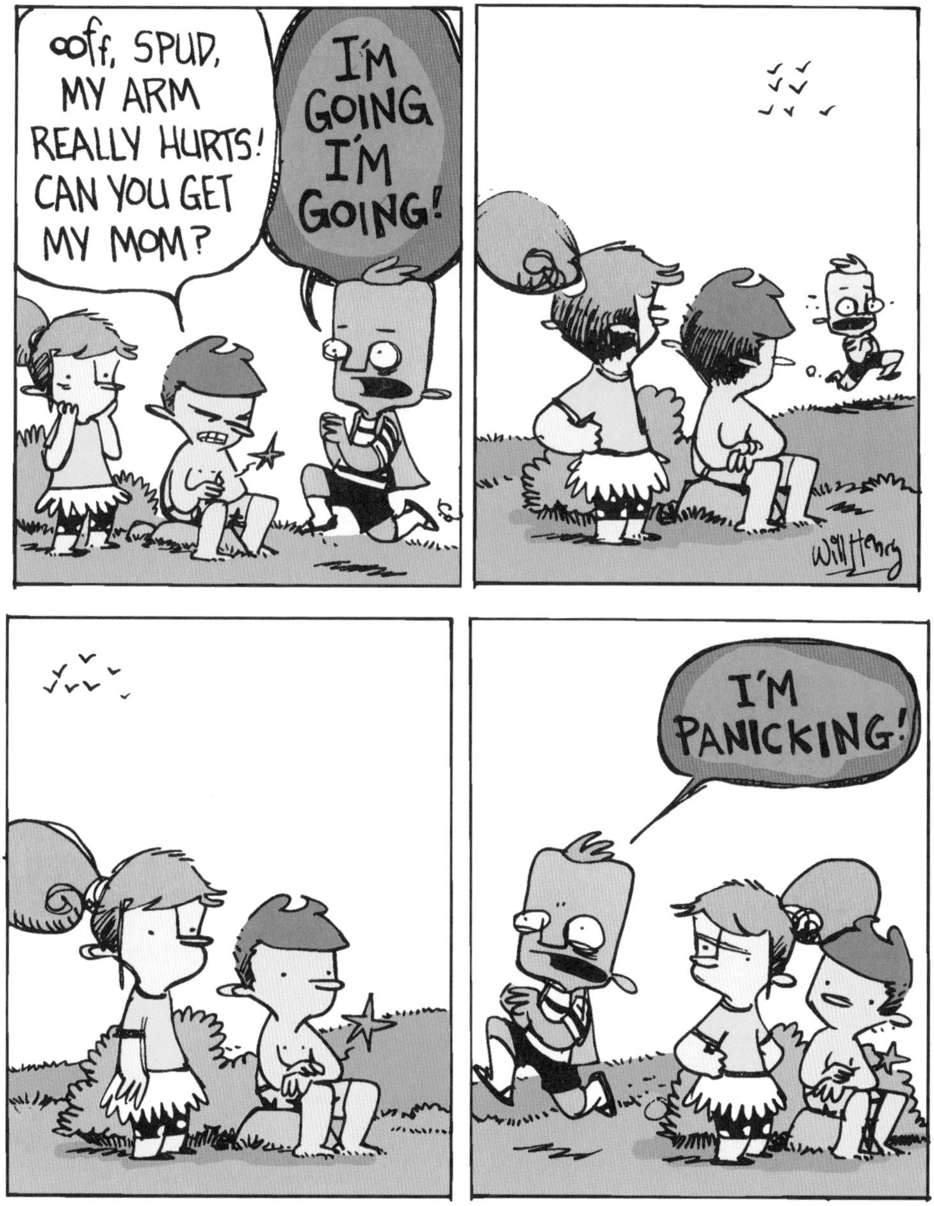

ooff, SPUD, MY ARM REALLY HURTS! CAN YOU GET MY MOM?
I'M GOING I'M GOING!
Will Henry
I'M PANICKING!

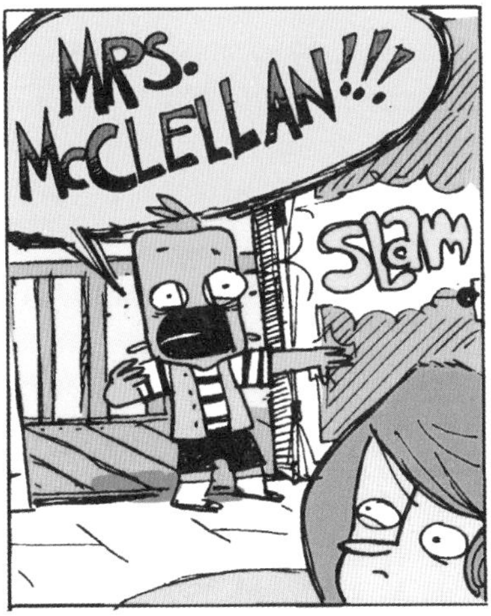
MRS. McCLELLAN!!!
SLAM

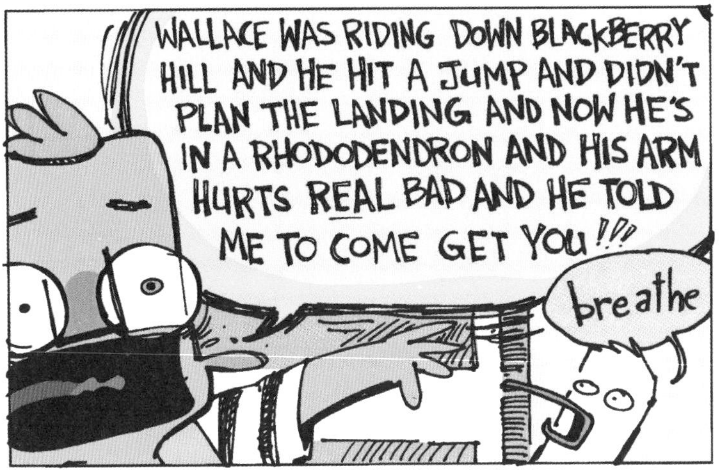
WALLACE WAS RIDING DOWN BLACKBERRY HILL AND HE HIT A JUMP AND DIDN'T PLAN THE LANDING AND NOW HE'S IN A RHODODENDRON AND HIS ARM HURTS REAL BAD AND HE TOLD ME TO COME GET YOU!!!
breathe

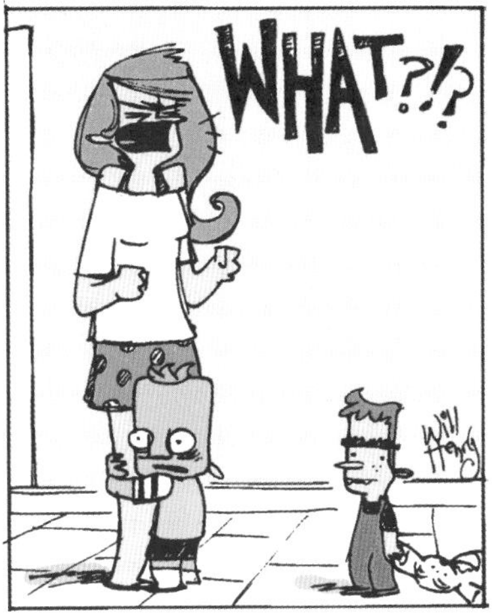
WHAT?!?
Will Henry

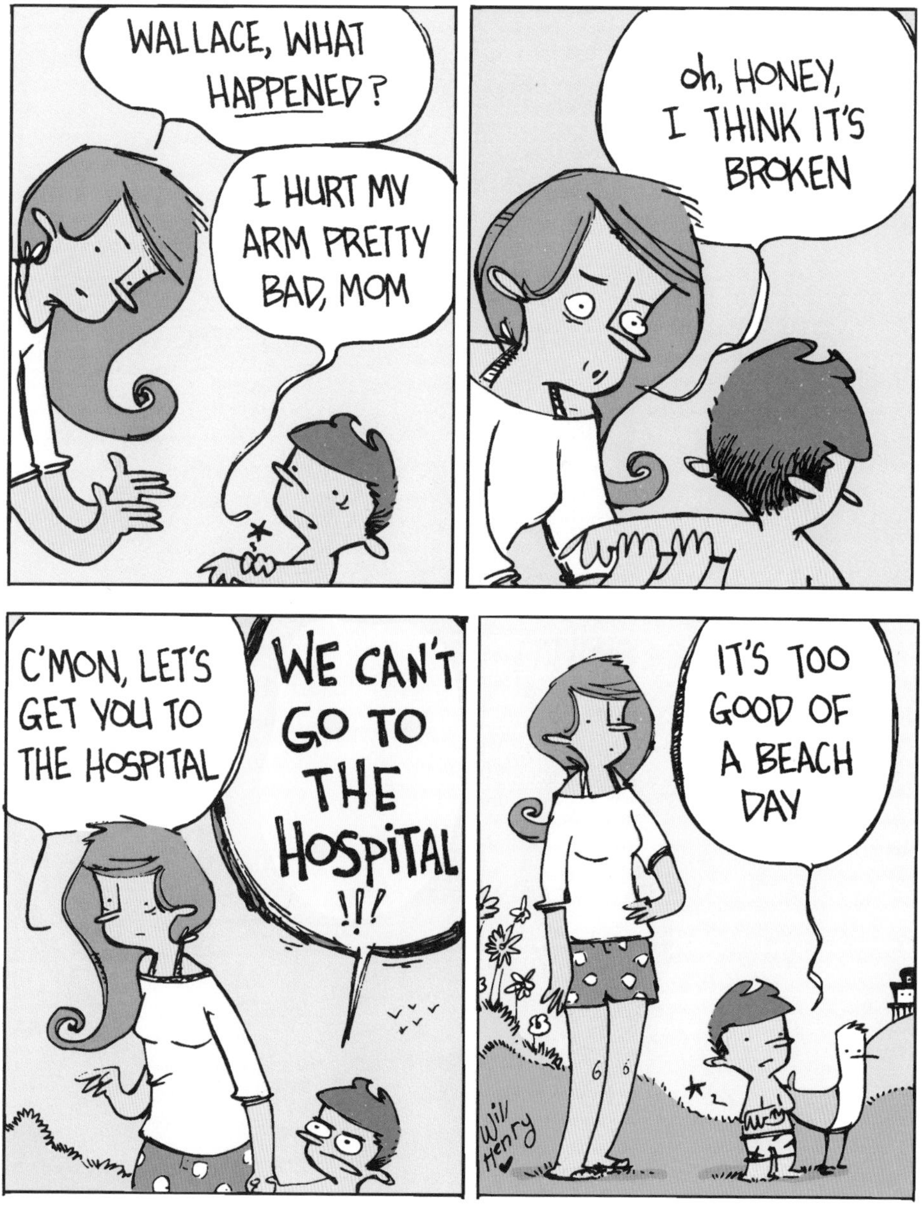
WALLACE, WHAT HAPPENED?
I HURT MY ARM PRETTY BAD, MOM
oh, HONEY, I THINK IT'S BROKEN
C'MON, LET'S GET YOU TO THE HOSPITAL
WE CAN'T GO TO THE HOSPITAL !!!
IT'S TOO GOOD OF A BEACH DAY
Will Henry

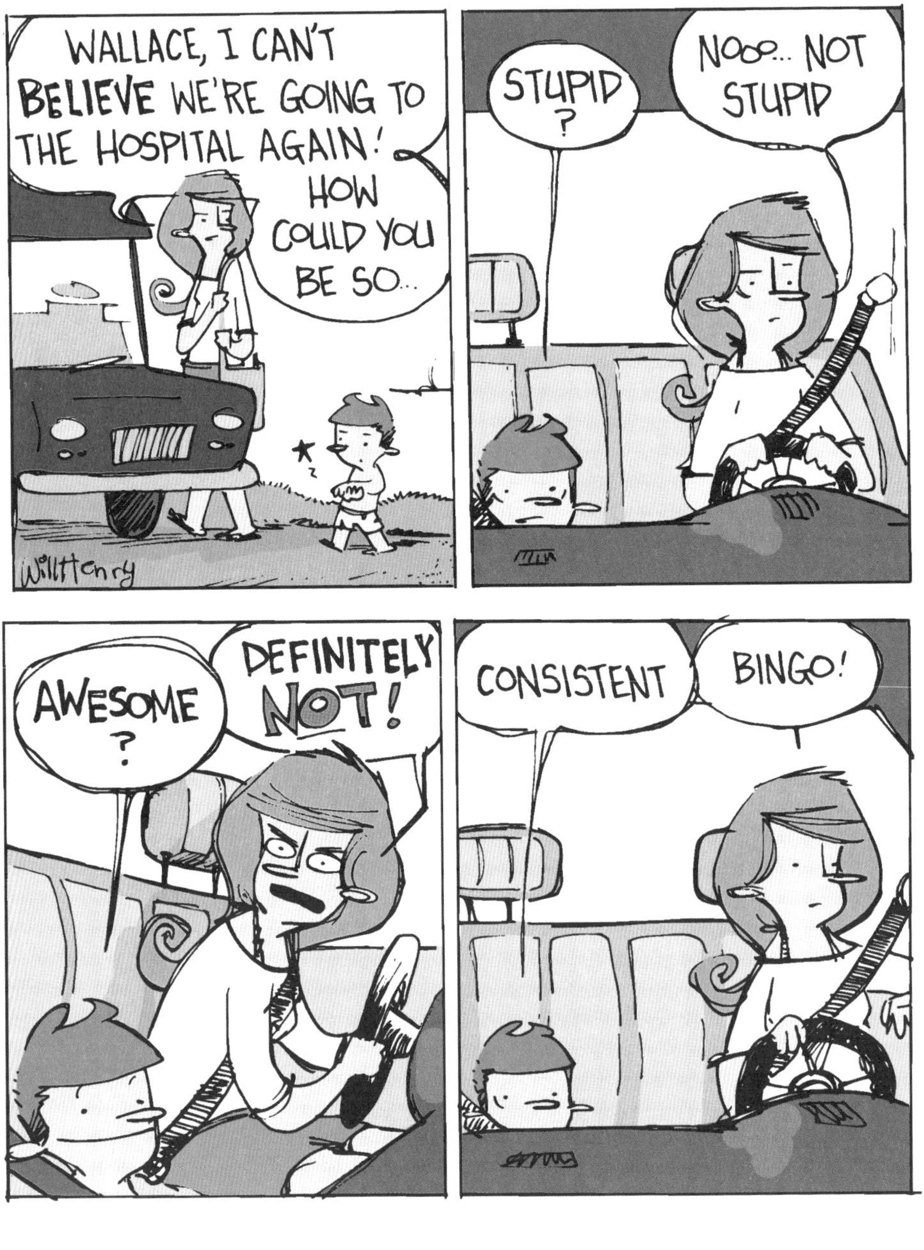
WALLACE, I CAN'T BELIEVE WE'RE GOING TO THE HOSPITAL AGAIN!
HOW COULD YOU BE SO...
STUPID ?
NOOO... NOT STUPID
AWESOME ?
DEFINITELY NOT!
CONSISTENT
BINGO!

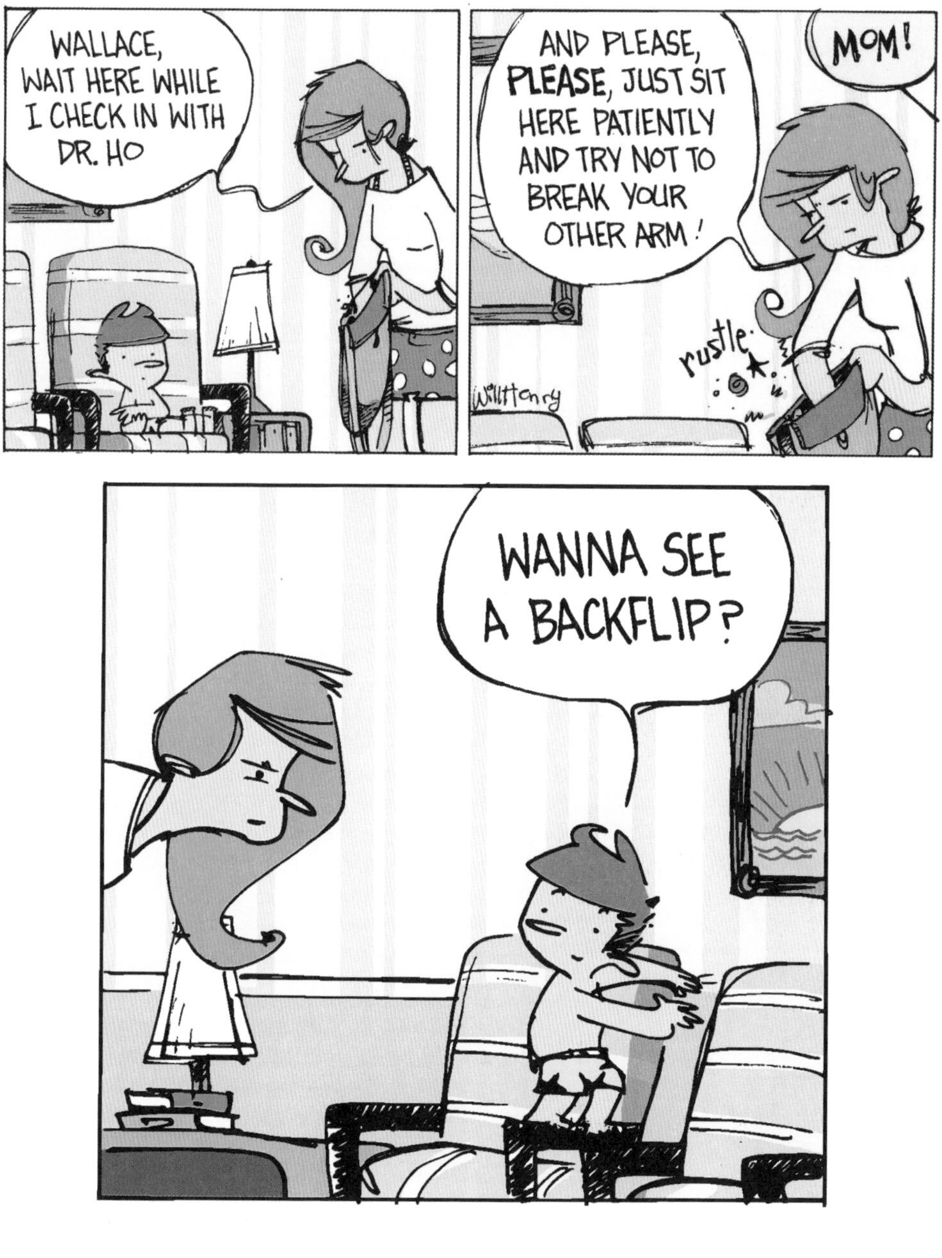
WALLACE, WAIT HERE WHILE I CHECK IN WITH DR. HO
AND PLEASE, PLEASE, JUST SIT HERE PATIENTLY AND TRY NOT TO BREAK YOUR OTHER ARM!
MOM!
rustle
WillHenry
WANNA SEE A BACKFLIP?

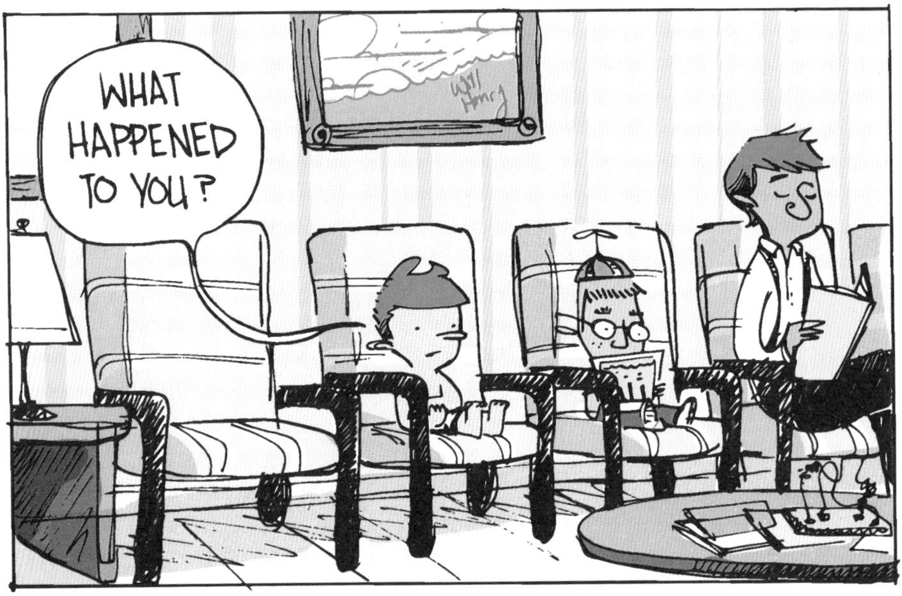
WHAT HAPPENED TO YOU?
Will Henry

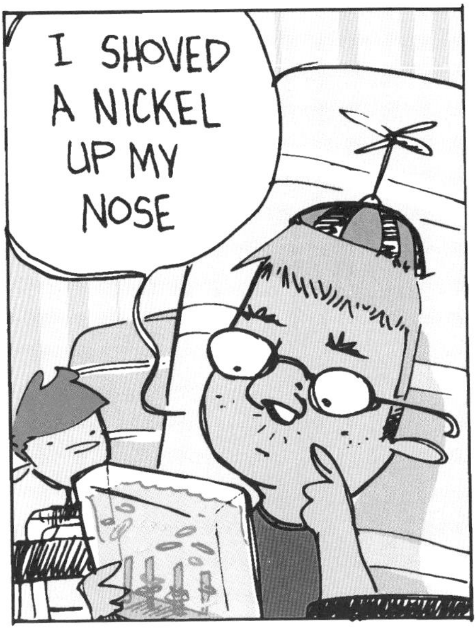
I SHOVED A NICKEL UP MY NOSE

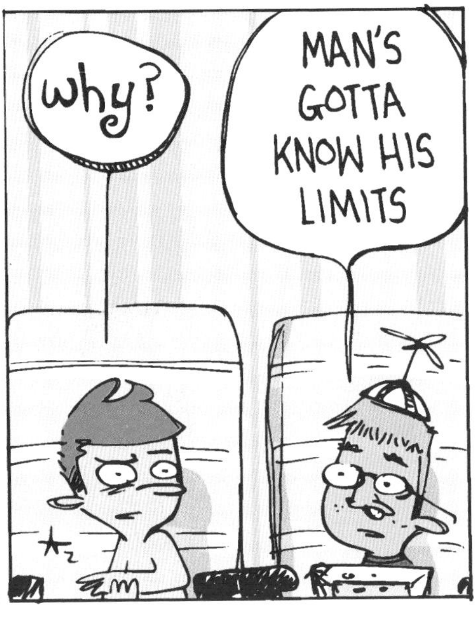
why?
MAN'S GOTTA KNOW HIS LIMITS

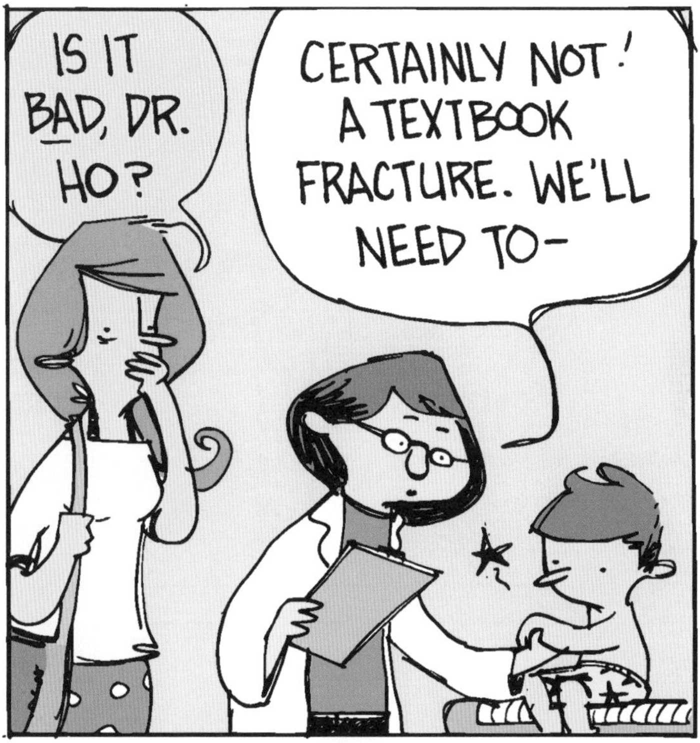
IS IT BAD, DR. HO?
CERTAINLY NOT! A TEXTBOOK FRACTURE. WE'LL NEED TO-

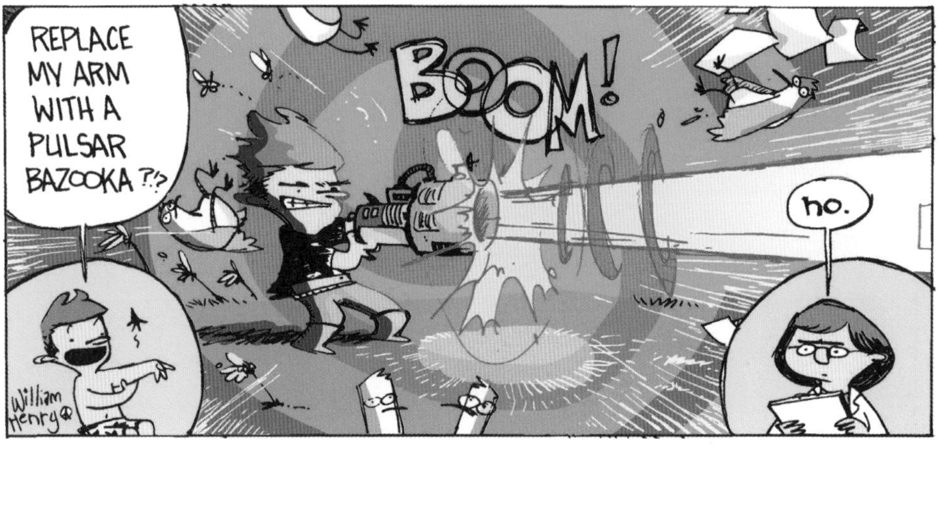
REPLACE MY ARM WITH A PULSAR BAZOOKA ?!?
BOOM!
no.
William Henry

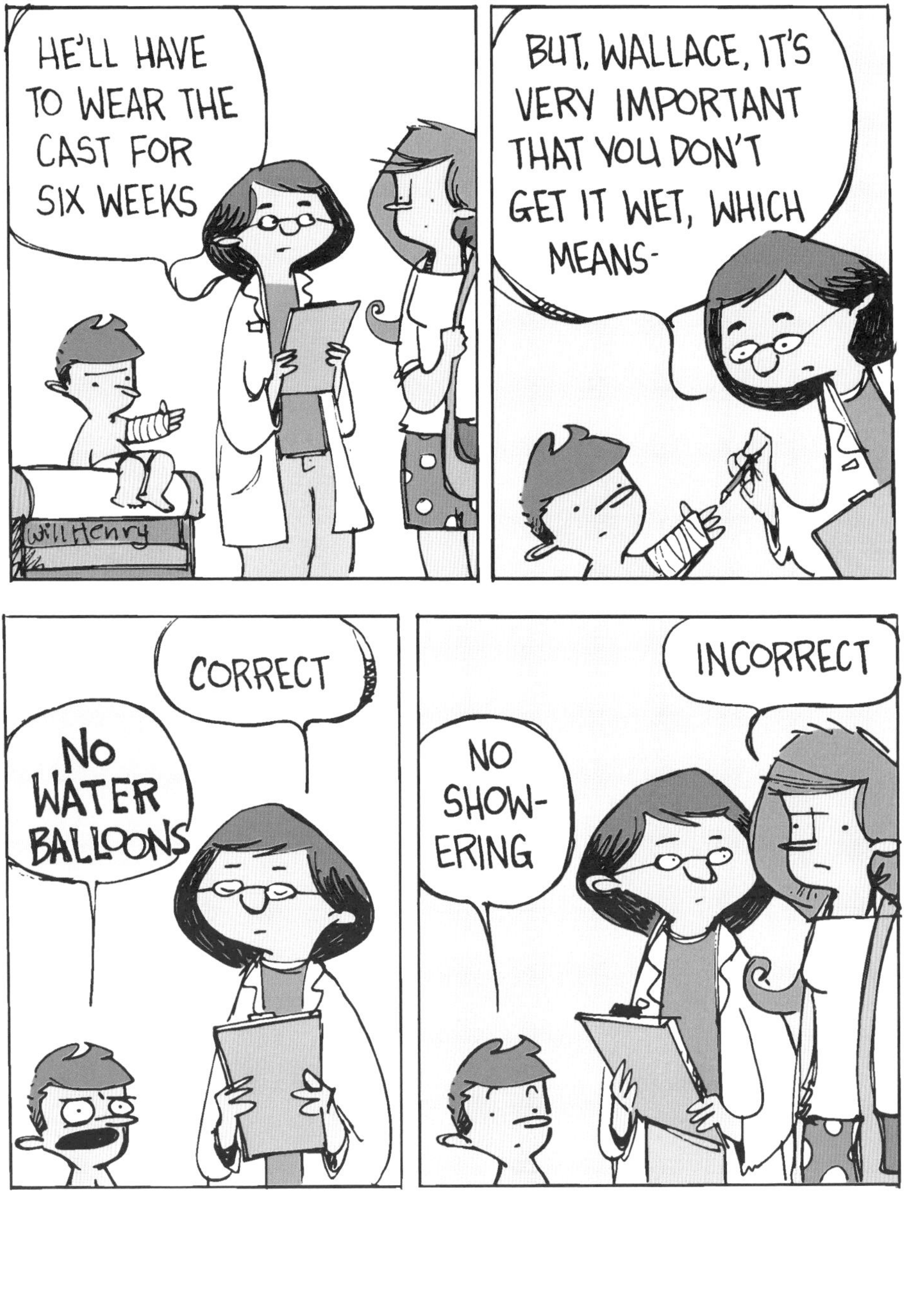
HE'LL HAVE TO WEAR THE CAST FOR SIX WEEKS
Will Henry
BUT, WALLACE, IT'S VERY IMPORTANT THAT YOU DON'T GET IT WET, WHICH MEANS-
NO WATER BALLOONS
CORRECT
NO SHOW-ERING
INCORRECT

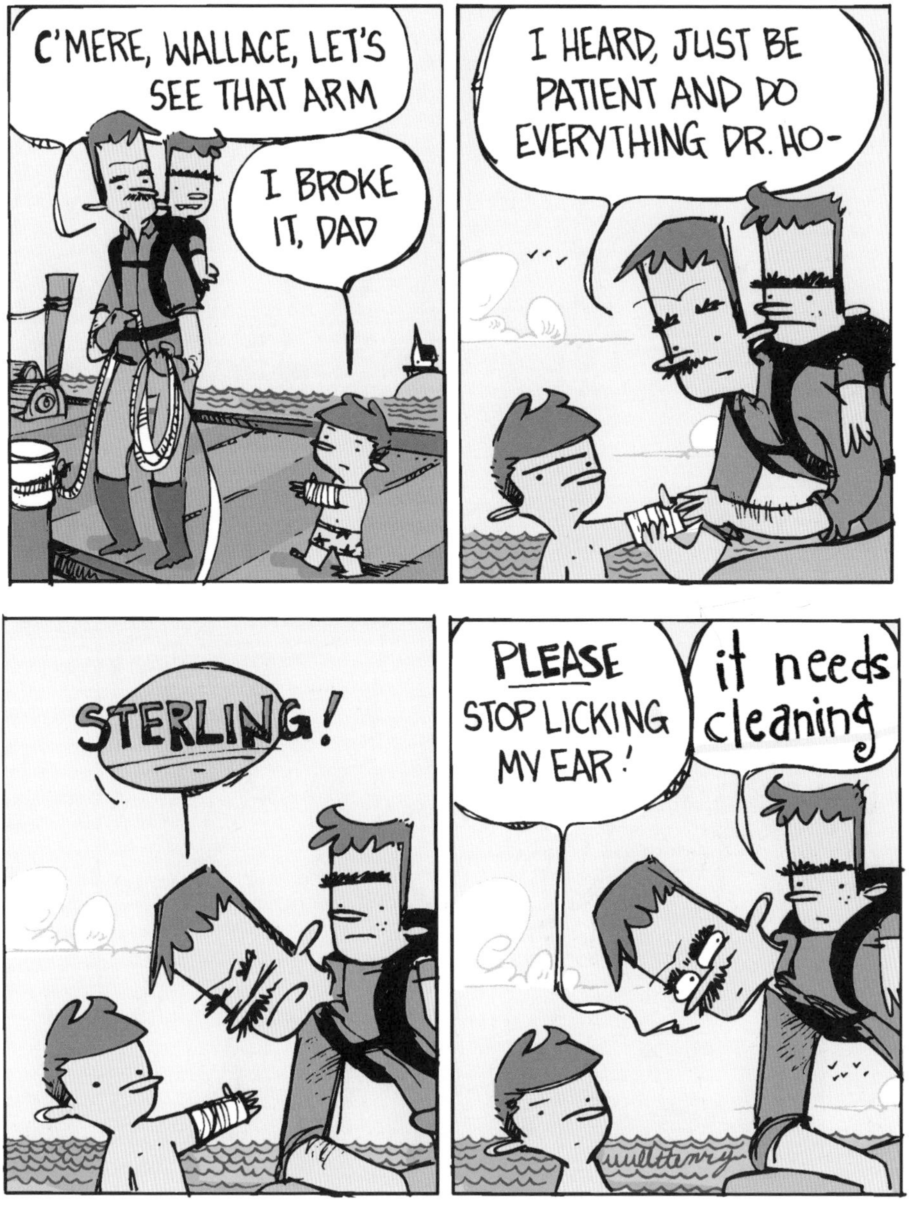
C'MERE, WALLACE, LET'S SEE THAT ARM
I BROKE IT, DAD
I HEARD, JUST BE PATIENT AND DO EVERYTHING DR. HO-
STERLING!
PLEASE STOP LICKING MY EAR!
it needs cleaning

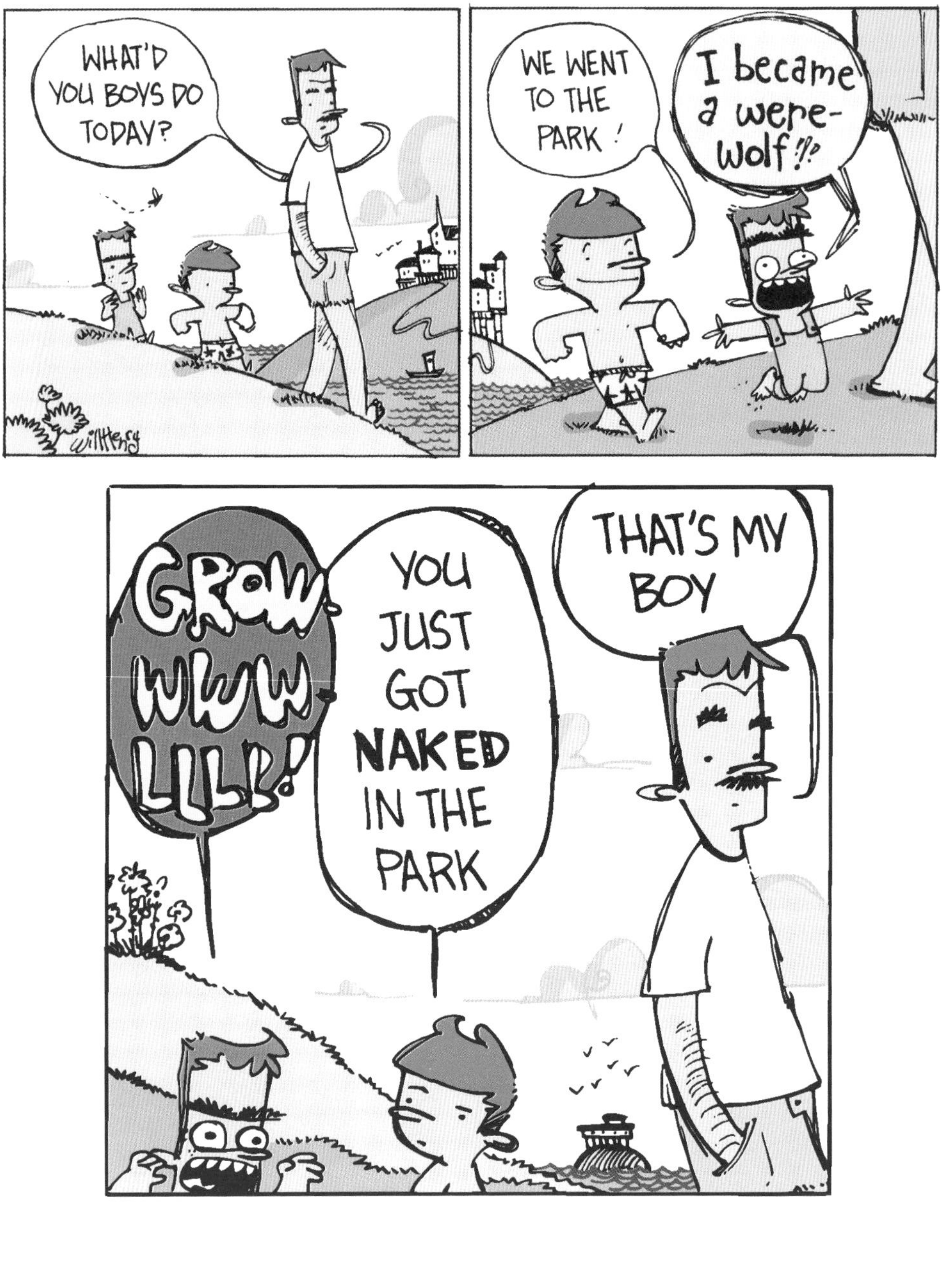
WHAT'D YOU BOYS DO TODAY?
WE WENT TO THE PARK!
I became a were-wolf!?!
GROWWWLLL!
YOU JUST GOT NAKED IN THE PARK
THAT'S MY BOY

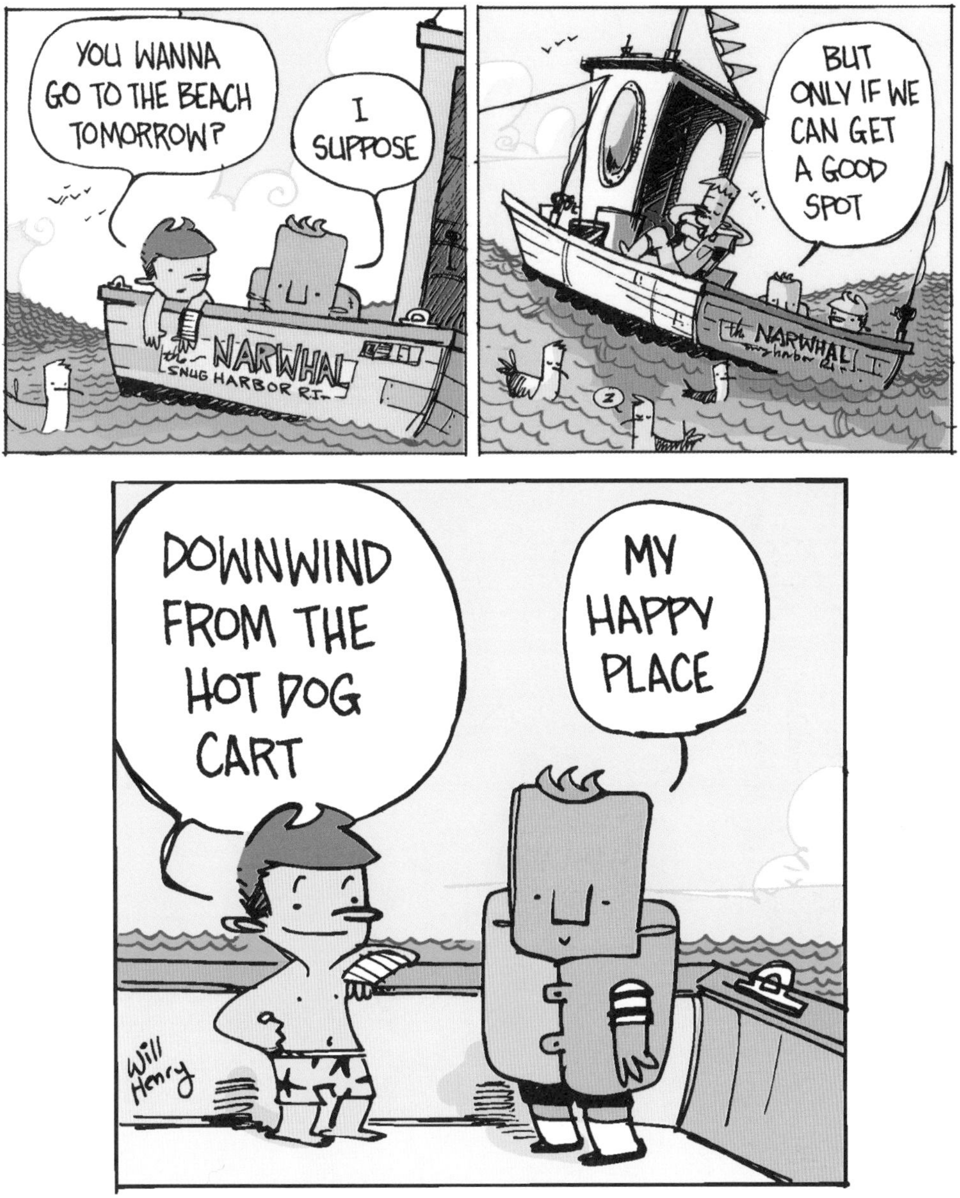
YOU WANNA GO TO THE BEACH TOMORROW?
I SUPPOSE
the NARWHAL
SNUG HARBOR R.I.
BUT ONLY IF WE CAN GET A GOOD SPOT
the NARWHAL
DOWNWIND FROM THE HOT DOG CART
MY HAPPY PLACE
Will Henry

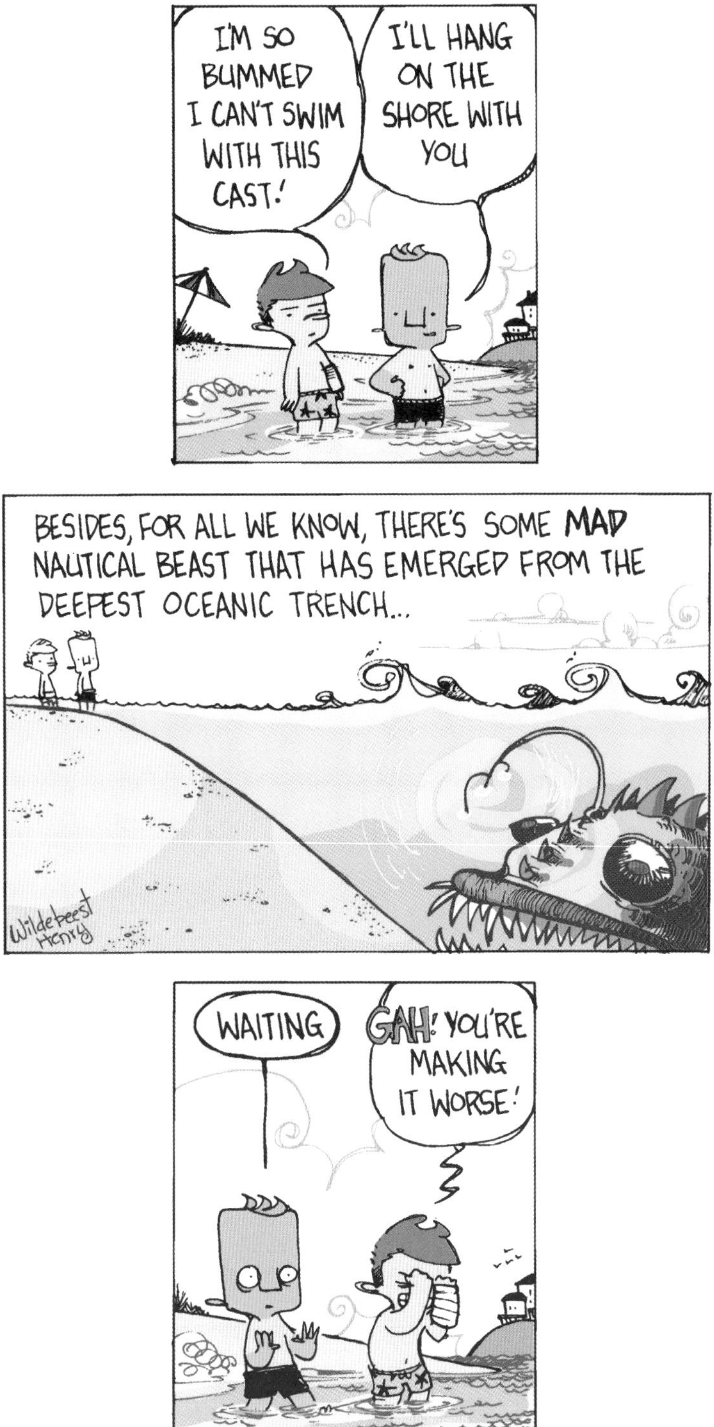
I'M SO BUMMED I CAN'T SWIM WITH THIS CAST!
I'LL HANG ON THE SHORE WITH YOU
BESIDES, FOR ALL WE KNOW, THERE'S SOME MAD NAUTICAL BEAST THAT HAS EMERGED FROM THE DEEPEST OCEANIC TRENCH...
Wildebeest Henry
WAITING
GAH! YOU'RE MAKING IT WORSE!

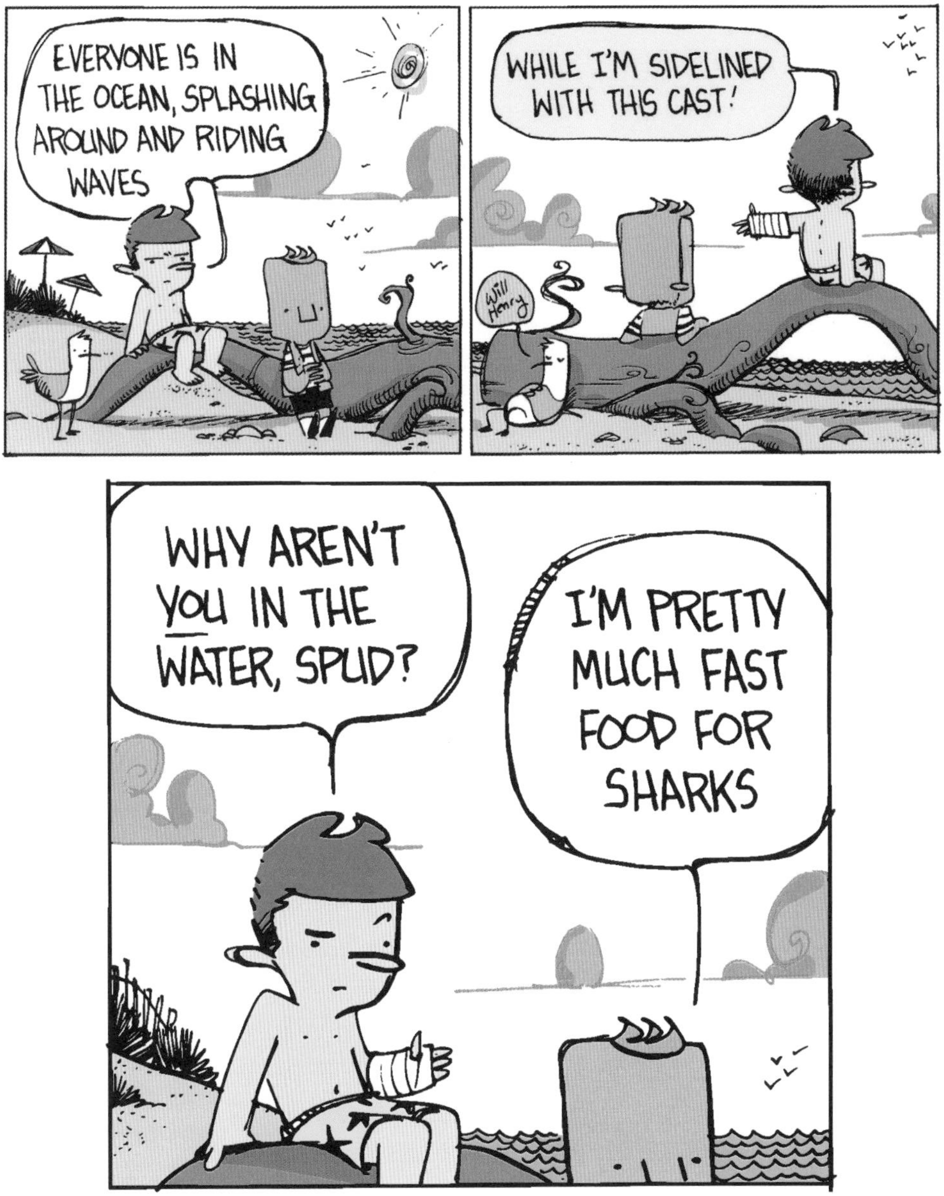
EVERYONE IS IN THE OCEAN, SPLASHING AROUND AND RIDING WAVES
WHILE I'M SIDELINED WITH THIS CAST!
Will Henry
WHY AREN'T YOU IN THE WATER, SPUD?
I'M PRETTY MUCH FAST FOOD FOR SHARKS

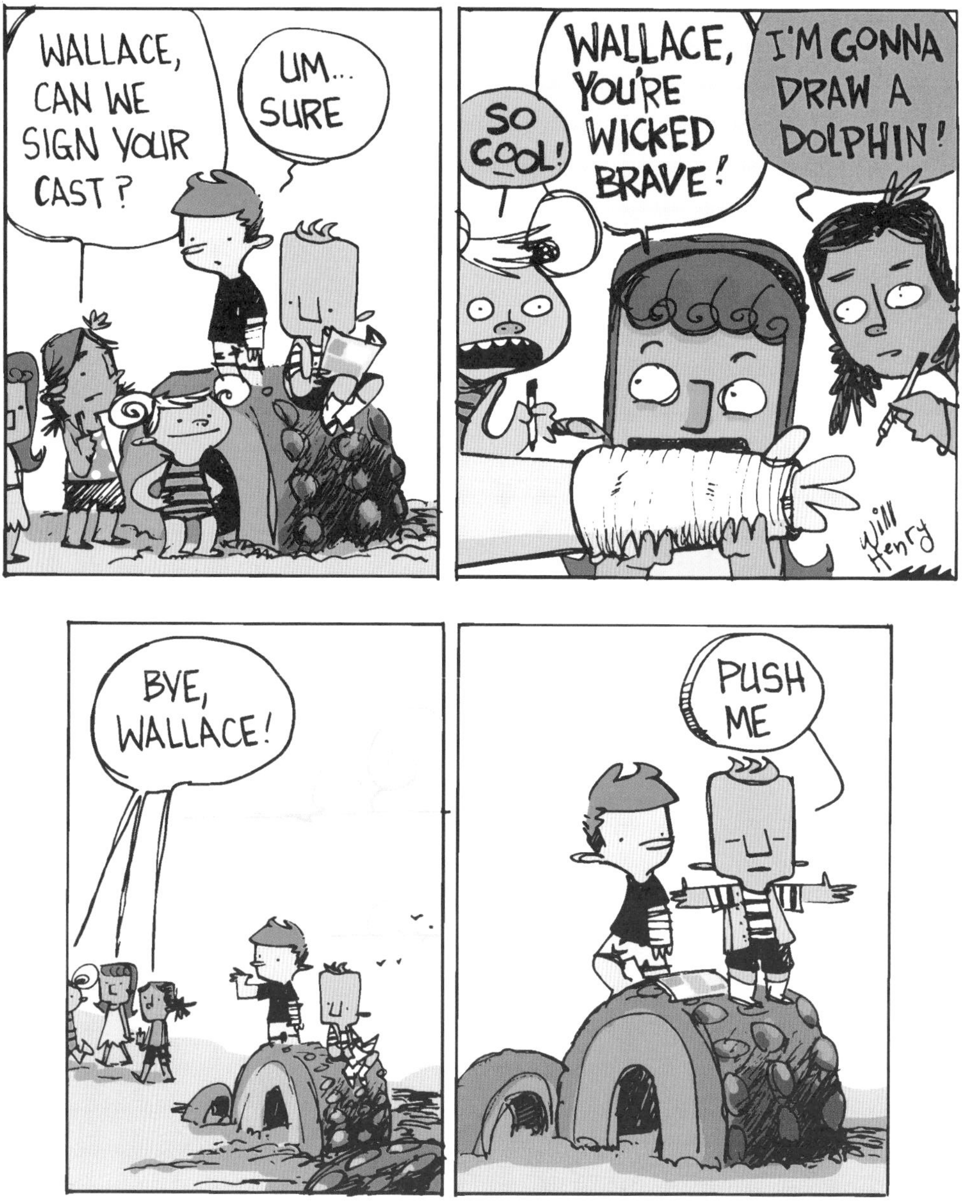
WALLACE, CAN WE SIGN YOUR CAST?
UM... SURE
SO COOL!
WALLACE, YOU'RE WICKED BRAVE!
I'M GONNA DRAW A DOLPHIN!
Will Henry
BYE, WALLACE!
PUSH ME

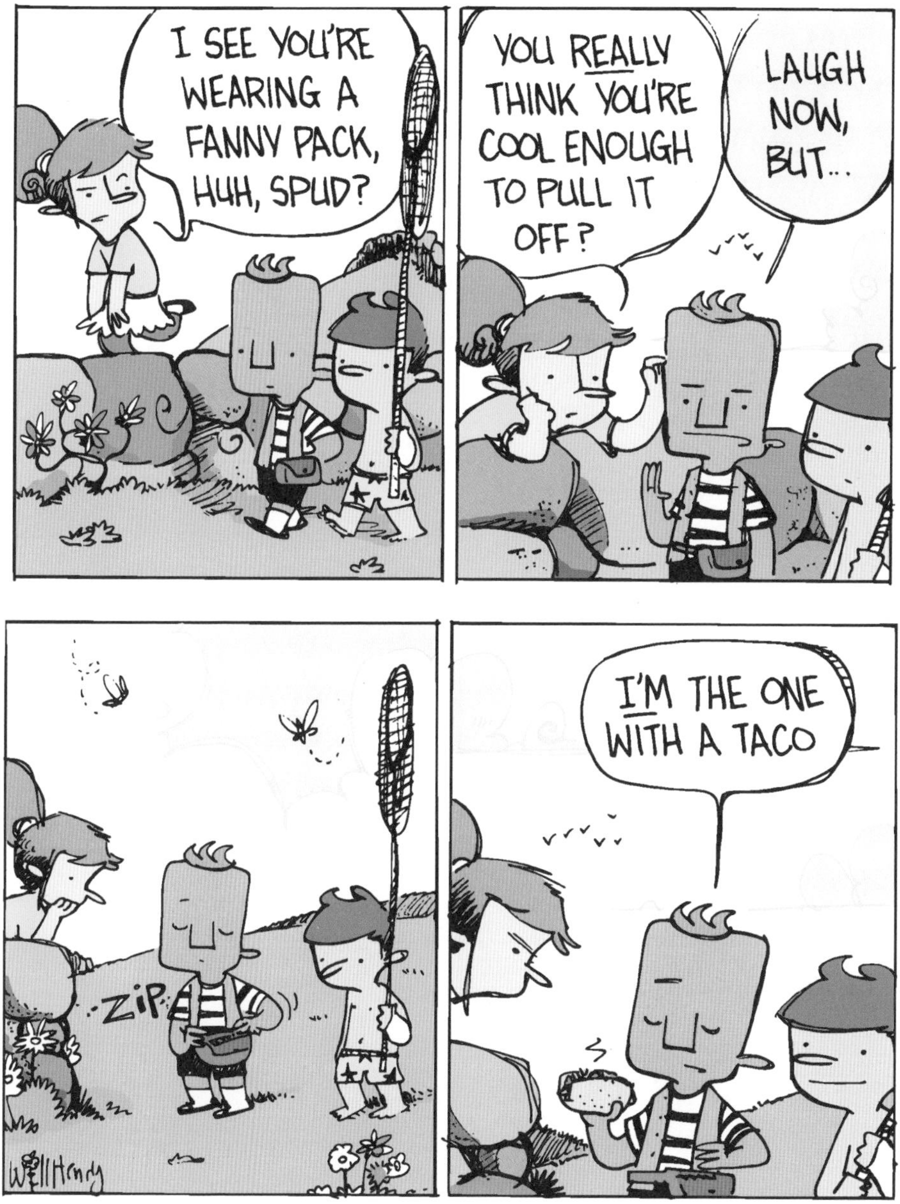
I SEE YOU'RE WEARING A FANNY PACK, HUH, SPUD?
YOU REALLY THINK YOU'RE COOL ENOUGH TO PULL IT OFF?
LAUGH NOW, BUT...
ZIP
I'M THE ONE WITH A TACO
WillHenry

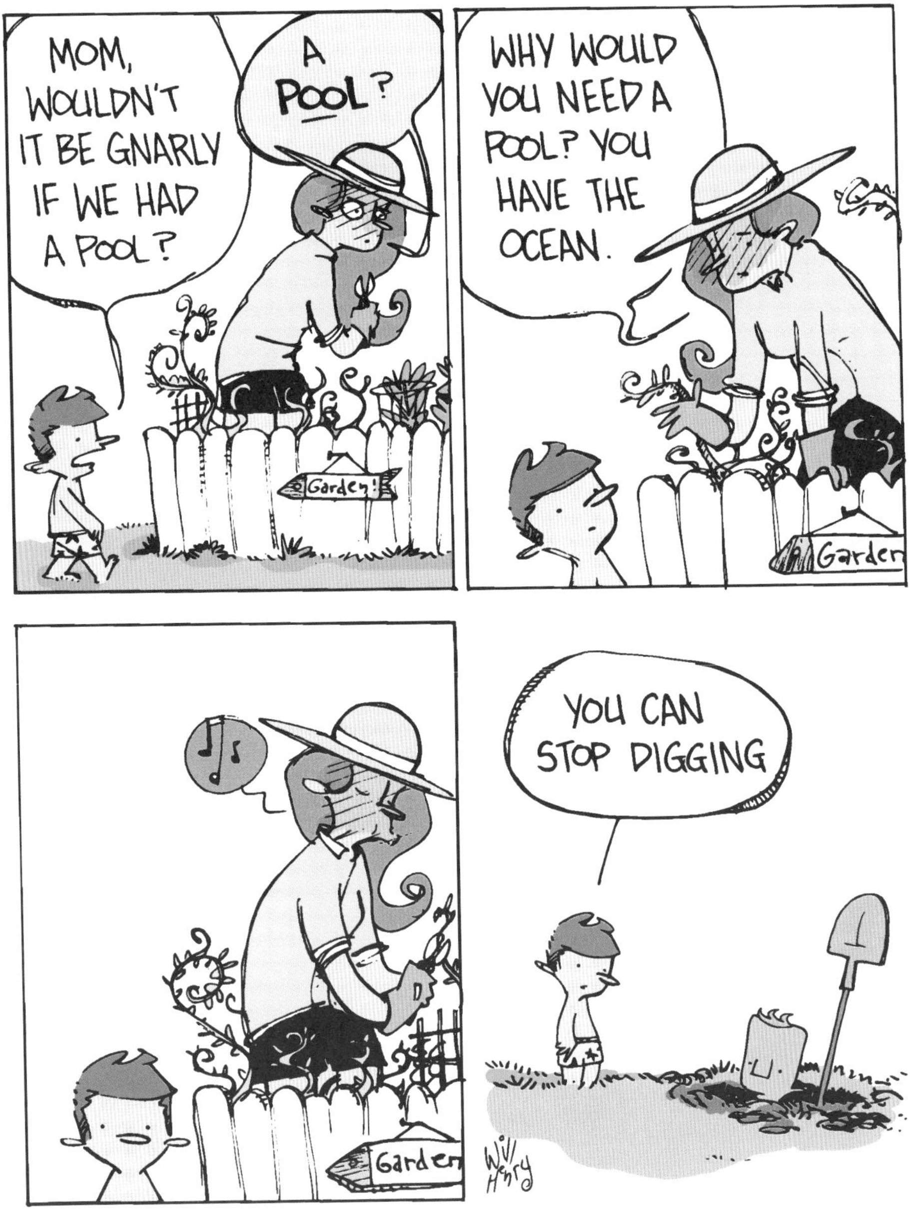
MOM, WOULDN'T IT BE GNARLY IF WE HAD A POOL?
A POOL?
Garden!
WHY WOULD YOU NEED A POOL? YOU HAVE THE OCEAN.
Garden
Garden
YOU CAN STOP DIGGING
Will Henry

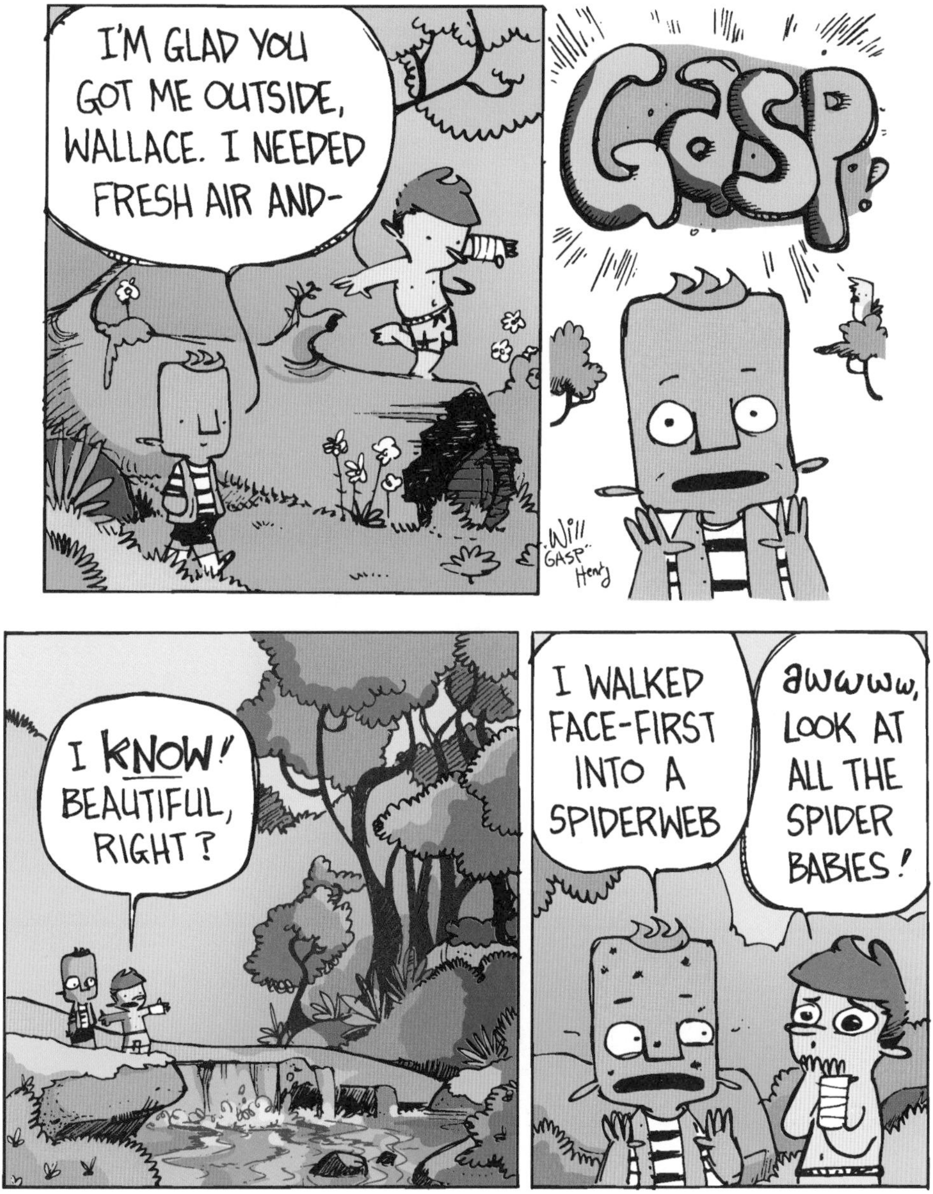
I'M GLAD YOU GOT ME OUTSIDE, WALLACE. I NEEDED FRESH AIR AND-
GASP!
WILL "GASP" HENRY
I KNOW! BEAUTIFUL, RIGHT?
I WALKED FACE-FIRST INTO A SPIDERWEB
awwww, LOOK AT ALL THE SPIDER BABIES!

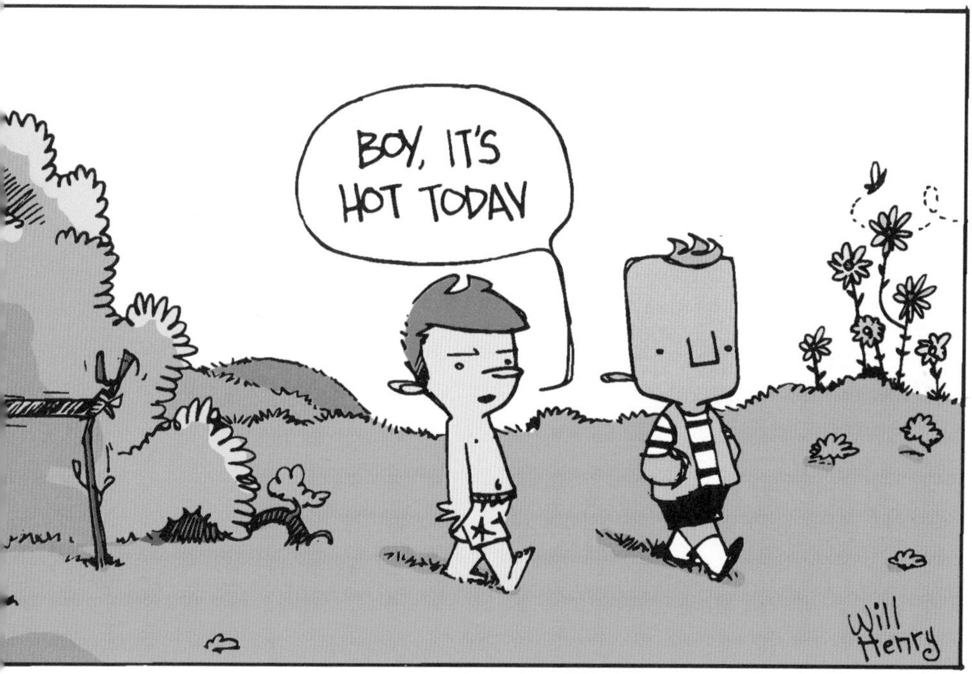
BOY, IT'S HOT TODAY
Will Henry

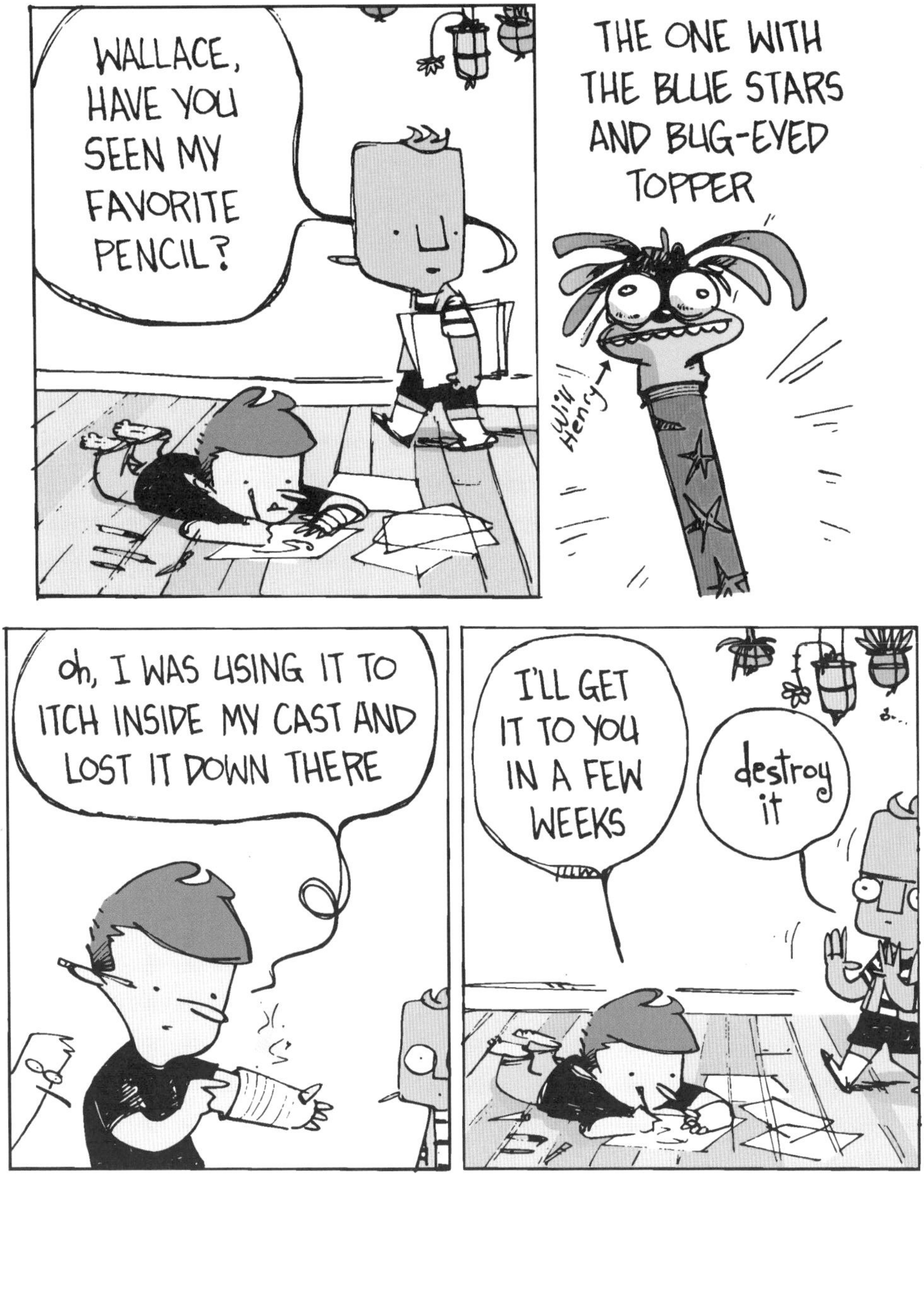
WALLACE, HAVE YOU SEEN MY FAVORITE PENCIL?
THE ONE WITH THE BLUE STARS AND BUG-EYED TOPPER
Will Henry
oh, I WAS USING IT TO ITCH INSIDE MY CAST AND LOST IT DOWN THERE
I'LL GET IT TO YOU IN A FEW WEEKS
destroy it

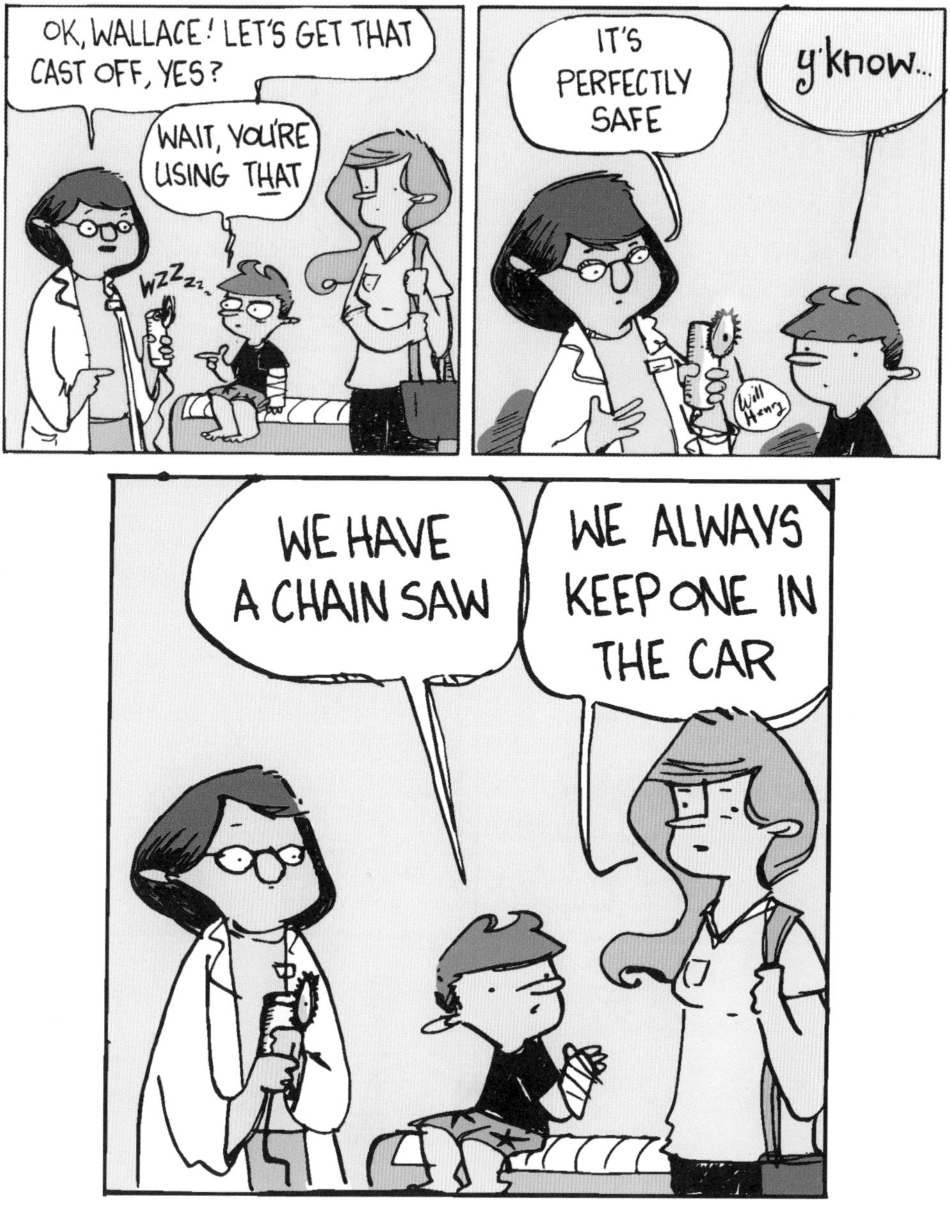
OK, WALLACE! LET'S GET THAT CAST OFF, YES?
WAIT, YOU'RE USING THAT
WZZzz...
IT'S PERFECTLY SAFE
y'know...
Will Henry
WE HAVE A CHAIN SAW
WE ALWAYS KEEP ONE IN THE CAR

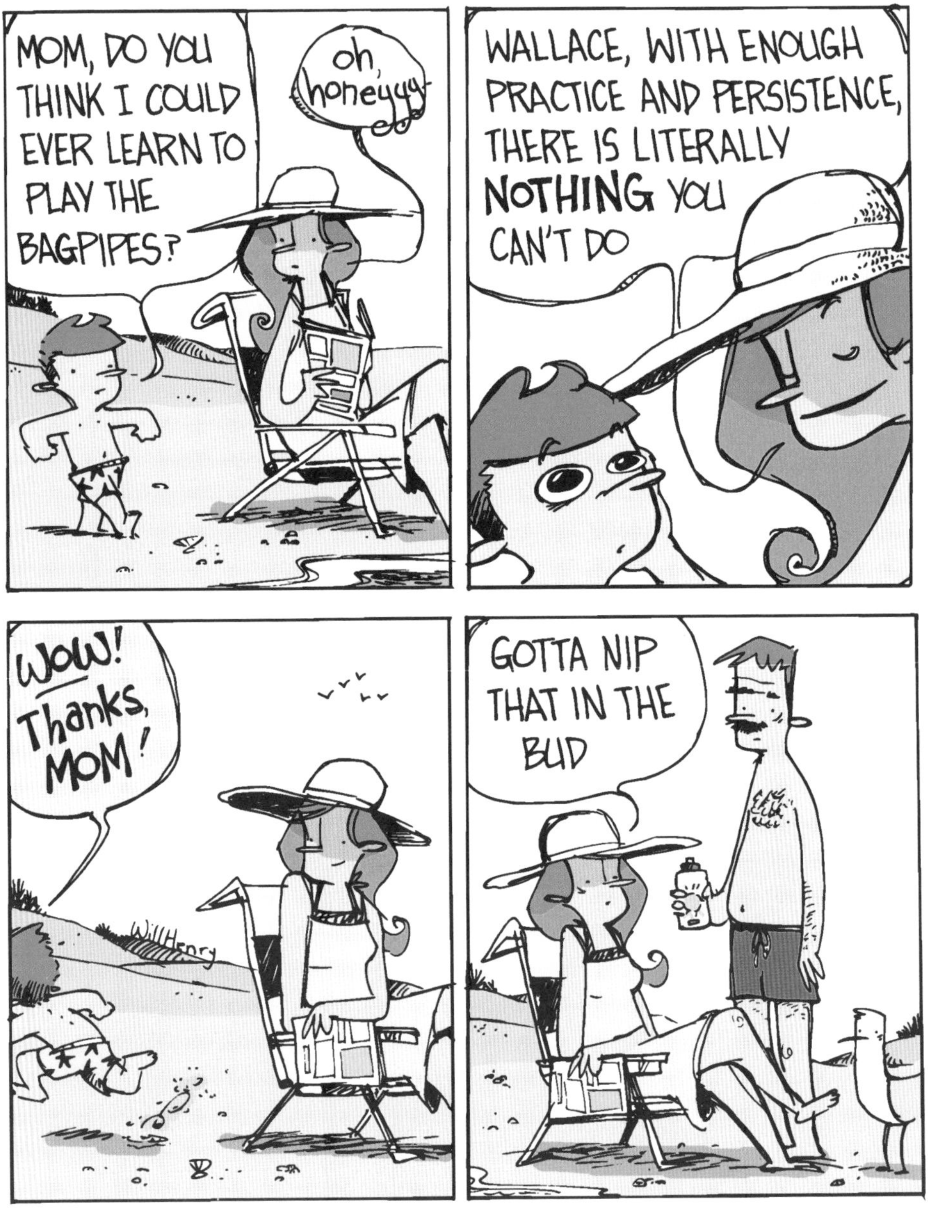
MOM, DO YOU THINK I COULD EVER LEARN TO PLAY THE BAGPIPES?
oh, honeyyy
WALLACE, WITH ENOUGH PRACTICE AND PERSISTENCE, THERE IS LITERALLY NOTHING YOU CAN'T DO
WOW! Thanks, MOM!
Will Henry
GOTTA NIP THAT IN THE BUD

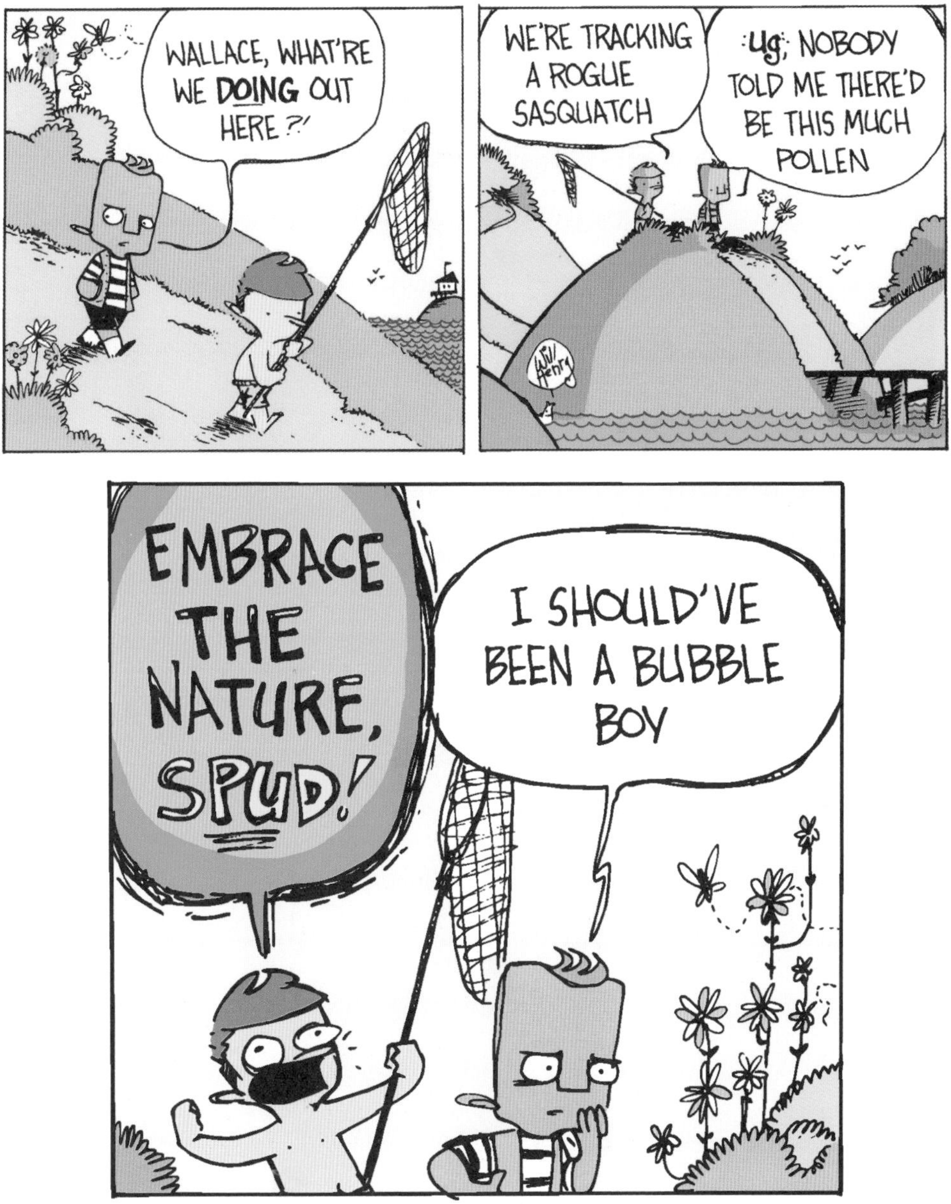
WALLACE, WHAT'RE WE DOING OUT HERE?!
WE'RE TRACKING A ROGUE SASQUATCH
:ug: NOBODY TOLD ME THERE'D BE THIS MUCH POLLEN
EMBRACE THE NATURE, SPUD!
I SHOULD'VE BEEN A BUBBLE BOY

WALLACE, WHERE ARE YOU TAKING US?
APRIL LUCAS SAYS THERE'S A SECRET HIDEOUT DEEP IN THIS RHODODENDRON PATCH
SHE SAYS THE SIXTH GRADERS COME HERE TO DRINK MOUNTAIN DEW AND MAKE PRANK CALLS
MAYBE THEY'LL ORDER ME A PIZZA
MAYBE A KNUCKLE SANDWICH

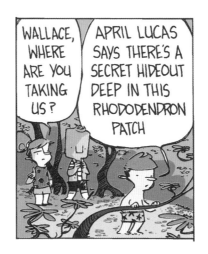

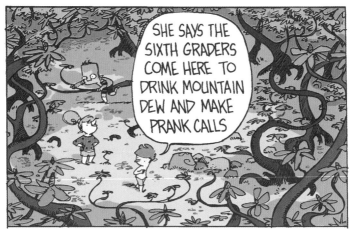

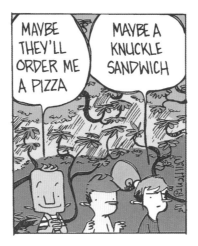

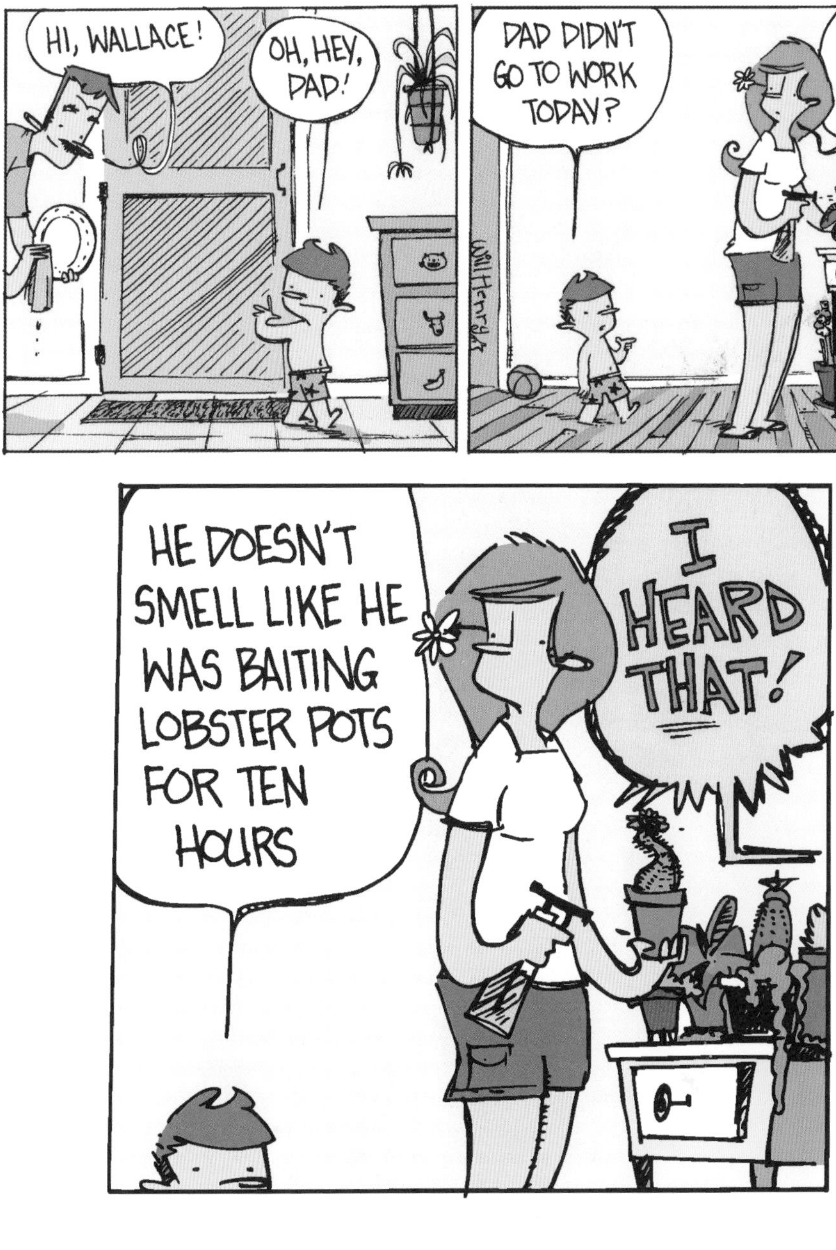
HI, WALLACE!
OH, HEY, DAD!
Will Henry
DAD DIDN'T GO TO WORK TODAY?
HOW'D YOU KNOW?
HE DOESN'T SMELL LIKE HE WAS BAITING LOBSTER POTS FOR TEN HOURS
I HEARD THAT!

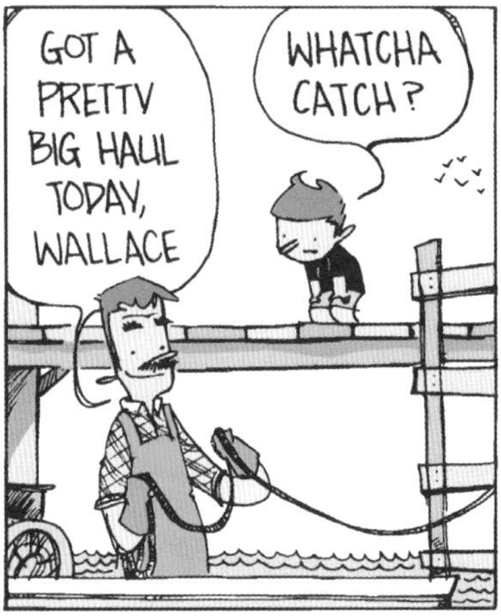
GOT A PRETTY BIG HAUL TODAY, WALLACE
WHATCHA CATCH?

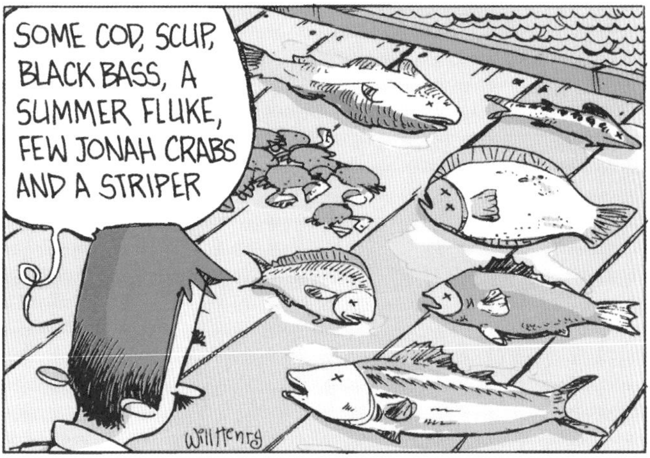
SOME COD, SCUP, BLACK BASS, A SUMMER FLUKE, FEW JONAH CRABS AND A STRIPER
WillHenry

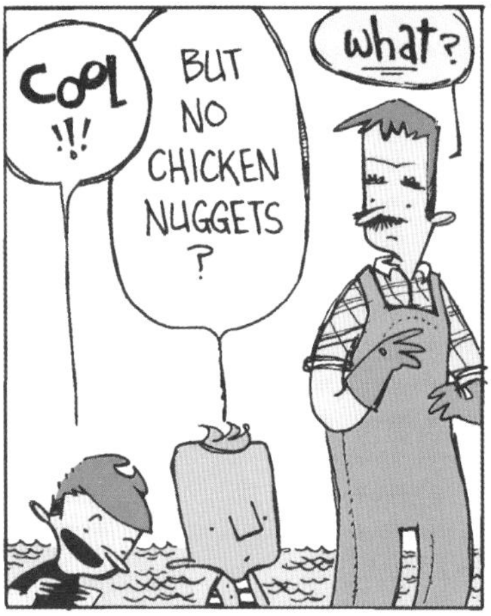
COOL !!!
BUT NO CHICKEN NUGGETS ?
what?

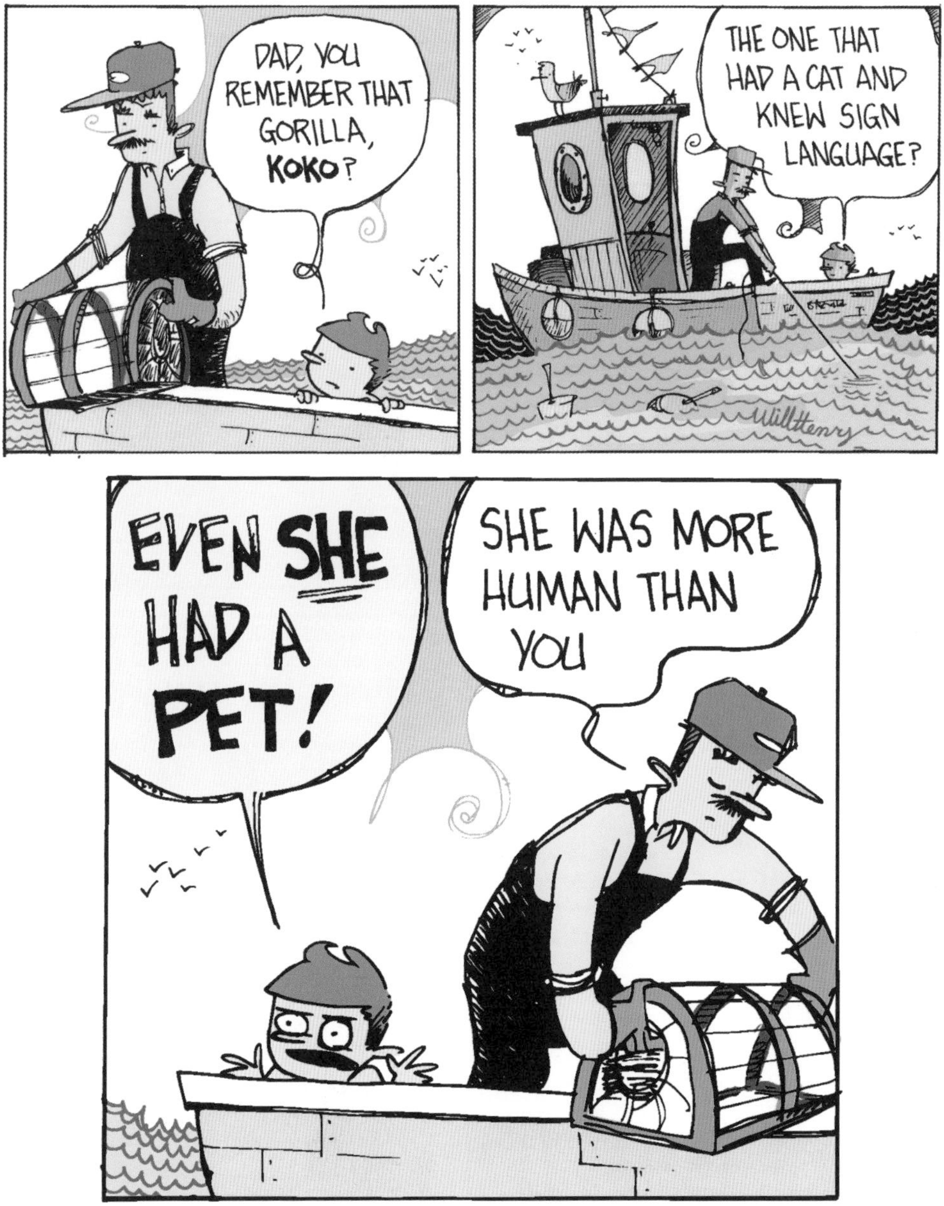
DAD, YOU REMEMBER THAT GORILLA, KOKO?
THE ONE THAT HAD A CAT AND KNEW SIGN LANGUAGE?
WillHenry
EVEN SHE HAD A PET!
SHE WAS MORE HUMAN THAN YOU

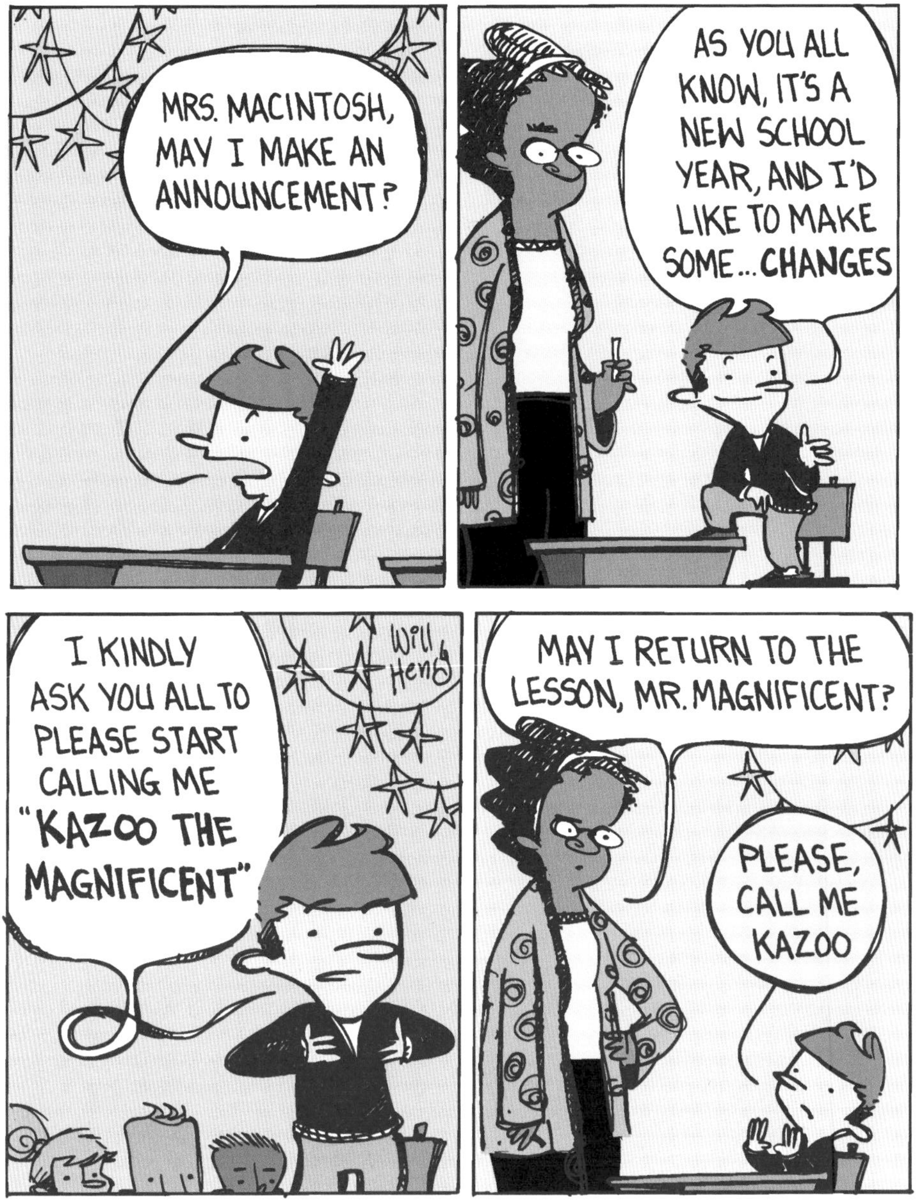
MRS. MACINTOSH, MAY I MAKE AN ANNOUNCEMENT?
AS YOU ALL KNOW, IT'S A NEW SCHOOL YEAR, AND I'D LIKE TO MAKE SOME... **CHANGES**
I KINDLY ASK YOU ALL TO PLEASE START CALLING ME "**KAZOO THE MAGNIFICENT**"
Will Henry
MAY I RETURN TO THE LESSON, MR. MAGNIFICENT?
PLEASE, CALL ME KAZOO

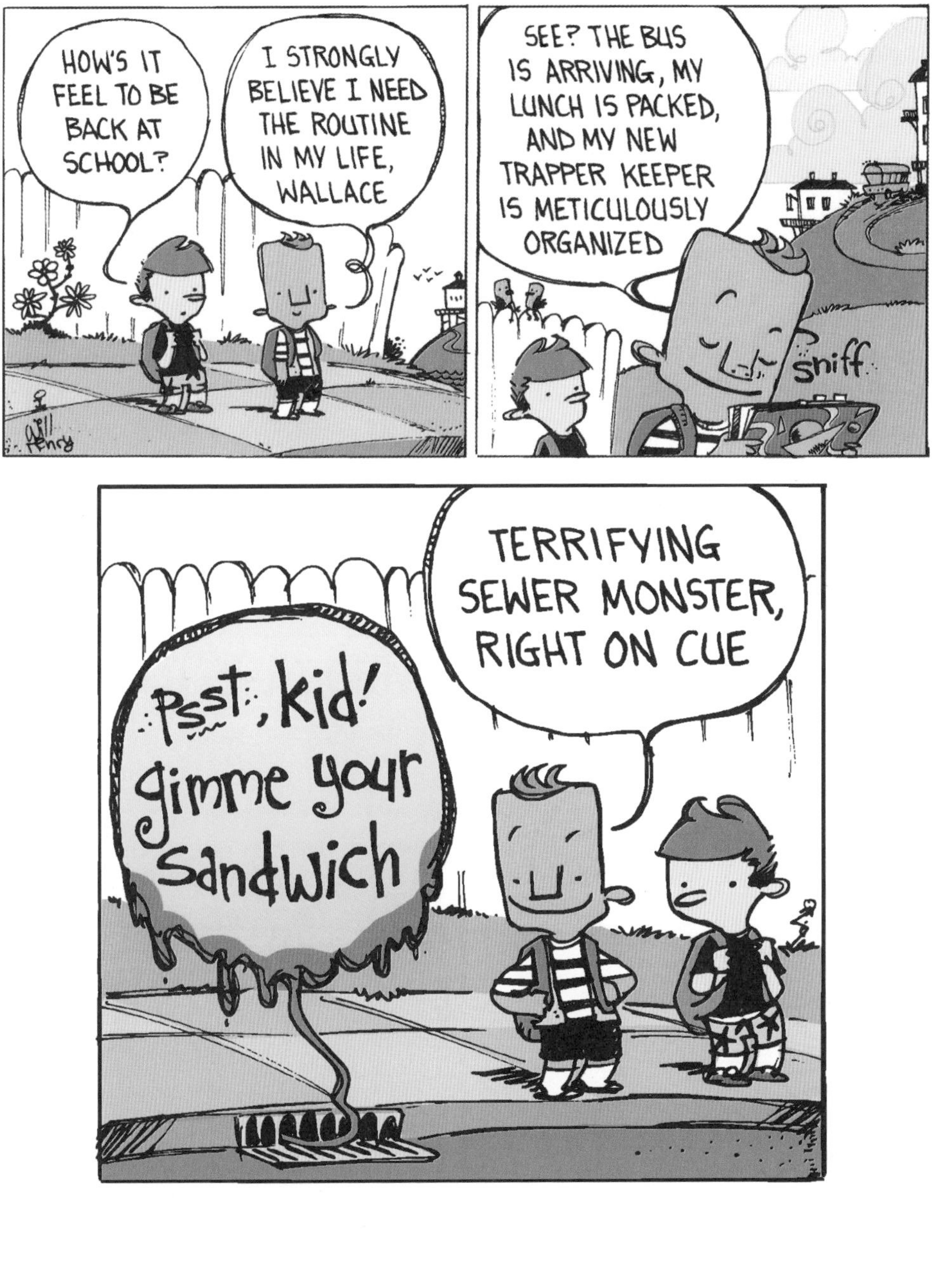
HOW'S IT FEEL TO BE BACK AT SCHOOL?
I STRONGLY BELIEVE I NEED THE ROUTINE IN MY LIFE, WALLACE
Will Henry
SEE? THE BUS IS ARRIVING, MY LUNCH IS PACKED, AND MY NEW TRAPPER KEEPER IS METICULOUSLY ORGANIZED
sniff
Psst, kid! gimme your sandwich
TERRIFYING SEWER MONSTER, RIGHT ON CUE

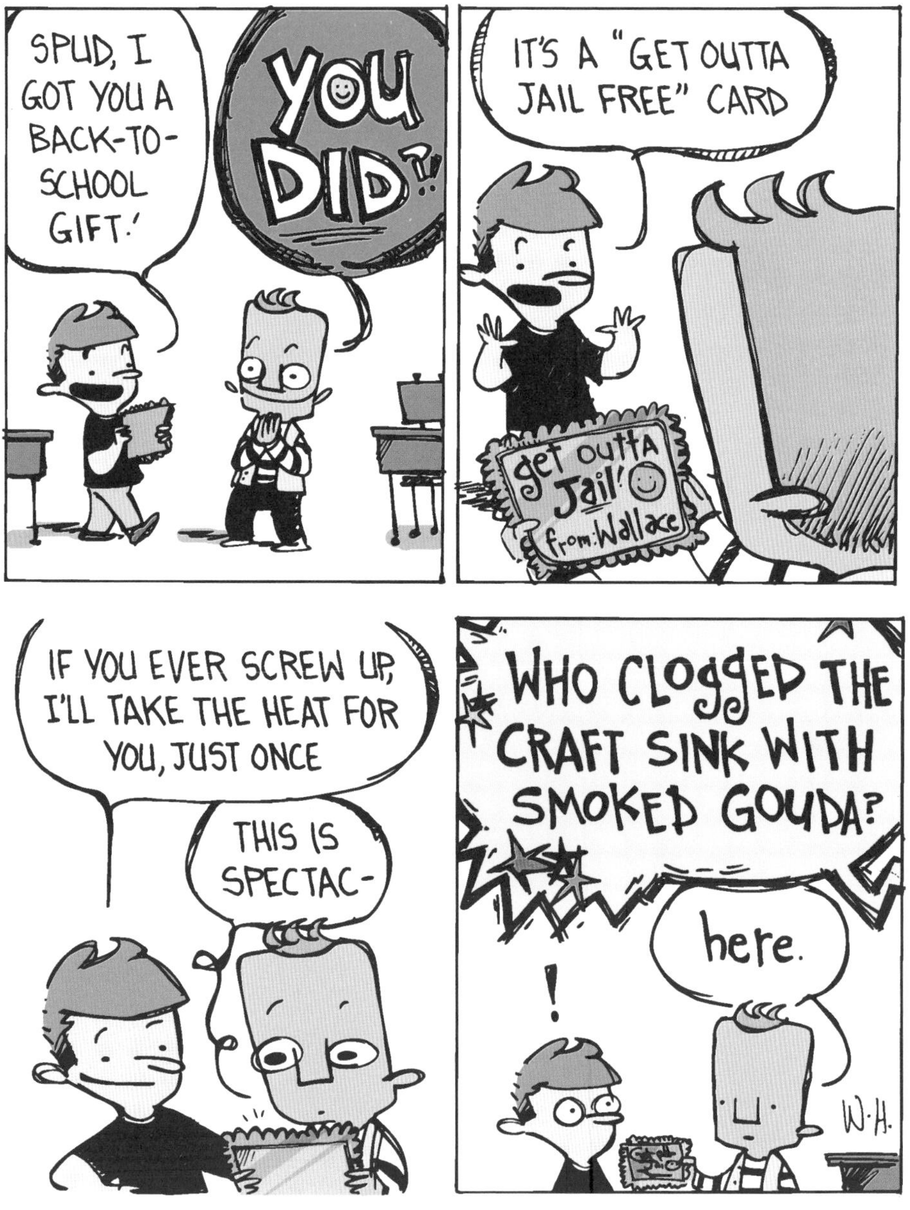
SPUD, I GOT YOU A BACK-TO-SCHOOL GIFT!
YOU DID?!!
IT'S A "GET OUTTA JAIL FREE" CARD
get outta Jail! from: Wallace
IF YOU EVER SCREW UP, I'LL TAKE THE HEAT FOR YOU, JUST ONCE
THIS IS SPECTAC-
WHO CLOGGED THE CRAFT SINK WITH SMOKED GOUDA?
here.
!
W.H.

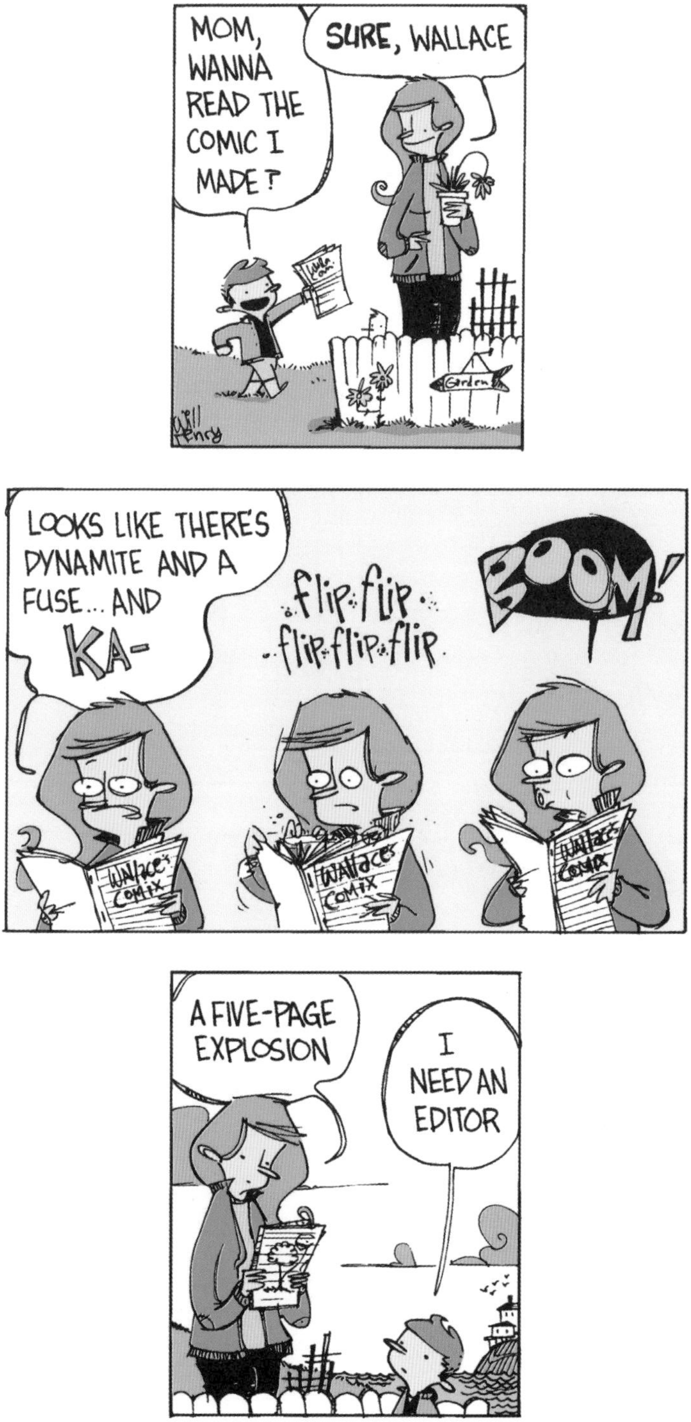
MOM, WANNA READ THE COMIC I MADE?
SURE, WALLACE
LOOKS LIKE THERE'S DYNAMITE AND A FUSE... AND KA-
flip flip flip flip flip
BOOM!
A FIVE-PAGE EXPLOSION
I NEED AN EDITOR

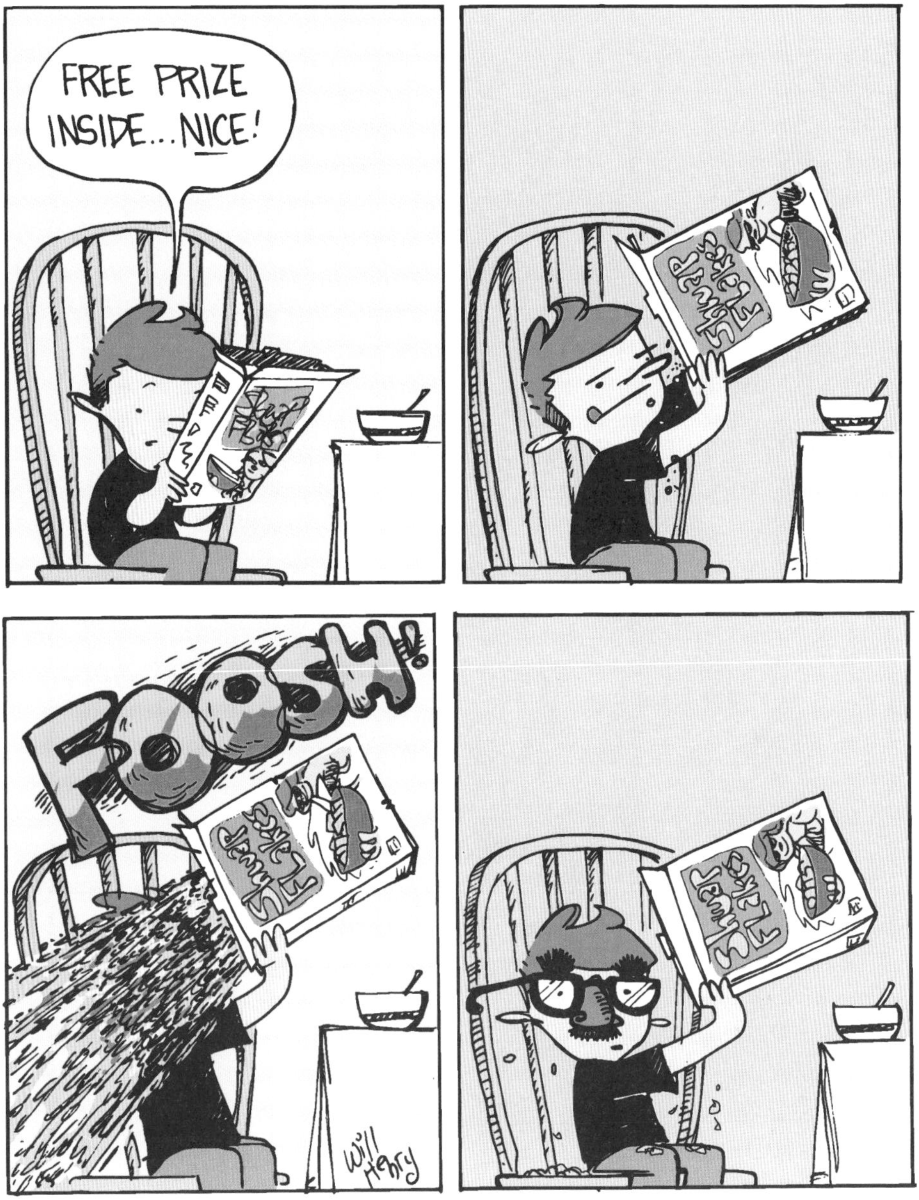
FREE PRIZE INSIDE...NICE!
FOOSH!
Will Henry

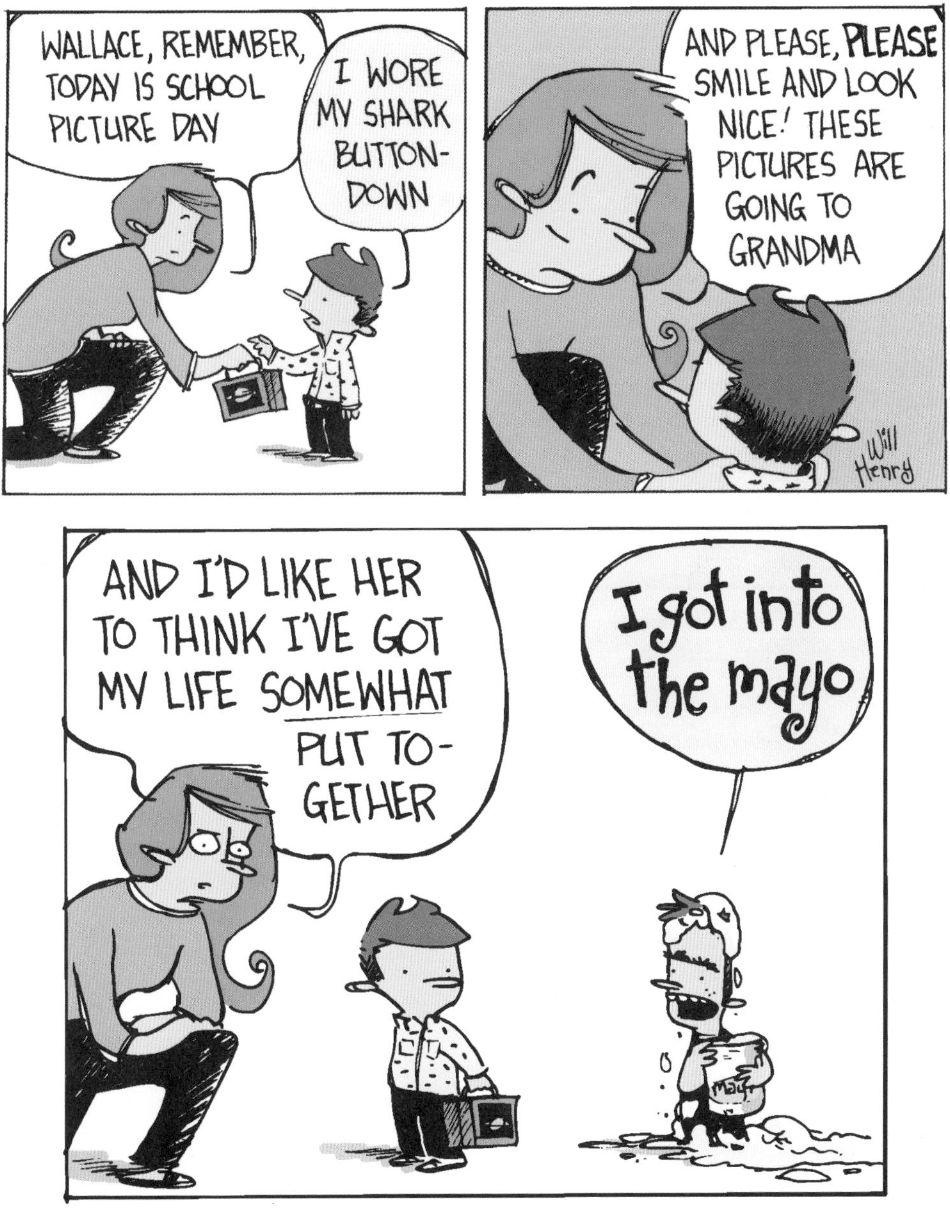
WALLACE, REMEMBER, TODAY IS SCHOOL PICTURE DAY
I WORE MY SHARK BUTTON-DOWN
AND PLEASE, **PLEASE** SMILE AND LOOK NICE! THESE PICTURES ARE GOING TO GRANDMA
Will Henry
AND I'D LIKE HER TO THINK I'VE GOT MY LIFE SOMEWHAT PUT TO-GETHER
I got into the mayo
MAYO

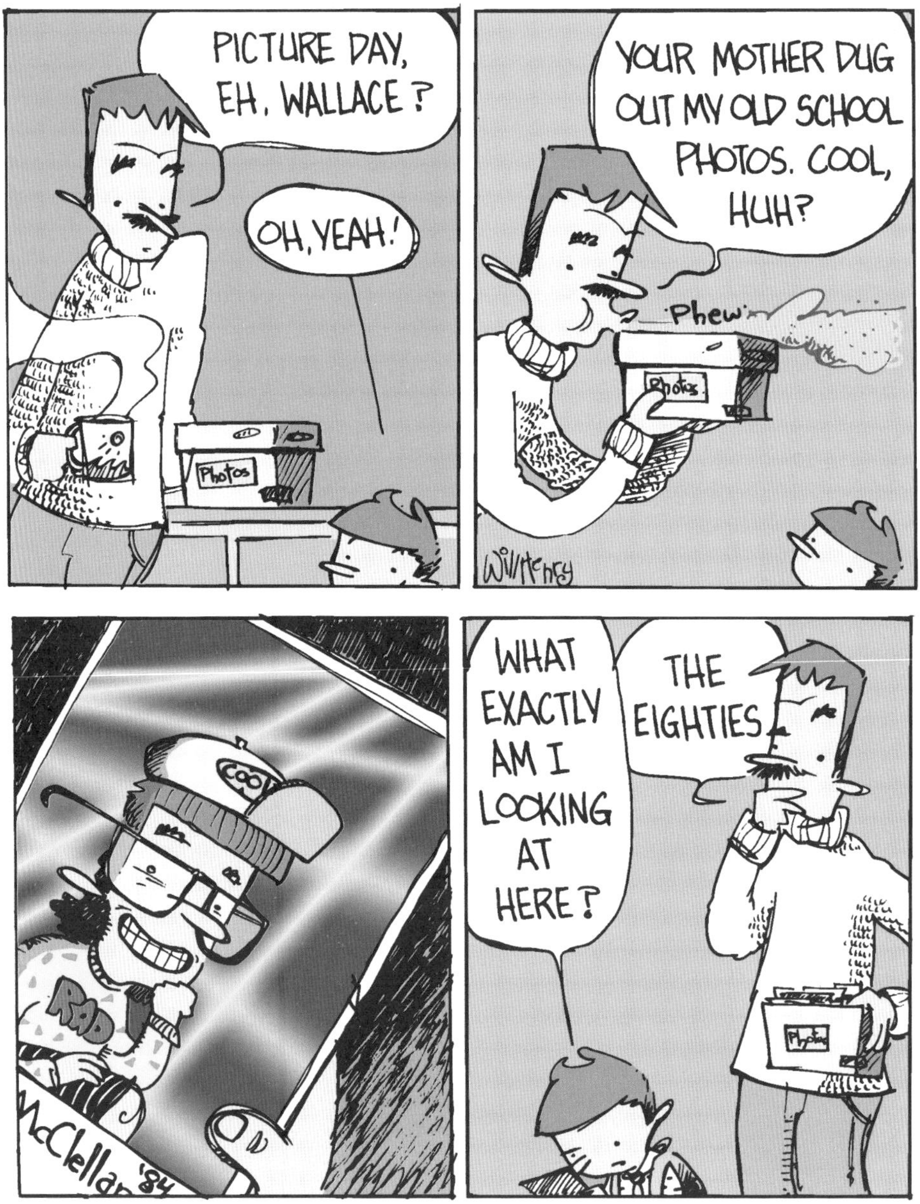
PICTURE DAY, EH, WALLACE?
OH, YEAH!
Photos
YOUR MOTHER DUG OUT MY OLD SCHOOL PHOTOS. COOL, HUH?
Phew
Photos
WillHenry
COOL
RAD
McClellan '84
WHAT EXACTLY AM I LOOKING AT HERE?
THE EIGHTIES.
Photos

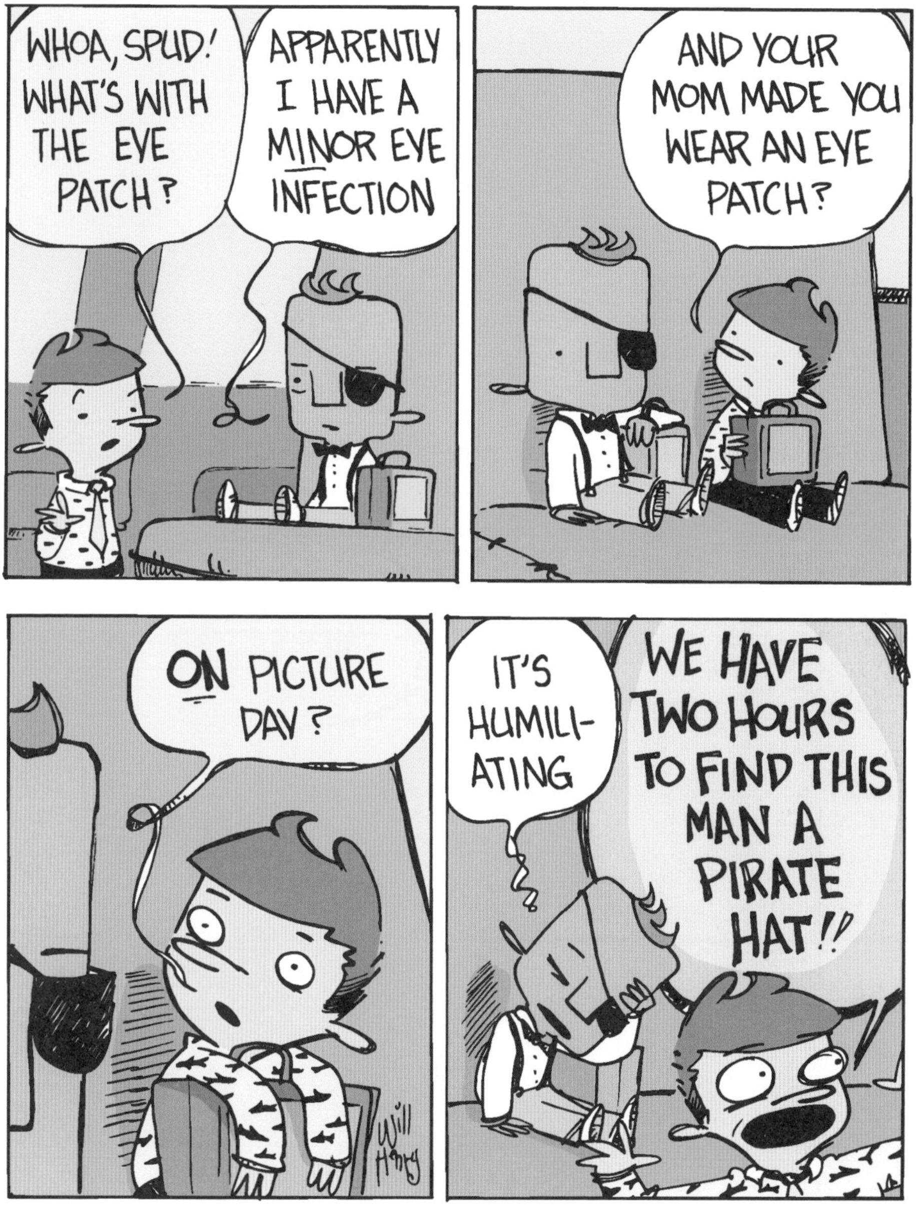
WHOA, SPUD! WHAT'S WITH THE EYE PATCH?
APPARENTLY I HAVE A MINOR EYE INFECTION
AND YOUR MOM MADE YOU WEAR AN EYE PATCH?
ON PICTURE DAY?
IT'S HUMILI-ATING
WE HAVE TWO HOURS TO FIND THIS MAN A PIRATE HAT!!

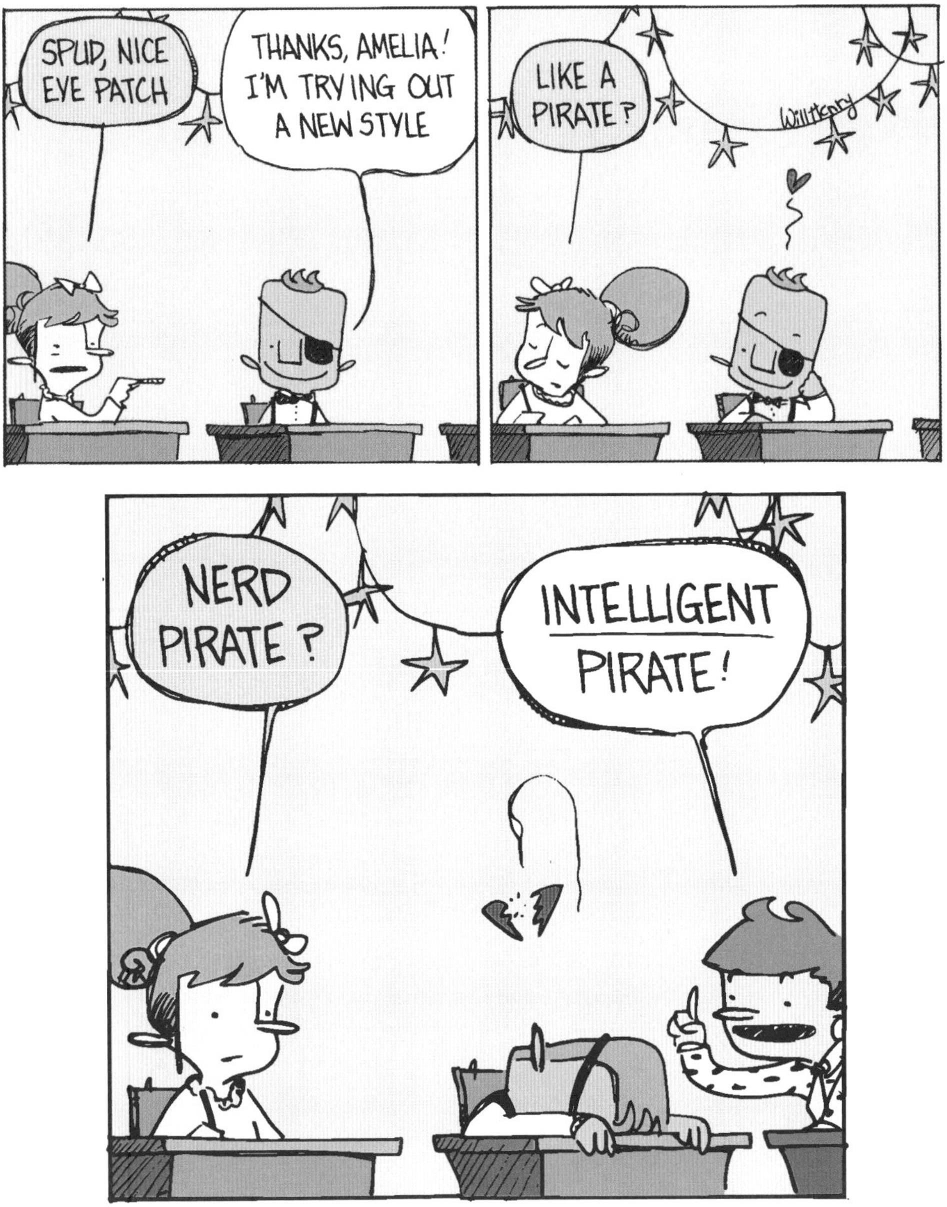
SPUD, NICE EYE PATCH
THANKS, AMELIA! I'M TRYING OUT A NEW STYLE
LIKE A PIRATE?
NERD PIRATE?
INTELLIGENT PIRATE!

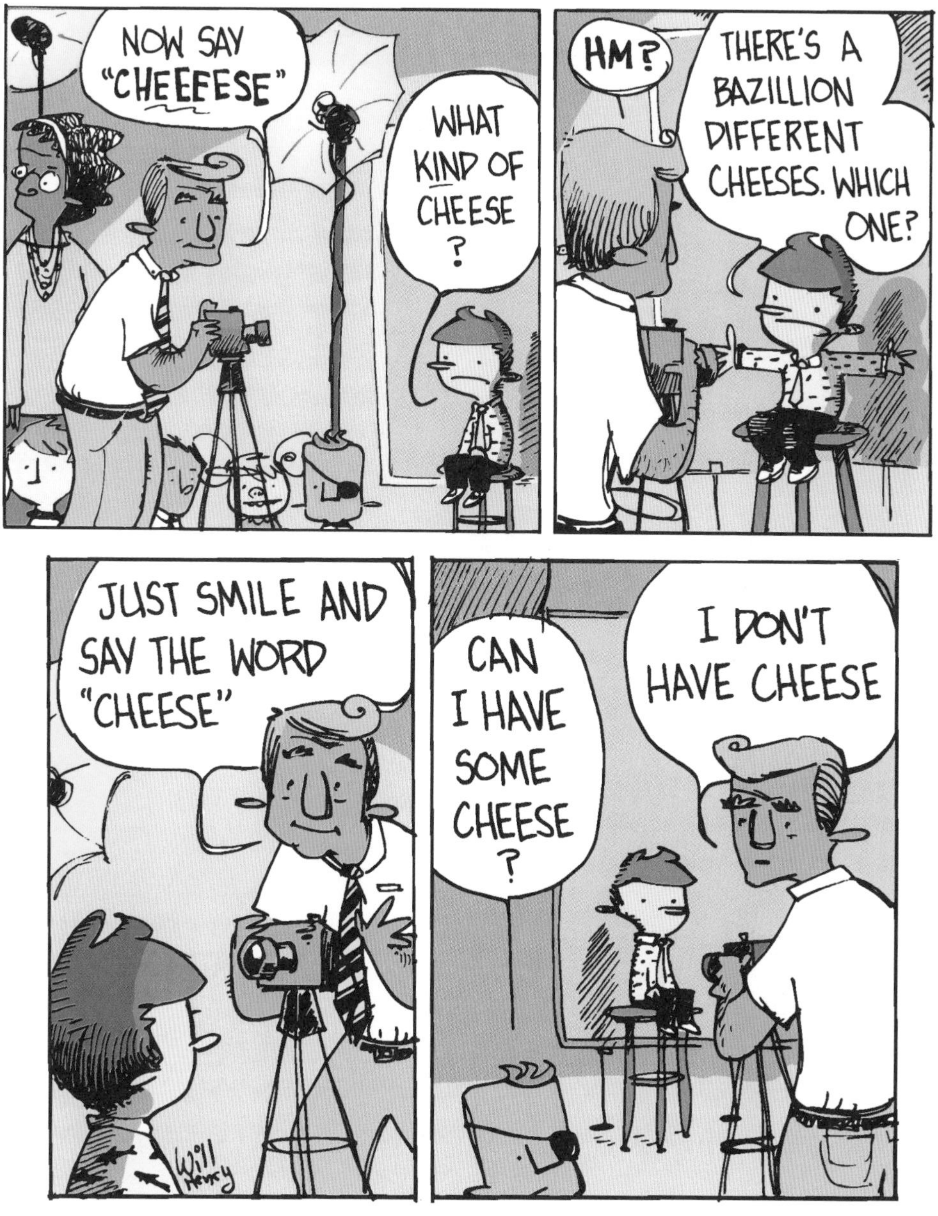
NOW SAY "CHEEEESE"
WHAT KIND OF CHEESE ?
HM?
THERE'S A BAZILLION DIFFERENT CHEESES. WHICH ONE?
JUST SMILE AND SAY THE WORD "CHEESE"
CAN I HAVE SOME CHEESE ?
I DON'T HAVE CHEESE
Will Henry

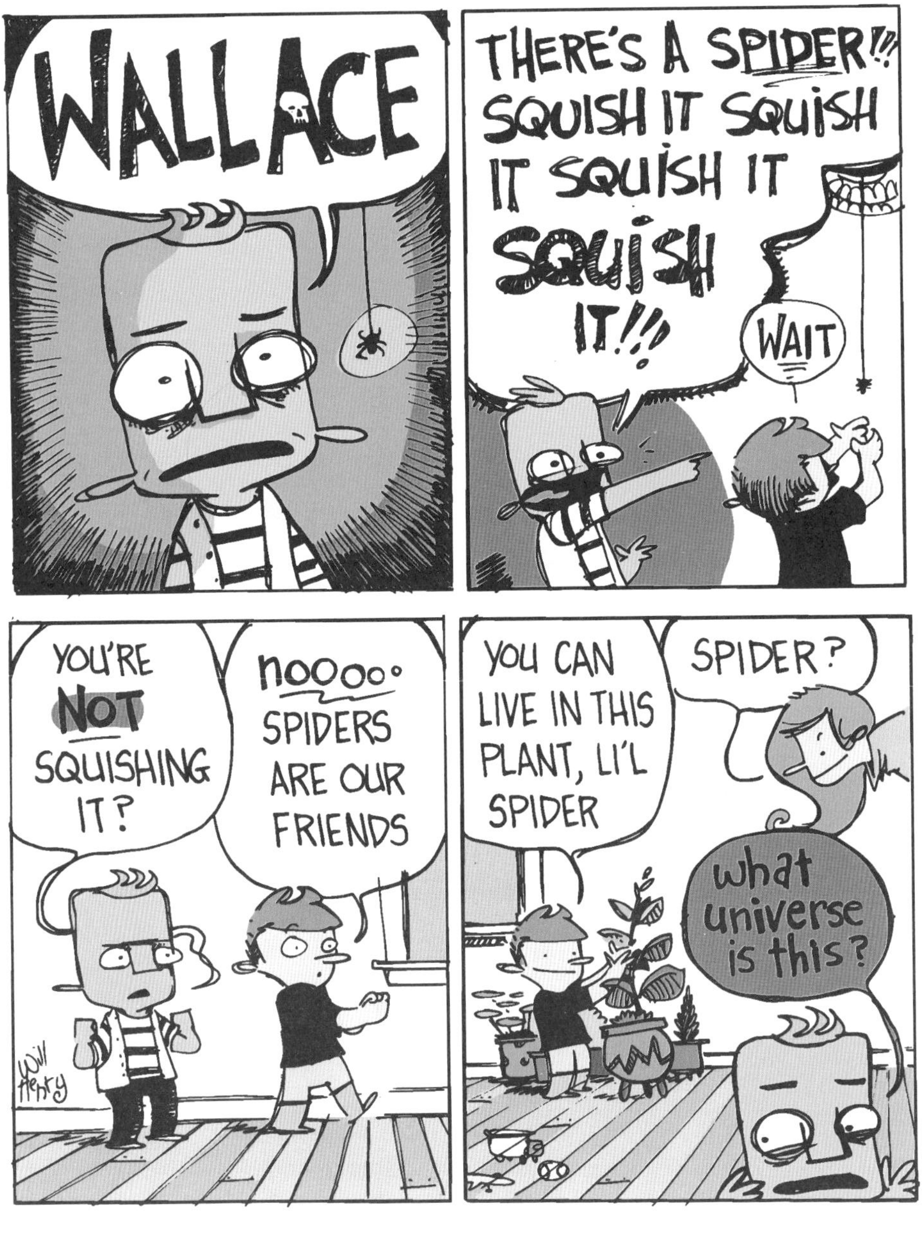
WALLACE
THERE'S A SPIDER!!! SQUISH IT SQUISH IT SQUISH IT SQUISH IT SQUISH IT!!!
WAIT
YOU'RE NOT SQUISHING IT?
noooo° SPIDERS ARE OUR FRIENDS
Will Henry
YOU CAN LIVE IN THIS PLANT, LI'L SPIDER
SPIDER?
what universe is this?

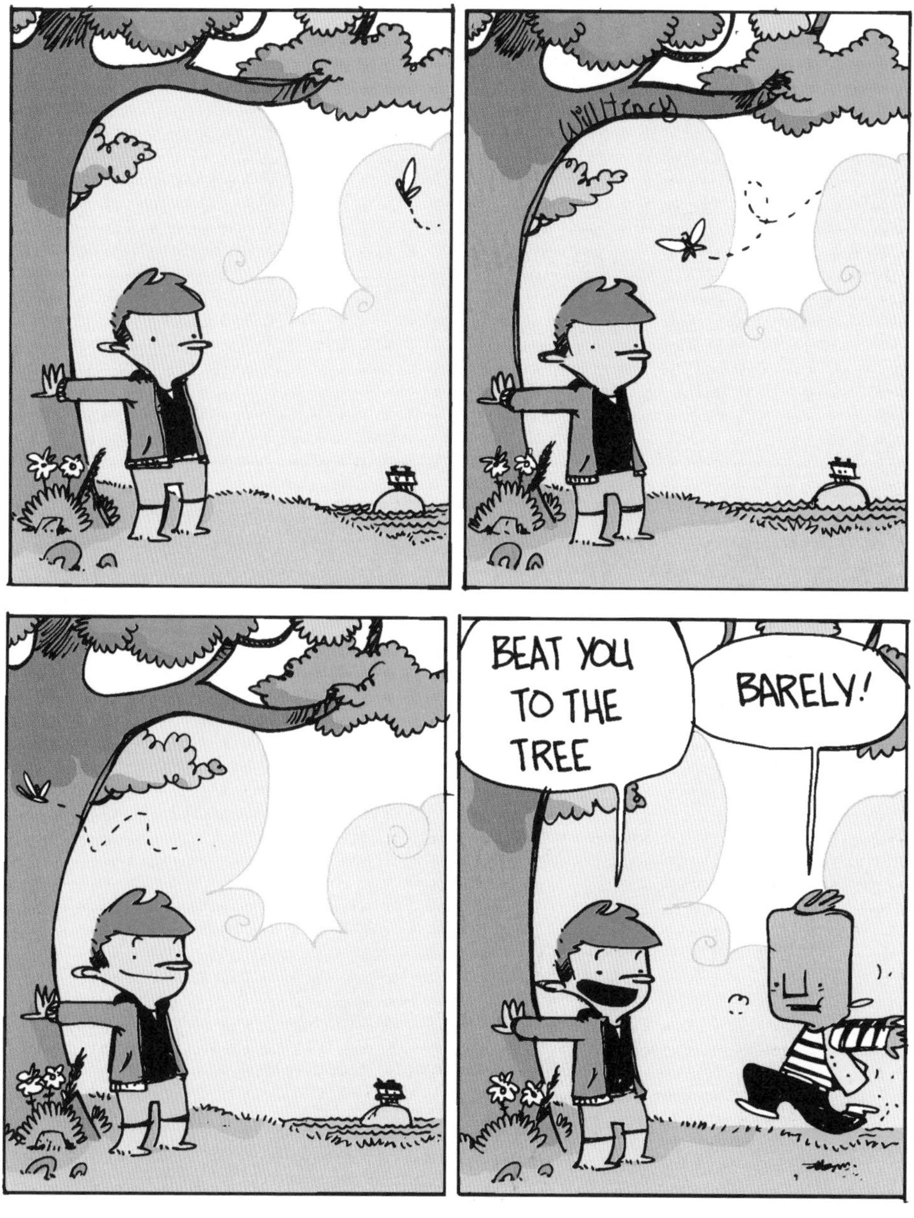
BEAT YOU TO THE TREE
BARELY!

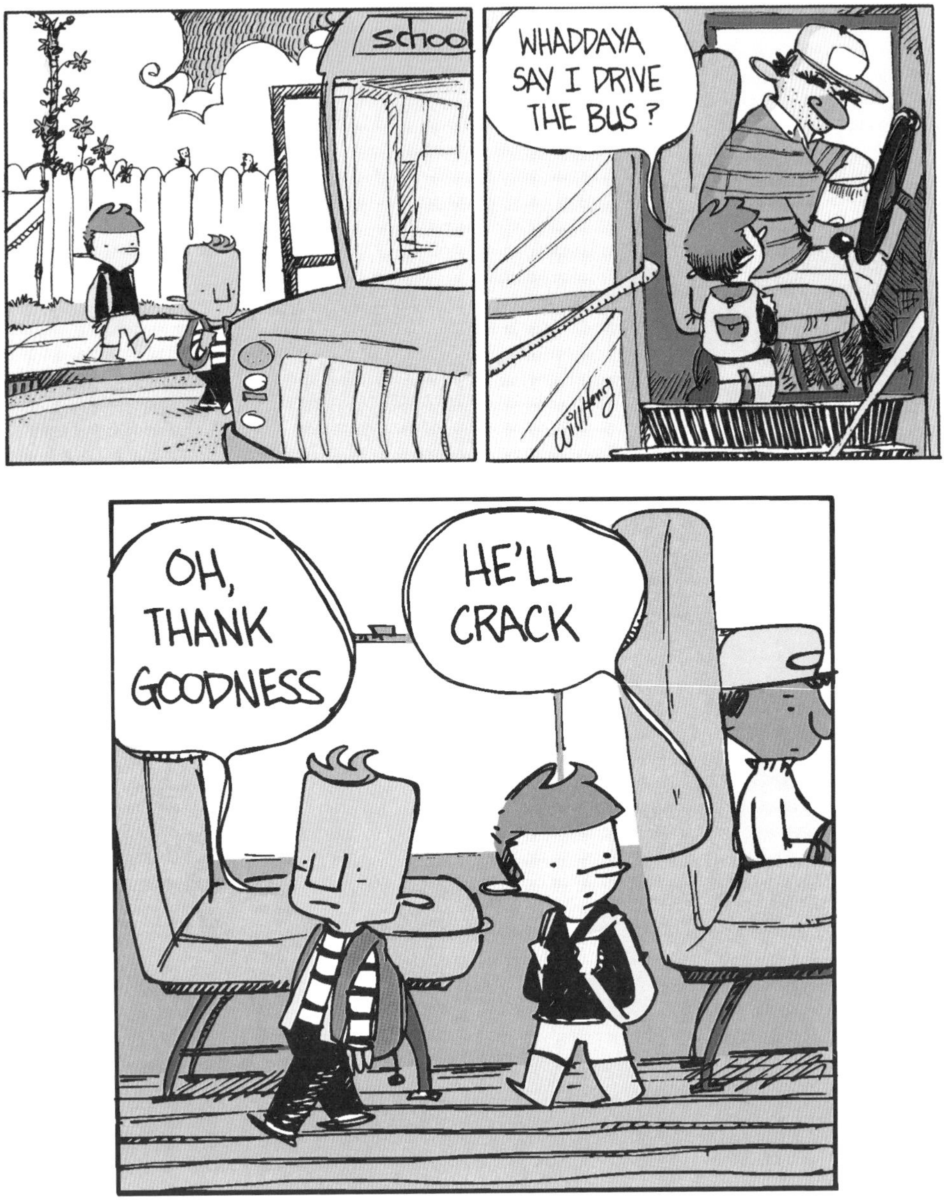
SCHOOL
WHADDAYA SAY I DRIVE THE BUS?
Will Henry
OH, THANK GOODNESS
HE'LL CRACK

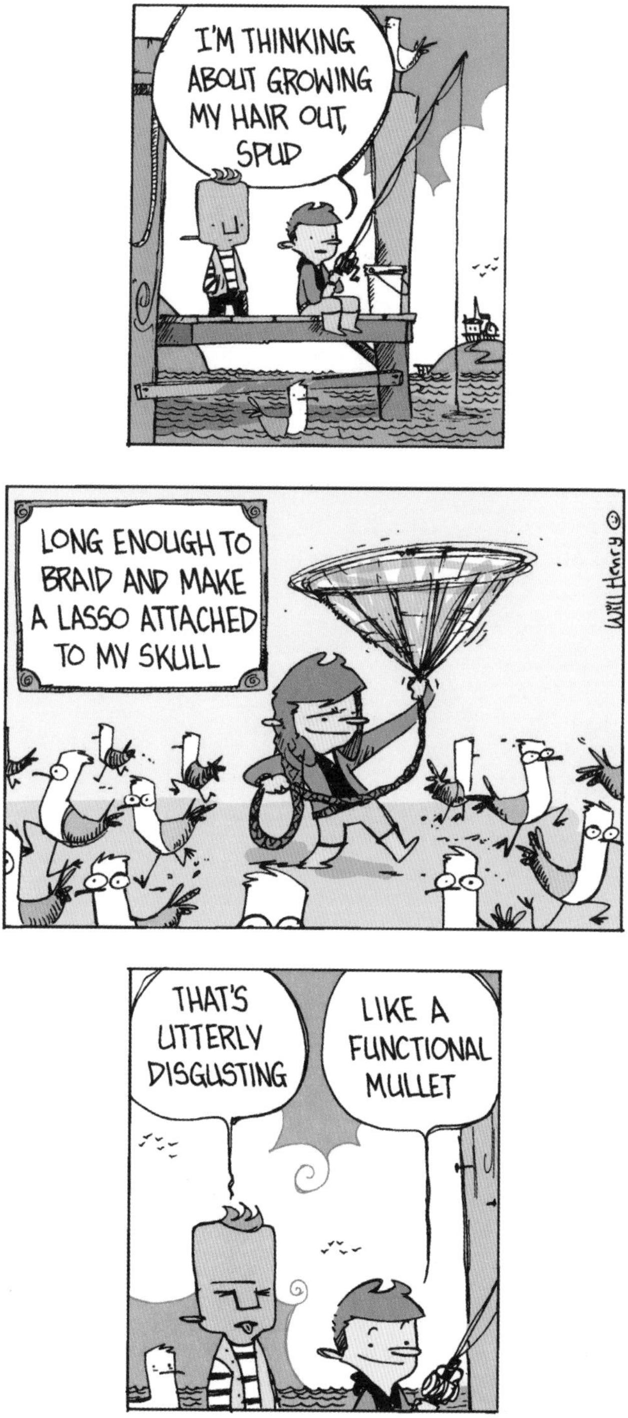
I'M THINKING ABOUT GROWING MY HAIR OUT, SPUD
LONG ENOUGH TO BRAID AND MAKE A LASSO ATTACHED TO MY SKULL
Will Henry
THAT'S UTTERLY DISGUSTING
LIKE A FUNCTIONAL MULLET

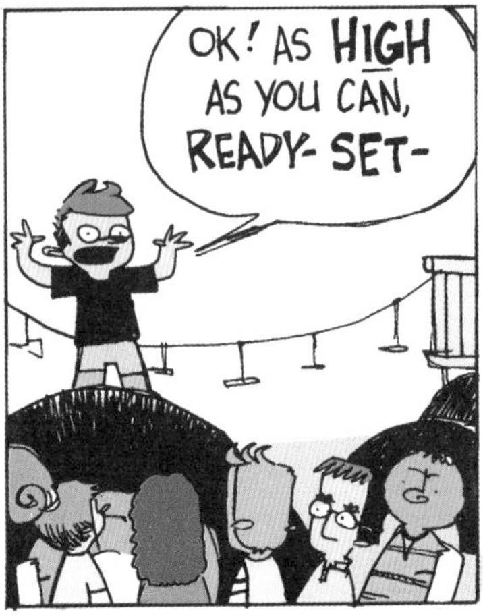
OK! AS HIGH AS YOU CAN, READY- SET-

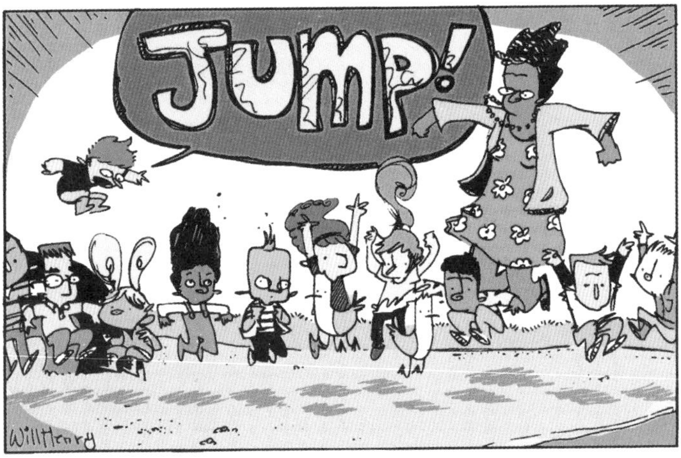
JUMP!

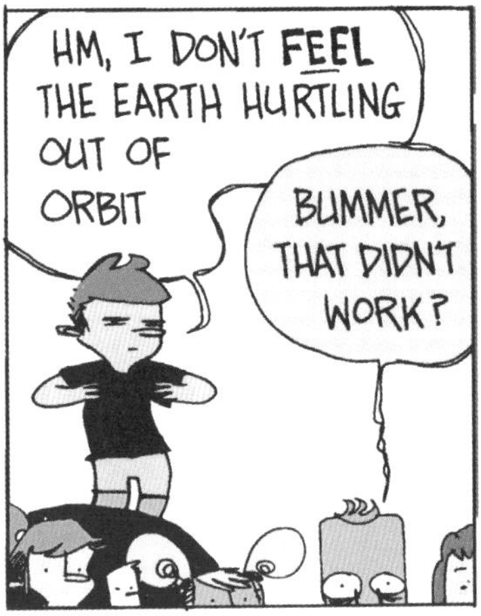
HM, I DON'T FEEL THE EARTH HURTLING OUT OF ORBIT
BUMMER, THAT DIDN'T WORK?

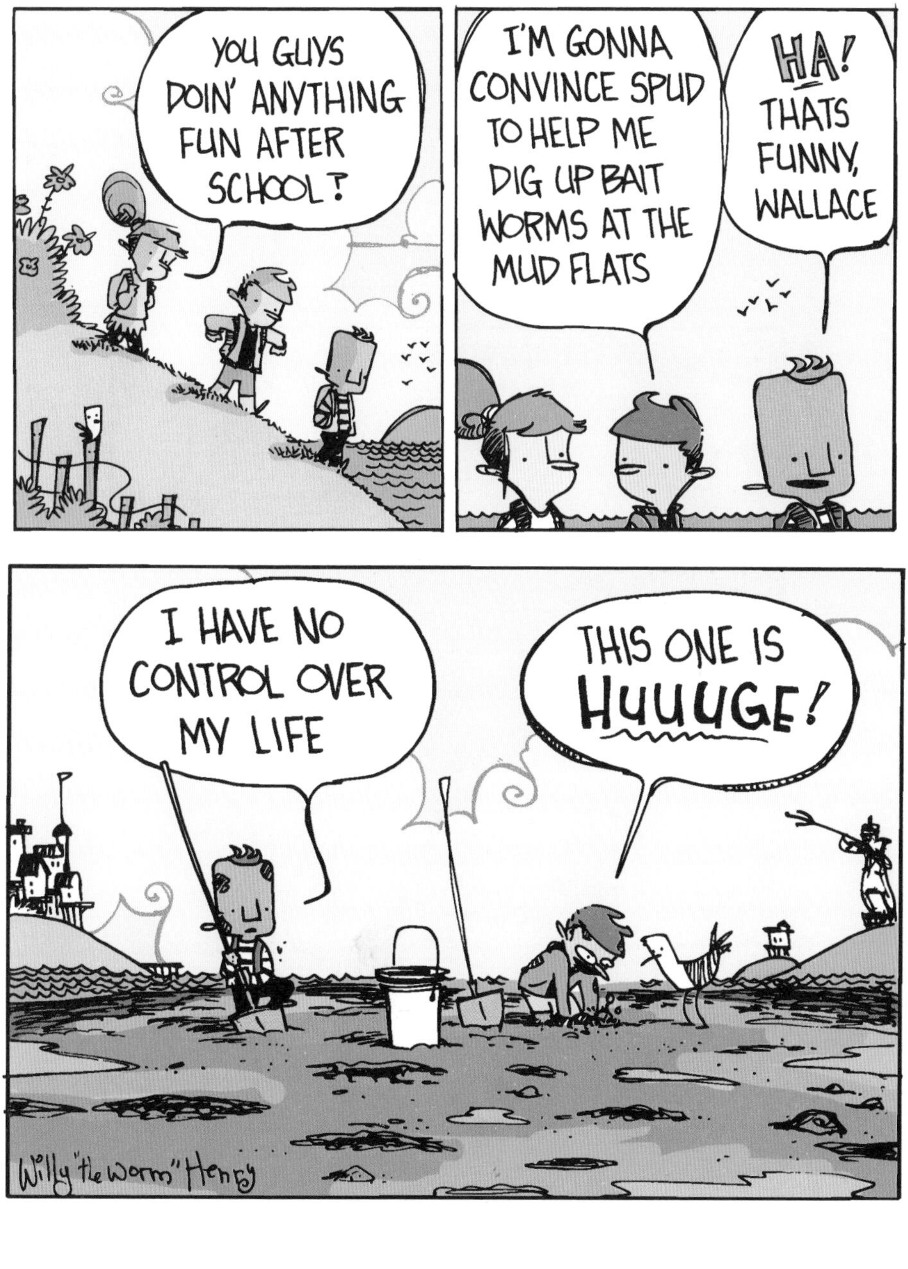
YOU GUYS DOIN' ANYTHING FUN AFTER SCHOOL?
I'M GONNA CONVINCE SPUD TO HELP ME DIG UP BAIT WORMS AT THE MUD FLATS
HA! THATS FUNNY, WALLACE
I HAVE NO CONTROL OVER MY LIFE
THIS ONE IS HUUUGE!
Willy "the worm" Henry

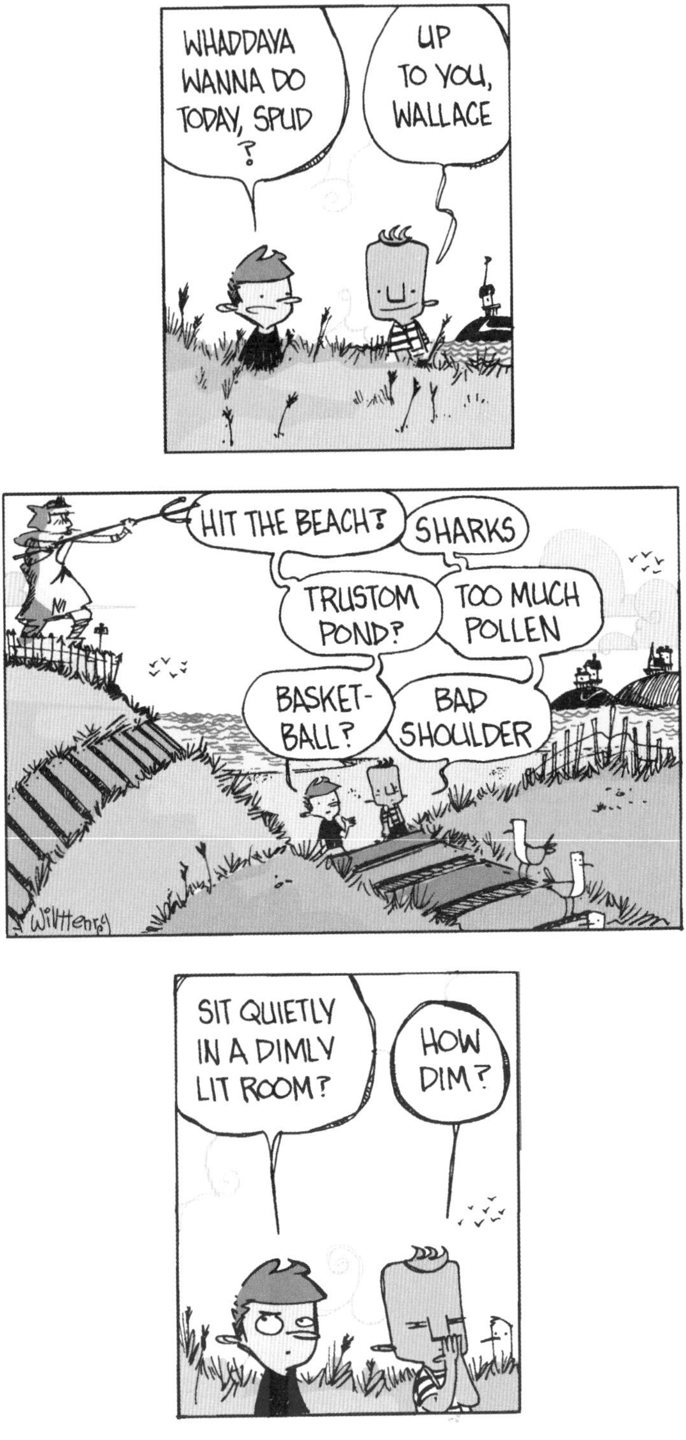
WHADDAYA WANNA DO TODAY, SPUD ?
UP TO YOU, WALLACE
HIT THE BEACH?
SHARKS
TRUSTOM POND?
TOO MUCH POLLEN
BASKET-BALL?
BAD SHOULDER
SIT QUIETLY IN A DIMLY LIT ROOM?
HOW DIM?

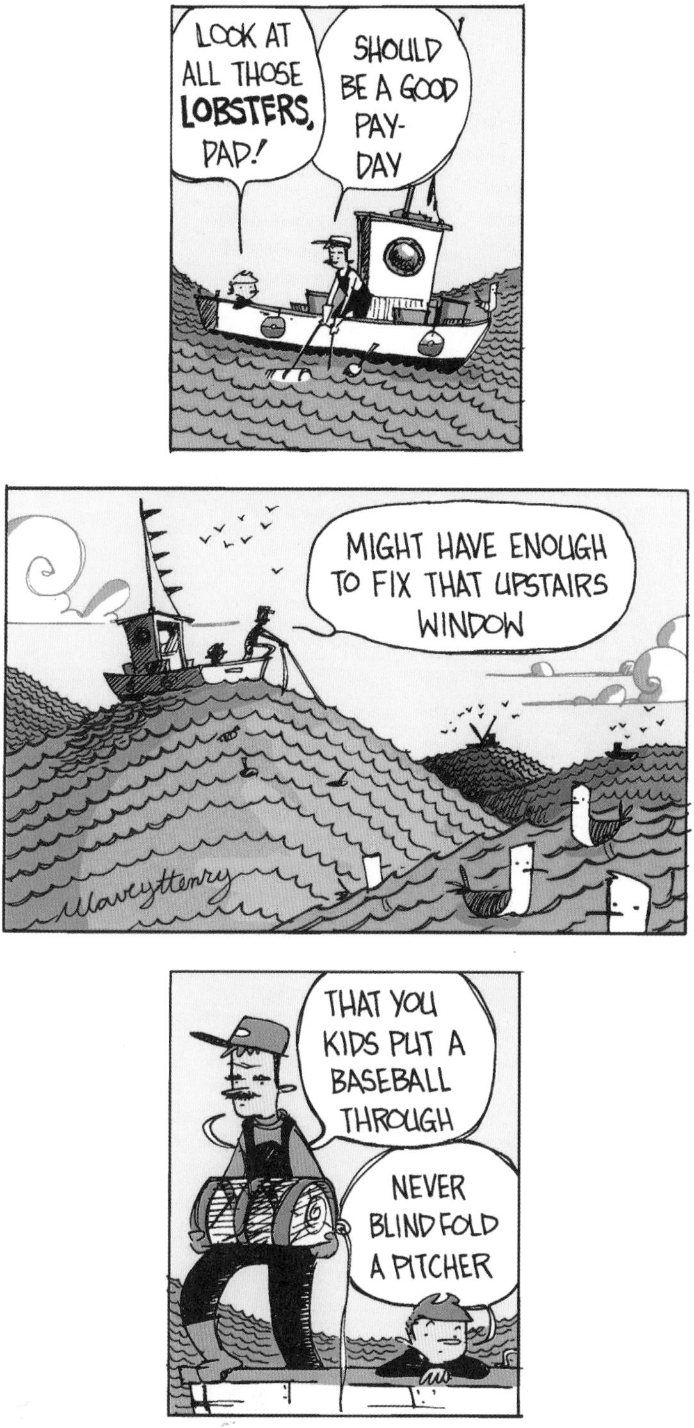
LOOK AT ALL THOSE **LOBSTERS,** DAD!
SHOULD BE A GOOD PAY-DAY
MIGHT HAVE ENOUGH TO FIX THAT UPSTAIRS WINDOW
THAT YOU KIDS PUT A BASEBALL THROUGH
NEVER BLINDFOLD A PITCHER

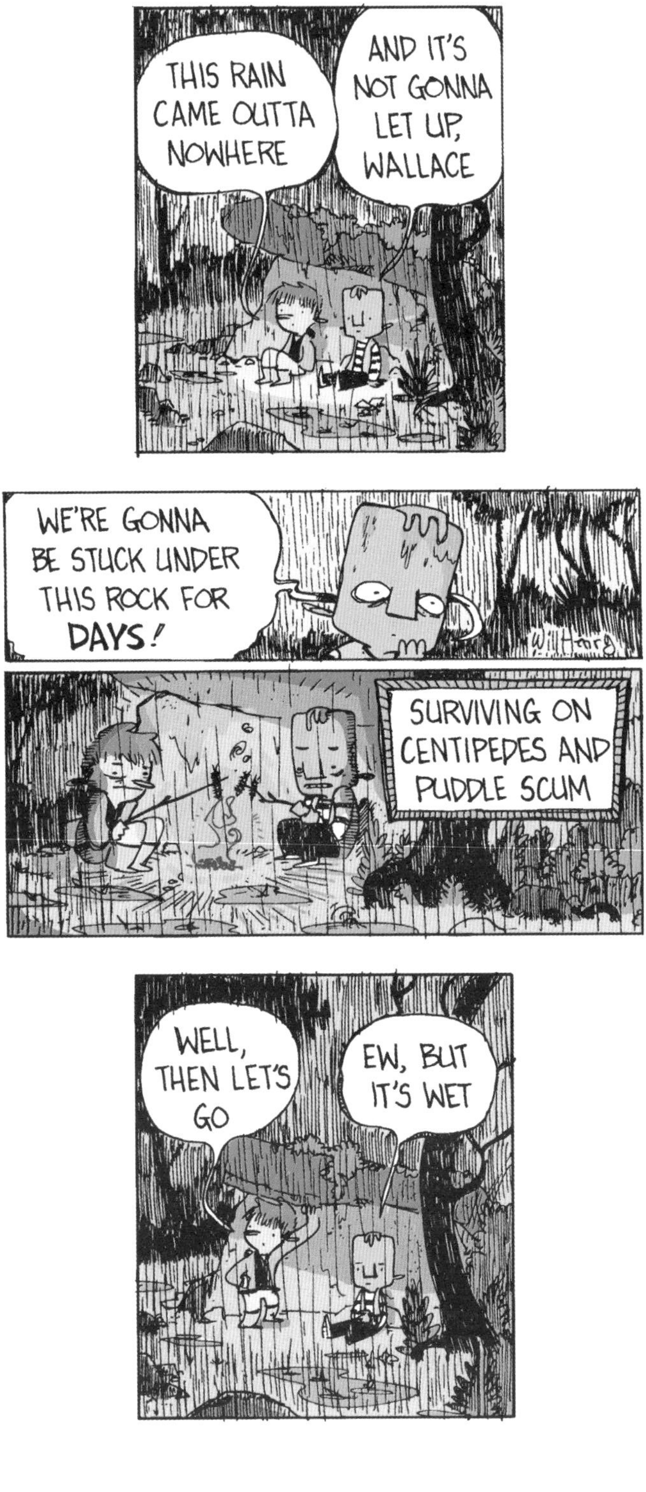
THIS RAIN CAME OUTTA NOWHERE
AND IT'S NOT GONNA LET UP, WALLACE
WE'RE GONNA BE STUCK UNDER THIS ROCK FOR DAYS!
SURVIVING ON CENTIPEDES AND PUDDLE SCUM
WELL, THEN LET'S GO
EW, BUT IT'S WET

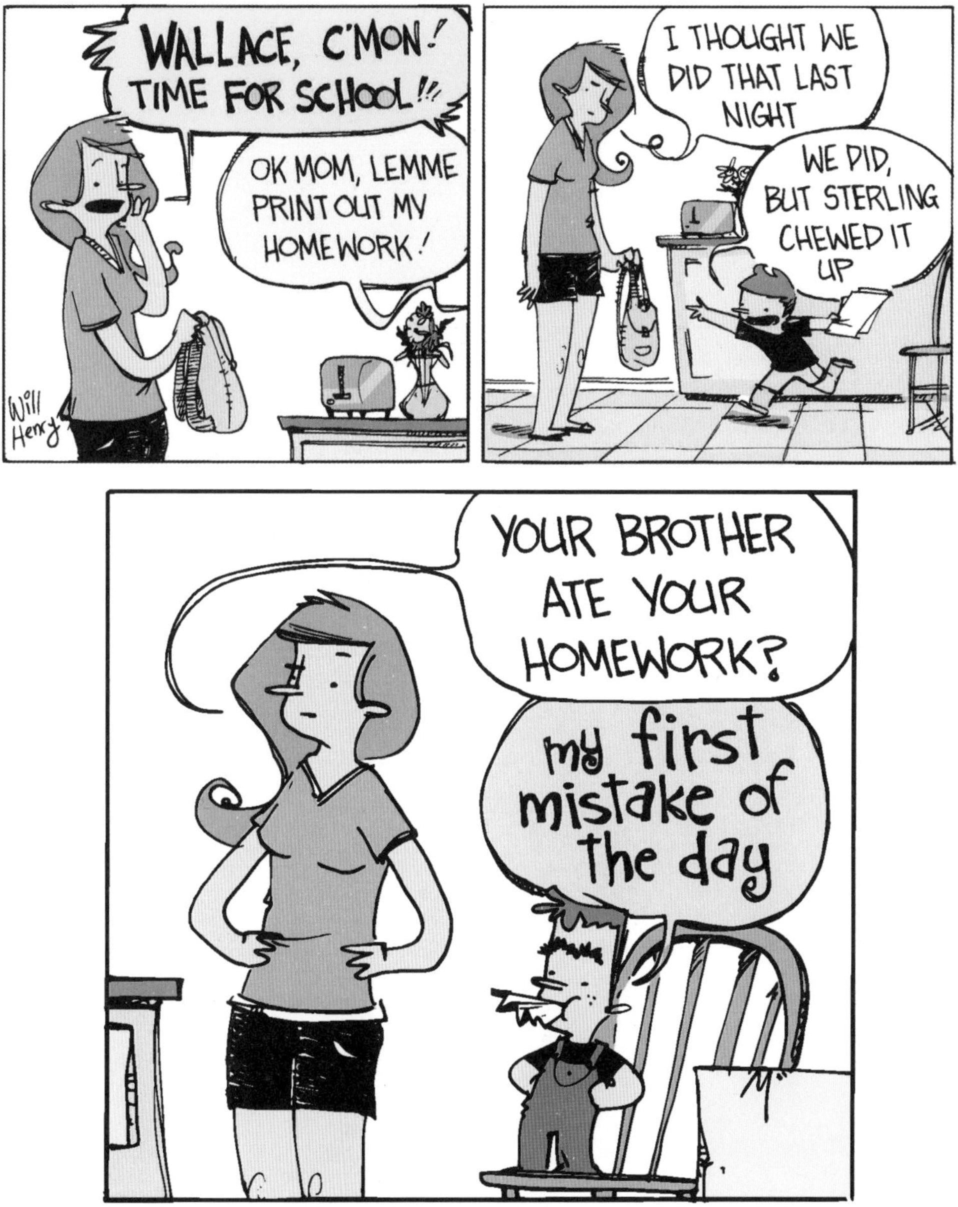
WALLACE, C'MON! TIME FOR SCHOOL!!
OK MOM, LEMME PRINT OUT MY HOMEWORK!
Will Henry
I THOUGHT WE DID THAT LAST NIGHT
WE DID, BUT STERLING CHEWED IT UP
YOUR BROTHER ATE YOUR HOMEWORK?
my first mistake of the day

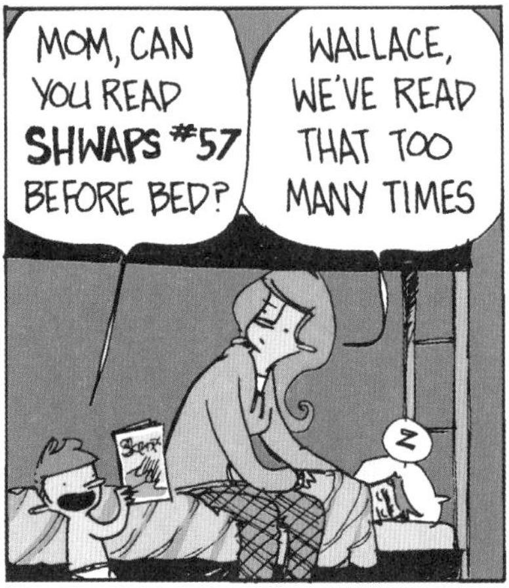
MOM, CAN YOU READ SHWAPS #57 BEFORE BED?
WALLACE, WE'VE READ THAT TOO MANY TIMES
Z

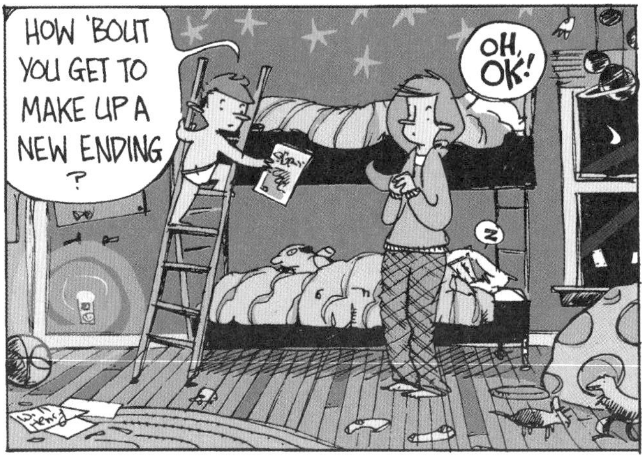
HOW 'BOUT YOU GET TO MAKE UP A NEW ENDING ?
OH, OK!
Z

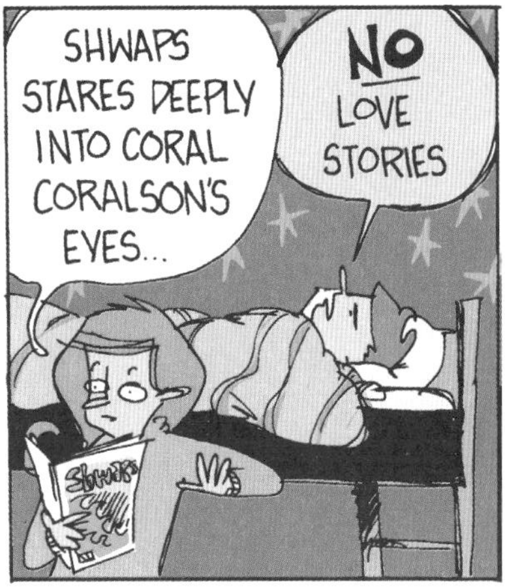
SHWAPS STARES DEEPLY INTO CORAL CORALSON'S EYES...
NO LOVE STORIES

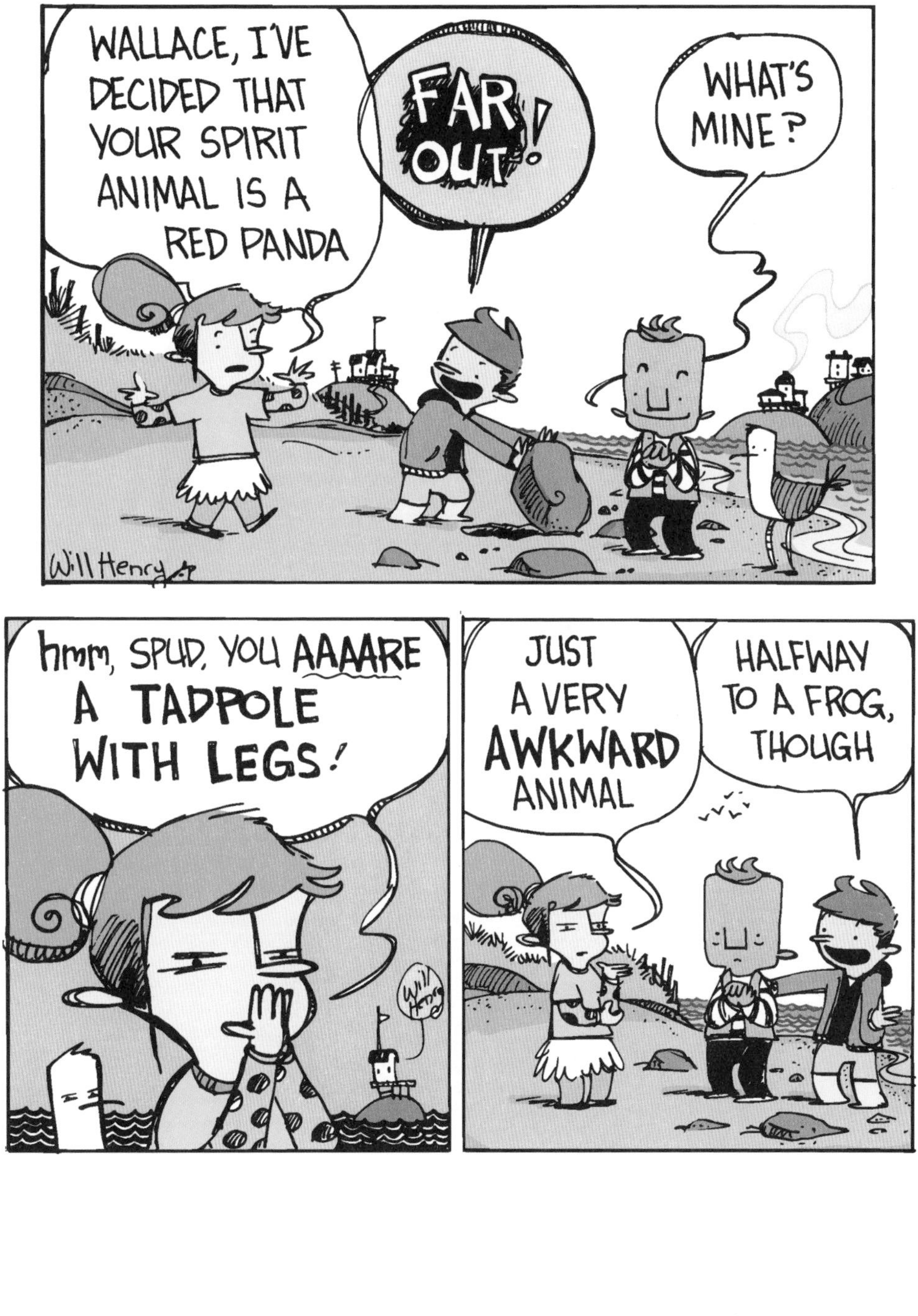
WALLACE, I'VE DECIDED THAT YOUR SPIRIT ANIMAL IS A RED PANDA
FAR OUT!
WHAT'S MINE?
Will Henry
hmm, SPUD, YOU AAAARE A TADPOLE WITH LEGS!
JUST A VERY AWKWARD ANIMAL
HALFWAY TO A FROG, THOUGH

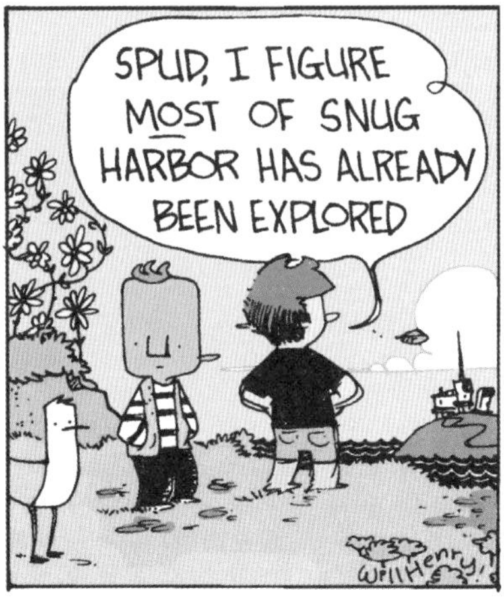
SPUD, I FIGURE MOST OF SNUG HARBOR HAS ALREADY BEEN EXPLORED
Will Henry

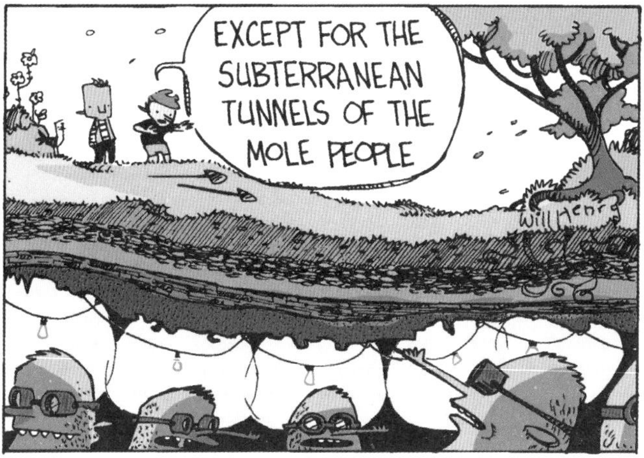
EXCEPT FOR THE SUBTERRANEAN TUNNELS OF THE MOLE PEOPLE
Will Henry

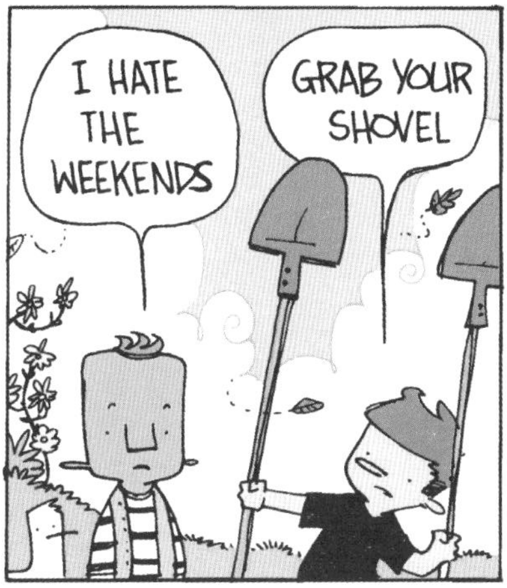
I HATE THE WEEKENDS
GRAB YOUR SHOVEL

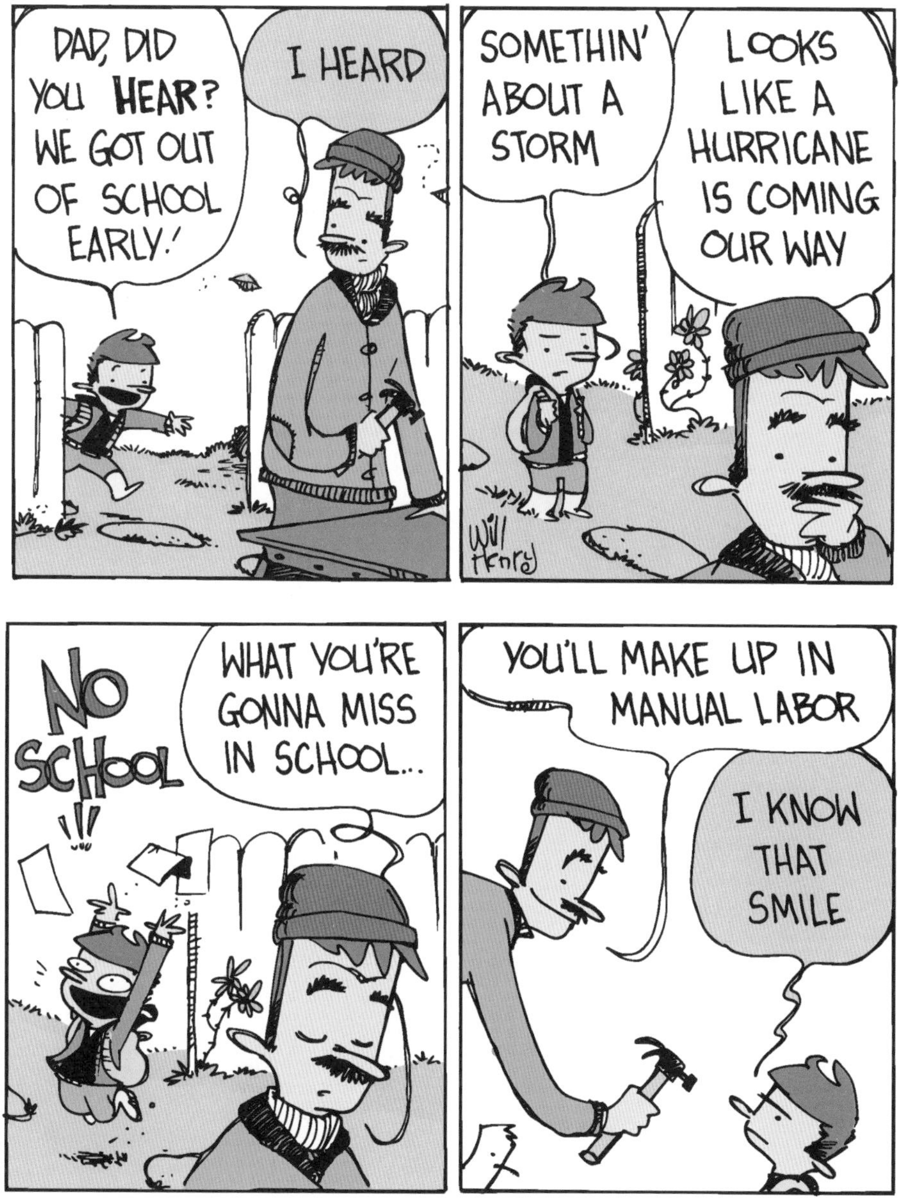
DAD, DID YOU **HEAR**? WE GOT OUT OF SCHOOL EARLY!
I HEARD
SOMETHIN' ABOUT A STORM
LOOKS LIKE A HURRICANE IS COMING OUR WAY
Will Henry
NO SCHOOL !!!
WHAT YOU'RE GONNA MISS IN SCHOOL...
YOU'LL MAKE UP IN MANUAL LABOR
I KNOW THAT SMILE

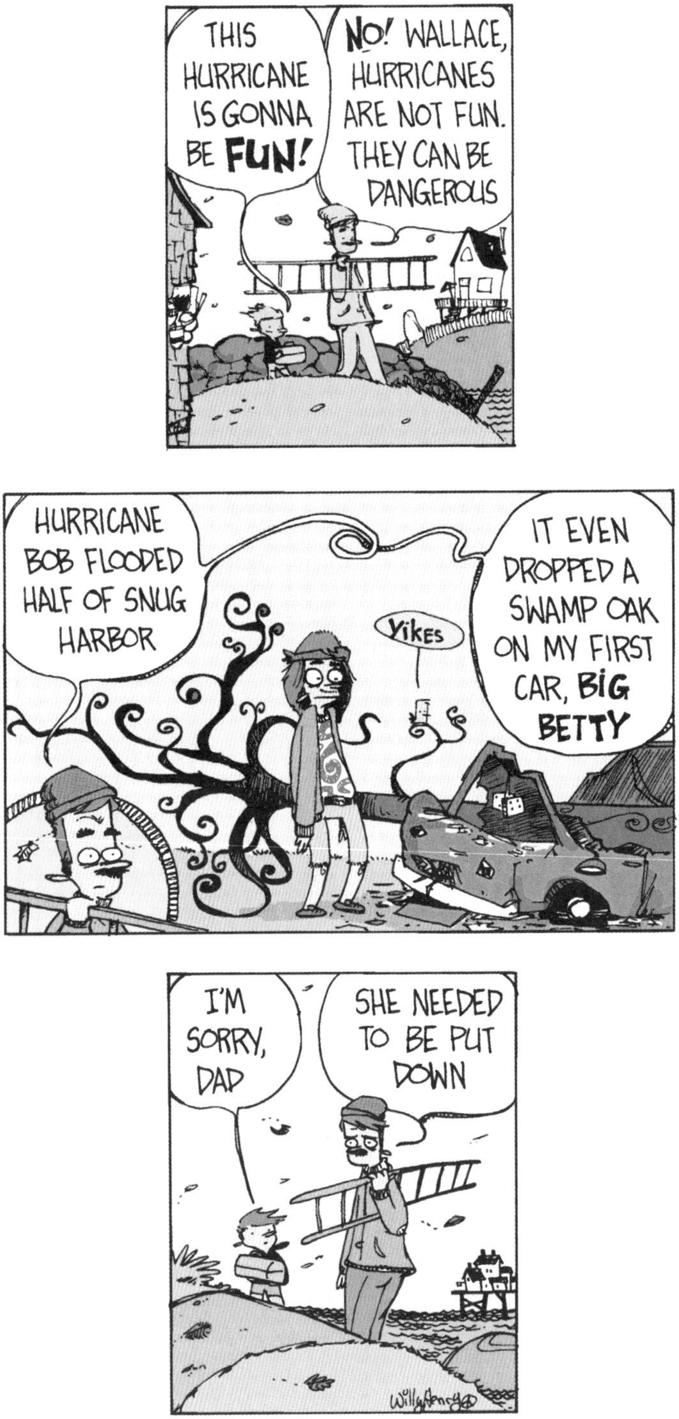
THIS HURRICANE IS GONNA BE FUN!
NO! WALLACE, HURRICANES ARE NOT FUN. THEY CAN BE DANGEROUS
HURRICANE BOB FLOODED HALF OF SNUG HARBOR
YIKES
IT EVEN DROPPED A SWAMP OAK ON MY FIRST CAR, BIG BETTY
I'M SORRY, DAD
SHE NEEDED TO BE PUT DOWN

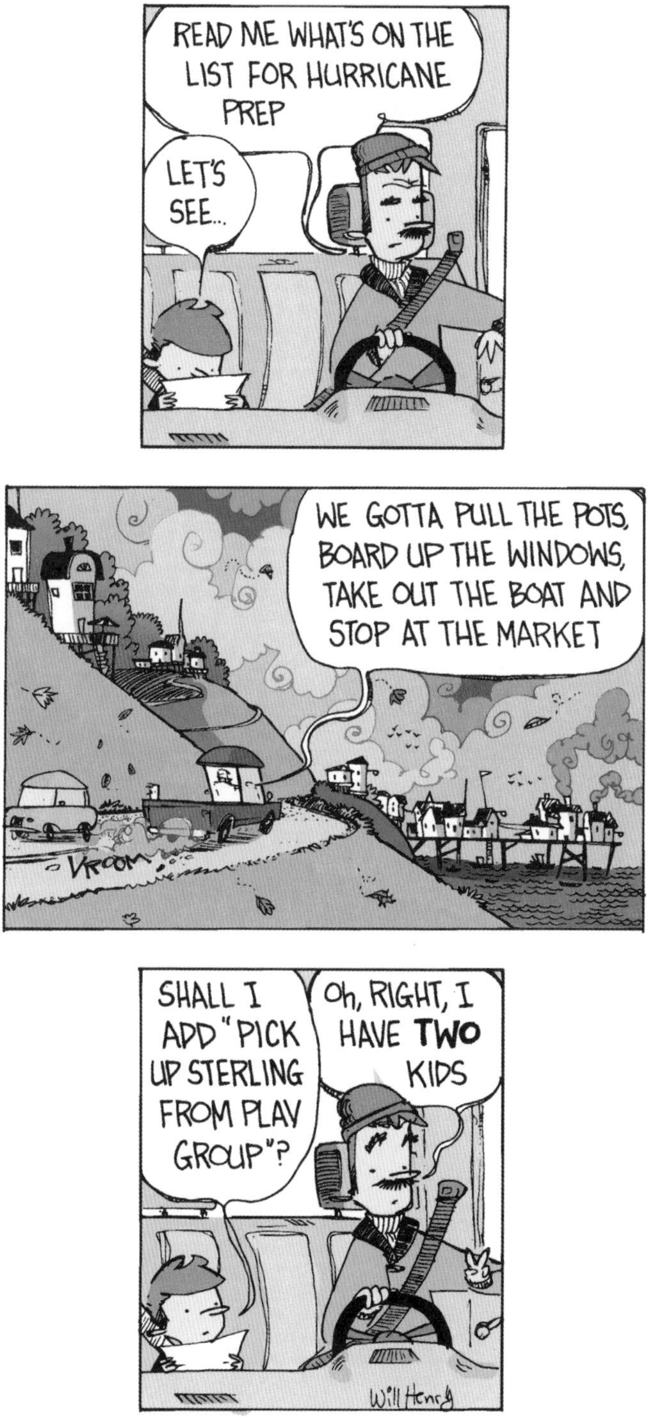
READ ME WHAT'S ON THE LIST FOR HURRICANE PREP
LET'S SEE...
WE GOTTA PULL THE POTS, BOARD UP THE WINDOWS, TAKE OUT THE BOAT AND STOP AT THE MARKET
VROOM
SHALL I ADD "PICK UP STERLING FROM PLAY GROUP"?
Oh, RIGHT, I HAVE **TWO** KIDS
Will Henry

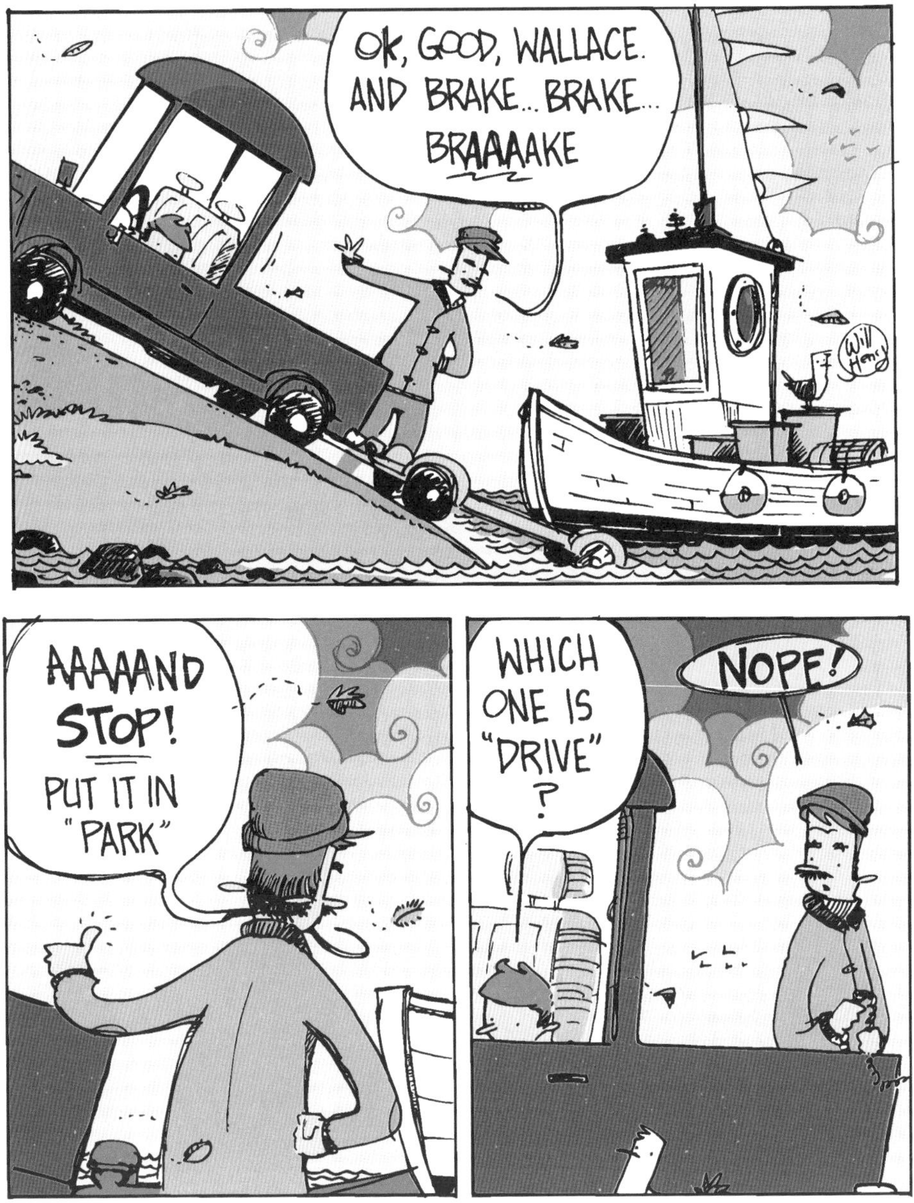

OK, GOOD, WALLACE. AND BRAKE... BRAKE... BRAAAAKE
Will Henry
AAAAAND STOP! PUT IT IN "PARK"
WHICH ONE IS "DRIVE"?
NOPE!

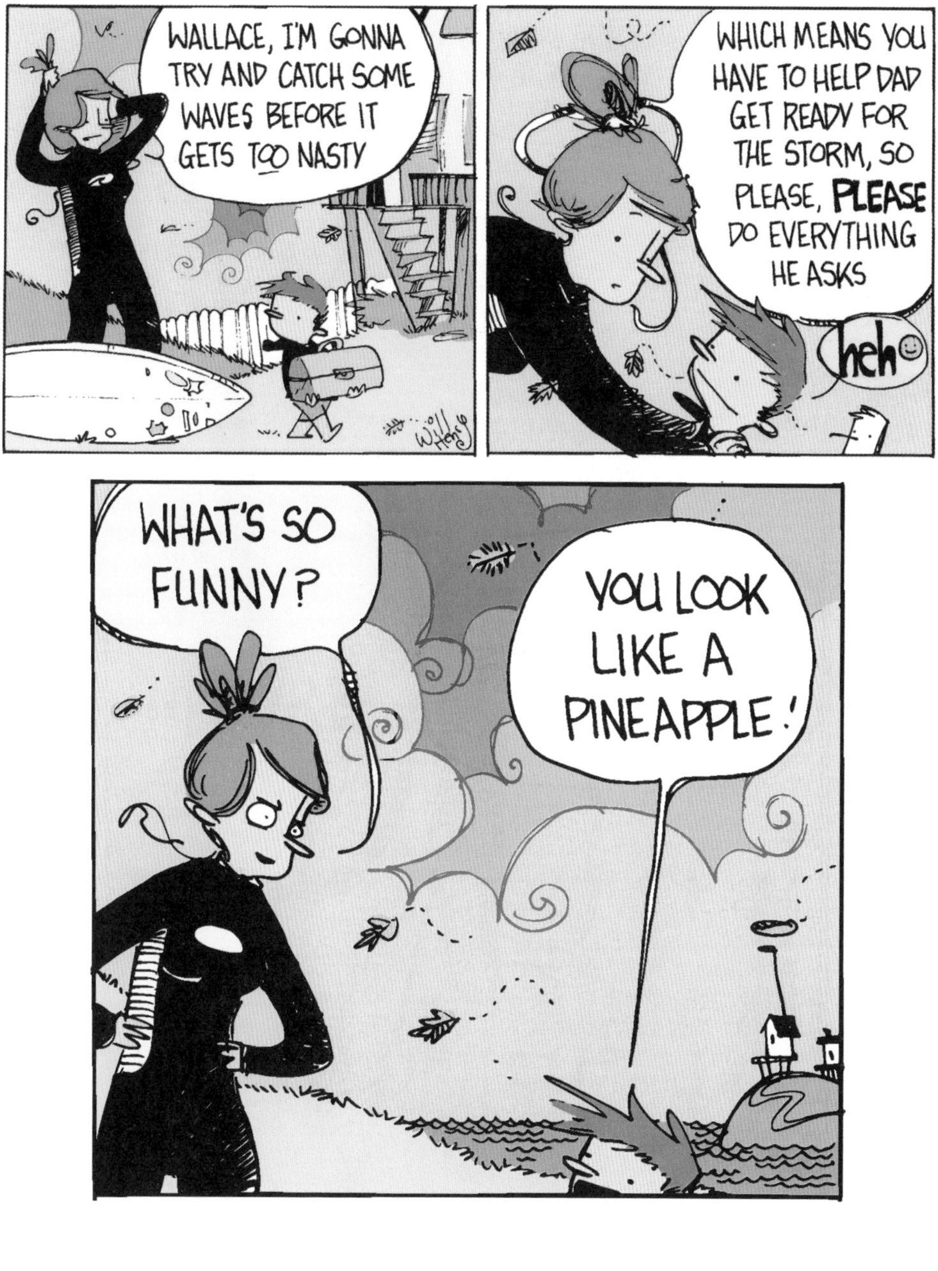
WALLACE, I'M GONNA TRY AND CATCH SOME WAVES BEFORE IT GETS TOO NASTY
WHICH MEANS YOU HAVE TO HELP DAD GET READY FOR THE STORM, SO PLEASE, PLEASE DO EVERYTHING HE ASKS
heh
WHAT'S SO FUNNY?
YOU LOOK LIKE A PINEAPPLE!

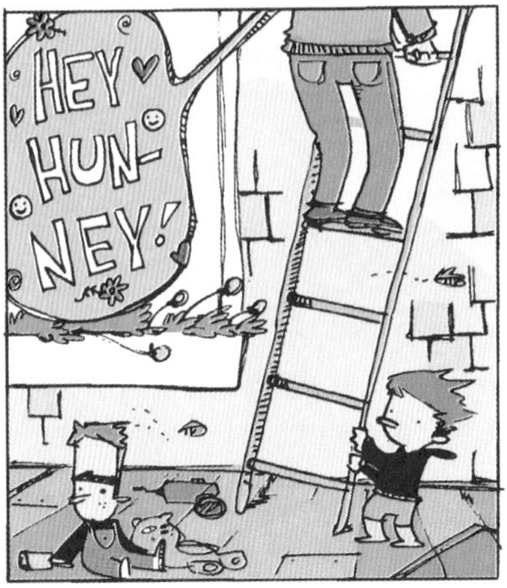
HEY HUN-NEY!

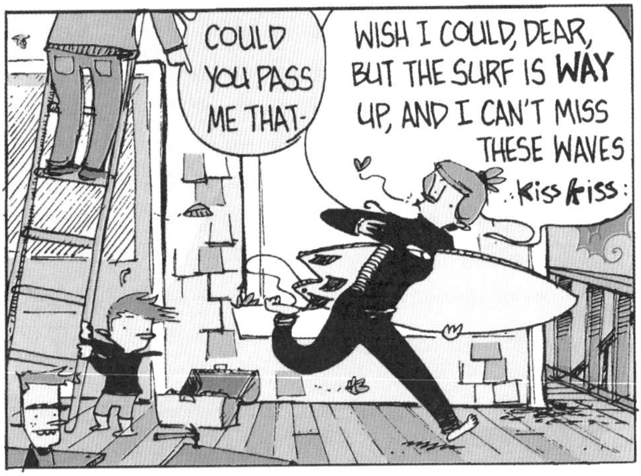
COULD YOU PASS ME THAT-
WISH I COULD, DEAR, BUT THE SURF IS **WAY** UP, AND I CAN'T MISS THESE WAVES :kiss kiss:

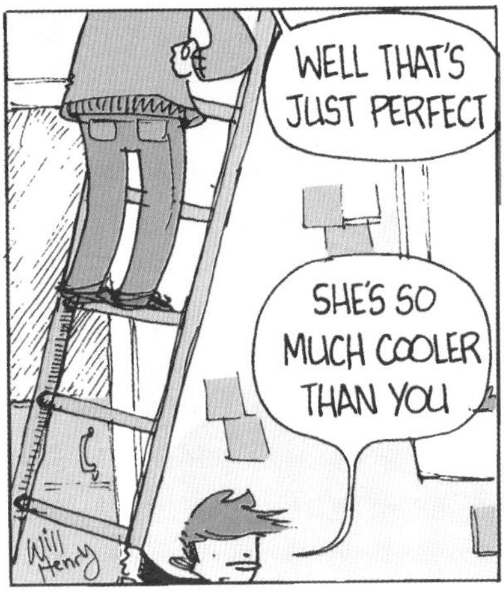
WELL THAT'S JUST PERFECT
SHE'S SO MUCH COOLER THAN YOU
Will Henry

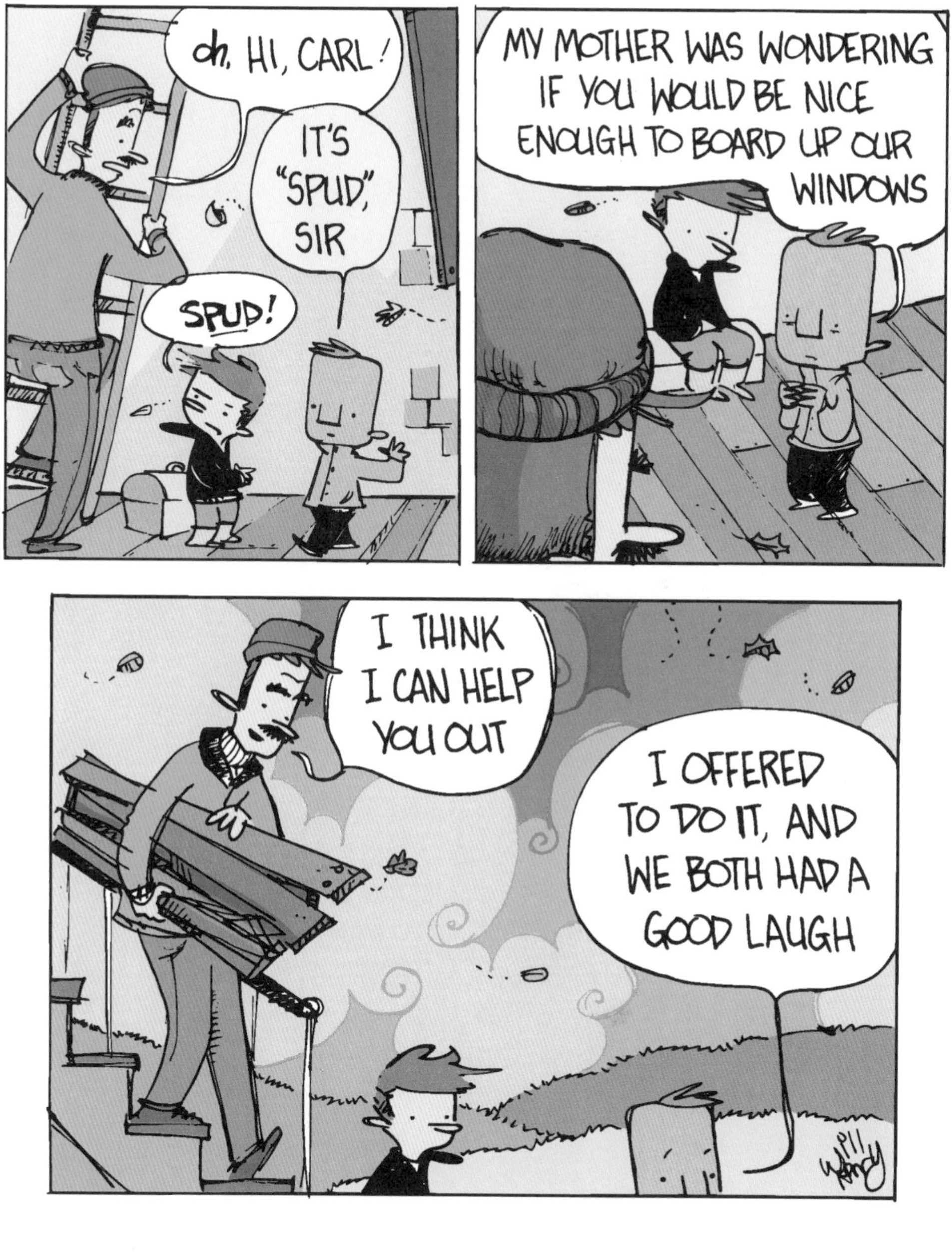
oh, HI, CARL!
IT'S "SPUD", SIR
SPUD!
MY MOTHER WAS WONDERING IF YOU WOULD BE NICE ENOUGH TO BOARD UP OUR WINDOWS
I THINK I CAN HELP YOU OUT
I OFFERED TO DO IT, AND WE BOTH HAD A GOOD LAUGH

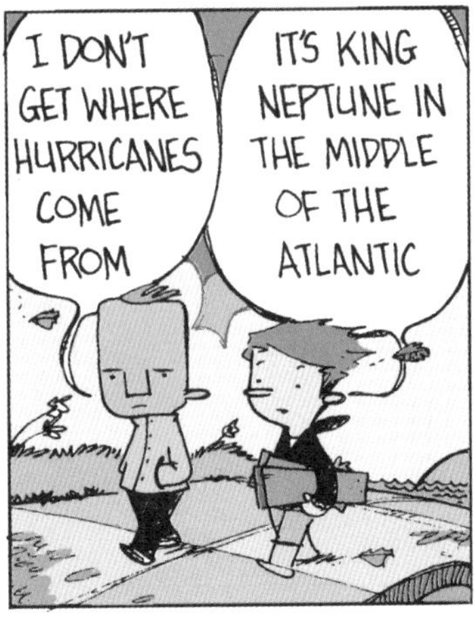
I DON'T GET WHERE HURRICANES COME FROM
IT'S KING NEPTUNE IN THE MIDDLE OF THE ATLANTIC

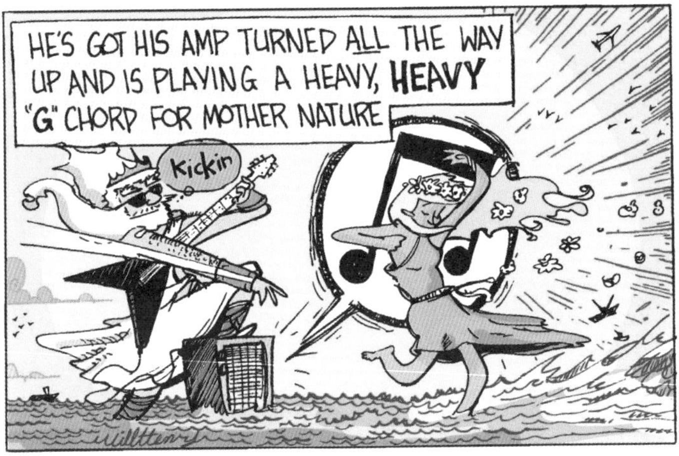
HE'S GOT HIS AMP TURNED ALL THE WAY UP AND IS PLAYING A HEAVY, HEAVY "G" CHORD FOR MOTHER NATURE
Kickin

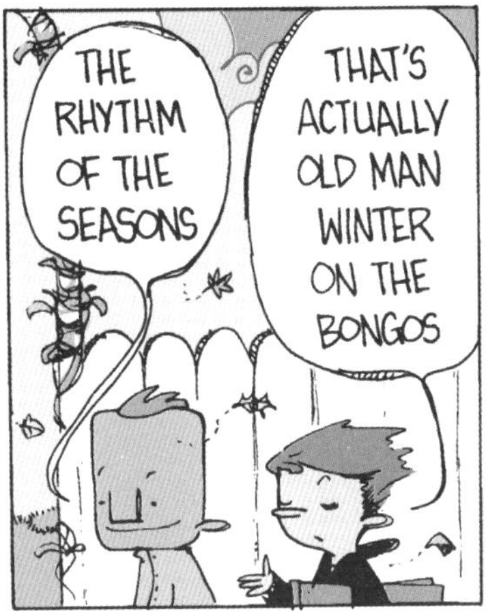
THE RHYTHM OF THE SEASONS
THAT'S ACTUALLY OLD MAN WINTER ON THE BONGOS

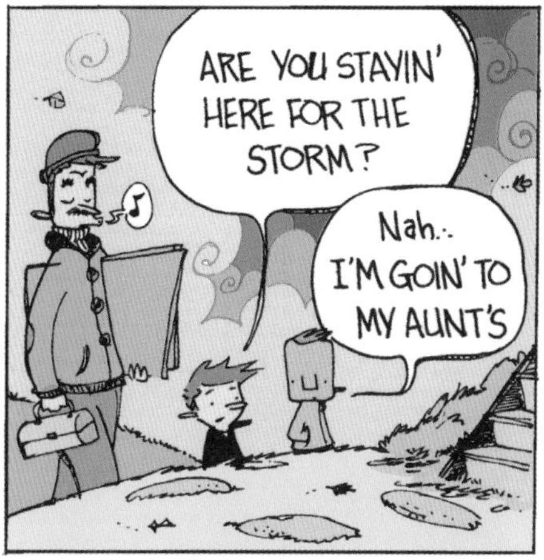
ARE YOU STAYIN' HERE FOR THE STORM?
Nah... I'M GOIN' TO MY AUNT'S

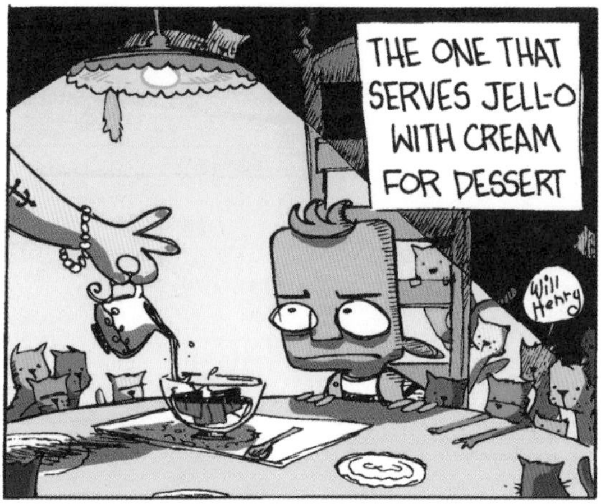
THE ONE THAT SERVES JELL-O WITH CREAM FOR DESSERT
Will Henry

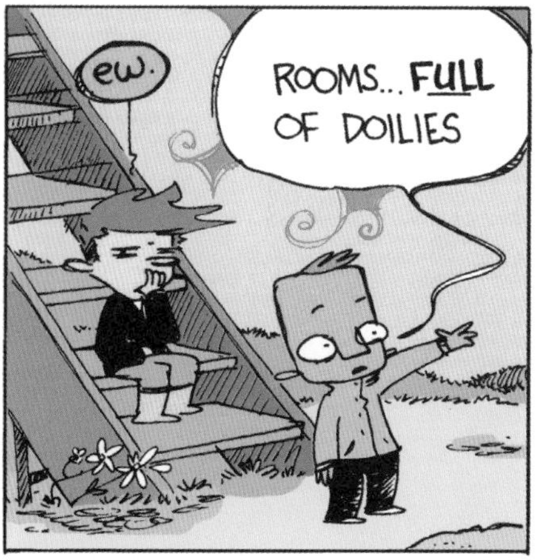
ew.
ROOMS... FULL OF DOILIES

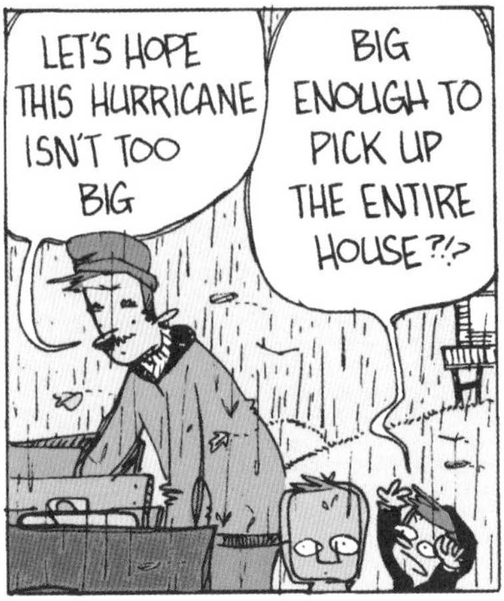
LET'S HOPE THIS HURRICANE ISN'T TOO BIG
BIG ENOUGH TO PICK UP THE ENTIRE HOUSE?!?

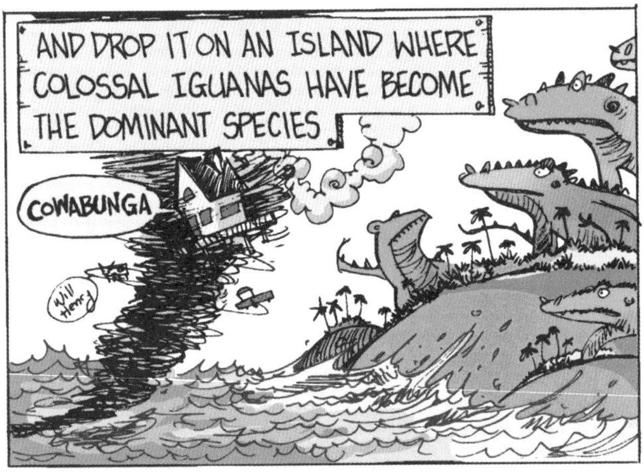
AND DROP IT ON AN ISLAND WHERE COLOSSAL IGUANAS HAVE BECOME THE DOMINANT SPECIES
COWABUNGA
Will Henry

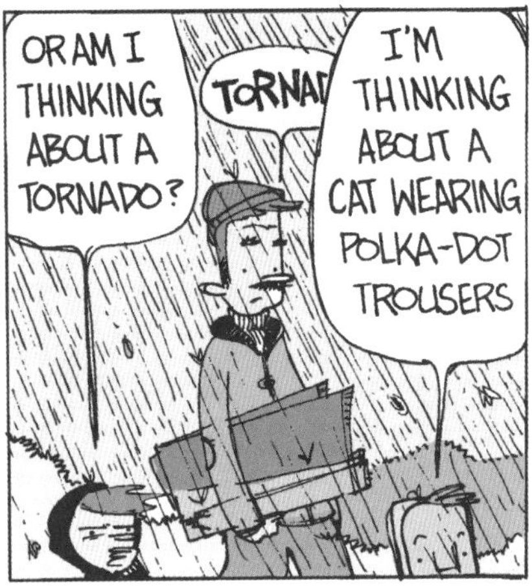
OR AM I THINKING ABOUT A TORNADO?
TORNAD
I'M THINKING ABOUT A CAT WEARING POLKA-DOT TROUSERS

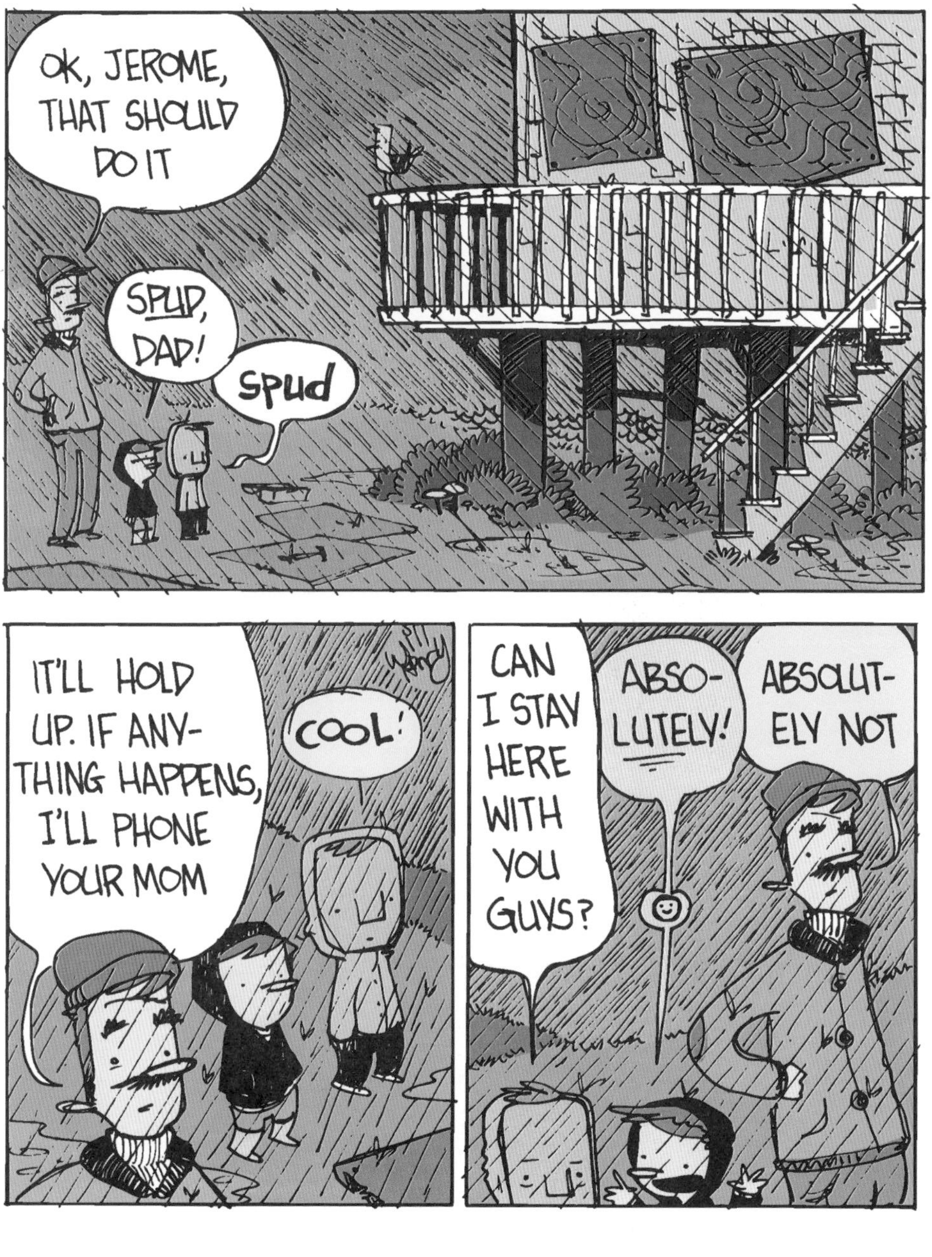
OK, JEROME, THAT SHOULD DO IT
SPUD, DAD!
spud
IT'LL HOLD UP. IF ANY-THING HAPPENS, I'LL PHONE YOUR MOM
COOL!
CAN I STAY HERE WITH YOU GUYS?
ABSO-LUTELY!
ABSOLUT-ELY NOT

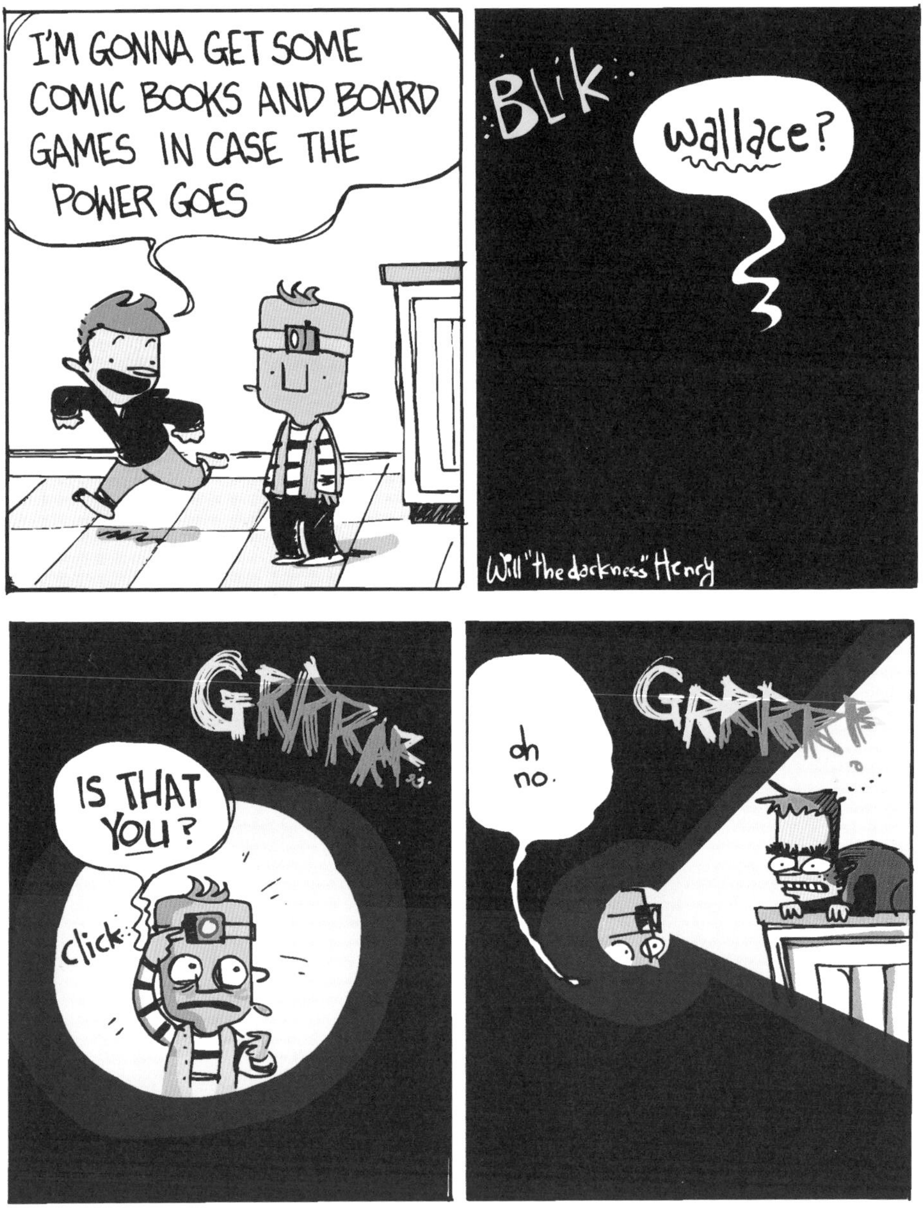
I'M GONNA GET SOME COMIC BOOKS AND BOARD GAMES IN CASE THE POWER GOES
BLIK
wallace?
Will "the darkness" Henry
GRRRRAR
IS THAT YOU?
click
GRRRRR
oh no.

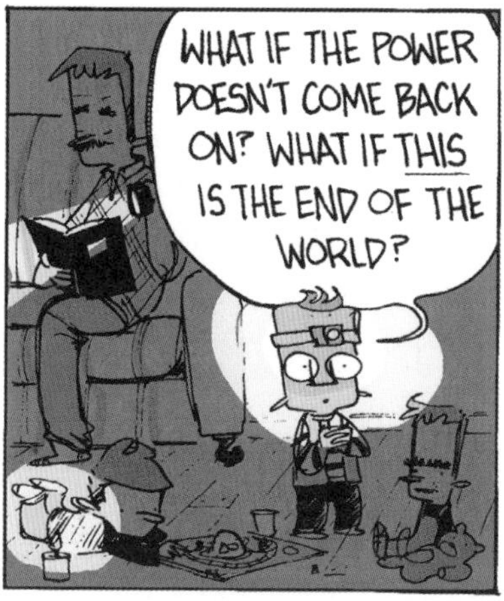
WHAT IF THE POWER DOESN'T COME BACK ON? WHAT IF THIS IS THE END OF THE WORLD?

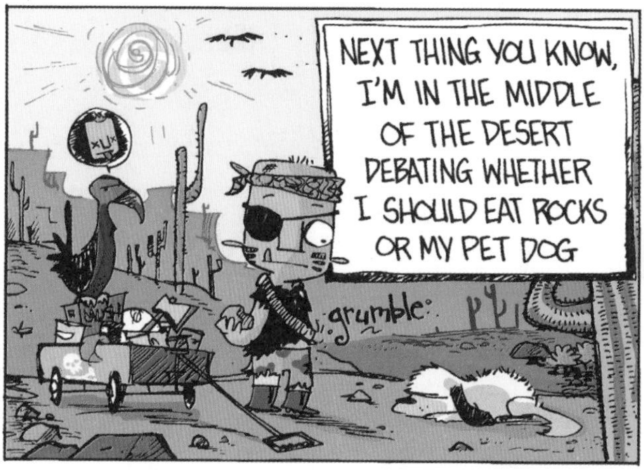
NEXT THING YOU KNOW, I'M IN THE MIDDLE OF THE DESERT DEBATING WHETHER I SHOULD EAT ROCKS OR MY PET DOG
grumble

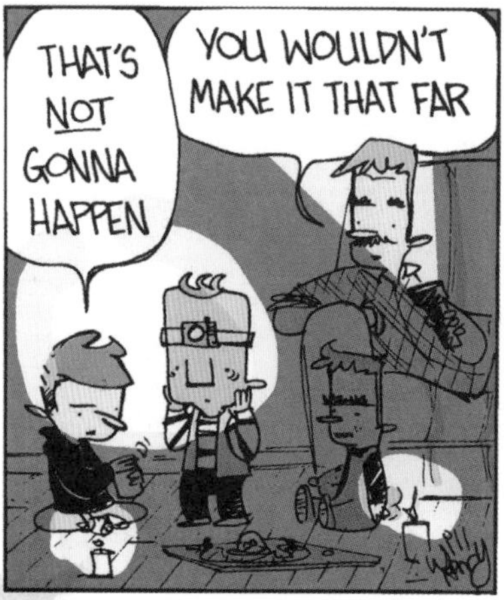
THAT'S NOT GONNA HAPPEN
YOU WOULDN'T MAKE IT THAT FAR

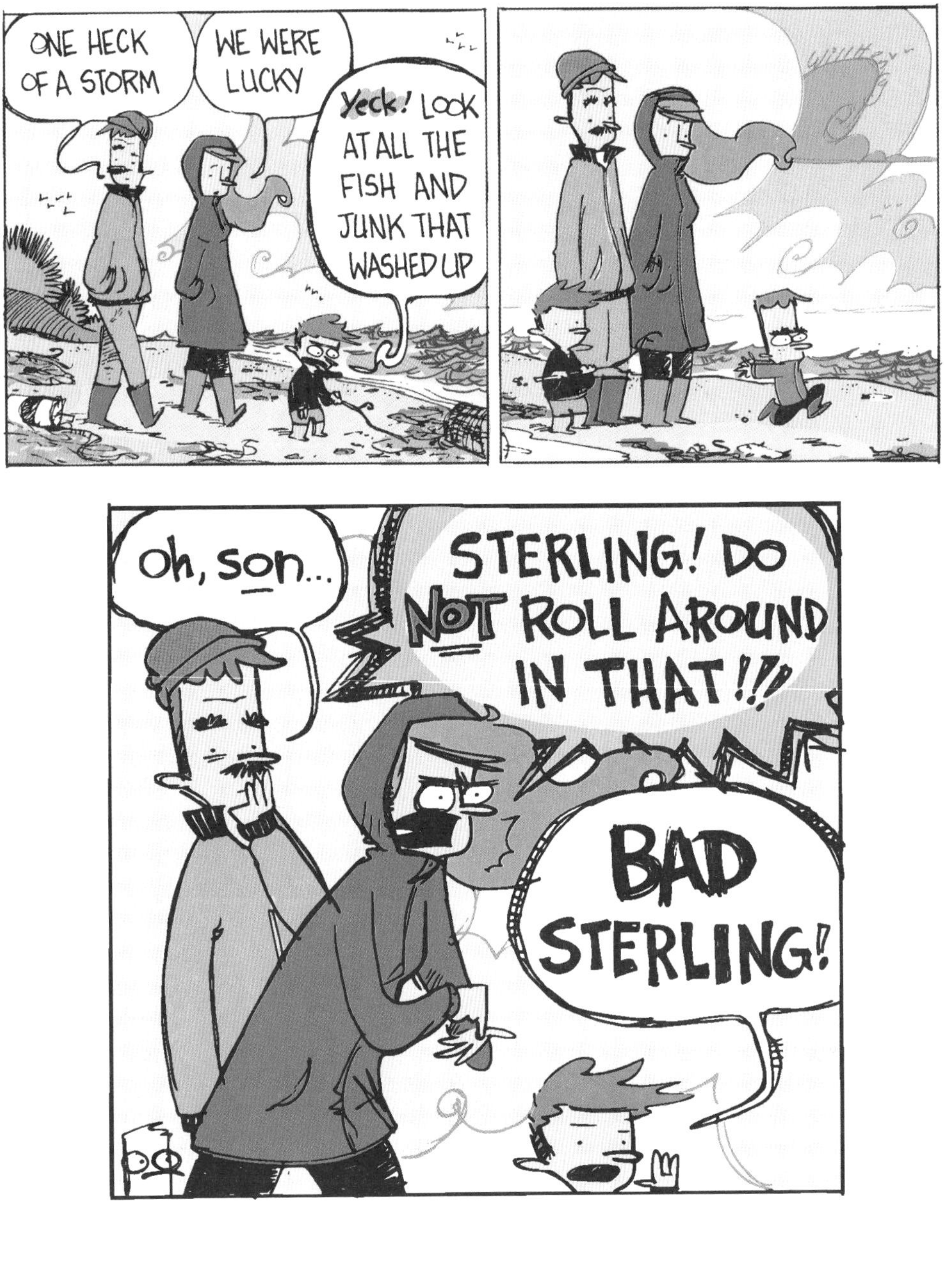
ONE HECK OF A STORM
WE WERE LUCKY
Yeck! LOOK AT ALL THE FISH AND JUNK THAT WASHED UP
Oh, son...
STERLING! DO NOT ROLL AROUND IN THAT!!!
BAD STERLING!

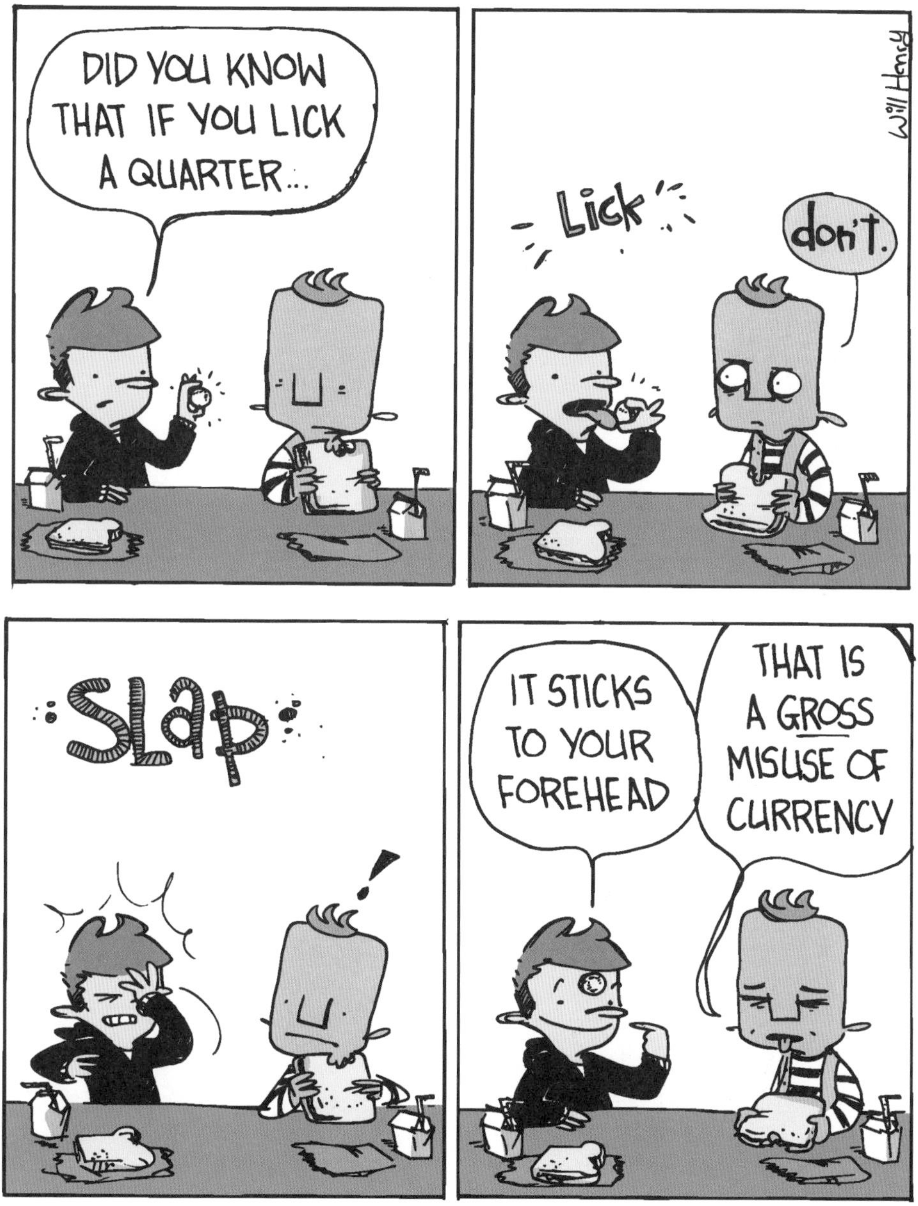
DID YOU KNOW THAT IF YOU LICK A QUARTER...
Will Henry
Lick
don't.
SLAP
!
IT STICKS TO YOUR FOREHEAD
THAT IS A GROSS MISUSE OF CURRENCY

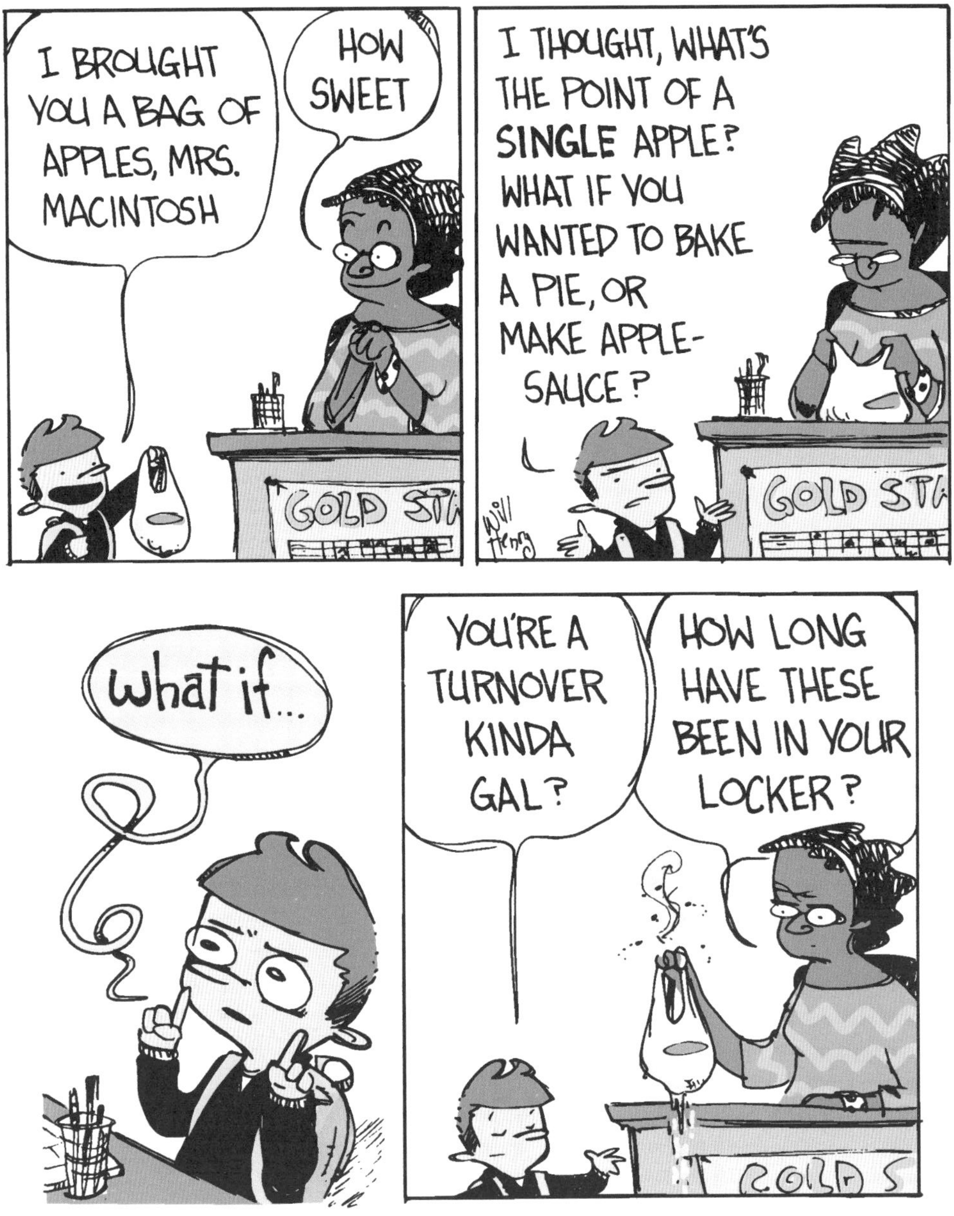
I BROUGHT YOU A BAG OF APPLES, MRS. MACINTOSH
HOW SWEET
I THOUGHT, WHAT'S THE POINT OF A SINGLE APPLE? WHAT IF YOU WANTED TO BAKE A PIE, OR MAKE APPLE-SAUCE?
GOLD ST
Will Henry
what if...
YOU'RE A TURNOVER KINDA GAL?
HOW LONG HAVE THESE BEEN IN YOUR LOCKER?

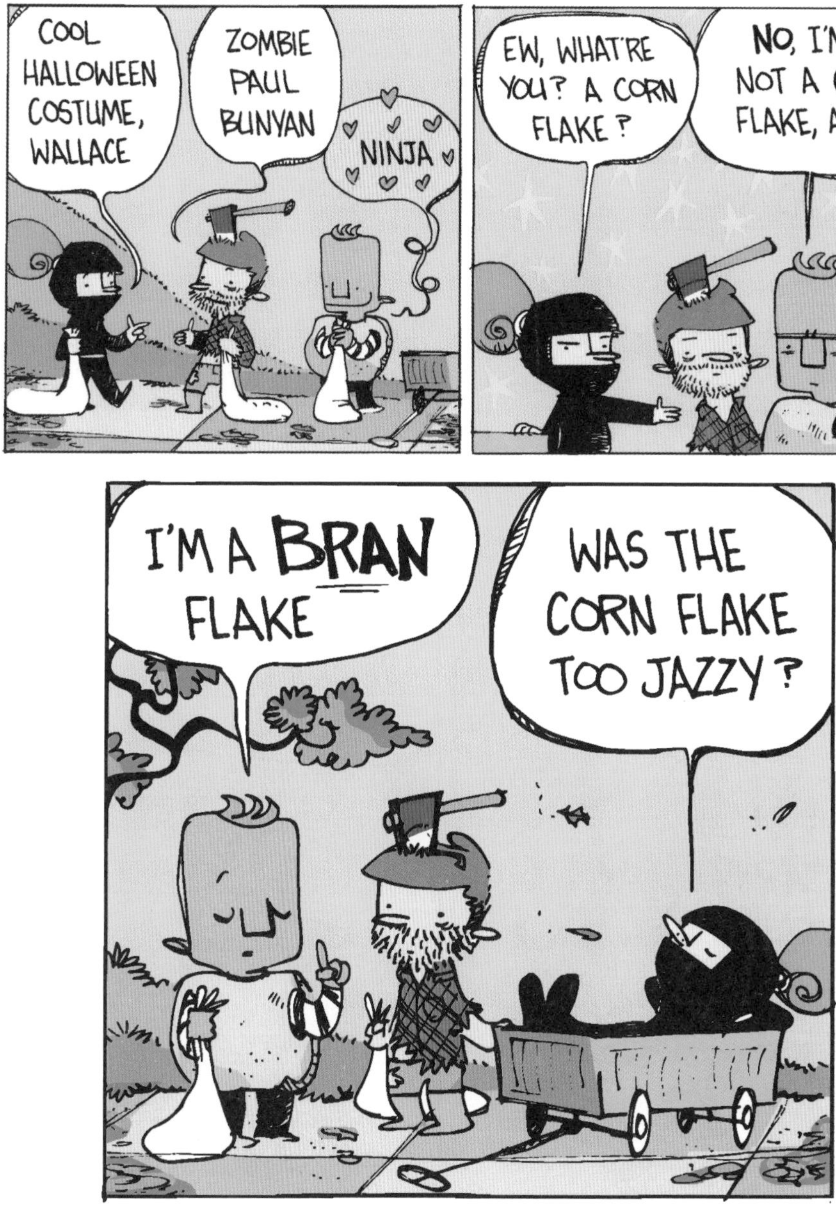
COOL HALLOWEEN COSTUME, WALLACE
ZOMBIE PAUL BUNYAN
NINJA
EW, WHAT'RE YOU? A CORN FLAKE?
NO, I'M NOT A CORN FLAKE, AMELIA
Will Henry
I'M A BRAN FLAKE
WAS THE CORN FLAKE TOO JAZZY?

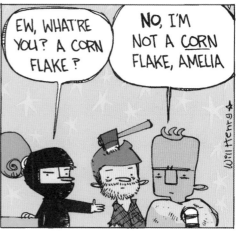

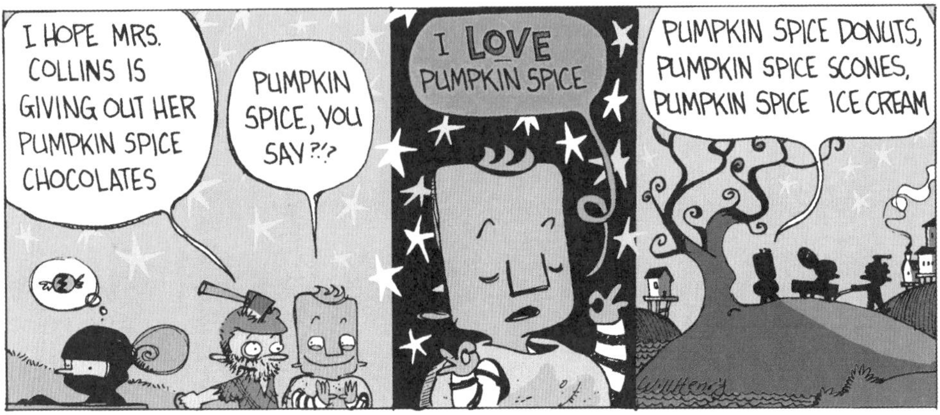
I HOPE MRS. COLLINS IS GIVING OUT HER PUMPKIN SPICE CHOCOLATES
PUMPKIN SPICE, YOU SAY?!?
I LOVE PUMPKIN SPICE
PUMPKIN SPICE DONUTS, PUMPKIN SPICE SCONES, PUMPKIN SPICE ICE CREAM

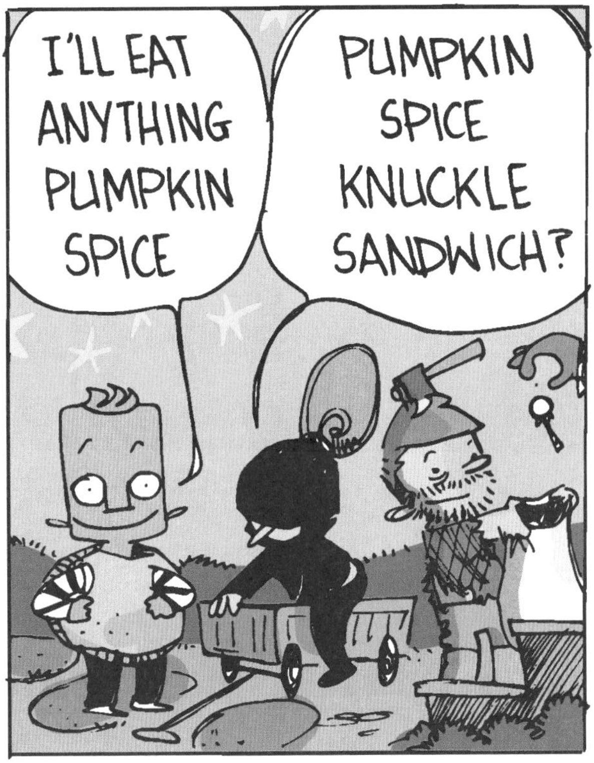
I'LL EAT ANYTHING PUMPKIN SPICE
PUMPKIN SPICE KNUCKLE SANDWICH?

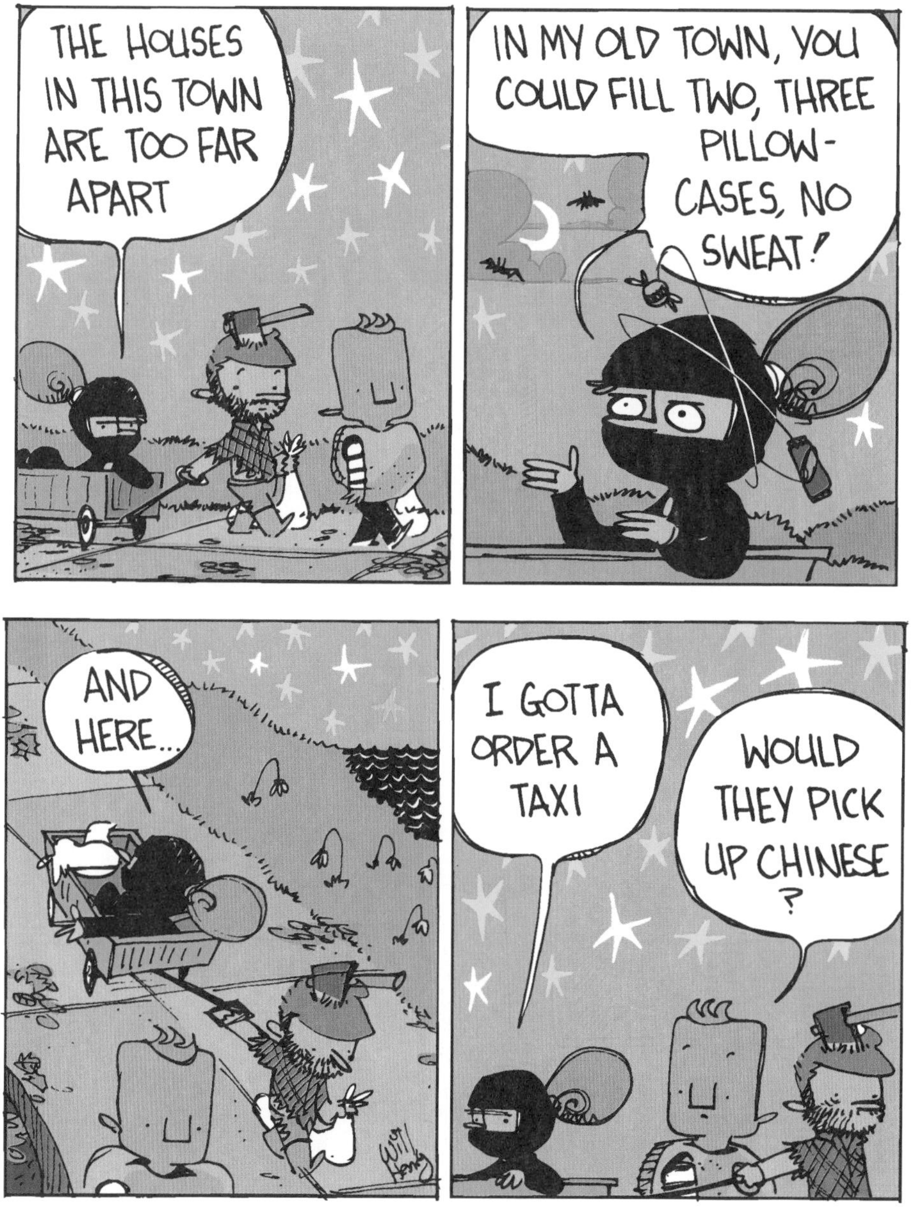
THE HOUSES IN THIS TOWN ARE TOO FAR APART
IN MY OLD TOWN, YOU COULD FILL TWO, THREE PILLOW-CASES, NO SWEAT!
AND HERE...
I GOTTA ORDER A TAXI
WOULD THEY PICK UP CHINESE?

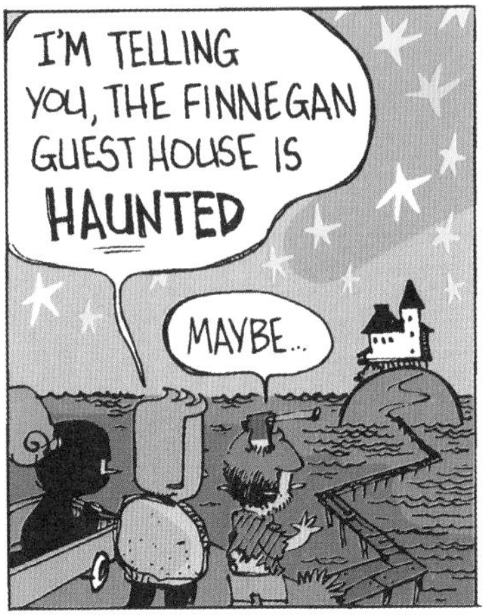
I'M TELLING YOU, THE FINNEGAN GUEST HOUSE IS HAUNTED
MAYBE...

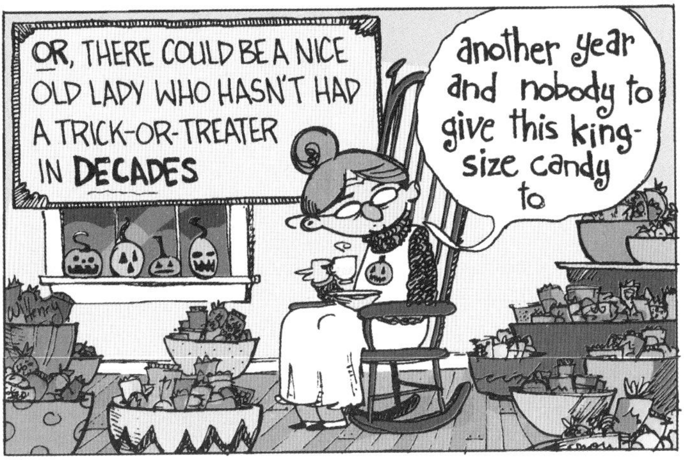
OR, THERE COULD BE A NICE OLD LADY WHO HASN'T HAD A TRICK-OR-TREATER IN DECADES
another year and nobody to give this king-size candy to

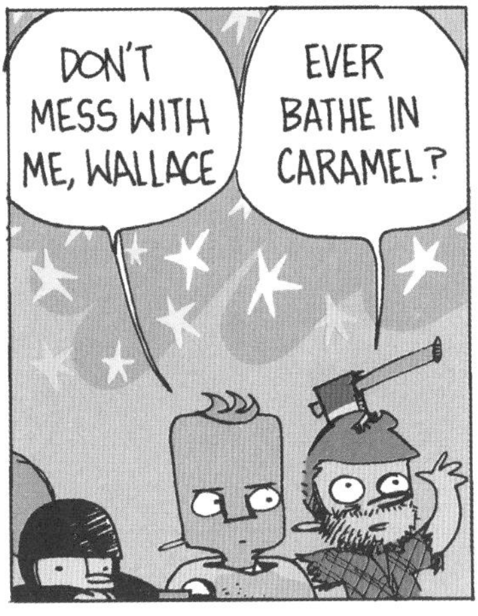
DON'T MESS WITH ME, WALLACE
EVER BATHE IN CARAMEL?

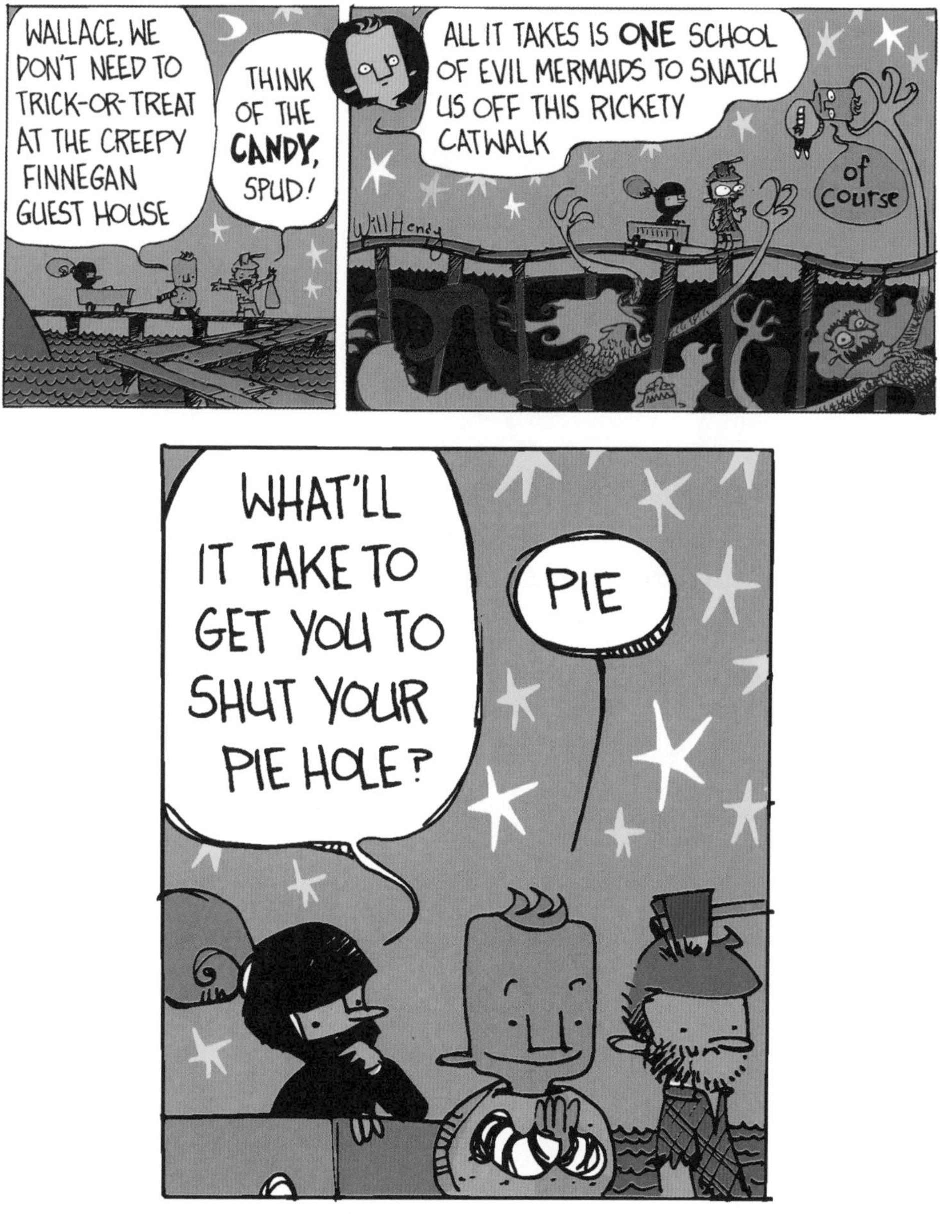
WALLACE, WE DON'T NEED TO TRICK-OR-TREAT AT THE CREEPY FINNEGAN GUEST HOUSE
THINK OF THE CANDY, SPUD!
ALL IT TAKES IS ONE SCHOOL OF EVIL MERMAIDS TO SNATCH US OFF THIS RICKETY CATWALK
of course
WillHendy
WHAT'LL IT TAKE TO GET YOU TO SHUT YOUR PIE HOLE?
PIE

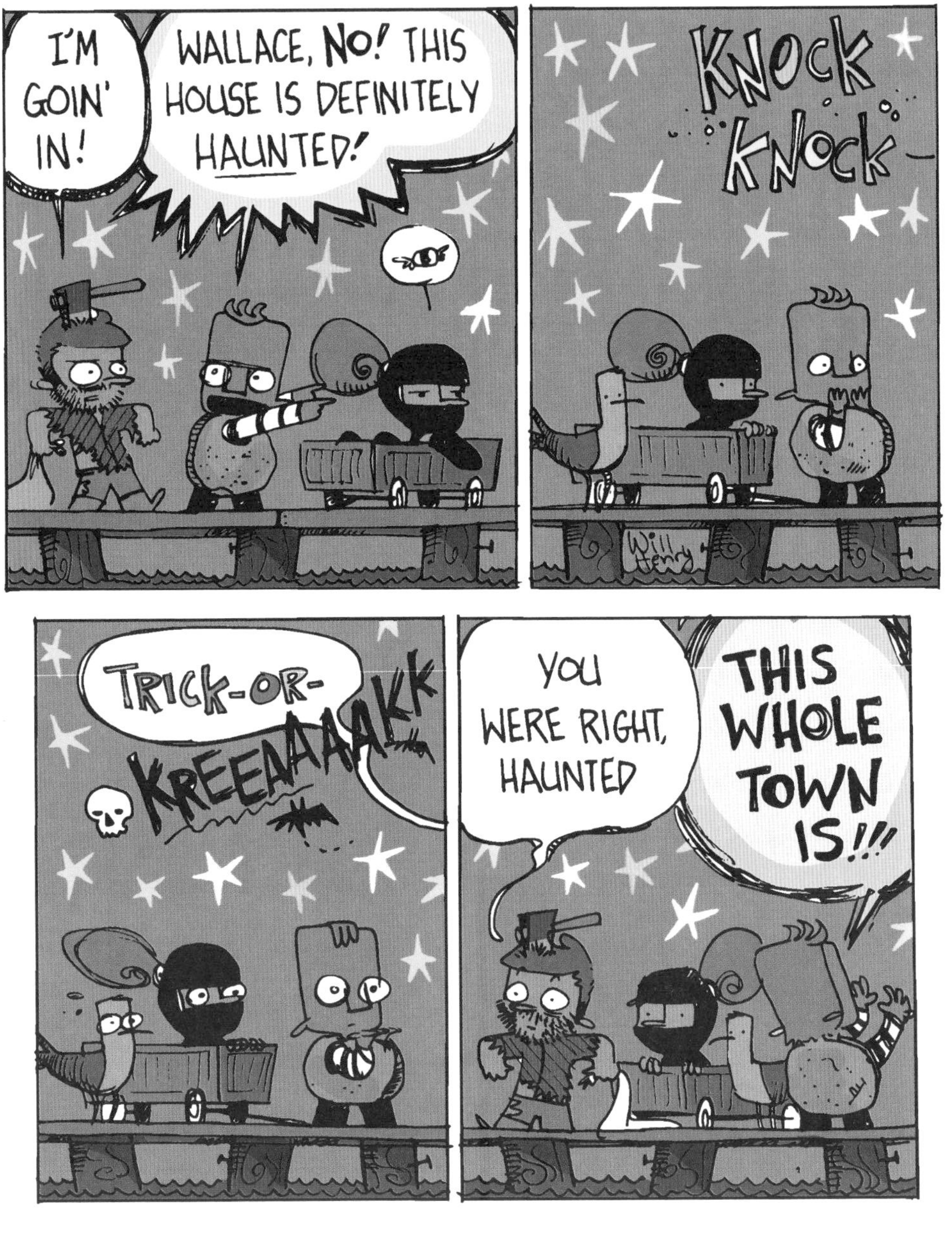
I'M GOIN' IN!
WALLACE, NO! THIS HOUSE IS DEFINITELY HAUNTED!
KNOCK KNOCK
Will Henry
TRICK-OR-
KREEAAAAKK
YOU WERE RIGHT, HAUNTED
THIS WHOLE TOWN IS!!!

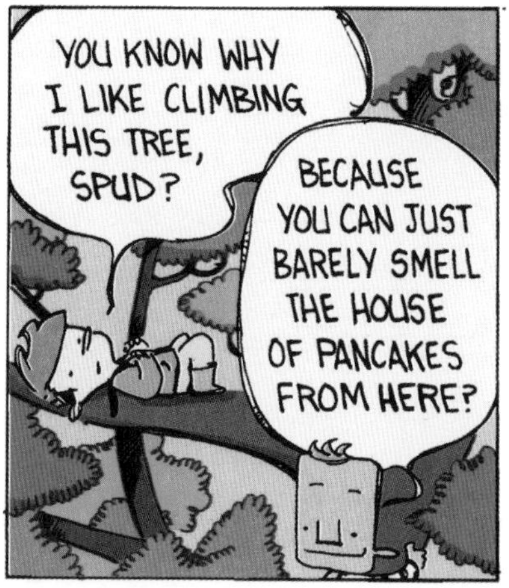
YOU KNOW WHY I LIKE CLIMBING THIS TREE, SPUD?
BECAUSE YOU CAN JUST BARELY SMELL THE HOUSE OF PANCAKES FROM HERE?

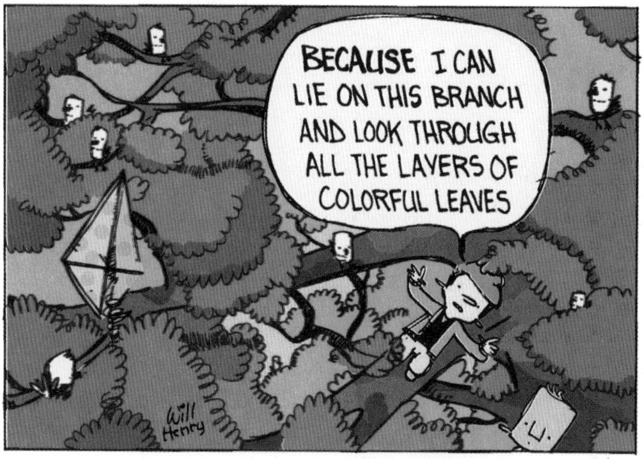
BECAUSE I CAN LIE ON THIS BRANCH AND LOOK THROUGH ALL THE LAYERS OF COLORFUL LEAVES
Will Henry

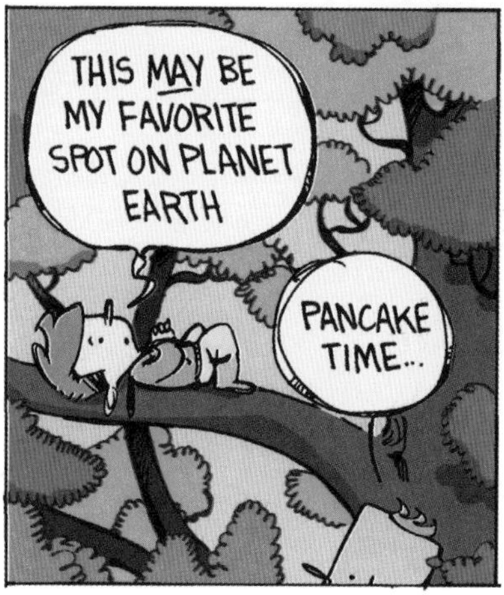
THIS MAY BE MY FAVORITE SPOT ON PLANET EARTH
PANCAKE TIME...

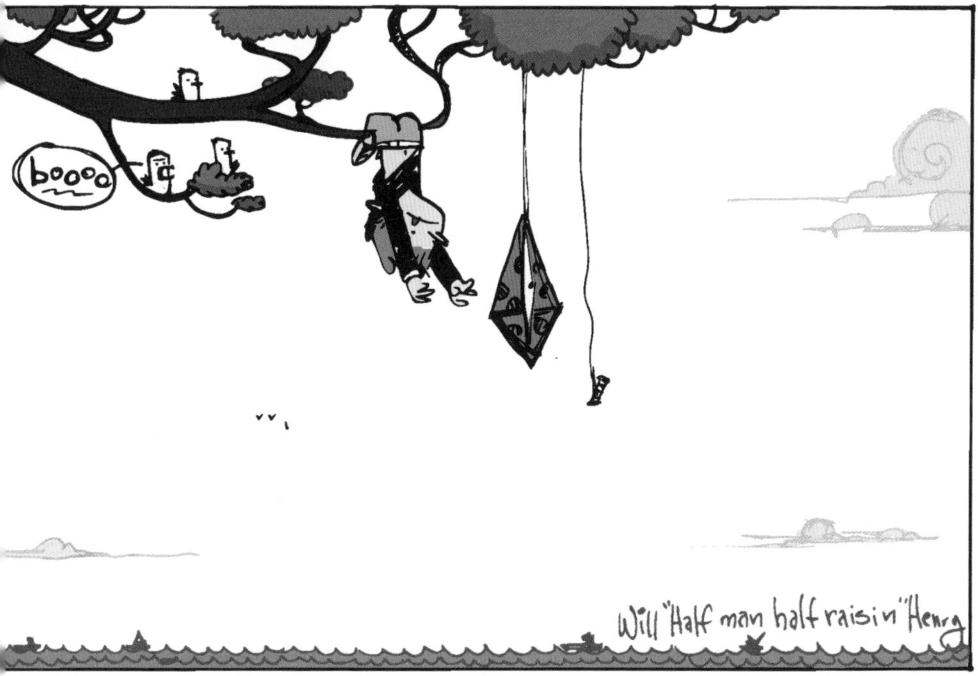
boooo
Will "Half man half raisin" Henry

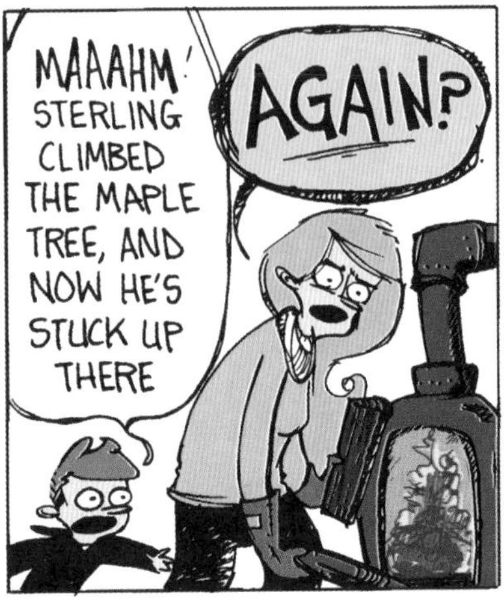
MAAAHM! STERLING CLIMBED THE MAPLE TREE, AND NOW HE'S STUCK UP THERE
AGAIN?

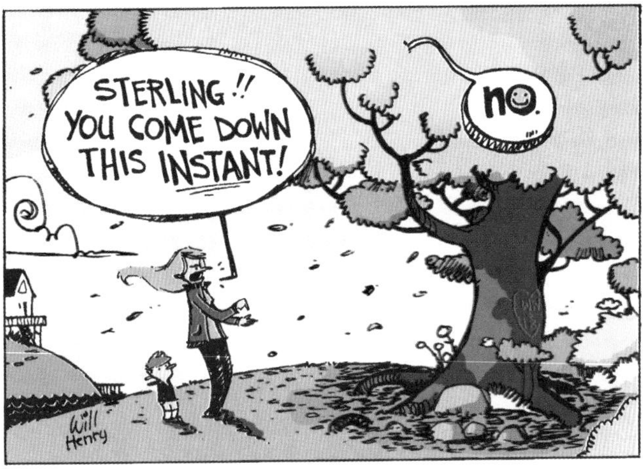
STERLING!! YOU COME DOWN THIS INSTANT!
no.
Will Henry

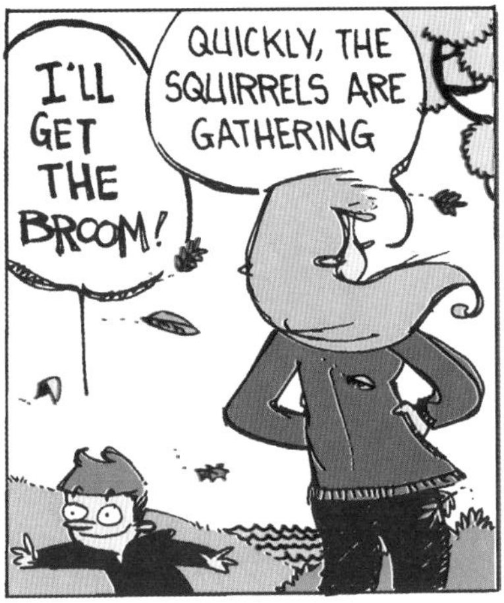
I'LL GET THE BROOM!
QUICKLY, THE SQUIRRELS ARE GATHERING

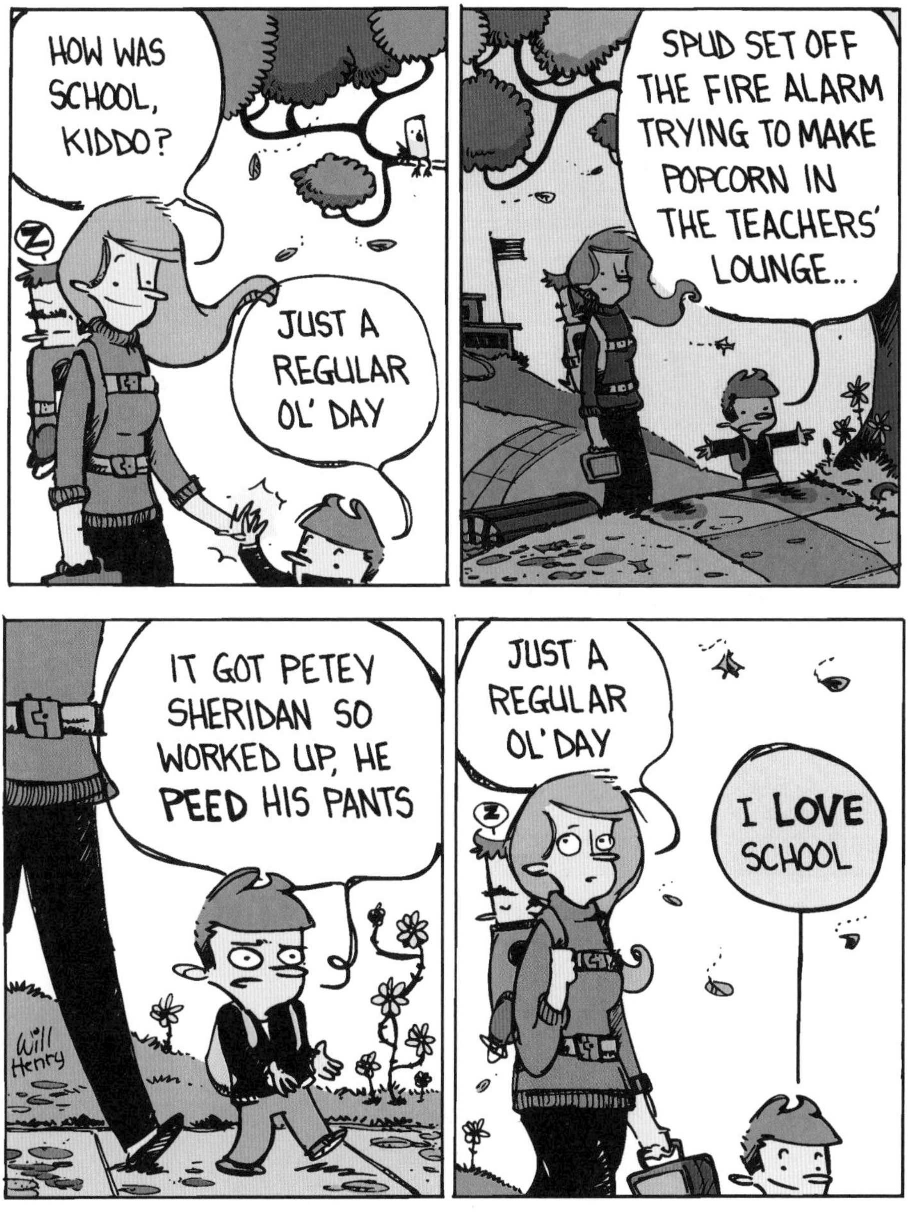
HOW WAS SCHOOL, KIDDO?
JUST A REGULAR OL' DAY
SPUD SET OFF THE FIRE ALARM TRYING TO MAKE POPCORN IN THE TEACHERS' LOUNGE...
IT GOT PETEY SHERIDAN SO WORKED UP, HE PEED HIS PANTS
Will Henry
JUST A REGULAR OL' DAY
I LOVE SCHOOL

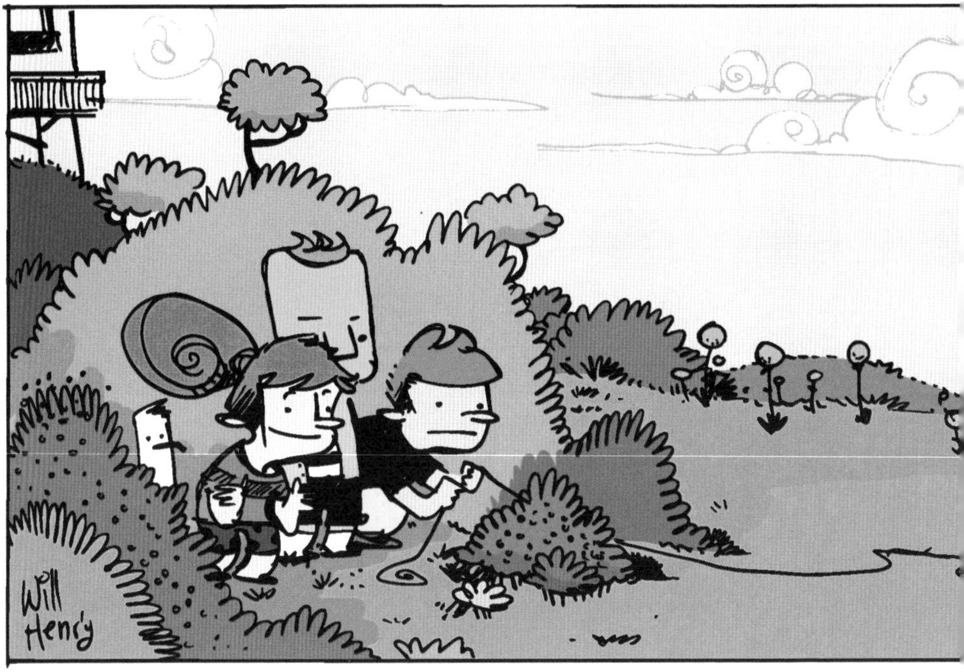
Will
Henry

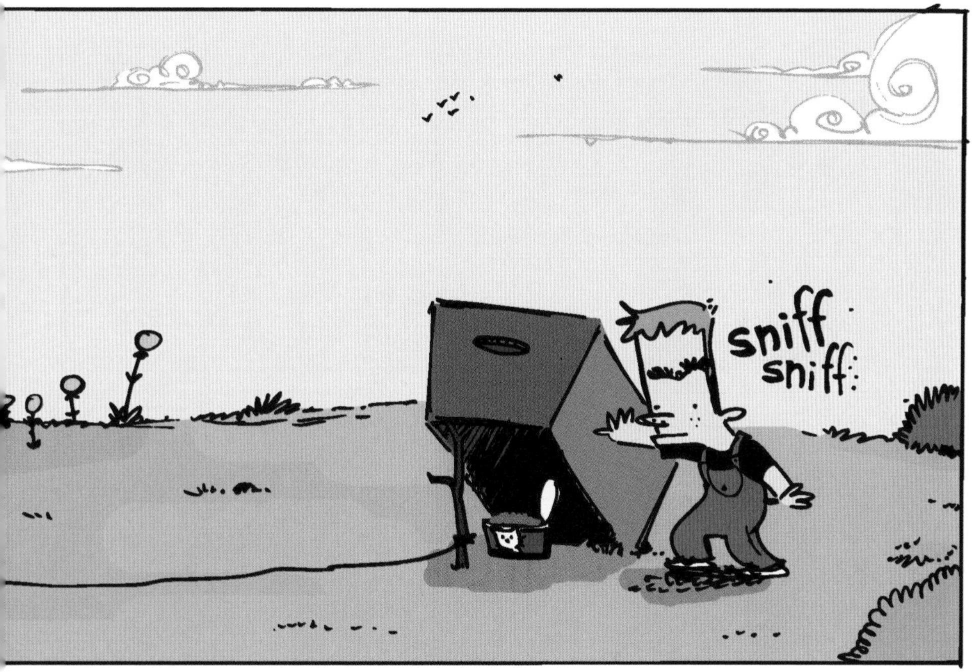
sniff
sniff

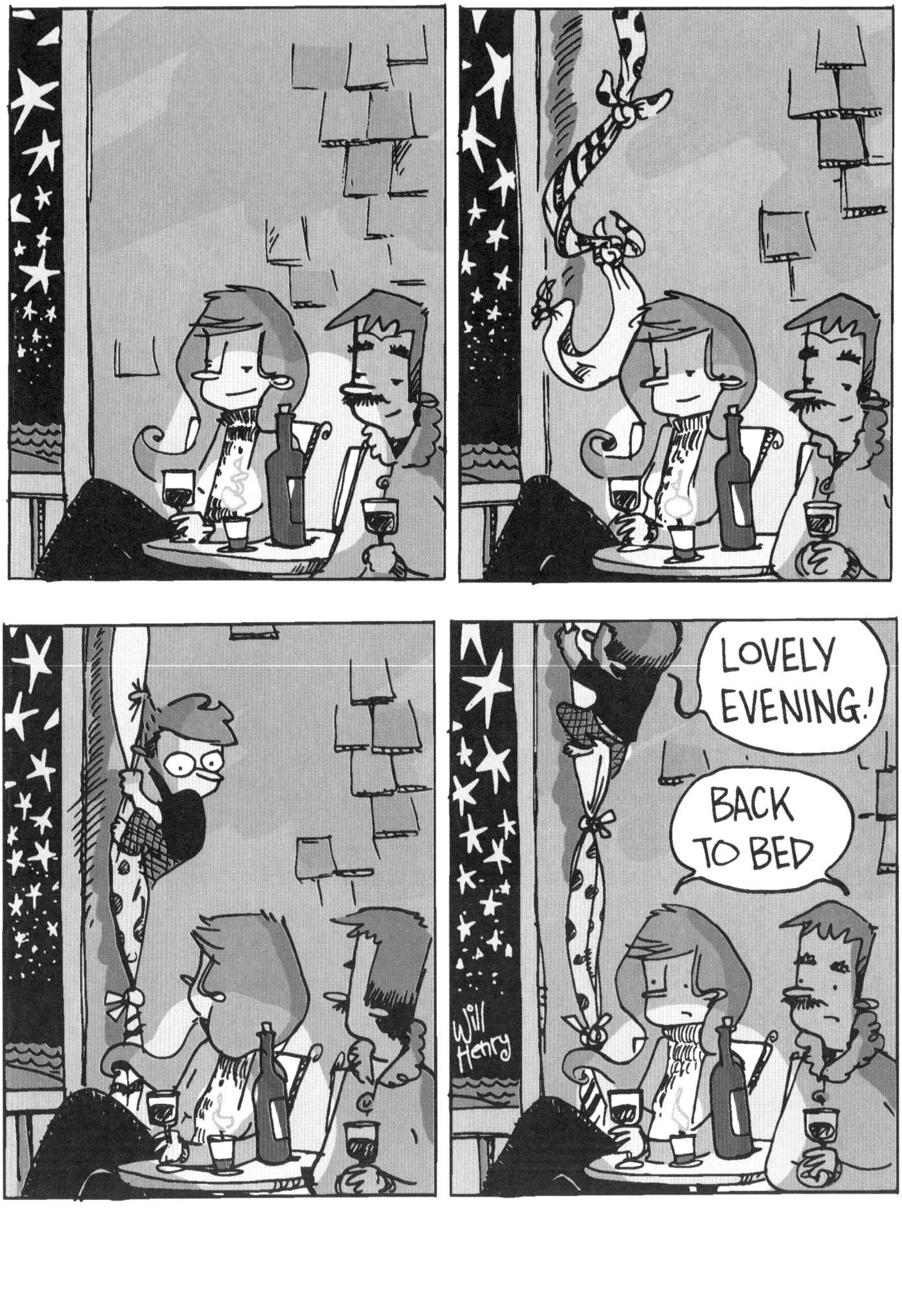
LOVELY EVENING!
BACK TO BED
Will Henry

Pine Cone Bird Feeder

WHAT YOU'LL NEED

Pine cone

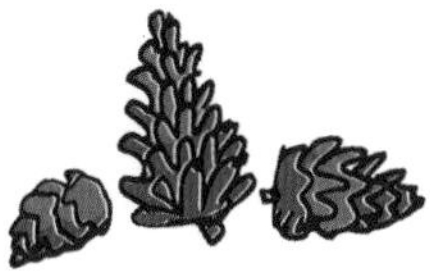

Peanut butter and butter knife

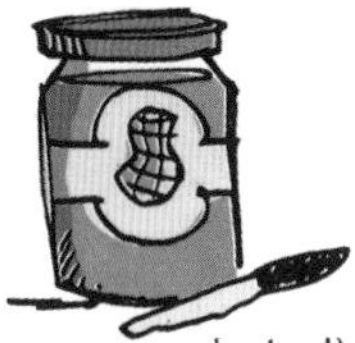

(hummus works too!)

String

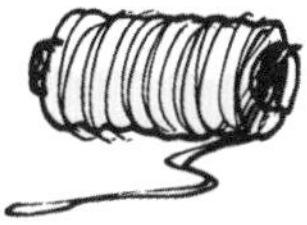

Birdseed

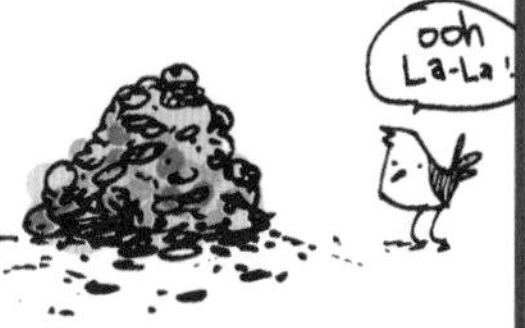
ooh La-La!

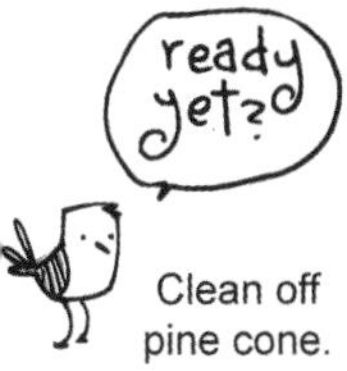
ready yet?

Clean off pine cone.

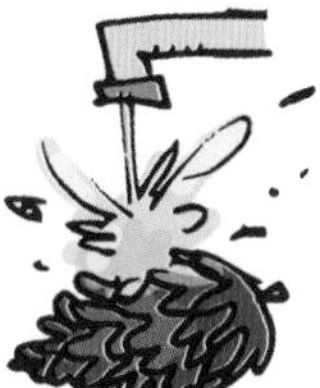

Tie string between the scales of the pine cone with some slack for hanging.

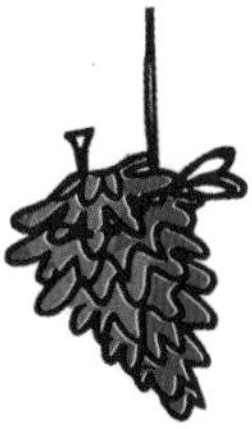

Using the butter knife, cover the pine cone with peanut butter, getting in all the nooks and crannies.

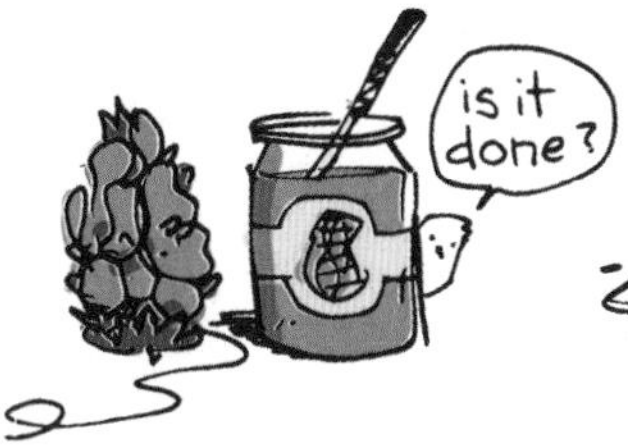
is it done?

Roll peanut butter pine cone in birdseed, getting good coverage.

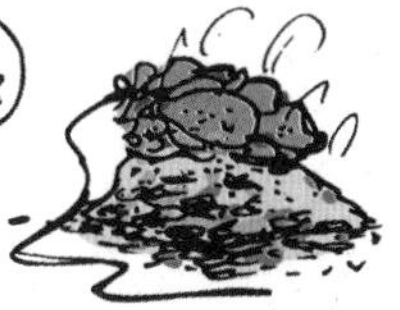

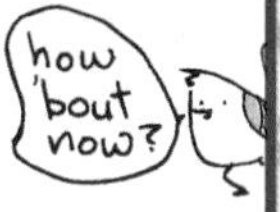
how 'bout now?

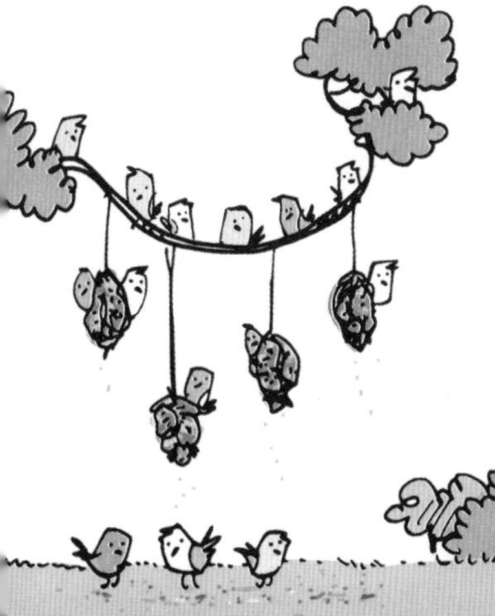

Hang your feeder in the park, by the woods, outside your window, or on your balcony and watch the action!

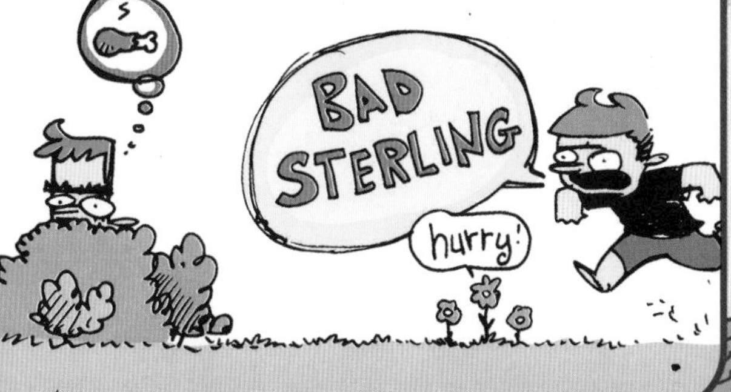
BAD STERLING
hurry!

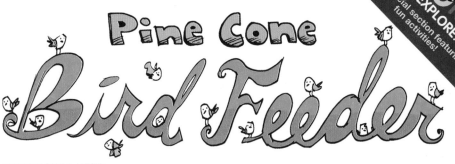

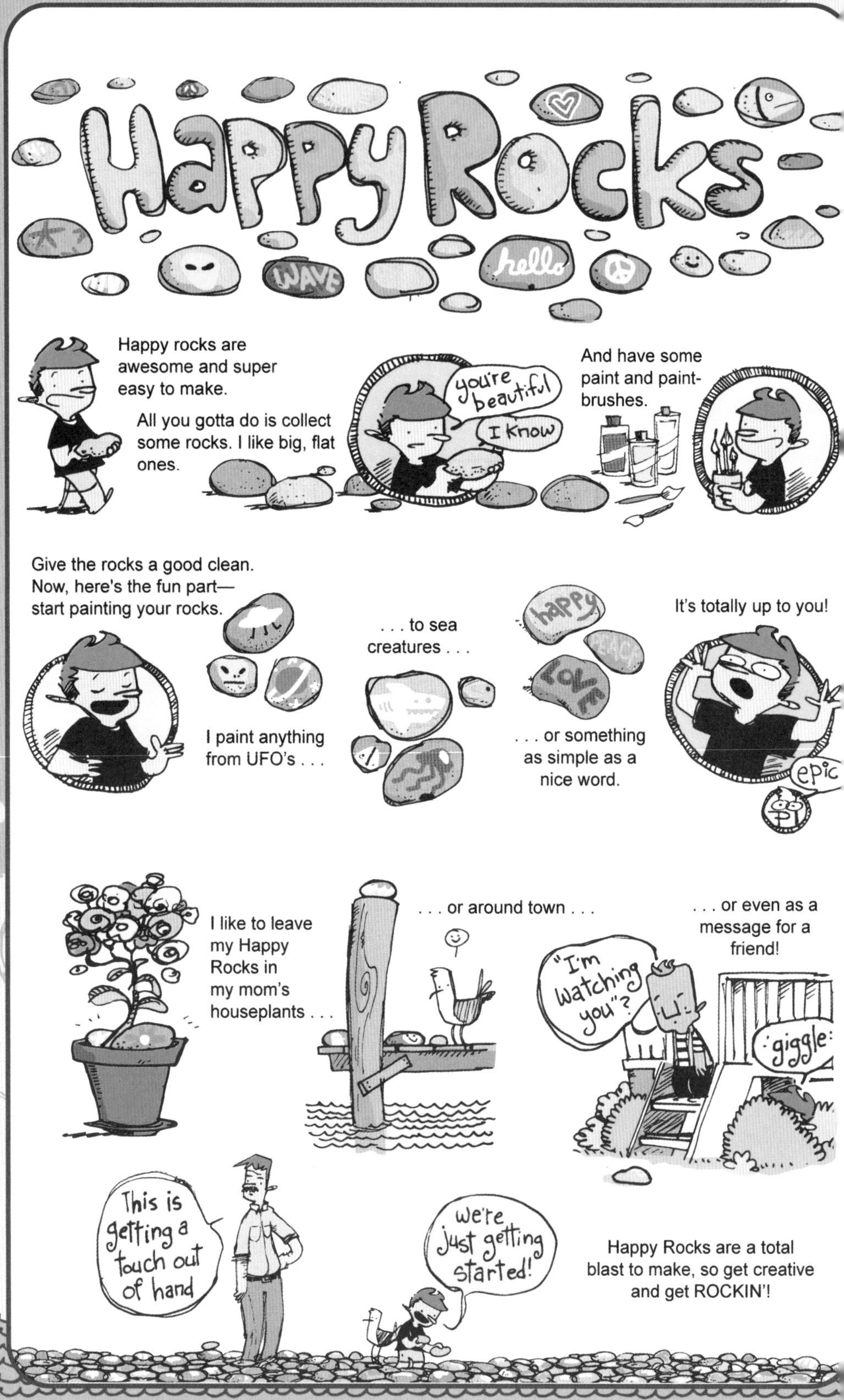

Happy Rocks
WAVE
hello
Happy rocks are awesome and super easy to make.
All you gotta do is collect some rocks. I like big, flat ones.
you're beautiful
I know
And have some paint and paint-brushes.
Give the rocks a good clean. Now, here's the fun part—start painting your rocks.
I paint anything from UFO's . . .
. . . to sea creatures . . .
happy
PEACE
LOVE
. . . or something as simple as a nice word.
It's totally up to you!
epic
I like to leave my Happy Rocks in my mom's houseplants . . .
. . . or around town . . .
. . . or even as a message for a friend!
"I'm watching you"?
:giggle:
This is getting a touch out of hand
we're just getting started!
Happy Rocks are a total blast to make, so get creative and get ROCKIN'!

Make your Own PAPIER-MÂCHÉ MASK!

WHAT YOU'LL NEED

Balloon

Bowl or Tupperware

Newspaper (cut into strips)

Scissors

Flour and water

String

Paint and brushes

Mix 2 cups of water to 1 cup of flour in bowl to create a paste.

Blow up a balloon to roughly the size of your head.

I'm gonna need a bigger balloon

Dip newspaper strips into the paste and lay them onto one side of the balloon until half the balloon is fully covered.

Let dry for 24 hours.

Pop balloon and pull away from mask.

Trim the edges of your mask and cut eyeholes.

Cut two holes on each side of your mask where you can attach a string.

Lastly, paint whatever you'd like on your mask. (IT'S YOUR MASK!)

I'm a tomato

We know

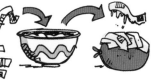

Wallace the Brave is distributed internationally by Andrews Mcmeel Syndication.

Wicked Epic Adventures copyright © 2021 by William Wilson.
All rights reserved. Printed in China. No part of this book may be used
or reproduced in any manner whatsoever without written permission
except in the case of reprints in the context of reviews.

Andrews Mcmeel Publishing
a division of Andrews Mcmeel Universal
1130 Walnut Street, Kansas City, Missouri 64106

www.andrewsmcmeel.com

21 22 23 24 25 SDB 10 9 8 7 6 5 4 3 2 1

ISBN: 978-1-5248-6507-8

Library of Congress Control Number: 2020944033

Made by:
King Yip (Dongguan) Printing & Packaging Factory Ltd.
Address and location of manufacturer:
Daning Administrative District, Humen Town
Dongguan Guangdong, China 523930
1st Printing—12/14/20

ATTENTION: SCHOOLS AND BUSINESSES
Andrews Mcmeel books are available at quantity discounts with bulk purchase for
educational, business, or sales promotional use. For information, please e-mail the
Andrews Mcmeel Publishing Special Sales Department:
specialsales@amuniversal.com

Look for these books!

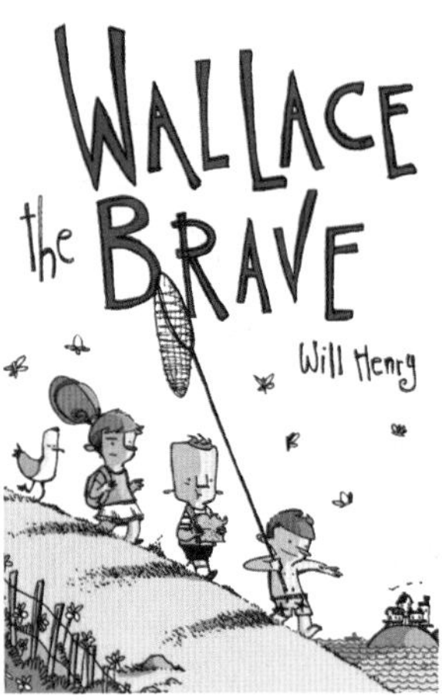
Wallace the Brave
Will Henry

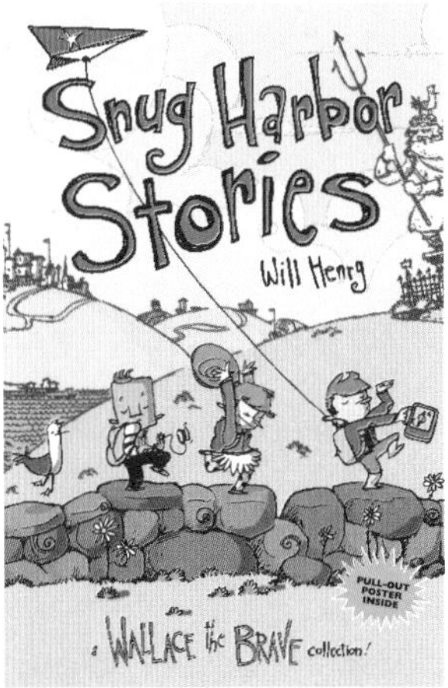
Snug Harbor Stories
Will Henry
PULL-OUT POSTER INSIDE
a Wallace the Brave collection!

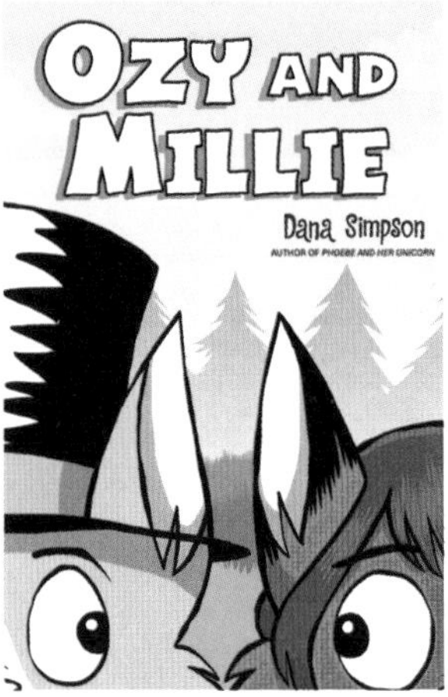
Ozy and Millie
Dana Simpson

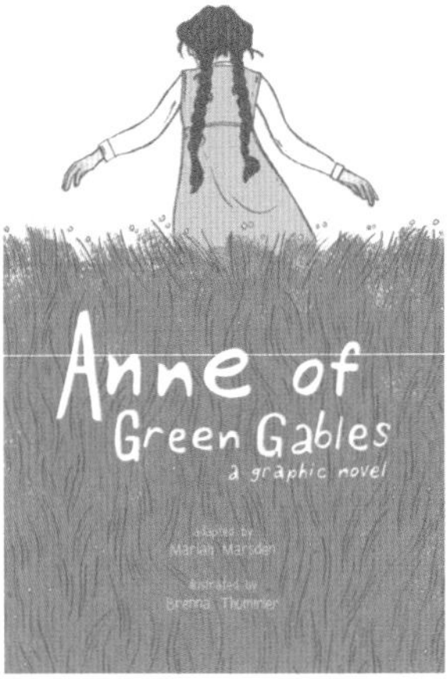
Anne of Green Gables
a graphic novel

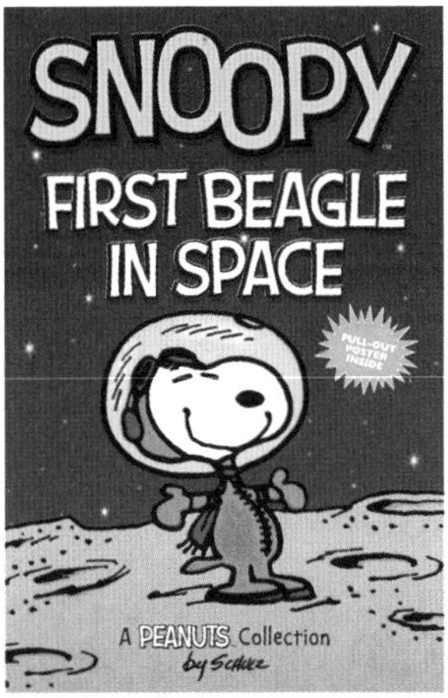
SNOOPY
FIRST BEAGLE IN SPACE
PULL-OUT POSTER INSIDE
A PEANUTS Collection
by Schulz

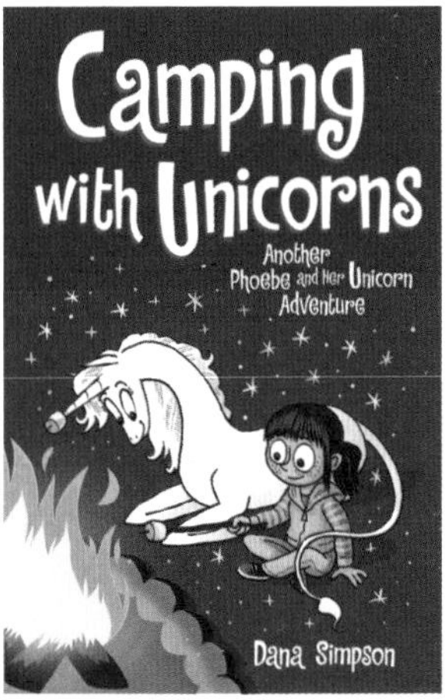
Camping with Unicorns
Another Phoebe and Her Unicorn Adventure
Dana Simpson

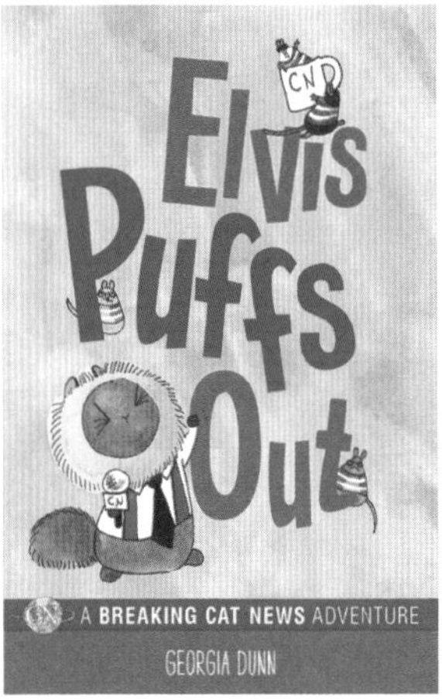
Elvis Puffs Out
A BREAKING CAT NEWS ADVENTURE
GEORGIA DUNN

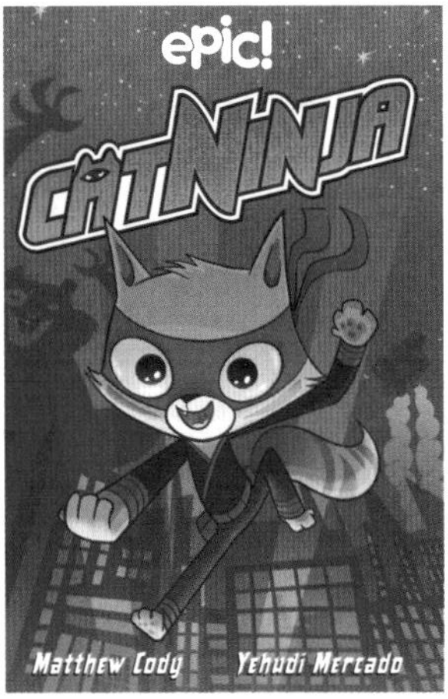
epic!
CatNinja
Matthew Cody
Yehudi Mercado

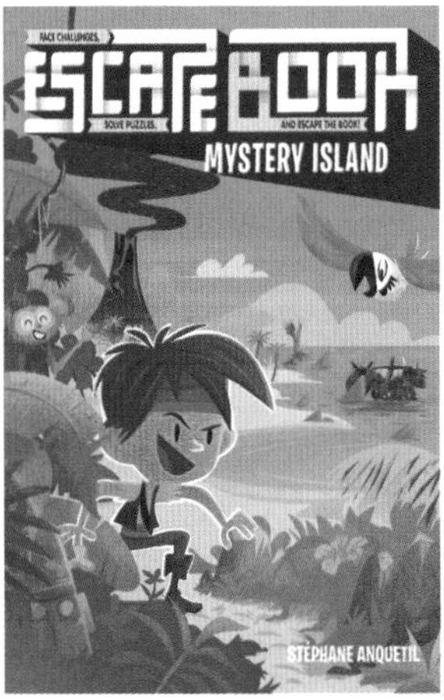
ESCAPE BOOK
MYSTERY ISLAND
STÉPHANE ANQUETIL